PRAISE FOR THE NOVELS OF GREGORY HARRIS!

THE ENDICOTT EVIL

"An intriguing central mystery."

—*Publishers Weekly*

THE DALWICH DESECRATION

"One of my favorite Victorian mystery authors. The author's research into the era is impeccable."

—*Historical Novels Review*

THE BELLINGHAM BLOODBATH

"A terrific story . . . both storylines come together in perfect symmetry, making for an incredibly pleasing mystery. The author nails it yet again!"

—*Suspense Magazine*

THE ARNIFOUR AFFAIR

"Colin has Holmes' arrogance but is dimpled and charming, while Ethan is a darker Watson . . . [T]he relationship between the leads is discreetly intriguing."

—*Kirkus Reviews*

"Pendragon matches Sherlock Holmes in his arrogance . . . he is redeemed, in part, by his brains and his gentle treatment of Pruitt."

—*Publishers Weekly*

"The mystery is extremely well done, the characters carefully drawn and the story moves quickly to a satisfying conclusion."

—*Washington Independent Review of Books*

Books by Gregory Harris

THE ARNIFOUR AFFAIR

THE BELLINGHAM BLOODBATH

THE CONNICLE CURSE

THE DALWICH DESECRATION

THE ENDICOTT EVIL

THE FRAMINGHAM FIEND

Published by Kensington Publishing Corporation

THE FRAMINGHAM FIEND

A Colin Pendragon Mystery

GREGORY HARRIS

KENSINGTON BOOKS
www.kensingtonbooks.com

KENSINGTON BOOKS are published by

Kensington Publishing Corp.
119 West 40th Street
New York, NY 10018

Copyright © 2018 by Gregory Harris

All Kensington titles, imprints, and distributed lines are available at special quantity discounts for bulk purchases for sales promotion, premiums, fund-raising, educational, or institutional use.

Special book excerpts or customized printings can also be created to fit specific needs. For details, write or phone the office of the Kensington Sales Manager: Kensington Publishing Corp., 119 West 40th Street, New York, NY 10018. Attn. Sales Department. Phone: 1-800-221-2647.

Kensington and the K logo Reg. U.S. Pat. & TM Off.

eISBN-13: 978-1-61773-892-0
eISBN-10: 1-61773-892-1
First Kensington Electronic Edition: June 2018

ISBN-13: 978-1-61773-891-3
ISBN-10: 1-61773-891-3
First Kensington Trade Paperback Printing: June 2018

10 9 8 7 6 5 4 3 2

Printed in the United States of America

For Carla Navas
One of a kind

CHAPTER 1

The sight before us was worse than anything I had ever seen. More than a dozen years trundling along in Colin's wake, watching him solve innumerable murders, extortions, malicious acts; none of it prepared me for what we saw when we entered Amelia Linton's Whitechapel room. The scene was so grisly that Superintendent Tottenshire, the man who had beseeched Colin and me to assist Scotland Yard with this murder, had demurred to join us, leaving us in the hands of his newly minted inspector, Maurice Evans. That alone should have forewarned me.

"The landlady, a Mrs. Simpson, found her this morning," Inspector Evans was explaining in a spare, rudimentary tone as Colin and I hovered just inside the doorway. "She had a part-time job at the Coventry flower market, but the landlady says Miss Linton went out most nights to earn extra wages. Told us she'd been sending money to her mother and siblings in Leith near Edinburgh. That's what brought Mrs. Simpson up to Miss Linton's room this morning. She says Miss Linton was never late for tea before she hurried off to the flower market each morning—no matter what she'd been up to the night before. . . ." The inspector's voice trailed off.

I found my eyes drawn back to the small dining table where

Miss Linton's mutilated body lay. Her head was thrown back as though she was in the midst of a great laugh save for the fact that there was no such expression on her face or in her eyes—which were diminished and unseeing as they bulged from their sockets. That was when it became evident that her head was cantilevered back not from merriment but because her neck had been carved nearly down to the spine, leaving its attachment to her body tenuous at best. The swath of blood that had rushed from the wound had stained the upper half of her chest, coating it with a black, viscous sheen that held an all too familiar metallic tang.

"She is quite like the superintendent told you the first victim was last week." Inspector Evans was still speaking. "She was also torn open from clavicle to groin with most of her innards . . ."

He did not finish his sentence, nor did he need to, for it was exactly as had been described to us not an hour prior. Miss Linton's torso lay open, her rib cage pried apart so it was plain to see that where her internal organs should have been, there was nothing but darkness and blackened gore—the whole of it flattened incongruously as a result of the unnatural void. If there could be any doubt about what we were witnessing it was quickly dispelled by the arrangement on the floor around the table, a tableau so gruesome that I believe my very breath ceased for a period of time.

Just as with the first victim, this woman's missing organs—one after the other—had been meticulously placed around the table's circumference: heart, lungs, stomach, liver, kidneys, a tangle of intestine, pancreas . . . I could not contain the gasp that rose of its own volition from my throat.

"It all looks so very particular," Colin muttered. "As if the killer was looking for something."

I blanched, glancing over at him to see whether he was trying to ease the thick tension, only to find an expression of thoughtful consideration on his face that was matched by a similar countenance on the inspector's.

"Only the Devil knows what lurks in the mind of a man capable of such a thing as this," Inspector Evans said after a moment.

Colin took a step into the room. "Then the challenge will be ours to discover the same thing."

I sipped a quick breath and stepped forward, stopping at the door to search its jamb for signs of forced entry, though truthfully I was doing everything I could to avoid looking at the carnage.

"How many of your men have already trampled over this scene?" Colin asked from somewhere near the table, his words disturbing the silence enough to make me jump slightly.

"Far more than you will like," came the answer, and I could tell by the tone of the inspector's voice that he was displeased himself. "I am afraid the superintendent does not hold to your opinion of contamination at these scenes. The more eyes pledged to a case, the more men committed to shifts walking these same streets, the better he feels."

"Look how well that served him during the Ripper murders," Colin murmured.

"You don't think—" The inspector was interrupted by a harsh, disapproving exhalation from out in the hallway before he could finish.

"What an appalling sight," Denton Ross hissed, tugging on the white lapels of his coroner's coat and stiffening his spine. But it was not lost on me that he was staring at Colin and not at the body.

"You will give us a moment," Inspector Evans snapped, obviously having noticed the same thing. "Are you finished here, Mr. Pendragon?"

"Have photographs been taken?" Colin asked, coming back toward me.

The inspector turned to one of the young bobbies standing just outside the door, ensuring that none of the uninvited curious gained entry, and the young man informed us that a photographer had been there not half an hour before our arrival. The news did not please Colin.

"So we will have photographs of a well-contaminated murder scene taken some seven hours after the discovery of the body. It scarcely seems worth the effort," he groused. "I should like to see your autopsy report as soon as you are finished, Mr. Ross," he said as he swept to the door.

"I do not report to you," Mr. Ross grunted as he moved over to the body, his assistant—the lanky, pock-marked Miles Kindall—following in his wake.

"Mr. Pendragon and Mr. Pruitt are here in an official Scotland Yard capacity," the inspector barked. "You will remember that, sir."

Mr. Ross *tsked* as he stood over the body. "Well, this is a buggered mess. Get some pans and a bucket or two, Mr. Kindall. This isn't going to go easily."

"Please proceed with restraint, Mr. Ross," the inspector warned. "You will notice the newspapers have yet to be notified."

A thin sneer tugged at a corner of Mr. Ross's rubbery lips. "You're worried that it's the Ripper again, aren't you. The Yard's unfinished business come back for its due."

"Are you an investigator now?" Colin asked, his voice tinged with distaste. "Because you are speaking absurdities."

Mr. Ross snickered, and the very sound of it made my stomach seize with fury. "So insistent, Mr. Pendragon."

"Enough, Mr. Ross," the inspector cut in. "I'll not have you inflaming this city with something we have no notion about."

"Oh, come now . . ."

"You will deliver your report first thing tomorrow morning, Mr. Ross," Colin spoke up, "or I will have the Yard assign your assistant to take the lead."

Mr. Kindall reappeared in the doorway as though summoned, a bucket hanging from each hand with various metal pans poking out and one tucked firmly beneath his right arm. "What?"

"You are on the verge of promotion," Colin answered, and was gone.

"That ruddy bastard." Mr. Ross seethed before Inspector Evans could hold up a hand.

"Collect the remains and get on your way," he reiterated. "And we *will* have the results of your autopsy first thing tomorrow."

I did not wait for the response but hurried to find Colin, having caught the sudden unsteadiness of his gait as he had left the room. There was no doubt that the wounds he had recently suffered at the hands of Charlotte Hutton—two bullets to the chest and a crack to the back of his skull—were still demanding their due. I feared it was too soon for him to take a case.

CHAPTER 2

⟫◦⟪

The ride back to our flat was silent, as I kept quiet rather than harangue him about the frailness of his health. I held my tongue, watching the neighborhoods slowly improve as we clattered from Whitechapel to Kensington, all the while pledging that I would shoulder the greater burden of this case.

"My father's here," he mumbled as our cab slowed, and I too spotted the black Town Coach with its team of horses and the Pendragon lion and griffin crest on its side.

"I wonder what he wants?" I said, though I was sure it was to check on Colin. Sir Atherton had been by nearly every day since Colin's release from hospital two weeks prior, though he always managed to scrounge up some alternate reason for coming.

When Colin and I reached our study at the top of the stairs, it was to find Sir Atherton in Colin's chair before the fire, as always, and Mrs. Behmoth across from him on the settee, the two of them deep in what looked to be overwrought conversation. There was a full service of tea laid out before them, as well as a plate of raspberry and lemon tartlets. One pleasant adjunct of Colin's well-wishers was the fact that Mrs. Behmoth had taken to baking daily. We were ever prepared for visitors now and even happier when there were none to share the spoils with.

"Well . . ." Sir Atherton's pale gray eyes drifted over to us as he smiled. "Here are my boys at last."

Mrs. Behmoth shifted around and scowled the instant her eyes fell on Colin. "Ya look like shite." Her eyes darted to me. "What're ya thinkin', keepin' 'im out 'alf the bleedin' day when 'e's still tryin' ta get well?"

"He is *not* my keeper," Colin informed her curtly as he dropped onto the settee next to her.

Her eyes narrowed. "Well, ya still look like shite."

"You do need to take care of yourself," Sir Atherton spoke up.

"Are you here for a reason, or are the two of you simply testing my patience?" Colin muttered, picking up two unused tea-cups stacked to one side of the tray and pouring us tea.

"Besides checking on how you are getting along, I am actually here on another matter," he answered just before he took a nip of his tea.

"Well, thank heavens. I'll not be coddled." He thrust my tea-cup at me.

"Yer too ornery ta be coddled," Mrs. Behmoth announced as she pushed herself off the settee, grabbed the teapot, and headed down the stairs.

"That woman is infuriating," Colin bothered to state as he turned back toward his father. "You were saying . . . ?" And if I hadn't already been aware of his flagging vitality I could most certainly hear it in his voice.

Sir Atherton gave a thin smile, and I suspected he had caught it as well. "Do you remember a gentleman by the name of Braxton Everclear when we were living in Bombay? He was a junior diplomat who worked in my office and used to come by the house quite a bit after your mother died. Had a son a few years older than you named Henry."

"I remember Braxton. He was very kind. But I don't remember a son."

"His boy never lived in India. I suppose they thought he might do better in London, but he got into quite a bit of trouble anyway and finally died some years back after living what can only be described as a wayward life."

"Wayward . . . ?" Colin repeated, though I was sure we both knew what Sir Atherton meant.

"He struggled with an addiction to alcohol and opium that brought him to a sorrowful end." Sir Atherton shifted his eyes to me and offered a gentle smile. "Henry did not have the fortitude to conquer his demons," he added for my benefit, though it was the love of his son that had truly made it possible for me to vanquish my own. "Braxton and his late wife were devastated. They pledged themselves to care for Henry's only child, a boy born out of wedlock named Quentin, though he could not be properly claimed as their grandson."

"What a horror to convention," Colin mumbled with distaste.

"Braxton has been sending the boy money ever since," Sir Atherton continued without comment, "encouraging him to attend university, but the lad has been drifting, and Braxton has struggled to have an impact."

"How old is Quentin?" I asked.

"Nineteen. He was living in Whitechapel with his mother until recently."

"Whitechapel . . ." Colin muttered thoughtfully. "Why isn't he living with her any longer?"

"She became ill and died. It has left the boy on his own."

"And has Mr. Everclear offered his grandson the refuge he deserves, or has propriety forbid him from doing so?" Colin asked, his tone disapproving.

"He has tried to do the best that he can," his father answered patiently. "You cannot judge him for the tenets of a society he does not control."

"You needn't speak to me of such things. Ethan and I would be their victim as well if we did not strive so for invisibility." He brought a thumb and forefinger to the bridge of his nose, and I could tell that he had reached the limits of his patience.

"You were telling us about Quentin Everclear," I said to Sir Atherton. "Does Braxton have some concerns about his grandson?"

"He does." Sir Atherton nodded. "He's not heard from the

boy in over two weeks now. And what he finds most distressing is that the first of the month has come and gone without word. He has been paying the boy's rent since his mother's death, but this month the lad failed to come around and pick it up. Braxton sent a messenger to inquire about the boy, but the man was turned away without a scrap of information. I just thought . . ." He hesitated, his eyes settling on mine, making his apprehension about asking anything of his ailing son clear.

"Your thought is well placed," I spoke up. "I will go down to Whitechapel myself and see what I can learn. Do you have an address?"

"I do." He pulled out a folded square of paper from his jacket pocket.

"The two of us will go," Colin said, his voice contrite as Mrs. Behmoth could be heard coming up the stairs. "We will find the young man and deliver him to his grandfather. You really mustn't mind me," he continued, "I do seem to be a bit short of patience today."

"Today?!" Mrs. Behmoth parroted as she reached the landing with the steaming teapot clutched in one hand.

"I have grown weary of healing," he allowed, throwing Mrs. Behmoth a fierce scowl as she settled back onto the settee and began refilling our cups.

"Then you should let Ethan handle this business with Quentin Everclear," Sir Atherton suggested. "I am sure it will amount to little more than a few questions. Nothing to trouble yourself over."

"And yet here you are asking for our help," Colin needled before releasing a sigh. "Besides, it is hardly a bother, as we have just accepted a case in Whitechapel anyway."

"Wot?!" While Mrs. Behmoth was the first to speak, I noticed the same question already forming on Sir Atherton's lips.

"We shall be working with Scotland Yard to solve two recent murders. One a week ago and the other last night."

"I don't remember reading about two murders . . ." Sir Atherton started to say.

"You ain't well enough ta be runnin' all over the place chasin' down some nutter. Are ya outta yer bloody mind?" Mrs. Behmoth swung her anger to me. "Wot in the 'ell are ya thinkin', lettin' 'im do that?!"

"Excuse me," Colin interrupted harshly. "Ethan does not *let* me do anything. I answer neither to him nor to you. I am perfectly capable of assessing my own health, thank you very much."

"Well, yer the color a wax and ya lost too much weight."

"Weight?!" Colin repeated, flexing an arm with a prideful scowl.

Mrs. Behmoth stood up and waved him off, scowling at Sir Atherton as she headed for the stairs. "'E's yer fault, ya know. You were too easy on 'im." And having had her say she stomped down the steps, notably disregarding the responsibility she'd had in helping to bring him up.

"Do I really look thin?" Colin asked as he pushed himself off the settee and stared into the mantel mirror.

"It's just a bit of weight," his father answered before I could derail the topic. "Now, what of these Whitechapel murders . . . ?"

"The Yard kept the first one quiet, but they'll have no such luck with this second," Colin replied in a single breath, turning and heading for the back of the room where my desk was—and his weights. "Two women carved up clavicle to pelvis with their insides removed." He snatched up the dumbbells, and I saw him wince as he tried to curl them toward his body.

"Their insides removed?" Sir Atherton's face curdled.

"The killer placed them around their bodies like some sort of ritual," I explained. "Should you be doing that?" I called to Colin.

"It was made to look like the work of the Ripper," Colin added, ignoring my question.

"The Ripper?!" Sir Atherton clanged his teacup back onto the table. "After all these years. Does Scotland Yard really think that maniac is back?" Colin did not answer, persisting in pumping the weights even though a sheen had already sprung up on his brow and his face continued to register obvious pain. "Put those damned things down!" his father suddenly roared.

Colin's arms hung at his sides, and his expression stung, though whether from surprise or contrition I could not tell. I busied myself topping off our tea and in a moment was aware that Colin had dropped back onto the settee. "Another tartlet?" I said to Sir Atherton, hoping I did not sound as awkward as I felt.

"I shouldn't." He gave me a stiff grin. "I am round enough already." He picked up Colin's teacup and held it across to him. "I want to know if you believe it is the Ripper."

Colin took the cup and leaned back, his fatigue evident. "It is extremely unlikely."

"Unlikely . . . ? Why?"

"A man driven by such urges to do what he did could not simply stop himself for seven years. Not unless he was in prison or committed to an asylum."

Sir Atherton let out a deep breath and shook his head. "This would indeed be a scourge. If that fiend has returned . . ."

"Which is why the Yard has sought my help." Colin glanced over at me, and the slightest grin crooked a corner of his mouth. "Me and Ethan."

"In that"—his father declared—"Scotland Yard has chosen wisely. But I must insist you see to yourself first. You will serve no one if you fall ill or aggravate your wounds."

Colin allowed a wistful smile. "Very well, but there is something I have been meaning to ask of you. . . ."

"And what would that be?"

"Charlotte Hutton," he said, his voice rumbling his distaste. "The last we know of her is that the train she was on the night she shot me was headed for Dover. We can assume she was headed for the Continent, since her funds remain frozen in Zurich, but how much longer will the Swiss agree to hold them? Can you continue to encourage them to cooperate?"

"I shall do whatever I can."

"Good. Because I should very much like to go to Zurich the moment this Whitechapel case is completed. It is well past time for that woman to pay for the deaths she caused and her attempt on my own life."

Sir Atherton flinched ever so slightly. "Wouldn't it be wiser to let the international authorities attend to that woman? You cannot be expected to remain dispassionate where she is concerned."

Colin's eyebrows rose. "You doubt my integrity?"

"Don't be absurd." Sir Atherton pushed himself out of Colin's chair and headed for the staircase. "I will do what I can with the Swiss authorities," he said when he reached the steps, "but I will have your word, Colin. You will take care. I will not lose you and neither will Ethan."

Without realizing it, I found myself holding my breath as I waited for Colin's response. What was it I feared that he might say? Yet when he did finally answer—"You have it"—I was unaccountably relieved. It was a promise to his father, and I knew the significance that held for him.

CHAPTER 3

The first eruption took place that very evening with the release of the *Times*'s late edition heralding the two Whitechapel murders. The tension throughout the city became immediately palpable as the once-familiar headline was again being shouted along the streets. However, the second, and worse, event came the following morning in the form of an unrelenting pounding on our door downstairs.

"What the bloody hell?!" Colin cursed as he bolted upright in bed in the span of an instant. "What time is it?"

I checked my watch on the night table with far less vigor than he was showing. "Nearly six," I managed to mumble.

He threw the covers back and popped out with more enthusiasm than I had seen from him since the shooting. I watched as he stormed around the room, pulling on his underclothes and then hurriedly shrugging into a suit. "Aren't you getting up?"

"There isn't anyone I want to see at this hour. I barely want to see you."

"Well, you'd best roust yourself, as this is not likely to be good."

"All right," I answered with a yawn before finally pushing myself into a sitting position.

The next voice to be heard was that of Mrs. Behmoth shouting from some distance, almost assuredly the midpoint of the stairs. "*Ya got about a dozen a them newspaper arses out on the porch. Ya want me ta tell 'em ta bugger off?*"

Colin yanked our bedroom door open before turning and glaring back at me. "Are you coming, or would you rather I line them up in here?"

I crawled from the bed with a great sigh and moved to the doorway next to him. "*Have them wait outside,*" I hollered back to Mrs. Behmoth. "*And tell them we'll join them shortly.*"

Colin looked me over, one of his eyebrows arched. "I wonder what they'll make of the sight of you."

I gave him a scowl before retreating into the room and yanking on a suit of my own. Within a handful of minutes I had joined him in the study, though I struggled to look as alert as he did.

"Whatever this is, we had best tread carefully," he warned as we started down the stairs. "These men will print anything to sell another of their paper."

"Now, ain't you two jest a sight," Mrs. Behmoth interrupted from the doorway to the kitchen, her sleeves rolled up to her forearms and her hands and apron already dusted with flour, a newspaper tucked under one arm. "I can't believe I'm seein' the two a you up before the milk's delivered. It's almost respectable."

"Do be sure to have the tea ready when we come back inside, or I'll not be respectable for long," Colin advised. And satisfied with his response he swept the door open and stepped outside without a further glance in her direction, missing the fact that she was now holding the newspaper out toward us.

"What . . . ?" I started to say, but it was too late. He was already outside, and before I could get a second word out of my mouth I heard a man fairly shout at him:

"*Is it true the Ripper's returned?!*"

Mrs. Behmoth gave a slim shrug as she tossed the folded newspaper onto the shelf of the hall tree and headed back for her kitchen. Even folded I could make out the bulk of Colin's name and the totality of the word *Ripper*. Our involvement, it seemed, had been leaked.

"Wherever did you hear such nonsense?" I heard Colin say in a distinctly disapproving tone.

"Are you saying it isn't true then?" the same voice pressed as I joined him on our small porch.

I was amazed to find that Mrs. Behmoth had not exaggerated, as there were indeed fourteen men hovering at the bottom of our steps, each carrying a notepad of one form or another and a pencil. There was little else to distinguish them, although I did recognize the gentleman from the *Times,* as he had once done a florid piece on Colin.

The man who had shouted the question was young and ordinary, save for the elaborate waxed mustache that curled out from the sides of his lips. "Can we quote you on that, Mr. Pendragon?" he pushed again.

"You and your conspirators have come pounding on my door at an ungodly hour with your agenda." Colin glared at him. "What is your name?"

"My name?" The young man looked taken aback as he glanced around for a moment, as though beseeching a cohort to lend a hand. "I'm Clement Triffler with the *Sun*. Now will you answer my question?"

Colin answered with a hollow laugh that carried not a shred of mirth in it. "By asking your name, Mr. Trifling, I have simply brought us to the same level: You know my name, and now I know yours. However, if you wish me to address your shouted questions you will first answer the single one I have put to you: Wherever did you hear such rubbish about Jack the Ripper?"

"It was the coroner." An older man standing to the side of the eager Mr. Triffler spoke up. "I'm Oswalt Northcliffe with the *Daily Telegraph*. I spoke with Mr. Ross last night once he'd completed the autopsy on Miss Linton, and he informed me that Scotland Yard believes the Ripper has returned. He said it's why they've brought you in to assist with the investigation. Is it true?"

"Thank you for your gallantry, Mr. Northcliffe," Colin replied, "but if you knew me at all you would know that I do not...*ever*...assist in an investigation. I work for myself, which means I assist no one. Nevertheless, I *was* consulting with Inspector Maurice Evans yesterday at the scene of Miss Linton's murder. He sought my opinion on a few matters. . . ."

"What sort of matters?" Mr. Triffler spouted before Colin could finish.

Colin slid his eyes to the young man once again. "Ah, Mr. Trifling . . ."

"It's Triff—" he started to correct, but Colin was not to be stopped.

". . . if Inspector Evans would like to discuss with you the matters he discussed with me, then he is free to do so, but I'll not relinquish his confidence. Which is why he sought my advice rather than that of Mr. Ross." He offered a thin-lipped smile.

"But Mr. Pendragon"—it was the man I recognized from the *Times*, Mr. Hatch or Thatch—"will you not give us any statement? If only to quell the public hysteria."

Colin's face soured. "If there is hysteria, it is the result of careless wordsmithing by you men. You clearly do not intend to report the truth when you print the ramblings of a man like Denton Ross without the slightest care. I'll not be quoted in the wake of him." And to ensure these men understood that he meant what he said, he turned and stalked back into the house, kicking the door shut.

"Nice going, Triffler," someone standing farther back grumbled.

"Would you be willing to give us a comment, Mr. Pruitt?" the man from the *Times* called to me. "Now that Mr. Pendragon has admonished us, it would be nice to come away with *something* for our efforts."

I suspected that Mr. Hatch...or Thatch...was the only one amongst this crowd who even knew my name. "Very well," I answered rather more brusquely than I had meant. "Let me tell you three things, two of which I hope you will commit to memory. First, I will remind the lot of you that Mr. Pendragon was seriously wounded not three weeks ago on the train platform at Victoria Station when he was shot several times during the escape of Charlotte Hutton. A bit of empathy would be appreciated before you pound on our door at this hour with your hyperbole."

I glowered at them before I continued. "Second, Mr. Pendragon has been a proponent of your periodicals for over a dozen years. In that time, with all of the news conferences he has given, explaining his cases and detailing their outcomes, I should think he has earned some level of courtesy that might keep some of you from being so eager to publish any bit of nonsense without checking with him first.

"And last of all . . ." But if I'd had a third point at the start of my scolding I lost it as my eyes fell on Mr. Triffler's unyielding face. "Last of all"—I heard myself repeat—"you are never again to bang on this door before eight unless the building is ablaze."

One corner of Mr. Triffler's lips ticked up, accentuated by his preposterous curling moustache, and to keep myself from attempting to remove the smugness of his grin I turned with the sharpness of a palace guard and hastened inside.

"It's on the front page of the *Sun* and probably every other paper," Colin groaned as I barreled inside, nearly colliding with him.

"I tried ta show ya," Mrs. Behmoth spoke as she exited the kitchen with a tray full of tea and warm scones, heading for the stairs.

Colin flipped the paper toward me, and I gaped at the headline: RIPPER RETURNS!—PENDRAGON AIDS GRISLY INVESTIGATION. It stared at me like an accusatory harridan. Colin was gripping the paper so tightly that his fingers were as white as his face. "Denton Ross is quoted throughout," he said in a flat, tight voice. "If I see him today I shall have to throttle him with my bare hands."

I winced, knowing he would exact some revenge if our paths did cross his today. "I'll go pick up the autopsy report," I said as I followed him upstairs. "And perhaps we should go to the Yard ... ?" It all felt uncomfortable given that our work was usually done outside of the public's focus.

"Yes ... of course ..." he answered distractedly. "Ruddy hell," he added, flopping down into his chair and fussing with the tea things Mrs. Behmoth had brought up. Finding only two cups on the tray he glanced over at her, a frown creasing his forehead.

"I already 'ad some," she said as she moved back toward the staircase. "And I don't fancy sittin' 'ere with you in a mood this early in the day."

He went back to preparing our tea without a word, and while I wanted to protest that he had good reason for his mood, I kept my mouth shut until I had fetched a scone and received my first cup of Earl Grey. "The Yard will have someone who will handle those newsmen. Inspector Evans will make sure they're kept at bay."

"It's hardly their fault." He sighed and leaned back, his teacup cradled in both hands. "The return of the Ripper is a story that would indeed merit full reporting by them. It is their duty. It is the reason they are paid. But it will also make this case very much more difficult. They'll forever be hovering about, demanding answers. Which is their bloody right."

"But the Yard will field their inquiries. It needn't be our concern."

He stared at me from over the rim of his cup, one of his eyebrows cocked in either amusement or annoyance, I couldn't tell which. "The Yard failed to apprehend the Ripper six years ago," he stated dryly, making his exasperation clear. "So do you really think the press will return to the same source for their information? Or will they pester the renowned detective who has been brought in to guide them?" He pointed to himself. "Personally, I would come to me."

I wanted to laugh, but I knew he was right. "They will be everywhere."

He nodded, snatching up a scone. "We will be investigating under a microscope." He shook his head and thrust his cup back onto the table. "And all the while the mood of the city . . . the fear . . . will only intensify."

My stomach sank even though there was no surprise in what he had said. "Are you sure you're up to this?"

He looked at me and smiled, his eyes twinkling with pleasure before slowly sobering up. "How could you ask such a thing?" he said after a minute.

CHAPTER 4

⟶◦◦◦⟵

Pandemonium reigned in front of the Yard by the time we arrived there several hours later. If we'd had a dozen newspapermen vying for answers at our flat, the steps leading up to the front doors of the Yard were besieged by four times as many, which did not include the greater than a hundred additional souls whom I assumed were there from the sheer terror of thinking the Ripper had returned. The mob was shouting for answers at a decibel even greater than that of the newsmen themselves.

Colin's ashen face grew paler as we approached, so it was without a second's thought that I ordered our cab driver to take us around to the back. Neither of us were prepared to wade into such a throng.

"Gentlemen . . ." Inspector Evans looked harried and tense when we reached his tiny office. "We seem to have lost control of this day already."

"Thank Denton Ross for that," Colin snarled as he dropped into a chair across from the inspector. "I suggest you order him gagged and trussed."

"Nothing would please me more."

"They were outside our flat before dawn. If Mrs. Behmoth were not an early riser I'm afraid we would this minute be visiting her in a cell charged with manslaughter." A scowl settled on his face. "They're just lucky I'm not up to snuff." His lament punctured my mood.

"Never mind those vultures," the inspector was quick to say. "Just refer them back to us. We've a woman on staff named Alice Kettle whose sole job it is to handle that rabble."

"A woman?!" Colin repeated. "How very clever."

"She's a relative of one of the commissioners, but don't be fooled. She is a sharp one and can hold her own with that lot."

"I've seen her quoted," I said.

"I'll let her know they've been by your flat." The inspector slid a folder across to Colin. "She'll straighten them out."

Colin nodded as he flipped open the folder, his face curdling at once. "These images do not diminish." He dug the photos out and held them toward me while continuing to stare down at an assemblage of papers.

"No, thank you," I said, tossing them—upside down—onto the inspector's desk. "I assume that is Mr. Ross's report on Miss Linton?"

"It is," the inspector answered. "Mr. Ross had Mr. Kindall drop it off early this morning. It would seem Mr. Ross was mindful enough not to show up here himself, though you will notice he has signed every page to ensure we know the work is his."

"Who else would do it?" Colin grumbled, slowly thumbing through the pages as his scowl deepened.

"Still . . ." Inspector Evans twisted his face into a glower. "I have a mind to request that Mr. Ross be put on suspension. Let Mr. Kindall cover for him."

"Do you think him capable?" I asked. "How long has he even been working in the coroner's office?"

The inspector sighed, running a quick hand through his thinning hair. "A year . . . year and a half, maybe. Long enough to know how to keep quiet. Something Mr. Ross seems incapable of doing."

"Any chance you still have the autopsy report for the first victim?" Colin asked as he passed the folder to me.

A rogue's grin bloomed across the inspector's face in an instant. "I thought you might wish to see that." He snatched up another folder with pride, tossing it to Colin. "Her name was Elsie Barrell . . ."

"I see that," Colin responded blithely as he poured himself into the file without a hint of acknowledgment for the inspector's prescience.

I turned my attention to Amelia Linton's file and read as much as I could stomach. Even without the photographs nestled within, I found the descriptions of her remains vivid enough to elicit memories I did not wish to relive. When the report began to tick off the organs placed outside of her body, I shut the folder and glanced back at Colin. "Are you looking for anything in particular?" I asked, knowing that he was.

"Similarities," he said, shutting the folder before holding it out to me. "I think you will see what I mean."

It took a moment before I could force my hand forward to grab the proffered file. There was no question that I should look at it, yet I could have lived the whole of my life without flipping it open. I tugged the raised flap and was instantly staring at the photograph of a young woman with dark, curly hair whose sternum had been split just as with Miss Linton. A second photograph revealed the same lumpy assemblage of dark masses arranged around the body that were, without question, her organs.

Before the imagery could emblazon itself upon my mind, I turned the photograph up and was relieved to see a page filled with nothing but words. Cold, analytical descriptions filled with medical jargon slid across my field of vision, and I did not even realize that I'd ceased to process what I was reading until I heard Colin say my name. "Pardon?" I looked at him with a dazed expression.

"Do you notice anything odd?" he asked for what I assumed was the second time.

"It's barbaric." I answered without a thought.

He stared back at me, his eyebrows hitching the tiniest bit. "Well . . . yes . . . so it is. Anything else?"

"They have both been gutted like animals," the inspector spoke up, giving me the feeling we were playing the most macabre sort of parlor game.

Colin nodded with a thin smile, continuing to stare at me. "Both of the victims are missing their wombs and a length of intestine. Now, whatever do you suppose that means?"

"The man is a lunatic," the inspector roared.

Colin flicked his eyes at him but did not respond. There seemed nothing more to say.

"Where do we begin?" I finally spoke up.

"Do you have a fresh contingent of men assigned to Whitechapel working undercover?" Colin asked.

"They were selected yesterday afternoon and are to begin their rotating assignments tonight."

"And women . . . ?" Colin pressed. "Are there any women you might use as decoys?"

Inspector Evans blanched and rubbed at his forehead. "And who would we get for a duty like that? Beyond Miss Kettle, the only women on the rolls at Scotland Yard are secretaries and recordkeepers. Would you really have us tart them up and risk their lives in the alleyways of Whitechapel?"

"Not unless they are capable of handling a firearm and defending themselves with skill. There are such women, you know."

"The superintendent would never approve it."

"These may quickly become desperate times," Colin pressed. "Now that Mr. Ross has raised the specter of the Ripper, we may all face a very public vilification if there is another murder. You already have an assemblage of terrified and infuriated citizens at your door. Their numbers will only grow until an arrest is made."

Inspector Evans stood up, a pained expression on his face. "Fine," he muttered as he came around his desk. "Did you want to come with me? We *are* partners, and you might do a better job of making your case."

"I'll go with you," I said to the inspector. I had promised to take the lead on this case, and I meant to do so. "Besides, I have spent a third of my life making pleas on Colin's behalf, why shouldn't I do so now?" I looked at him as the inspector went out into the hallway. "Go home. Let Mrs. Behmoth fuss over you for a while."

Colin looked startled as he stared back at me, and I feared I had embarrassed him or made him angry. "Very well, then," he said after a moment, but the only sound I heard in his voice was weariness.

"If I can have a moment . . ." I said to the inspector.

"Of course. I'll meet you at the stairwell. Take your time." He paused and gave us a sideways grin. "But not *too* much time."

We all laughed—it felt good—as the inspector bustled off.

"You aren't worried about me, are you?" Colin asked.

"No!" I answered with far too much insistence.

Colin kicked the inspector's door shut with a boot, an accusatory scowl leveled on me. "I am fine, Ethan. Do not fret over me. I have my father and Mrs. Behmoth to do that."

"Whether you like it or not I am a part of that list, just as you would be had I been shot." The lines on his forehead softened, as did his eyes. "Now go home. I'll be there soon."

"All right," he muttered, and it made my heart rupture. "What did you want to tell me?"

I sucked in a tremulous breath. "I wanted to tell you that I'm stopping by Saint Paul's on my way back to our flat. I intend to find Paul and ask him to keep his ears open while he and his lads are running about Whitechapel. That boy can collect more information than anyone who has ever helped us. Perhaps he will be useful to us again now."

A smile edged onto Colin's lips, setting a glimmer behind his eyes. "An excellent idea."

"I thought I'd also have him make an inquiry at the boardinghouse where Quentin Everclear lives. If young Mr. Everclear really has gone missing, then no one will think twice about a boy asking a question or two. He'll be presumed to be nothing more than a messenger."

Colin's smile grew as he looked at me. "Well, now, you are simply making me feel superfluous."

"Good." I gave him a smile of my own. "Now go, and I shall see you in a short while." Without another word I hurried out the door and down the hall after Inspector Evans, feeling well pleased with myself as though maybe, just this once, I was actually the least bit in charge: a folly if there ever was one.

CHAPTER 5

As usual, Paul was a fount of chatter and information, which suited me since, just as the inspector had suspected, Superintendent Tottenshire had refused to consider using women as decoys no matter how much logic I brought to bear. Women, he insisted, were simply unsuitable for such a task. I was certain Mrs. Pankhurst and her suffragettes might have something to say about that.

"I was plannin' on comin' by anyway," Paul was explaining as we rattled toward Kensington in an open cab. "I ain't seen Mr. P since 'e got 'ome from 'ospital." I had him pegged at twelve or thirteen, though in truth I didn't really know how old he was. But whatever he counted in years one thing was certain, over the time Colin and I had come to know this lad, he was far shrewder and more clever than I had ever been at a like age.

"I think you will find him improved," I said. I hadn't intended to bring Paul back to the flat, but he had been so relentless in his concern for Colin that I thought he should come and see for himself.

"I was so 'appy ta see they was bringin' Mr. P on to the Whitechapel case. 'At's when I knew everything was gonna be a'right."

"You read the papers?"

"Nah," he snorted. "But I see the 'eadlines when I'm runnin' about. I know what's 'appenin'."

I chuckled. "I'd say you know better than most." Which was true, but the deed that had earned him my truest allegiance was his selfless display on the train platform in the wake of Charlotte Hutton having shot Colin.

"'At's why you and Mr. P keep 'irin' me. There ain't nothin' goes on I can't find somethin' about. 'Cept these ruddy murders."

"Don't you worry. Mr. Pendragon and I will solve this."

He looked at me curiously but didn't say anything further. It took another moment before I realized that this proud, egotistical boy was amused at my having included myself in credit for unraveling the case.

The cab pulled to the curb by our flat, and Paul bounced out before I finished paying. For some reason he felt compelled to knock on the door, so Mrs. Behmoth was already pulling it open by the time I reached the porch.

She gave a feigned scowl as she stared at Paul. "Wot's this urchin doin' 'ere?"

"He's come to see Colin," I answered.

"Well, 'e ain't 'ere, but ya might as well come inside anyway," she went on, dragging Paul across the threshold. "I just made some scones, and they ain't gonna eat themselves." In spite of her bluster I knew Paul had also earned her affections.

I stopped at the bottom of the stairs as Paul scampered up to the study. "Where did he go? He said he was coming right back from the Yard."

"'E did come back," she muttered, swinging the door shut and heading for the kitchen. "And then 'is father came by in a dither. The two of 'em took off a while ago." She stopped in the doorway and stared back at me. "Didn't say where they was goin'."

I sighed, my frustration well in evidence. "How long ago did they leave?"

"'Bout an hour, I s'pose." She disappeared into the kitchen, leaving the door swinging in her wake.

I grumbled, determined to let Colin know how foolish he was being as soon as he returned. "I don't know when he's due back, but you are welcome to wait for him."

Paul looked back at me from the settee with a broad smile. "I can't believe that old lady is fetchin' me some tea and scones. She don't like me."

I could not help but laugh. "After what you did for Mr. Pendragon I would say she likes you better than most now."

He shrugged. "Well, I ain't seen 'er treat you all that good anyway."

"*'E get what 'e deserves,*" she hollered as she began her ascent.

"There you have it," I said. "Mrs. Behmoth may be our housekeeper and cook, but she also helped to raise Mr. Pendragon. So she does what she chooses." I could see confusion on Paul's face. "It's complicated."

"It ain't complicated," she said as she rounded the corner from the landing with the tea tray in her hands. "This is a right respectable 'ousehold and we all got our jobs." She set the tray down and flopped onto the settee next to Paul, taking the liberty of pouring for us. "Though I can't always tell wot this one does," she said as she thrust a cup toward me. "'E showed up on the doorstep 'bout a dozen years ago and never left." She passed another cup to Paul. "Don't break that," she muttered under her breath as she shoved the plate of scones toward him before standing up again. "This is all ya get in case Sir Atherton comes back, so don't ask for more." She offered what passed for a smile and headed back down the stairs.

"Wot did she mean 'bout you showin' up and never leavin'?"

I shook my head and let my face curdle, but before I could answer, the front door opened and closed beneath our feet. "That must be Colin," I said, rising and moving to the landing. He came pounding up the stairs alone, his usual zeal absent, and as he crested the landing I realized why. His face was gray, his lips thin and pursed, and he appeared to be moving somewhat unsteadily with one hand brushing along the wall.

"Ethan . . ." he started to say as Paul bounced off the settee and turned toward him with a brilliant smile on his boyish face. "Paul."

"Mr. P! I came ta see 'ow yer doin'."

I followed Colin as he came around and lowered himself into his chair, not even bothering to try covering the wince that darted across his face. "I have had better days," he answered with a dry chuckle. "But what of you? Are you going to be able to assist us by poking around Quentin Everclear's boardinghouse?"

"A course I am." He beamed. "I'll 'ave information for ya later today."

"Outstanding," he said, but the word sounded hollow as he accepted the teacup that I held out to him. "And what do you hear around Whitechapel with regard to these recent murders?"

"All the ladies is scared. Most of 'em is keepin' ta small groups and won't 'ardly talk to a bloke. But they can't keep that up fer long, 'cause they gotta eat and pay fer their rooms. It's bad." He shook his head, yet his face suddenly broke out in an incongruous smile. "But I see they got you workin' the case now. Smartest thing them shites at the Yard ever done."

"Yes. Mr. Pruitt and I will do what we can."

I was taken aback by Colin's statement, so filled with self-doubt and pessimism that I found myself on my feet before realizing I had intended to stand. "You really must get to Mr. Everclear's boardinghouse," I said to Paul without a shred of finesse. "We need to figure out whether his disappearance is even a disappearance at all." I plucked at Paul's shoulder and hustled him toward the landing after pressing two of the scones into his hands. "Come back as soon as you've had a chance to ask around." He dutifully started down the stairs, but I grabbed his arm before he could get out of my reach. "And be careful, Paul. Don't do anything foolish or get yourself into trouble. Just a few questions here and there, and then come back and tell us what you've learned."

Paul smirked at me, making me feel like the foolish one. "I know wot ta do," he assured, and then thundered down the stairs and out the door.

I supposed he did.

In the next moment I turned on Colin. "You have done too much," I scolded. "Where did you go with your father? You have *got* to start taking better care of yourself. . . ." I let my voice die out as he held up a hand and stared back at me with an undeniable lack of vitality.

"Not now, Ethan. I am done in. You can lecture me later."

I sat down next to him and sucked in a breath, fully aware that he would not like what I was about to say. "We are going to tell Inspector Evans that we cannot work on these Whitechapel murders. I shall tell him myself. I will make him understand."

Colin looked at me, his blue eyes void of their usual eagerness. "And who will tell the Queen?"

"What . . . ?"

He put his teacup down and ran a hand through his hair, exhaling harshly. "That's where my father and I were. She requested to see me."

"What?!" I said again, suddenly incapable of following what he was telling me. "Who wanted to see you?"

"Our sovereign," he answered dully. "Victoria . . . ?" He pushed himself to his feet. "She fears a grand-nephew may be caught up in these Whitechapel killings. She swore my father and me to secrecy but demands to know whether he is guilty." He gave a labored shrug. "If he is, she will have him committed without a word, but heaven knows what we would tell the newspapermen. Such a scandal against the Crown is unthinkable."

"But . . ." I wanted to say something insightful and uncompromising, yet nothing would spring to my mind as he gave me a forlorn smile before heading back to our bedroom.

CHAPTER 6

I lasted about thirty minutes before deciding I had to get out and do something. I'd been pacing back and forth across the parlor more times than I dared admit, alternately worrying about Colin and convincing myself there was nothing to fear, before finally realizing that I couldn't continue to just wait there without risking losing my mind. The only choice I had was to get out onto the streets of Whitechapel and see what I could learn. If I intended to offer Colin some relief on these cases, then I had little reason not to start at once.

With the stealth of a cat on the verge of pouncing, I hurried down the stairs and into the kitchen to inform Mrs. Behmoth of my intent. Her disinterest was abundant, ceasing at the point of whether I would be back in time for dinner.

Thirty minutes after that, I was disembarking from a cab, having arrived just off Limehouse Street, a distance the driver had agreed to only because night had not yet thrown its cloak over the city. I would need to make sure not to tarry, or I'd have to walk back at least as far as Tower Bridge to get a ride home again.

I had not chosen Limehouse arbitrarily. I was going to visit the one person I knew who would most likely have information about what was being whispered along the alleyways of White-chapel. I was going to see my old caretaker, Maw Heikens.

I crossed the street and hurried down the decimated block, soot-blackened row houses lined up like rotting teeth. It had been better than a year since I had last come to call on Maw, as Colin did not approve of her or the sort of care she had provided me. Still, she'd proven vital during the Bellingham case, and it seemed foolish to ignore a potential resource when we were facing a case that was already setting the newspapermen and the public on edge.

Maw's building looked unchanged from my last visit with the exception of a small wooden sign hanging just outside the building's entry that read MAW'S CLUB. Though it was less than a year old, it already suffered from chipping paint and severe fading. Nevertheless, given the neighborhood I presumed it was likely enough to rekindle her business. My last visit had found her tipping toward destitution and every bit as decayed as her building.

I swung the door open and entered, and was instantly struck by the thick, earthy scent of opium. If any changes had been made inside I could not tell, as it remained as ill lit as ever, its patrons loath to engage with one another. The memory of it all—the smell, the people—made it feel as though time had ceased to move forward. In that moment I was once again struggling toward adulthood under an opiate cloud, doing Maw's bidding for room and board and whatever dregs of opium I could beg, pilfer, or scrounge from the used pipes.

The main room opened to my right, revealing itself in its hazy opacity. There were small clusters of people scattered about, but as I glanced around I could not find Maw.

"I ain't seen you here before," a young woman said as she approached me from out of the smoky vapor.

"I would like to speak to Maw," I answered, perhaps a bit too harshly. While I had no quarrel with this woman—in fact, I did not recognize her in the least—I could already feel the slithering poke of the opiate as it wormed into my brain—so welcoming, so familiar.

"Who wants ta know?" she pressed, her brow splitting into

a smooth frown that made me realize she was younger than she looked.

"Ethan Pruitt. I lived here once. I used to work for Maw. I used to help take care of this place."

She laughed, displaying a mouth as filled with gaps as it was teeth. "Took care a this place, did ya? Well, ya did a shite job of it."

And now I did have a quarrel with this woman. "Where's Maw?"

"Gone."

"Gone . . . ? Gone where?!"

I received a look that seemed equal parts amusement and disbelief. "You'll have ta ask the Devil that."

I'm not sure why, but it took another moment before I realized what she was telling me. It's not that Maw wasn't old or hadn't lived the hardest of lives, it's that she had always seemed somehow indestructible, including the last time I had seen her, when she'd warned me not to come back again. "How long ago?" I finally managed to ask.

She gave a slight shrug. "'Bout a year, I guess."

I felt myself wince, struck by the timing of her death in relation to my last visit. It made me grateful to have seen her one last time, to have been able to rearrange old ghosts, at least somewhat. "And how is it that you've come to run this place?"

"Yer a man with a lot a questions," she shot back, eyeing me with closer consideration. Clearly aware that I was not a potential customer.

"I told you, I lived here once. Maw looked out for me. She was . . ." My mind raced through a hundred possibilities before I finally settled on, ". . . a friend."

The woman laughed, and I could hardly blame her. "A friend, eh? Where were you when she was dyin'?"

I could do little more than glance away from her piercing gaze.

She waved me off like a pestering gnat. "Why'd ya want her anyway?"

I sucked in a quick breath. I had come all this way and wasn't about to fail without even trying. "Maw used to help me out from time to time. Fill me in on details about Whitechapel. Nobody knew more about what was happening here than her."

"What'd you say yer name was?"

"Ethan Pruitt."

To my surprise a slow grin spread across her face. "I know who you are. Yer that bloke what works with that Pendragon bloke. The one who's always solvin' cases."

"I am," I answered with some pride.

"Ya came here ta ask Maw about the Ripper, didn't ya?"

"The Ripper?" I studied her face. "Is that what you're hearing? Does everyone believe that twaddle being printed in the papers?"

"The papers?" She laughed again, making me feel ever more the fool. "You think any a this lot gives a shite about what's written in them bleedin' papers? You been gone too long." She started to turn away from me, dismissing me, but I refused to be so easily disdained.

"Is that what *you* think?" I said. "That the Ripper has returned?"

She looked back at me, and I was amazed to find that her face looked grim. "It's him, all right. Makin' a right mockery a you and yer feckin' Yard. Nobody gives a ruddy shite what happens down here, so he's come back ta do what he pleases jest like the last time."

"Then why do you think he stopped the first time?" I demanded before she could try to move away from me again.

Her eyebrows caved in. "'Cause the Devil works in his own time. Now I've got payin' customers ta tend to. . . ."

"Fine. One more question then. Have you ever heard of a young man named Quentin Everclear?"

She shook her head and tossed me a frown. "Nah. But we ain't much fer names 'ere. I think ya'd know that."

"Of course." I reached into my pocket and pulled out a pound note, offering it to her. "Thank you for taking care of Maw."

She looked at the proffered note and then at me, her disapproval on full display. "That ain't gonna do 'er any good now," she said with noticeable contempt before turning and walking away, leaving the pound dangling from my fingers like an offense.

I stuffed it back into my pocket and cast my eyes around the blurry room, noting the small clusters of people dispersed about, each lost to their own deliriums. I wondered if any of them might be Braxton Everclear's grandson, but I no longer felt the eagerness to find out. Paul would report back tonight, and we would see if the young Quentin Everclear was even missing at all. As it was, I could no longer tolerate the opium smoke stinging my nose and throat, and at least that fact pleased me.

I hurried back out to the street and was surprised to find it far more crowded than usual given that it was only just starting to ease toward late afternoon. It took a moment before I abruptly realized the reason: There was fear here. Real fear. With the night drawing closer, most people did not wish to be caught by the darkness. The Devil, it seemed, really had returned.

CHAPTER 7

—⟫•⟪—

Dinner was dispatched without fuss. In an effort to promote Colin's health, Mrs. Behmoth had set herself to making steak and kidney pie, a concoction I find rather horrid. To make matters worse, Colin did little more than pick at, his appetite having yet to reassert itself. I shared what few rumors I had heard about the Ripper while in Whitechapel, and he succeeded in not rebuking me for having gone to see Maw. When I told him she had died, he even managed to feign a hint of sorrow, though I was certain some part of him was relieved. It was as if he feared I might actually go tumbling back one day.

We had both shoved the odorous pies back and forth on our plates countless times, and I was just about girded to face Mrs. Behmoth's wrath by whisking it all downstairs when a rapid pounding struck the door below.

"That will be Paul," Colin said as he pushed himself up from the table in our parlor and wandered over to the fireplace. "I hope he has something to report about Quentin Everclear."

I heaved a sigh in spite of myself and began to collect our dishes. We didn't often take our meals up here, but with Colin's weakened constitution we had been doing so since his return from hospital. That fact had compelled Mrs. Behmoth to resume harping about the installation of a dumbwaiter, and quite frankly I did not blame her.

Before I could make the least headway with the cleanup, Paul came bounding up the stairs, his eyes widening in unabashed longing at the bounty of food about to go to waste. "Steak and kidney pie," he mumbled.

I looked at him—dark-haired, scrawny, face perpetually smudged, cap being wound and unwound between his fingers—and stopped what I was doing. "Would you like some?"

He did not need to be asked twice. "Ain't ya gonna eat this?" he asked as he plopped himself down at Colin's place and snatched up his fork.

"Let me get you a fresh place setting. . . ." I started to say, but it was too late. The boy had already tucked himself into Colin's leftovers without a second thought. "Right." I sat down across from him, and a moment later Colin came over and lowered himself into the chair at the end of the table.

"Mrs. Behmoth will be happy," he said.

"I ain't 'ad somethin' like this in forever," Paul managed to say with a mouth full of food. "Yer missus really knows 'ow ta cook." He glanced over at my plate, half-eaten and sullenly spread asunder. "Ya done with that?" He reached over and snatched the plate before I could answer, scraping its contents onto his own. "Ya shouldn't be wastin' good food," he scolded.

"No wonder I like this lad." Mrs. Behmoth spoke up from the landing, startling me as I had not heard her climbing the stairs. "'E knows wot's good." Paul beamed, a rather unsightly vision given the dribbles of gravy streaking his chin. "We got berries and cream for dessert, if ya want."

Paul's eyes ignited again. "Yes, Mum," he answered at once, and only then turned to look at Colin and me. Colin chuckled, and as Mrs. Behmoth headed back down the stairs I thought I heard her chuckling as well.

"I see that working on the Everclear case has stoked your appetite," Colin said.

"It 'as." He nodded heartily as he continued to shove great forkfuls of steak, kidney beans, and pastry into his mouth. "'Cause I found 'im."

Colin bolted upright in an instant, his attention immediately riveted. "You what?!"

"I found 'im," Paul repeated with a grin so wide I could have counted his teeth. "'E were livin' right where ya said, actin' big as a dog wot's 'ead a the pack."

"How extraordinary. . . ."

"Did you engage him?" I asked.

Paul tossed me a vacant look as he struck the bottom of the plate. "Wot?"

"Did you speak with him?" I corrected, glancing over at Colin. "I don't think we wanted him to know he was being sought. . . ."

"I didn't say shite to 'im," Paul answered before Colin could, and then, ignoring the napkin next to his plate, pulled a sleeve across his mouth. "I know 'is landlady. A right slag wot used ta toss me da' when he weren't totally sotted." The sound of Mrs. Behmoth ascending the stairs could be heard in the brief silence as Paul finished off the glass of water next to the plate.

Mrs. Behmoth rounded the landing carrying a small dish filled with sliced strawberries and cream. "Ya sure got a mouth on ya fer such a little shite," she informed him, nevertheless setting the dish in front of him and removing the emptied plates.

"Yes, Mum."

"Yes, Mum," she repeated with a shake of her head. "Ya boys is all the same." And to my surprise she shot a sideways glace at Colin before gathering the rest of the things and heading back down to the kitchen.

"So you know Mr. Everclear's landlady. . . ." Colin prodded, though Paul was already scarfing down his dessert as though one of us might try to take it from him. "What did she tell you?"

"That 'e were a sod but 'e pays 'is rent on time."

"Does he? And has he paid this month's?"

"I s'pose." Paul shrugged as he picked up the little bowl and drank down the pink-hued cream. He licked his upper lip and gave a smile. "She didn't say 'e 'adn't."

"Did she mention whether she had seen him recently?"

"Didn't 'ave ta." Paul's grin widened as he shoved himself back from the table and stood, taking a languorous stretch. "I saw 'im meself." He laughed, keenly aware that he had our rapt attention as he walked over to the settee and flopped down as though we were visiting in his home. "She told me 'e's a reg'lar at the opium clubs. 'Specially the ones down near the Thames. Weren't 'ard ta find 'im. Skinny little bugger 'bout the size a me wrist."

"You have done a remarkable job," Colin acknowledged, lowering himself into his chair with yet another all too familiar wince fleeting across his face. "Mr. Pruitt will see to it that you are appropriately compensated."

"Wot?" Paul turned his gaze to me.

"I shall pay you," I answered, pulling several crowns from my pocket and handing them over. "For a job well done."

Paul reached forward and snatched them from my open palm before leaning back again, his smile never wavering. "That ain't all," he added. "The cheeky bugger was tossin' money about like 'e made it 'imself."

"What do you mean?"

"Payin' ta fill the pipes a 'alf the place."

"You went inside?!" I blurted before I could manage to still my tongue.

Paul leveled a look at me that seemed intended to suggest I had lost my mind. "Well, I weren't gonna find the bloke standin' outside in the alley. Besides, I know the chippie wot runs 'at club."

"Of course you do."

"What you aren't aware of," Colin cut in as he turned to Paul, "is that his grandfather is a man of some means, so it is entirely possible that young Mr. Everclear has saved a sum over time to feed his habit."

"No, no." Paul waved him off. "'E 'ad a roll a pound notes on 'im that I could 'ardly get me fist around."

"You what?!" I erupted.

"I put it all back." Paul rolled his eyes. "'E didn't even know I took it. It weren't outta 'is pocket but a minute." He shrugged. "Maybe two."

Colin reached for his vest pocket, no doubt to grab a coin to flip through his fingers while he ruminated some internal consideration, but the sudden movement made him wince again, and as I watched, his hand dropped without completing its task. "It's all quite curious," he said after another moment. "It seems we will need to pay this young man a visit ourselves. If we are to report back to his grandfather, we had best have the whole tale."

"Do ya want me ta follow 'im?" Paul asked, an overabundance of enthusiasm marking his words.

"I think you have done more than enough for now," Colin answered. "Why don't you let us handle things from here, and we will let you know as soon as your services are required again."

"Ya swear?!"

"You are the only person we come to for assistance."

"Damn right," Paul crowed as he popped off the settee. "Ya keep feelin' better, Mr. P, and I'll come round ta check on ya."

"You mustn't trouble yourself," Colin said with something of a wan smile. "I shall be fine."

"I ain't really worried 'bout you," Paul said with a snicker. "I just thought I'd come by at suppertime."

"You absolutely must do that," I spoke up. "I know Mrs. Behmoth will be pleased to have a guest with such an eager appetite."

Not three minutes later Paul slammed the door on his way out, but not before I heard Mrs. Behmoth press a satchel of bread, cheeses, and fruit into his hands and, almost assuredly, a few biscuits or tarts. I looked around to find Colin gazing toward the fireplace, his brow creased, and felt relieved that he was thusly engaged. "Are you wondering about Quentin Everclear?" I asked. "I doubted he would be so easily located, or even alive."

"I feared the same. We shall have to go and speak with him tomorrow. I cannot help but be intrigued by the bundle of cash

Paul found on him, and I am certain Braxton will want to know as well. . . ." His voice trailed off for a moment as he continued to stare at the fire before abruptly pushing himself to his feet with a grimace. "We must get down to Whitechapel tomorrow and begin our investigation properly. My name has been fed to the press. I'll not have another murder on my watch."

"Do you really suppose you can capture this madman so easily?"

He looked at me with his familiar determination, as though trying to comprehend how I could ask such an absurd thing, but I was not fooled. For behind his eyes, deeply imbedded so as to cover the fact even from himself, I could tell that something had changed with the momentum of his recovery. Before I could remark on it, however, he mumbled that he was retiring for the night, and in that moment I knew I was right.

CHAPTER 8

I was dreaming, I think, about ghosts. Miserable, haunted souls corrupted by one manner of unfinished business or another, leaving them cursed to wander the realm of the living moaning and lamenting their fate. Or so our friend, Lady Dahlia Stuart, professed to those who came to partake of her theoretical clairvoyance. What clawed at me was the unnerving sounds of their spectral grief—so real, so alarming, that they woke me from my slumber with a jolt. And that was when I realized I could still hear them.

In less than an instant, even as my brain struggled to attune itself to wakefulness, I realized it wasn't ghosts at all—it was Colin. I pushed myself up on an elbow and peered at him through the darkness. He was on his back and seemed to be asleep, though an audible groan was released with his every exhalation. "Colin?" I muttered in little more than a whisper, but he did not respond.

I slid closer to him, becoming aware of the dampness of the sheets from his head to his waist as I did so. His hair was matted and wet, and his face glistened in the refracted moonlight as though he had been doing one of his physical workouts.

"Colin?!" I said again, the tone of my voice ratcheting in tandem with the pounding of my heart. I reached out and touched his forehead, and felt at once that he was burning up.

I was out of the bed and yanking on some undergarments before I knew I was moving, stumbling to the door and flinging it open so hard that it slammed against the perpendicular wall. "*Mrs. Behmoth!*" I hollered, struck by the fact that my voice sounded controlled in spite of my rampaging heart and the numbness that had seized my head. "*I need you to get outside and flag a cab. We must get Colin to hospital.*"

I hurried back into the room and snatched up a cloth, dunking it into the pitcher across from our bedside and wringing it out in a single movement. "Colin?" I now said in full voice as I turned up the light by the bed and drew the cloth across his forehead. "Can you hear me?"

His jaw was taut, and I could tell that he was gritting his teeth, but his eyes did not open. They did not so much as flutter.

I wiped his face, dabbing the cool cloth across his skin, but still there was no response other than the guttural groans that continued to escape from his mouth. The whole of his body was radiating heat, leaving me little choice but to quickly re-wet the cloth and begin dragging it across his chest and arms, trying to cool him off and bring his wretched fever down.

"Wot's 'appenin' . . . ?" Mrs. Behmoth called as she came pounding down the hall.

"He's burning up. He's not answering. We've got to get him to hospital."

"It's those ruddy wounds," she cursed. "I told 'im 'e were pushin' 'imself too 'ard."

"Please," I said, tamping back my panic, "just get a cab."

To my relief she did not utter another word, but turned and fled, moving with a nimbleness and speed that both consoled and distressed me.

"I'm going to get a nightshirt on you," I told Colin, neither expecting nor receiving any acknowledgment. "We have to get you to hospital," I continued, knowing that had he been awake or even the least bit aware he would have protested the idea, if not flatly refused. But no such argument ventured forth from his throat. There was only that same abhorrent sound as though his body was struggling to cheat death.

I set the cloth on his forehead before rushing over to his armoire in three resolute steps, flinging the doors wide and digging through the pile of items strewn across the bottom, fumbling for one of the seldom used garments. I could find every manner of undergarment and enough hosiery to cover his feet into the next millennium, but there were no nightshirts.

"Dammit to bloody hell," I seethed, slamming the doors shut and bounding over to my own armoire. At least there I knew I would find what I wanted. In less than a moment I yanked a gray nightshirt out by its collar.

I hurried back to the bed and was struck again by the sight of him. It was terrible, ever more so given the desperate guttural sound that continued to issue forth. It gripped my heart and stole my breath, so I started talking to him, chattering really, as soon as I sat on the bed, saying the words I needed to hear and hoping he would find them comforting as well. "It's going to be all right. Everything is going to be fine."

I lifted him into a sitting position, cradling his head within the crux of one arm so I could coax the nightshirt down over his shoulders. With the bulk of it bunching around his neck, I leaned him against my body and worked his left arm through the first arm hole, working as quickly and carefully as I dared, all the while fearing that I might be causing him further distress even though he had yet to reflect so much as a whisper of lucidity.

I worked his right arm through the appropriate opening and, before I pulled the whole of it down over his body, stopped to take a fast look at the wounds marring his chest. There were two of them, along with a single exit wound under his arm that I could not see. While both of the chest wounds looked puffy and reddish, neither appeared any the worse than when he had left the hospital, which prompted a dreadful chill to careen down my spine as I tried to imagine what might have happened to so suddenly render him in such a state.

"I got a cab waitin'," Mrs. Behmoth announced as she came rushing back into the room. "'Ow's 'e doin'?"

"Help me get this on him," I answered, ignoring her question.

She reached over me and, while I held him around the shoulders, continuing to cradle his lolling head, she pulled the nightshirt down to his waist. "'Ow are we gonna get 'im downstairs?"

"I'll carry him."

"Wot?! You'll never make it. 'E's too 'eavy."

"Don't be absurd," I snapped, but I was the one being foolish. While I had leverage over Colin by virtue of my height, he carried the musculature that would have been a godsend at this moment.

I threw the covers back so sharply that they took flight and sailed off onto the floor in a heap. "I'm going to lift you up," I told him in a voice so soft I could barely hear it myself. I swung his legs around and let his feet strike the carpet. "Hold him a minute," I instructed. Mrs. Behmoth stepped forward and placed one meaty hand on each of his shoulders, letting his head rest against the softness of her belly. The very sight of it made me want to laugh and cry.

"Let me get in front of him so I can lift him from under the arms," I said, convincing myself it was the right thing to do even as I settled on the plan. "Then I'll squat down and put him on one of my shoulders. That's how I'll get him downstairs."

To my surprise Mrs. Behmoth did not say anything other than to give a silent nod as she shifted to one side. I slid my arms into the crux beneath Colin's arms and heaved him up, grateful for the shove Mrs. Behmoth planted on the middle of his back. His groan suddenly stretched into something that sounded living and tortured, but it was too late to stop, so without allowing a further thought I planted my right shoulder at his waist, hefting him up as though I might actually have the wherewithal to do such a thing. It felt like the whole of my body registered its outrage in an instant. I realized I was going to crumple to the floor, until I felt Mrs. Behmoth's hands grip the arm I had wrapped around Colin's waist pinioning me in place.

I stood there, Colin dangling over my shoulder, and the only sound I could hear was his shallow, unsteady breathing. That, more than anything else, terrified me.

"Can ya walk?" Mrs. Behmoth hissed in a whispery tone.

"Of course," I insisted, before taking the smallest step forward and realizing that I really could. "Guide me. I'll need help getting down the stairs."

Mrs. Behmoth did not answer. She didn't need to. We both understood what had to be done.

She walked backward from the bedroom, down the hall, through the study, and across the landing, her hands on my elbows, tugging a little left or right depending on the direction I needed to go. Through the length of it she would mutter where we were as though I could not tell, and repeatedly questioned how I was doing. I did not answer her. Not once. I could not risk the energy. All I could do was set my feet down, one after the other, and know that I was moving ever forward.

"Step . . ." she said, and her grip tightened on my elbows. I could feel her descending ever so slightly and knew we were facing the worst of it.

The ball of my foot reached the abyss, and I let my bare heel scrape against the riser as I lowered myself, slamming down onto the next step much more severely than I had expected.

"Step . . ." she said again, as though I did not know there were thirteen more.

On we went until we reached the waiting cab and its driver, who suffered an immediate upbraiding from Mrs. Behmoth until he scrambled down and helped me lower Colin safely inside the waiting vehicle. By the time I stood up again, out of breath and belatedly aware of the chill and how underdressed I was, Mrs. Behmoth was already scurrying back out the door, a robe around her shoulders and another hanging from one arm with a pair of slippers clutched in a hand. I had no idea how she'd gotten them so quickly.

She hiked the robe over my shoulders, and we both fell into

the carriage, me sitting next to Colin, his head cradled on my lap. *"To Saint George's!"* I yelled to the man as though he could not already imagine where we were headed. "And be quick," I bothered to add. And for the first time since I had awoken from my ruptured sleep, my voice sounded on the verge of breaking.

CHAPTER 9

Sepsis.

It was a new word, a word I had only heard once before, a nightmarish word. It referred to the infections so often attendant with a wound, only this sort of infection—sepsis—meant it was rampaging throughout the entirety of the body. The prognosis was grave. The doctors carefully tempered their reports, giving little indication as to the likelihood for recovery, assuring they would remain faultless should the worst transpire. An outcome I refused to conceive.

I knew Mrs. Behmoth held the same view, as each morning she showed up at Saint George's bearing a sack of fresh shortbreads and several small meat pies. "'E needs ta get 'is strength back," she would say, and Sir Atherton or I would agree. It did not matter to any of us that consciousness continued to elude him.

For two days the three of us sat by his bedside, waiting for him to rouse himself, and by the end of both days Mrs. Behmoth had no choice but to give the food to the night duty nurses. Just the same, when dawn cracked on the third day she showed up again, another basket of treats clutched in her hands, an identical look of determination etched on her broad face, and I could not have been more grateful for it.

"You need to go home and get some rest, Ethan," Sir Atherton suggested that third day, but he had no room to talk. He'd been at Colin's bedside with me from the moment the messenger I'd dispatched had reached him three mornings prior, though the two of us took turns during the nights. One of us would doze while the other watched Colin, and as I looked across at him—brilliant white hair askew, face as rumpled as the clothing he wore, eyes wearied and ringed with red—I could only imagine the sight the two of us made. The proof of it was in the fact that Mrs. Behmoth had brought me some proper clothing the third day.

"I'm fine right here," I answered. "He'll be cross when he wakes up and finds himself here. I'll not leave you to explain that to him."

We both chuckled, though the totality of the sound was dry and hollow. It brought no solace, and when I noticed the flicker of pain that darted behind Sir Atherton's eyes it caught my breath.

"'Ow is 'e?" Mrs. Behmoth bothered to ask, hope evident in her voice as she sat down in the third chair already arranged at his bedside. Neither Sir Atherton nor I answered. There was nothing to say—nothing new anyway.

At least he had ceased the mournful sounds he'd been making. While I was thankful for that, I could see little else the doctors had, or were, accomplishing. Leeches had been applied to his wounds on the first morning, and shortly thereafter one of the doctors had begun giving him shots of saline solution into the veins in his arms. They told us the shots were intended to help flush out the infection along with the cleansing the leeches were doing at the sites of the wounds themselves. The exit wound under his arm, the one I'd been unable to see, had turned out to be the worst. The injustice of that fact made me angry, though I cannot say what I would have done differently had I known it.

Colin's fever continued to spike and rage, and I would swab alcohol on his skin to wrestle it back down, but only after Sir Atherton informed the doctors that it was his wish for me to do so. I knew I was an oddity to the hospital staff—this friend of Colin Pendragon's who doted over him like a brother yet was nothing of the sort. But it mattered not a whit as long as Sir Atherton gave his consent.

"I made pigeon and venison pies," Mrs. Behmoth informed us as she set the basket at the foot of the bed. "'E loves those," she added, as if we might not know that. "An' I saw yer inspector when I was comin' in. 'E were talkin' ta one a 'is bobbies they got posted downstairs."

"Bobbies?" I repeated, and saw that Sir Atherton was as surprised as me.

"Ain't ya seen the papers?" She flicked her eyes between me and Sir Atherton. "Course not," she answered herself with a wearied exhalation. "Another a them girls got 'erself killed last night."

"Oh God," I heard myself say as my throat went dry.

"Them news blokes is crawlin' all round that lobby downstairs, demandin' ta talk ta—" Mrs. Behmoth stopped herself and sagged back into her chair, the impossibility of her statement seizing her own tongue.

The three of us sat there, immobile and silent, each lost to our own thoughts, until Inspector Evans knocked on the doorjamb, a look of expectation on his face. "Is it okay if I come in?"

"Of course," Sir Atherton said before I could, reminding me that it was not my place to do so.

He stepped into the room soundlessly, as though to make any noise might roust Colin from a much-needed sleep. "How is he doing?"

"My son is strong," Sir Atherton replied. "If anyone can fight this, it will be him."

"I have no doubt of that. There are days I still find him intimidating." The inspector gave a hesitant chuckle that Sir Atherton joined in on, but I could not force myself to engage. "Has he woken up yet?"

It was an unsettling question; nevertheless I was very much gratified by his use of the word *yet*. "There has been little change." I finally spoke up so that Sir Atherton would not have to carry the burden of this conversation on his own. "Soon enough," I hastened to add, and I swear that my heart skipped an actual beat as I proclaimed it.

"Ya want a shortbread?" Mrs. Behmoth held out the basket to him. "You can 'ave *one,* but I'm savin' the rest for 'im."

"I'm fine, thank you," he answered, though he did not look fine. While he remained as polished as ever, the consummate professional, his face was drawn and pale, and his eyes betrayed the fact that he had almost certainly managed no more than the briefest flirtation with sleep in a lengthy span of time. Which was how I knew what was coming. "Mr. Pruitt"—he sounded forlorn and wearied—"might I have a word for a moment?"

"I see no point." It came out harsher than I had intended, but there was nothing he could say that would move me from Colin's side.

"Ethan . . ." I was startled by Sir Atherton. "You have no cause to speak to the inspector in such a way. You said yourself that you and Colin have been working in partnership with him and Scotland Yard."

In the more than a dozen years that I have known Sir Atherton, I do not remember him ever scolding me, yet that was how it felt in that moment. It sent a wave of embarrassment coursing through me. "My apologies," I mumbled as I stood up, intending to head for the door.

"No, no." Sir Atherton pushed himself out of his chair and waved to Mrs. Behmoth. "We will go and stretch our legs while the two of you talk. I have been sitting far too long this morning and need to get some exercise before I become fused to this seat." He trundled to the door and held it wide for Mrs. Behmoth before turning back and looking at me. "Do remember," he said with a nod of his chin toward the bed, "I believe he can hear us." And then they were gone.

"Do you suppose that's true?" the inspector asked as he sank down into the seat Mrs. Behmoth had vacated.

"I don't really know. All of this . . ." I had no idea what to call any of it so I settled on a shrug.

"Well, it is certainly understandable. I can only imagine how his father must feel."

"Yes," I agreed, as there was no surprise or offense meant in his statement. I was but a friend with little need for consolation, and in that moment I wished that was true. "What is it you wanted to discuss?"

"I'm sure you can imagine," he responded, and I noticed a slight flush color his cheeks. "It is this case. There was another killing on Framingham last night, right in the center of Whitechapel."

"So I heard."

He cleared his throat before plunging ahead. "I am hoping you will come back with me to the young woman's boardinghouse. You will find the scene nearly untrampled. I have worked hard to ensure you get a proper look before too many of our lot start pillaging about. I know how important you and Mr. Pendragon believe that to be."

All I could think to do was sit there a minute and pretend I was considering his request. The thought of leaving Colin, even to fulfill an obligation he had pledged us to, felt inconceivable. The Yard would have to fend for itself.

"Your faith in me is misplaced," I finally said, though I found it impossible to look at him. "Colin is the sleuth. I am simply the one who takes the notes and reminds him of the names."

To my surprise Inspector Evans allowed the hint of a smile. "And I would say that it is your lack of faith in *yourself* that is misplaced, Mr. Pruitt. I cannot imagine that after all the years you have been following Mr. Pendragon from one end of this city to the other, you've not learned a great deal. A great deal indeed. I would even go so far as to state that you know a far sight more than most of the men at Scotland Yard. So you would do me an enormous turn if you would come and have a look—give me your perspective."

It was my turn to offer the slightest of smiles, to let him know that I was affected by his kind words though my mind would not be changed, but before I could demur again the door popped open and Sir Atherton returned, not with Mrs. Behmoth at his side but with Paul. The two of them looked so incongruous together that I did not immediately realize that Paul's face was smudged with black streaks that tracked across his face from his eyes to his chin. He had been crying.

"You will pardon the interruption," Sir Atherton said as he ushered Paul inside. "Mrs. Behmoth informed me that this is the young gentleman who did such a kindness for Colin the afternoon he was shot. It is an honor to finally be able to thank the noble lad," he continued, nodding his head and bowing like the refined diplomat he was.

Paul flushed, looking like his eyes might pop out of their sockets. "I ain't never met a real sir before," he muttered.

"You will find us very much like any other," Sir Atherton responded with a smile. "Now go on, tell Mr. Pruitt what you told Mrs. Behmoth."

Paul cuffed a hand across his cheeks before settling his gaze on me, shuffling from one foot to the other. "'Ow's Mr. P?" he asked in a voice far softer and more hesitant than I had ever heard from him before.

"He's going to be fine," I said, as much for myself as for him. "Now, what did you want to tell me?"

He scrunched his face up and shrugged Sir Atherton's hand from his shoulder before starting to speak again. "That woman wot was killed last night . . ." He paused a moment, though he kept fidgeting from side to side as though he needed to use the loo. "She were me mum."

"Your mother?" I racked my brain yet could not ever remember a single time he had mentioned his mother. "I . . ." But I could think of nothing else to say.

"Delphine Materly was your mother?" Inspector Evans asked in the midst of my bewilderment.

Paul glanced over at the inspector with an expression that held little willingness to engage. In an instant his eyes flicked back to mine, the misery floating behind them as familiar as that which I was feeling. "Are ya gonna find 'im? Are ya gonna make that bugger pay fer wot 'e did?" The scruffy boy stared at me, holding my gaze and daring me to deny him his due.

"Paul . . ." I started to say, unsure of what point I intended to make, when Sir Atherton spoke for me.

"Of course he will. You cannot continue to sit here, Ethan. Colin would not have it. Mrs. Behmoth and I will stay right here. It is for us to do. You come back when you can. You will find the three of us waiting for you."

I dared not speak, as I did not trust my heart or head to release the words unburdened. So I nodded, first to Sir Atherton and then to Inspector Evans, and with a grip to Paul's shoulder I turned him about and the two of us left. And all the while I took care not to give a backward glance, for I knew that would be the undoing of me.

CHAPTER 10

There was a sting in the air of fresh blood, metallic and sharp. That there was such a scent became understandable as soon I caught a glimpse of the volume and breadth of the stuff splattered almost as far as I could see across the dark, cramped space. Delphine Materly had put up a good fight, that much was evident, but if there remained an ounce of the life-giving liquid left within her veins I would have been surprised.

Inspector Evans and I were standing at the bottom of a short set of cellar steps that ran beside the blackened brick building Delphine Materly had lived in. The structure stood at the corner of a row of similar three-story flat-fronted buildings, all indistinguishable from one another, all covered in soot and grime and the rampant dereliction this neighborhood was fraught with. The crumbling cement steps that led down to a cellar barely high enough for a man to stand in were all that delineated this particular building from any of the others on this end of Framingham Street. And at this moment they were smeared by a swath of blood the width of my two hands.

True to his word, the inspector had a contingent of constables lined up along the front of the building that stretched right around the corner, keeping the crowd back behind the stanchions that had been rushed into place long before the two of us had arrived. Tempers were high amongst the assembled lot, so it had been a delicate task to wend our way through them. Fortunately neither the inspector nor I had been recognized, and for just an instant I had been glad that Colin wasn't with us.

I was also relieved that I had insisted Paul stay with one of the bobbies at the farthest periphery of this scene. He had begged to tag along, insisting it was what he needed to do, but I had been adamant. This was no place for a boy and most certainly not the son of the victim, no matter that she had abandoned him in his infancy, which he had admitted on the ride over.

"I would say that he attacked her on the street and dragged her down into the cellar," I said to the inspector, eager to make sure that he was seeing what I was.

"That was my thought too," he agreed, and I suspected we were both pleased by the confirmation.

"The killer is becoming bolder."

The inspector removed his hat and mopped at his face with his handkerchief in spite of the morning being cool and overcast. Strain was evident behind his eyes, but I thought I could also detect fear. "Or more careless," he finally said. "And I do believe the people here are losing their patience. We cannot have another debacle like we did six years ago."

"We won't," I insisted, though I was not sure I believed it myself.

"Do you think it could really be the Ripper again?"

I continued to stare into the claustrophobic space at the bottom of the steps, the harsh tang of the musty air daring me to move forward. I could feel the inspector's eyes on the side of my face, watching me, waiting to gauge my answer. "No. It isn't. The man known as Jack the Ripper is in Leavesden. Colin had him committed to the asylum, and I have already confirmed that he is there even now."

"*What?!*"

"He is an immigrant from Poland. A barber highly skilled with scissors and razors."

"Kosminski," the inspector blurted. "He's one of the men *we* were watching."

"I know. But Colin was able to do more than that, though he was never able to procure the proof a magistrate would have needed. So he had the man committed and the murders stopped." I glanced at him. "Nevertheless, in spite of what you and your colleagues must think, Colin has never sought to make the Yard appear inept."

"I know that, but . . ."

"He will be infuriated if he finds out that I have told you."

"But this news—"

"Matters not a whit unless Mr. Kosminski had been released from the asylum, which he has not. I told you, I have already checked. So what we are dealing with is somebody new. A copycat of some sort perhaps, or maybe just another man with a vendetta against the working-class women of our city. You and I will discover which." I glared at him and was pleased as a new determination began to settle upon his face. "I will ask you to maintain this secret with my promise that should it ever have a bearing, I will release you from your vow."

Inspector Evans released a labored sighed. "Very well. I appreciate your confidence, Mr. Pruitt." Before I could say anything further he stepped back and hollered up the stairs. "*Get those blasted lights over here.*" He turned back to me and nodded toward the murkiness awaiting us. "You are going to like this. We shall bring daylight into that cellar so we can have a proper look."

A carriage with a wagon attached was rolled forward, and upon the wagon sat an unwieldy contraption that turned out to be a steam generator. Connected to it by way of a black braided cord was a metal stand possessing four bare electric bulbs along a crossbar. The whole of it was delivered by a man dressed in coveralls. I had seen the Yard use something similar, if markedly larger, in the field behind the Connicle estate, and it was a godsend.

The inspector took it from the man and swung it around,

stabbing it toward the entry of the cellar just as he would have a lantern, only this apparatus lit that underworld as handily as if he held a dozen lanterns. "Shall we?" he asked grimly.

I nodded, the gesture filled with a mixture of curiosity and trepidation, and the two of us moved forward.

The room, such as it was, brightened obediently. It was little more than a crudely finished concrete rectangle with narrow pillars spaced evenly to support the structure above. The walls were streaked with grime and stains, the source of which one could only guess at, and as the glaring lights reflected on them, many could be seen to glisten and sparkle, an indication that they still oozed whatever was feeding them. Black mold bloomed in patches across much of the surface, lending a fuzzy, dimensional look that made the walls appear to be alive where it proliferated. Yet even in this unnerving setting it was obvious that something much more sinister had occurred.

"This way," Inspector Evans said, though it took a moment before either of us moved away from the entrance.

The air was dank and musty, that coppery smack of blood prevailing. It was clear by the broad trail of slick, blackened blood that the killer had dragged Delphine Materly back from the entranceway after having sliced her throat at the top of the steps. There were thin, uneven markings on either side of the wide swath of blood, and I was certain they were signs of the young woman's struggle to try to keep from being drawn out of sight. But it had been for naught. Her life had ended fifteen feet back from the doorway, slumped against the wall, her head lolled unnaturally far to one side and her entrails spilling from a gash in her belly that looked to have nearly split her in half. Her dress, slips, and underthings were slashed in what looked to be a haphazard frenzy, and her legs gaped in a display I was certain was meant to repel. The indecency wrought upon this woman curdled my insides.

"This man," I said in a barely discernable tone, "takes great relish in his work. In that he is very much like the Ripper."

Inspector Evans looked grim. "If the Ripper was that barber, what was his motive?"

"If?" I could not stop myself.

"I only meant that he was never properly convicted," he defended. "You must concede that fact no matter how dubious it may seem."

"He is a lunatic," I answered with little regard for his concession. "I have been assured the man is kept well sedated and is said to be unable to make so much as a trifle of sense anymore. What else could be expected of such a fiend?"

"Then do you suppose we are seeking the same sort of man now?"

I shook my head. "I should think it could be even worse. A copycat would be a more calculated individual, driven as much by his brutal thoughts as by his resolve to mimic another madman."

"But he *is* mad," the inspector protested.

"Doubly so," I corrected.

I turned back to the gruesome sight of Miss Materly and struggled to think how Colin would proceed. The facts, I reminded myself. He would be collecting the facts, nothing more.

"What do you know of Miss Materly's death so far?" I asked, even as I forced myself to take a step forward and kneel down by her body.

Inspector Evans removed his hat and wiped at his brow again, but he did not come any closer. "Her landlady says she went out at around ten last night, apparently the same as she does most nights. Doesn't know when she came back, but around twelve-thirty one of the girls who has a room just above the street at the front of the building said she heard a man and woman laughing outside. She didn't think anything of it until a couple minutes later when she says she heard some sort of scuffle." He stabbed his hat back onto his head and shifted the bar of lights slightly. "But she didn't do anything about it anyway because she says it stopped as quickly as it had begun. Says she figured one of the girls was just having it off with a customer. She was not alone herself," he added needlessly.

"At least we know the woman is telling the truth then. Had she claimed anything else . . ." I did not bother to finish my sentence as I stared at Delphine Materly's profile, her skin waxen and colorless, dark eyes open and staring down at the wreck of her entrails as if in dismay. Wisps of curly brown hair poked out from beneath a flowery, well-worn hat that was sitting askew atop her head. Her features were delicate, her face round, her chin firm. Was there something of Paul in her looks? "Did the woman say whether she or her customer bothered to look out the window?"

"No. She says they were busy."

"I'm certain of that. She is not paid to be idle. Have your constables questioned the man she was with?"

"We're looking for him," he answered, and I heard a touch of embarrassment in his voice. "She says she doesn't know his name and—"

"Yes, yes." I cut him off. There was no doubt that she would make that claim, but I knew that many of these women lived off the visits of recurrent patrons. "I should like to speak with her. Today." I knew it was what Colin would do.

"Of course," the inspector answered with the sharpness of a well-trained subordinate, making me flinch at having caused such a reaction.

I turned my attention back to Miss Materly and leaned in slightly to look at the slash across her throat. It started just below her left ear and ran all the way across as far as I could see, leaving a great wash of sticky blood sloughed across her upper chest and arms. Her failing heartbeat had forced out the life-giving cascade even as the killer had rendered her torso wide open, spilling her entrails onto her own lap.

Just as with the second victim, Miss Materly was split from the breastbone to the crux of her womanhood, her garments torn well aside so there could be no mistaking the savageness of the wound beneath. This scene was unique because her entrails had spilled forth yet had not been placed around her body in any sort of tableau as had been done with the first two. It appeared that everything remained in the vicinity of where it belonged, though I could take no more than a cursory glance.

"He was interrupted," I said as I pushed myself away from her, startled to find my legs unsteady as I stood up.

"What . . . ?!" The inspector turned the string of lights on me.

"He did not have time to complete his usual ritual," I explained, quickly stepping out of the electric glare. "She has been killed in the manner of the first two victims, yet he did not have time to remove her organs or arrange them around her body. It also does not appear that he has taken any part of her, though Denton Ross will have to determine that." I realized I was rubbing my palms against the sides of my coat and allowed myself to take a further step away as I cast my gaze around the otherwise dark space in an effort to get the vision of Miss Materly from burning into my brain.

"Which means someone may have seen or heard something after all."

"We must hope so," I agreed, though I heard little of that hope in my voice. "I'm afraid there is little else to go on. Now, I trust you will excuse me as I must get back to Saint George's. Please send word when I may speak with that woman who professes to have heard the scuffling. I will come to the Yard to interview her. And I should very much like to see the autopsy report on Miss Materly as soon as Mr. Ross has it prepared. We may yet be able to learn something about this killer by what he did and did not do."

"I'll send a man to fetch you as soon as we have the woman collected, and I shall bring the autopsy report by myself this evening. You may count on me to be appropriately demanding with our Mr. Ross."

He turned slightly, casting the yellowish light back toward the doorway, and that was when I saw it, set apart like a black smudge against the rust-hued trails of blood. I knew what it was at once, since I had watched Colin balance the whole of the Bellingham murders on just such a clue. "A shoe print," I said in a hushed tone as though the timber of my voice might cause it to evaporate like a mirage. "You must have it photographed without delay. Perhaps one of your men might even make a tracing of it."

Inspector Evans drew in a stilted breath as he came up behind me, jostling the lights to fully illuminate the part of a toe and heel from a man's right shoe that had been captured by the slick viscosity. "I'll not let another person down here until we have it fully captured."

"Very good." I did the best I could to summon a smile, but it proved a difficult entreaty. I would do my best on this case, to keep any other women from losing their lives in this heinous way, but for the moment I was consumed by the need to get back to Saint George's. The thought that Colin might have improved, that I could finally discuss this case with him, drove me from that dreadful place with the first stirrings of hope.

CHAPTER 11

In the midst of my own distress I had forgotten about Paul. Only as I headed toward the line of bobbies, my head hung low in an attempt to avoid eye contact with anyone in the gathered crowd, did I spot him. He was just where I had left him, at the side of a young bobby who looked very much peeved to have pulled such a duty.

I called to the lad. He scrambled over to me before his attendant could so much as register what was happening, and I steered him toward the area off to one side where several cabs stood waiting. I suspected all of them were set there at the behest of the gathered newspapermen who had descended upon the scene in an effort to ferret out something their competitors could not. I stepped over the stanchion while Paul ducked beneath, certain we were going to get away unmolested, when I suddenly caught my name being called.

I knew it was not the inspector so, for a moment, decided I would feign to have not heard. But the beckoning persisted, drawing ever closer as I tried to hail one of the waiting drivers, until I was finally forced to glance around. In an instant I saw the thick, black handlebar mustache of Clement Triffler from the *Sun* bearing down on the two of us.

"*Mr. Pruitt . . . !*" he called again, elbowing his way crosswise through the crowd that, until that second, had paid me little mind. "*You must let me assist you,*" he insisted, which only annoyed me further.

"*You needn't trouble yourself,*" I hollered back as yet another driver informed me that he was already engaged and waiting for his return fare. "I shall pay you double whatever you have been promised," I hissed up to the man, "if you will take us as far as Saint Paul's."

"That'd be the last fare I'd get from this lot and they're forever goin' from place ta place," he informed me, shaking his head with a gap-toothed grin. "I ain't daft."

"Three times!" I barked, swiftly becoming aware of a few people standing nearby turning my direction in the face of Mr. Triffler's encroaching assault. Even so, a laugh was the only answer I received for my efforts.

"Ain't you that one wot works for Colin Pendergone?" I heard a man ask from somewhere behind me with what sounded like derision.

"Wot ya runnin' from?" a woman growled. "The Ripper ain't after the likes a you, 'e's after *me!*"

And as though to endorse the woman's sentiment a cluster of people abruptly turned and surged toward Paul and me so that when I heard Mr. Triffler's voice again, this time very near me, I did not think twice about shoving Paul up into the coach. "You will move this carriage immediately," I roared at the startled driver, "or you will face the unbridled wrath of every constable from here to Scotland Yard."

My answer came in the crack of reins followed by a frantic bawl, which set the cab in motion. Our progress was tenuous, with much halting and swaying of the vehicle as the crowd pounded their fury on the doors and body of our rig until, thankfully, the din was pierced by the sound of shrill whistles, and I knew someone had ordered the constables to clear our way. In another minute we sprang free, the driver taking full advantage of our unexpected liberation to stir his horse to immediate speed.

"I'm sorry about that," I mumbled to Paul as I settled back, coaxing my heart and breath to cease their racing.

"Eh . . ." he muttered, his face plastered against the window with a look of amused indifference. "They're all a bunch a feckin' toads who only give a shite about themselves. I was about ta clear the bloody lot of 'em ta get you out."

I wanted to laugh at his bravado yet did not doubt that he would probably have found some way to do so. "They are scared. And they have every right to be. We know so little right now."

"When's Mr. P gonna wake up? We need 'is 'elp."

"Soon," I vowed. "Why is it I've never heard you mention your mother before?"

"Because I ain't never said more than 'allo ta 'er once, and I don't think she even knew 'oo I was."

"I'm sure she did."

Paul glanced at me with an expression that left no doubt that he was not buying my overearnest supposition. "She were bloody well drunk and tol' me ta piss off 'cause she 'ad a fish on 'er line." He returned to the view wheeling past our windows before adding, "She were just a slag but she were me mum."

His statement made me cringe. "Might you be wrong? How are you so certain she was your mother?"

"'Cause me dad were right fixed on 'er. 'E'd get ta drinkin' and start blubberin' 'bout losin' 'er. Right pitiful."

"Then he must be taking her death very hard."

Paul craned back and tossed me another disbelieving look before giving a halfhearted shrug. "Sure," was all he said.

"Why don't you let me take you to your flat. Make sure everything is all right."

He stared at me, his face appearing both boyish and regrettably hardened at the same time. It took a moment before he gave a coarse chuckle. "I ain't some nob wot needs ta be walked 'ome, ya know."

"Did I say you were?" I shot back.

A full minute passed before he finally muttered, "Suit yerself."

I wasted no time in pounding on the roof of the cab. "What's your address?" I asked.

"Warwick Lane," he mumbled without the slightest hint of interest. "Just past White Hart Street."

I called out the new destination to our driver before settling back in my seat, pleased to have a diversion that felt right. It would be good to meet Paul's father, I told myself, though I hoped I would not be dismayed when I did.

The cab began to slow as soon as we turned off Ludgate onto Warwick even though White Hart was still two blocks farther. In truth, Warwick was hardly more than a narrow passageway, more mud than cobbles. Despite its close proximity to Saint Paul's, the street was lined on both sides by tightly packed buildings, each looking more derelict than the next. If an ounce of care had ever been paid to these structures it could not now be seen. They seemed to be looming over the street like giant monoliths, blocking out the sun and ensuring that the air remained rife with the confined stench of humanity.

"Stop," Paul shouted as he flung himself out the door long before the driver could bring the coach to a halt.

"Thank you." I thrust a handful of change at the driver, to which he gave a satisfied smile. He had done us a great service, so I did not care that I had grossly overpaid him.

I jumped down, taking care to avoid landing in any discolored puddles, and hurried after Paul. He was stalking back the way we had come, hands stuffed deep within his trouser pockets, eyes raking the ground, looking as though he had been well chastised for one reason or another. I wondered whether his mood was a product of my determination to come here. Not halfway down the block he turned and bounded up a short set of steps to one of the ragged buildings.

The majority of its windows were either cracked or stuffed with cardboard where the glass was missing entirely, and all manner of garments hung from the smudged sills of many of the rooms, the linens stained by the soot-filled air. Even the building's front door looked ravaged, covered with hairline cracks and suffering from a bend that could have rivaled an archer's bow.

When Paul threw it open hard enough to slam against an interior wall, I understood why.

"Ya little pisher," I heard an old woman's voice shriek. "Ya keep doin' that and I'll set yer bleedin' arse on fire."

"Bugger off," he shot back, but there wasn't a speck of contempt in his tone. It was, I assumed, a ritual for them.

He leapt up the stairs by twos, hands still buried deep in his pockets, and I could tell this was something he did countless times a day. I followed closely, taking care not to touch the stair railing, which looked as coated with filth as the building itself. Paul flew past the second floor, and then the third, and just as I thought he might be about to lead us out onto the rooftop he turned and banged open a door that led into a small space that had once been nothing more than an attic.

Crudely finished and markedly small, it was further diminished by a sloped ceiling and enough clutter tossed about that I could not have said what the floor looked like, or any piece of furniture for that matter.

"'At you, boy?" A gravelly male voice pierced the silence from somewhere unseen.

"'Oo the 'ell else would it be?"

"Don't start with me, ya little shite." A short man with a soft body dressed in a pair of rumpled trousers and an undershirt, both wholly soiled, lumbered into the room from somewhere unseen—a water closet? . . . a bedroom? . . . I did not know. But when he saw me he stopped moving at once and narrowed his eyes with venom. "'Oo the feck are you?"

"I am an acquaintance of your son's."

"You plan on layin' a hand on 'im and you'll pay me for it first," he warned.

"What?!"

"Shut up, ya sot," Paul snarled as he threw himself down on a pile of clothing that apparently had a chair beneath it. "This 'ere is Mr. Pruitt like I told ya 'bout. Works fer Mr. Pendragon. They're the ones wot pays me ta 'elp 'em out. They're the ones keepin' you in yer bloody drink, so don't be a feckin' twat."

The man's face seemed to calcify for an instant before it

slowly crumbled into what I presumed was meant to be a look of welcome. He reached a hand up and shoved it through his tangle of hair to little avail before lurching fully into the room. "Well, why the 'ell didn't ya say so? Come in, come in," he spouted, waving an arm with enough force that I thought for a second he might lose what equilibrium he had and topple forward. "Can I get ya a drink, sir? Get me bottle, ya nob," he ordered out of a corner of his mouth, and to my surprise Paul popped right up and disappeared into the room his father had just come out of.

"Nothing for me," I demurred.

"Well, I 'ope ya don't mind if I 'ave a wee taste meself. It's med'cine, ya know. Keeps me gout in check." He beamed at me with a grin filled with gaps and rotting teeth. His mouth had to bring him constant pain, but I doubted he had ever lived the life of a man who would suffer from gout.

"I understand," I answered anyway. When Paul returned, ramming the bottle into his father's soft gut on his way back to the concealed chair, I noticed he had not bothered to bring any glasses. "Your son has been very helpful to Mr. Pendragon and me," I pointed out, the earnestness of my tone forced even to my own ears.

The man held the bottle in the crux of one arm, almost as though he was cradling a baby, and did not bother to look at me when he spoke again. "Glad 'e's good for somethin'. 'E don't do shite round 'ere."

"I am sorry for your loss," I said, increasingly eager to be finished here.

"Wot loss?"

I glanced over at Paul, who seemed to be paying no attention whatsoever, before looking back at his father. "Your wife . . ." I started to say.

"Ain't got a wife," he answered with finality. "If ya mean that slag wot shoved that twisted bit a shite into the world"—he gestured with his chin toward Paul—"then ya ain't got nothin' ta feel sorry for. She got wot she deserved."

"Wot the 'ell kinda thing is that ta say," Paul groused.

"Feck off, ya little bugger. Ya don't know nothin'. She didn't give a shite about you." He turned his glazed eyes toward me as a sneer broke out across his face. "Left me ta raise 'im meself. Didn't care two shites 'bout anyone but 'erself." He took a quick pull from the bottle. "They're all the same. A pox on every one of 'em."

"Did you know the other two women?" I asked, a terrible thought stirring in my mind.

"Maybe," he snarled. "Don't give a shite about any of 'em."

"So I gathered." I glanced toward Paul again and found him gaping at me. Had I been so obvious in asking the question? "You should come by the hospital tomorrow," I told Paul, hoping to cover for my clumsiness. "I know Mr. Pendragon will be pleased to see you."

"The boy's got work ta do," his father cut in. "'E can't be piffling off ta no 'ospital. If ya gave a ruddy piss about 'im ya'd give 'im a crown or two ta 'elp out. I can't work, ya know. Me insides ain't right."

"None a you is right," Paul scoffed.

"I only drink ta keep me stomach settled."

"Till tomorrow then?" I said to Paul, who returned a silent nod.

I let myself out and hurried back to Saint Paul's, where I was able to hail a cab with little effort. The trip to Saint George's was mercifully brief. Upon arriving, I noticed there was still a small crowd assembled near the front entrance as we turned the corner onto Blackshaw Road. While it was nothing like the swarm on Framingham, I had no desire to be pelted by questions.

"Pull around back," I instructed the driver.

He gave a grunt as we sailed past the cluster of people before turning at the far corner. Yet, as we rounded the back of the building near the small rear entrance, I realized that a handful of men were waiting there as well. While most held notepads, one had set up a camera as though I might be enticed to stand still for a photograph. My stomach clutched as the carriage slowed.

"Ya want me ta stop?" the driver asked.

"Yes." There was a chance these men would not know who I was. They were far more likely to be looking for Inspector Evans or Superintendent Tottenshire, or even Sir Atherton. "Here is fine," I said, selecting an area as close to the door as possible.

I paid the man and hopped down, and almost before my feet touched the ground I heard a man shout my name.

"*Mr. Pruitt!* Is it true that Mr. Pendragon is dying? That you'll now be working on this case alone with Scotland Yard?"

Four men raced toward me, each cradling a pencil and paper, making it impossible for me to tell which of them had possessed the gall to press such an inquiry on me. I did not recognize any of them as I glanced at their faces, momentarily struck mute by the coldness of the question. It took another moment before I even realized the men were continuing to pelt me with queries, so I did the only thing I could think to do: I lowered my chin and began barreling toward the door, a destination that seemed to only recede farther with my every step.

"*Gentlemen . . . !*" It was a woman's voice. It cut through the harsh masculine tones with ease, making me look up to find a tall, slender woman with rosy-blond hair swept back from a lovely face. Yet in spite of her obvious youth, there was a hardness behind her pale blue eyes that appeared to contain a steely confidence. "Have I taught you nothing in all the time we have been working together?" she continued with a smile, though I could hear a note of scolding in her tone. "You must come to me for your answers. You will get nothing from Mr. Pruitt. He is not here to speak with you. That is *my* curse." She laughed, and to my surprise, the men laughed with her.

"Thank you," I whispered as I sidled past her.

"Alice Kettle," she replied, sticking out her hand.

"Miss Kettle."

She did not allow me to slow in the least, swinging her other hand up onto my shoulder and propelling me forward until we were at the door. "I shall wish to speak with you later," she said under her breath, her lips barely moving. "I can be of use to you if you will allow me."

"Of course," I answered, even as she pressed me through the door. "Of course." And then she was gone, swallowed by the small phalanx of men who seemed quite happy to be haranguing her.

I made my way up to Colin's room and let myself in, trying to tamp my expectations lest I should be disappointed again. Sir Atherton seemed to be napping, but Mrs. Behmoth was wide awake, staring at Colin as though she might coax him to consciousness by the sheer force of her will.

Things had indeed changed since I had left. It seemed impossible, but Colin looked even paler than before, the color of his skin as monochromatic as the sheets he was lying on. His left arm was propped above his head with a small metal pan resting under his armpit. As I peered into the container I could see a layer of something thick and muddy yellow clotted across the bottom, like a soft cheese that had curdled. It smelled foul and stung my eyes as I tried to understand what it was.

"Infection," Sir Atherton spoke before I noticed that he had opened his eyes. "They have lanced the wound and applied a fresh battalion of leeches."

"Eight," Mrs. Behmoth added.

"Eight," Sir Atherton repeated with a grave sigh. "They are doing all they can," he muttered, and I wondered for whose benefit he had said it.

I sank into the empty chair and struggled to keep my composure. I wanted to say something reassuring, consoling, but I could not find the words, nor did I trust my own voice. I was afraid the very sound of it would betray me.

"No matter what," Sir Atherton spoke up again, "you and Mrs. Behmoth will always have the flat. You are my son, too, Ethan."

His words—meant to relieve me—cut me to my soul, and I could do no more than sit there, hollowed of anything but the inherent need to breathe.

CHAPTER 12

—————⊰•◦•⊱—————

Just as he had promised, Inspector Evans stopped by Saint George's with the autopsy report for Delphine Materly tucked under an arm before the afternoon had fully waned. It came as a welcome reprieve given what had been happening here. Colin's fever had spiked yet again, and while the doctors seemed inexplicably heartened by it, I could see little to take refuge in. They were injecting some sort of saline solution into his veins with renewed frequency, and the nurses continued to fuss with the open wound under his arm, swabbing it with alcohol on an hourly basis. Leeches were applied and removed as they became bloated, and a seemingly limitless supply of opiates were injected into Colin's body to ensure that he was not suffering.

The inspector arrived just as Sir Atherton, Mrs. Behmoth, and I were being run from the room so another troop of doctors could perform an examination and have their say. Only after the three of us stepped out into the hallway was I reminded of the putrid smell of infection continuing to ooze from his wound, and I prayed for the thousandth time that it had not been discovered too late.

"Mr. Pruitt!"

"Inspector." It was a relief to see him. He represented something beyond all of this, and even though his business was the worst sort of evil, it was distracting and that was enough.

He made his salutations to Sir Atherton and Mrs. Behmoth, enquiring after Colin's health and giving the requisite words of encouragement. I found myself buoyed by the simplicity of his words. It could be so. It *would* be so.

"What have you made of the report on Miss Materly?" I asked once I had led him away from Colin's room.

"I was right about you, Mr. Pruitt. The wounds were just as you described them. He sliced her open on the street, but she did not die there. Mr. Ross believes that she bled out as he dragged her into that cellar. He says she had passed away by the time he sliced her throat, just as you suggested." He shook his head. "There was no reason for him to have done that."

"Was anything . . . missing . . . ?"

He ran a thumb and finger in opposing directions across his brow, and I was certain his head must be aching. "Her womb," he said after a moment, his eyes fixing on mine with a sickened fury. "Mr. Ross says the man fished in amongst her entrails until he found what he was after and cut it out. He apparently had more time than we expected."

"Unless he knew exactly what he was doing. We must be careful to consider everything. And what of the shoe print? Did you get any pictures of it? Were any of your men able to capture any sort of tracing of it?"

The inspector gave a slow nod, a hint of pride tickling at the corners of his eyes. "The pictures are in here," he said, handing the report's folder over to me. "And I bribed the artist from the *Times* to go down there and draw the shoe print, tracing it *exactly*, by promising to alert the *Times* first when an arrest is made."

"Outstanding."

"And I agreed they could get an exclusive interview with you," he sheepishly added.

"What? I don't do that. That's what Colin . . ." but I stopped the rest of the sentence from bolting from my throat.

"Miss Kettle will be with you the whole time. She's a master at dealing with those people. She'll take care of you. And it did get us the print that you wanted. . . ."

I forced myself to steal a calming breath. He was right. At the moment we had no other lead. "Of course." I forced the words from my mouth. "You did the right thing. This could be critical."

"I've already got a couple of my men checking with a cobbler I use. I'm hoping he can tell us the size and type of the shoe. See what we can learn."

"An excellent idea."

"There is something else," he continued, his eyes watching me as though testing to see whether I remembered what it was. "I have arranged for you to speak with Jacklyn Unter. She's at the Yard now. If you want . . ." He gave a shrug and waited for me to catch up.

"Yes. The woman who heard the scuffling at the time of Miss Materly's murder. Let us go at once," I said, surprising both of us. There was nothing for me to do here but worry, and I did not need Sir Atherton to reiterate that Colin would expect me to be working on the case.

I let him know where I was off to and was graced by a smile that assured me I was doing precisely what he thought I should. He even reminded me of Braxton Everclear's grandson, Quentin, and suggested I might check on him before I returned. I readily agreed, grateful to have things to do—critical, useful things.

For the second time I left Sir Atherton and Mrs. Behmoth to watch Colin, but not before peeking through the tiny window in the door, where I was heartened to see the bevy of doctors still buzzing over him. They were not giving up, and that was all I could ask.

"Have you given any thought as to how we're going to get out of here?" I asked Inspector Evans as we clambered down to the first floor. "The newspapermen are getting exceedingly impatient."

"Don't you worry about them," he answered with a confidence I feared could be misguided. "Miss Kettle will take care of it."

"You have great faith in her."

"Indeed, I do," he said with a laugh as we reached the entrance hall. "She is quite something."

And as though she had realized our impending need, Miss Kettle appeared from around a corner and headed right for us, a warm smile lighting her face. "Gentlemen," she said. "How is Mr. Pendragon faring?"

"He is the same," I answered blandly, and decided she could make of that what she would.

"May I confirm to the newsmen that you are assisting with the Whitechapel case, Mr. Pruitt?"

"You may assure them that Mr. Pendragon and I are continuing our services to the Yard on this case," I snapped before forcing myself to summon something of a smile for her. "Forgive me."

She shook her head and held my gaze, her ice-blue eyes searching my face and leaving me to feel somehow exposed. "It is a difficult time," she said graciously. "Perhaps it would be more useful if I told them that you and Mr. Pendragon are unable to continue while he recuperates. That will be the surest way to get them to stop hounding you, and then the two of you will be able to do your work without their constant scrutiny."

"Ah . . ." Inspector Evans smiled. "I like that."

"Will they believe it?" I asked, charmed at her inclusion of Colin.

"They will," she answered with absolute conviction. "Your carriage is round back. I have cleared the men out, but you had best not dally. There is only so much one woman can do." She gave us a playful smile, highlighting her striking beauty and assuring me that there was *much* this woman could do.

"Very well." The inspector gave a nod as the two of us hurried out the back of the building, where his coach and driver waited.

"We'll not be bothered when we get to the Yard," Inspector Evans said as we got under way. "There is a gated entry around back where prisoners are brought in and out. We will not have to face a single question hurled at us." He gave a dry chuckle, but there was little levity in his tone. It was such bad business. All of it.

He was right about the rear entry at the Yard. We flew down the driveway, the gates yawing wide the instant the men stationed there spotted the inspector's carriage, and I was elated not to have to face the newspapermen, photographers, and anxious East Enders demanding answers we did not have. As we pulled in under the great brick building, the clatter of our horse and carriage echoing shrilly within the confined space, I looked back and watched several bobbies heave the gates closed and lock them again. There was a mixture of electric lighting and gas lamps down here, but none of it did much to dispel the sense of dread any prisoner would feel upon arrival. I only hoped the devil carving up the women on Framingham Street would suffer this journey soon enough.

"Thank you," the inspector called to his driver as the two of us went in through the single thick door barred with steel.

The hallway was narrow and plain, and what few doors interrupted the smooth corridor contained small, barred hatches at eye level, ensuring that no one was allowed ingress or egress until they had been well scrutinized. A single photograph of the Queen endeavored to brighten this passage, yet given her matronly profile and dour expression, I did not find it the least bit successful. So I was happy when Inspector Evans finally pushed through one of the doors and started up a staircase.

"If you were a prisoner, this entire hallway would be locked down," he informed me over one shoulder.

"I hope never to endure the experience."

"Inspector Varcoe was forever threatening it against Mr. Pendragon." He gave a chuckle. "The two of them could be so impatient with one another."

"Patience has never been one of Mr. Pendragon's better qualities. I can only imagine how he is going to react when he finally wakes up," I added with a smile of my own, buoyed by the thought of having to confront his displeasure.

The inspector led me out into a huge corridor bustling with bobbies and plainclothes workers. "Here we are, then," he muttered as he ducked down a side hallway that was far less chaotic.

"I will have them bring Miss Unter in." He swung a door open onto a stark white room with a single table and four wooden chairs set around it. "Make yourself comfortable, if that's possible. We should only be a minute or two."

"Would you mind"—I asked as I stepped across the threshold—"if I spoke with her alone? I am hoping she might be more candid when she realizes I do not work for the Yard."

The shadow of a crease ghosted across the inspector's brow before he gave his answer. "Are we truly equal partners on this case, Mr. Pruitt? I shall not have a repeat of what happened on the Hutton case. I will not be played the fool twice. So do I have your word that you will not edit a single sigh of your conversation with her?"

I felt abashed by his hesitation and knew Colin and I had earned it. "You have my word."

"Very well, then," he agreed, nary a further hint of reluctance evident. "I shall fetch her myself and leave you to it." He started out the door before abruptly turning back. "I will be right outside in the hallway should you need anything. . . ." He seemed to be considering his words before he finally added, "You would do me a distinct service if you did not mention to Superintendent Tottenshire that we are handling Miss Unter in this way."

"You may count on me."

He gave a solemn nod and was gone.

I settled in for what I assumed would be a wait of some minutes, laboring to keep my thoughts on the task at hand, but my mind insisted on turning back to Saint George's and the fact that I had left for the second time this day. So it was with great relief that the door suddenly swung wide to reveal Inspector Evans and a young woman.

"Miss Unter," the inspector announced with all the charm I would have imagined he might use had she been a titled lady, "may I present Mr. Pruitt. He is assisting Scotland Yard in the capture of the man who killed your friend, Delphine Materly. Your cooperation with Mr. Pruitt is viewed as cooperating with Scotland Yard itself." Having made his pronouncement, and looking well pleased at having done so, he gave a nod to the two of us before sliding back out into the hallway and pulling the door shut.

Jacklyn Unter stared at me, seemingly disinclined to either come any farther into the room or flee back out into the hallway. Hers was a diminutive figure, though well rounded where it needed to be, and I presumed she had no trouble attracting a steady clientele. She had an explosion of blond curls piled upon her head and spinning around her heart-shaped face, which highlighted an apple-cheeked plumpness, giving her the look of a snowy milkmaid from some baronial estate.

"'Oo are you again?" she asked.

"Ethan Pruitt," I answered, taking advantage of her confusion to lead her to a seat. "I work with the detective, Colin Pendragon. Perhaps you have heard of him?"

"Ya," she shot back, flicking her eyes around the room as though she might spot him hiding amongst the chair legs or pressed in a corner. "'Ow come 'e ain't 'ere? Ain't I worth 'is time?"

"Mr. Pendragon is regrettably indisposed. You must believe me when I tell you that no one would rather be here than him."

"That right?!!" She beamed at my statement, certain that it was meant as a compliment. "You'll 'ave ta bring 'im round, then."

"Just as soon as it is feasible."

"Wot?"

"Miss Unter . . ." I said, seating myself across from her. "What I really need to ask you about is what you heard last night around the time we believe Miss Materly was attacked."

"Oh . . ." she murmured, tugging at the collar of her high-necked dress with an unconscious sort of defensiveness. "Well, I didn't know nothin' about 'er bein' attacked. I was just mindin' me own business. That ain't nothin' ta do with me."

I understood how she meant to play this and had no time for or interest in her charade. "When you say you were minding your own business, I assume you were entertaining a client. Is that accurate?"

Her gray eyes went steely. "Well, ain't you cheeky."

"Three women have been murdered, Miss Unter. Butchered with their organs left strewn about. It is the most horrific thing I have ever had the misfortune to see. So if you are offended by my cheek I will remind you that until we find this monster, no woman walking around Whitechapel will be safe."

She snorted. "Like you and this lot give a shite about any woman walkin' round Whitechapel. Look 'ow well ya did catchin' that feckin' Ripper the first time 'e were 'ere."

And there it was, just as I had known it would come. I leaned back in my chair and stared at the defiance burning in her eyes. But I was ready. "I used to live on Limehouse Street myself, just around the corner from your building. Almost ten years. I worked for a woman who ran one of the largest opium clubs in the East End, an establishment known for its discretion. I did whatever she asked because I myself was an addict. Nevertheless, that woman saved my life many times over. So do not dare tell me that I don't care about the women who live and work in Whitechapel."

Miss Unter's eyes narrowed almost imperceptibly. "Wot woman didja work for?"

"Nettie Heikens."

"Maw?!" she said with obvious disbelief. "Ya worked for Maw Heikens?"

"I owe her my life," I corrected sharply. "I stopped in to see her—"

"She's dead," Miss Unter interrupted.

"Yes, I discovered that. Now let us get back to the matter at hand. You were with a customer last night. . . ." I prodded, trying to maintain some level of patience even though I was beginning to feel quite at the end of my tether.

"'E weren't no customer, 'e were a reg'lar," she sniffed with a note of pride. "I ain't potty, ya know. I ain't shaggin' any ol' sot off the street when there's a nutter carvin' up ladies."

"It is unfortunate Miss Materly did not feel the same."

"Things weren't so easy for Delphine. She was always sick

and couldn't 'ardly work enough ta take care a 'erself. So when she was feelin' good she 'ad no choice but ta go out. Ain't nobody handin' out free meals, ya know."

"What was she suffering from?"

She screwed up her face, sending a scowl my direction. "That weren't none a me business," she answered irritably, but I knew she was lying.

"When I lived with Maw, the women who worked for her tended to know one another like sisters. They had to. In most cases they were all any of them had. We were a family of necessity. So you will tell me what she was suffering from."

Miss Unter rolled her eyes. "She was havin' lady problems," she sniped. "And on top a that she 'ad a 'usband wot was always showin' up drunk every couple a months and threatenin' 'er."

"I see."

"But it weren't like ya think." She waved me off sourly. "Delphine said they wasn't ever really married. But 'e carried on like 'e owned 'er; yellin' for 'er one minute and then beggin' 'er, all blubbery and full a shite the next. When none a that worked 'e'd start 'ollerin' that 'e was gonna cut 'er up if 'e ever caught 'er with another man." She let out a high-pitched laugh that was full of contempt.

"What did he look like?" I asked, knowing she was about to describe Paul's father to me.

"Tall, no meat on 'is bones, a right beak of a nose." She puckered her face again. "Nothin' ta set a girl's 'eart ta beatin'. I don't know 'ow Delphine got addled by 'im in the first place."

"Tall . . . ?" I blurted out of my surprise. "Slender?"

She stared at me as though I was daft. "A right beak of a nose," she repeated brusquely. "That were 'im."

"Forgive me, but I was introduced to a man earlier today who claimed to have been as good as Miss Materly's husband, yet he is short and rather portly of stature. Clearly not the man you describe."

Miss Unter gave a disinterested shrug. "Lot a blokes think that way 'bout a lady. Don't mean nothin'. Makes no difference ta the way we live."

"When was the last time the man came to see her?"

"I don't know . . . couple weeks ago, I s'pose."

"Would you recognize him again if you saw him?"

"A course." She gave a ribald snicker. "I got some a 'is money a few times when 'e couldn't find Delphine. I ain't no fool."

If she had said anything else I would have known she was lying. "And last night? What exactly did you hear?"

Her face sobered up as she absently tugged at the cuff of her sleeves. "They was laughin'," she said, her tone rigid and tense.

"Who?"

"Delphine and some man."

"Did you get a look at the man?"

"Why would I?" she shot back defensively, her guilt given the aftermath well apparent.

"Of course." I nodded. "You were with a customer. What was his name? I shall need to speak with him as well."

"Like 'ell."

In spite of my ill temper I managed to keep my voice smooth and low. "We are in the midst of a triple murder investigation, Miss Unter. One that includes the savage death of your friend, Delphine Materly. I do not make my request out of idle curiosity. I will have his name."

Her gaze darkened. "If you really worked for Maw Heikens, then you know I ain't never givin' you nothin' 'bout 'im."

"Maw took care of her girls. She took care of me. She would never have turned her back on one of us."

Miss Unter's defiance vacillated the thinnest margin, and I was certain I had struck her with the truth. "You can come ta me room and talk ta 'im there. 'E wants ta tell ya 'is name, that's 'is business."

"When?"

"This Friday. Come by at ten and don't be late. 'E don't spend the 'ole evenin' with me, ya know. 'E's got a wife ta go home to."

"I shall be there exactly on time," I assured her. "What did you hear after the laughter?"

She exhaled and gave a *tsk*. "A scufflin', like they was dancin' or somethin'."

"Dancing?"

"I'm jest sayin'," she sniped, clearly aware of what little she had to offer. "I didn't think nothin' of it. Ya 'ear all kinda sounds at night round there. Wot of it? If I went runnin' outside ever' time I 'eard somethin' I'd never earn a bloody farthing."

"And that was it?"

"I told ya I didn't know shite. I been sayin' it all day."

"What time did your companion leave?"

"'Ow do I know? I can't see Big Ben from me bed."

"Before dawn?" I pressed, at the end of my patience.

"Ya. I told ya 'e don't spend the 'ole night. 'E don't pay me enough fer that anyway."

I bit the inside of my cheeks to keep from upbraiding her. "Did you hear anything after that? Something beneath your floor that may have come from the cellar?"

"No."

"And what about in the few minutes after you heard the scuffling? Did you hear anyone leaving? Perhaps someone walking quickly away . . ."

"I 'ear carriages and 'orses goin' by the 'ole bloody night."

I released a tight exhalation that I hoped would telegraph my dissatisfaction with her answers. "I will be by to see you this Friday night. You and your regular visitor had best be there, or you will have the Yard so deep in your business you will be desperate to pay them to bugger off."

"That ain't fair," she groused. "I ain't done nothin' wrong."

"Tell that to your friend Miss Materly."

Before she could raise any further objections I left the room, nearly crashing into Inspector Evans as I escaped into the hallway, allowing the door to slam shut behind me.

"That can't be good," he said.

I shook my head and beckoned him to follow, not because I felt the need for privacy but because my frustration would not allow me to stand still.

"There is much to be done," I said, and for once I truly felt the burden of these words that I had heard Colin say so many times at the beginning of a case.

"Of course," he agreed, confusion covering his face as he hurried to keep pace with me.

I had learned almost nothing and was floundering with no real idea how to proceed. The inspector would be disappointed, though not more than I already was, and the very thought of it infuriated me.

CHAPTER 13

The sky had darkened and the scent of rain was thick in the air by the time I left Scotland Yard. I had told Inspector Evans everything about my conversation with Jacklyn Unter other than the particulars of my time spent in Whitechapel during my youth. It wasn't that I was ashamed of what I had done, but then neither was I proud. He had shared my disappointment at our inability to learn much of value from her, reminding me how little we had to go on with these cases. I told myself it was enough that we would go back to her flat on Friday night to speak with the man she'd been with at the time of Miss Materly's murder. Perhaps he had seen or heard something more. How very pitiful that after three killings we still had so little.

I caught a cab back to Whitechapel in spite of the fact that all I really wanted to do was return to Saint George's. Sir Atherton was right, however; there was nothing I could do there beyond agonizing every minute Colin did not stir. If any decisions needed to be made on Colin's behalf, only Sir Atherton would be consulted. Mrs. Behmoth and I were not family. We had no rights. Thank God Sir Atherton was alive and well and in London. The thought of it made me shiver, though I blamed it on the chill that had settled over the city.

Late afternoon was waning, which meant I was once again forced to bribe the cab driver to take me into Whitechapel by promising an extra stipend. So I was not surprised when we reached our destination in laudable time, the carriage pulling to a stop in front of a short brick building discolored by the thick, black soot. It was just off of Framingham on a street that looked like little more than an alleyway. The building had almost certainly been constructed as a warehouse before being converted to housing at some point over the ensuing years. It stretched some length down the narrow passageway and was only two stories in height. Its appearance was sorrowful given that there hadn't been so much as a passing attempt made to coax it toward something more residential.

"Are you sure this is the place?" I called up to the driver as I fumbled in my pocket for the address Paul had given me.

"'At's it," he responded with a decided lack of interest. "Ya wanna go somewhere else, fine by me."

"No, no." I climbed out and handed up his fare. "Thank you." He returned a disinterested grunt as he spurred his horse forward, careening back out onto Framingham as though he were running at Ascot.

I looked back to the unlikely building and then let myself inside, using a nondescript door as black as the walls since there didn't seem to be any dedicated front entrance. An ill-lit hallway lay before me, spreading away on both my left and right, doors with numbers in chipped white paint peppering its length. Walls of yellowed plaster rose to the ceiling, failing to meet at any true angles, confirming my suspicion that they had been added at some later point. Even as I stared down the corridor I could see that it was bowed, listing vaguely from side to side, proving not only its subsequent addition but the lack of concern applied when it had been completed.

I checked the scrap of paper for Quentin Everclear's room number and started forward. If I did not find him at home, Paul had also given me the name of the pub where he had initially spied the young man, but I was hoping not to have to spend that much time here just now. When I heard rain abruptly let loose outside, that idea became even less appealing.

Number 304 came up on my right side, and I checked my paper one last time. There seemed to be no sense to these numbers. If the three hundreds were on the ground floor, then I wondered what numbers were in use upstairs.

I knocked on the door and was startled when it opened with the rapidity of someone having been standing right there waiting for me. I stared into the face of a young man of medium height and slender build, his shoulders rounded forward as though he could not be bothered to properly set them back. His short brown hair was swept away from a face set with doughy brown eyes that looked as untroubled and indifferent as that of any noble heir. Yet here he was, residing in the heart of the East End, beholden to a grandfather he barely knew and with whom he was not clever enough to align himself.

His expectant face rumpled at the sight of me. "You've got the wrong room," he said as he made to close the door.

"Are you Quentin Everclear?"

"Who's asking?"

I could not help the smirk that tugged at a corner of my lips. That he would be a suspicious man was in keeping with what I had expected to find, though his lack of cunning did not speak well of his depth of intelligence. "I am an emissary for your grandfather, Braxton Everclear. He has sent me here."

The man's gaze darkened, and if he had been able to force his youthful face into a scowl I was sure his forehead would have been crowded with lines. "What for? I haven't asked him for anything. . . ."

"It is your silence that has caught his attention. He has been fearing for your safety."

Quentin finally stepped back from the door, shaking his head as he continued to move into the tiny space. He threw himself down onto a badly worn, overstuffed chair. "Well, come in," he barked at me. "Don't stand out there like a dolt. Just don't expect any tea and biscuits." He gave a snorted laugh. "A shot of whiskey and a bit of opium perhaps. . . ." His laugh turned into a leer, and I realized he thought me a buffoon.

"That sounds better," I answered, returning a sneer of my own.

He was surprised by my response, just as I had meant him to be, but only for an instant. Quentin Everclear was not bright but neither was he a fool. "Well, then . . ." He popped out of the chair and moved the few steps to a short bookcase that, while filled with a clutter of odds and ends, held no books, then pulled out a slim wooden pipe the length of his forearm. Just as he had promised, there was a half-empty whiskey bottle on top of the bookcase and another on a battered side table next to the disheveled bed shoved against the rear wall. The room held nothing else beyond a scatter of clothing and undergarments, leaving the place feeling claustrophobic with an oily rankness in the air.

He held the pipe and a tiny linen pouch toward me, a look of excitement alighting his face. "Let's have one for my grandfather," he said.

I told myself that it wasn't my dread over the tenuous state of Colin's health but rather the necessity that I *bond* with this scoundrel, get him to *trust* me, that finally made me grab the items from him. "Yes," I heard myself mutter as I brusquely tamped down what remained of my dignity.

A high-pitched chortle leapt from his throat, and I knew that he was already well within the shackles of the drug. "I cannot believe you work for my grandfather," he rasped like a mischievous child.

"I cannot believe he *is* your grandfather," I murmured as I took a pinch of opium from the little satchel and dropped it onto the ashy screen fitted inside the pipe's bowl. He handed me a box of matches before I could ask for it, and I drew the pipe to my lips while igniting a single match with my other hand. It was a skill that I had apparently not lost.

I gazed across at young master Everclear, his eyes wide with anticipation, and brought the match to the bowl, hanging it just above the delicate opium so that it would get heated without actually burning. It started to bubble almost at once, and as I drew in a mouthful of smoke, I thought Quentin Everclear was going to soil himself with eagerness.

"Here then . . ." He gave a reedy whine as he reached forward and tugged the pipe from my fingers. "Let me have some too."

I choked out a laugh, forcing the majority of the smoke out of my lungs as I did so, knowing he would not notice as he concentrated on fumbling for his dose. *How clever of me,* I thought, just as the sweet, smoky flavor began to curl around my tongue and tug at my brain. It had been so very many years.

"What did you say you do for my grandfather?" he asked as he lit the pipe and tugged hard, his eyes rolling upward with his pleasure.

"This and that," I said with a fool's grin.

"Well, whatever it is that you do I should say you are quite good at it." He gave a hearty guffaw and seemed pleased with himself as he handed the pipe back to me.

I went through the same motions again, reheating what was left at the bottom of the bowl—which, quite expectantly, was very little—and allowed it to accumulate in my mouth as best I could. "You mustn't tell him," I said, releasing the preponderance of it as I did. Even still, I knew that I had ingested enough to sense the intoxicating embrace that had once held me so close. It was comforting, gently easing the worry that had been gripping me since Colin's hospitalization. Why had I let this go?

"Tell him?!" Quentin Everclear said with a snicker. "I don't even speak to the old prig. He doesn't really even give a bloody piss about me anyway. I'm a bastard you know. Sprung from the loins of his only son and some pitiable prostitute from whom the Pennyroyal and Tansy wouldn't rinse my sorry soul away."

"And yet your grandfather pays for your room," I pressed ahead, the absurdity of my statement not lost on me given the rampant meagerness of his surroundings.

The young man laughed. "And do you suppose his generosity is simply a gift? That it comes without any expectation?"

"Tell me," I coaxed as I held the pipe back out to him.

A harsh pounding on the door brought Quentin Everclear to his feet in an instant, upheaving my heart to somewhere in my throat. "Bugger!" he hissed. "You have to get out!"

It was an absurd statement given that there was nowhere to go, but even so it brought me to my feet. "Hang on, mate," he called out before pressing a finger to his lips with one hand and pointing to his bed with the other. "Get under it," he demanded tonelessly. "*Now!*"

I started to shake my head, convinced he was not serious, and then he seized my sleeve and shoved me the few steps to his mess of a bed. Another ferocious pounding at the door was enough to eject the reticence from my drug-muddled brain, sending me skittering beneath the sagging cot, for I could see now that it was hardly a bed at all. If his visitor dropped himself onto it I would be suffocated without a sound.

"Open this bloody door, or I'll kick it in and tear your insides out with my bare hands."

I pulled my knees up to my chest and pushed myself into the farthest corner, though I was still within easy reach of an average man's arms. If I were discovered I would not only look a fool but guilty as well, though of what I had no idea.

I heard Quentin Everclear begin to release the latch, but before he could fully disengage it, the distinctive roar of a door bursting open froze me. There was a rapid scuffle and a strangled intake of breath, and as I peeked between the disgorged blankets dangling over the side of the cot, I watched Quentin's scuffed shoes back into the wall directly in front of me, driven there by a pair of spotless black leather boots with gray felt spats and pearl-looking buttons along their outsides. These were the shoes of a gentleman.

"If you ever leave me out there again," the man raged, "it is the last thing you shall ever do."

"Yes, sir . . . yes, sir," Quentin mumbled, his voice oddly high-pitched, making me wonder if the intruder was clutching him by the throat. "I was just getting dressed."

"Don't you lie to me." The other man's voice was as much a growl as it was a deep-set tone. "You have been feeding your filthy little habit. I can smell it."

"I have . . . I have. . . ."

I kept still, drawing no more than the most shallow of breaths, my eyes fixed on the two pairs of shoes, waiting for what would happen next. It seemed to take forever, time ceasing or perhaps sliding sideways in spite of the laws that declared its rigidity, but at last the gentleman's boots took a slight step back.

"I had work for you tonight," he said. "There are women to be found. But now you have broken a rule." The gleaming shoes stepped back again, giving Quentin Everclear a bit of room though never outside of his reach. "Was there some confusion? Have I been unclear?"

"No. . . ." Quentin sounded as though he was on the verge of tears. "No. I just . . . I forgot."

The gentleman laughed. It was the first sound he had made that did not carry the whiff of a threat in it. "You forgot," he repeated. "And do you know why you forgot?"

I watched Quentin shuffle his feet and could feel his fear as if it were my own. He did not answer, however, leaving me to imagine the dread that must be written upon his face, since I felt filled with it myself. Tucked beneath this sorrowful cot in this squalid place, I was panicked and hardly knew why.

"You are a slave to your habit," the man seethed. "And for that you are of no use to me. Pity. You were showing such promise. There was much money to be earned."

"Please . . ."

But Quentin Everclear said nothing further. I watched as the man took a single step toward him, approaching from the side. There was a subtle noise, not more than a brief intake of air, and then the pristine boots quite suddenly hastened away, the door slamming shut in an instant.

I started to unfurl myself and was startled when Quentin Everclear dropped to his knees before abruptly toppling forward, his eyes huge and round. He was staring at me as though about to beseech my aid when a great wash of blood hemorrhaged from his severed neck, striking me in the face and blinding one of my eyes.

CHAPTER 14

Great sheets of rain were erupting from the sky, which meant that I was confined to the hallway of Quentin Everclear's boardinghouse instead of pacing outside, which is what I was desperate to do. At some point one of the constables had brought an old wooden chair for me to sit on, but I'd found that it matched my mood, groaning every time I shifted position, so I disdained it and allowed myself to start pacing the corridor again.

A light blanket had been tossed over my shoulders the moment the constables had arrived and enticed me out of the rain, where I'd run to summon them. Even so, I knew the ribbons of blood across the top of my white shirt and gray jacket made me look like a victim, or perhaps the perpetrator, of the crime. I assumed the pelting rain had washed most of it off my face, though since I'd yet to find a mirror I feared I might be left with an unnaturally pinkish hue across my skin.

"Mr. Pruitt . . . ?" Inspector Evans emerged from Quentin Everclear's tiny room with one of his constables right behind him. "Would you mind coming inside one more time? I want to make sure our man gets the appropriate photographs."

"Of course," I heard my own voice drone, startled by the weariness there as I followed the two of them back into the room.

"That rag?" the inspector asked, pointing around the camera's tripod toward a deep umber-colored cloth waded into a ball next to the bed.

"It was one of Mr. Everclear's shirts," I explained again. "It was the first thing I grabbed once I had extricated myself from under the bed. I was trying . . ." It all sounded so foolish as I stared down at the waxen color of the young man's profile and hands. "There was little use," I bothered to add, since anyone could tell by the extent of the rupture to his throat that he was likely dead by the time his knees struck the floor.

"Of course." The inspector nodded. His cohort scribbled some notes and the camera flashed, turning the stark scene into something sickening and garish for an instant.

"And that was when I ran out," I continued, reiterating what I had already told him. "I was shouting the entire time and yet never managed to rouse a single person in this building." A curious thought suddenly struck me. "Does anyone else live here?"

"It seems that while most of the flats are rented"—Inspector Evans dropped his voice to a timbre of disapproval—"the people who live here are not accustomed to getting involved with one another."

"No doubt that is doubly true when someone is carrying on the way I was."

"And that is a sorry state of affairs."

"At least I didn't have to go any farther than a block and a half before I stumbled on a pair of your bobbies. That your presence here has increased was a godsend."

Inspector Evans winced. "I must apologize again for their having attempted to arrest you," he said under his breath as though the young officer standing behind him might not hear, which was absurd given the diminutive size of the room.

"You have nothing to apologize for," I answered in a similar tone. "My clothes were quite covered with blood, and your men would have been reckless not to consider me suspect under those circumstances."

"He should have recognized you," he insisted.

I turned around to face another young constable hovering in the doorway and the photographer fussing behind his camera. "I should like you both to answer a question for me, and you must be honest. When you opened your eyes this morning, if you had seen my face would you have been able to identify my name?"

The poor constable looked alarmed, his gaze flicking from me to the inspector and back again, and the photographer did not even deign to pull his head out from under the draped cloth behind his camera.

"Thank you." I turned back to the inspector. "No harm done," I reassured him, having proven what I always knew to be true. "Once the confusion was sorted, and it really only took a minute, your men reacted admirably, blasting their whistles and summoning the help we needed." I looked back at Quentin Everclear's body and felt my heart sink. How was I ever going to tell his grandfather what had happened?

"Tell me again about the shoes," Inspector Evans prodded.

"Boots," I corrected. "Black leather with gray felt spats and pearl-like buttons along the outside. Short heels. Spotless. Refined."

"Anything else?"

I could not keep the sigh from my lips. "I didn't know what was going to happen. Mr. Everclear told me to get under the bed and keep still. That he had business and it was important I not be found there. I . . ." I stopped myself, glancing at the two constables and the photographer lingering in the small room. "Might we have a moment alone?" I asked, but it was the nod from the inspector that sent the three men back out into the hallway.

Another protracted sigh escaped me before I could force myself to continue. "I was trying to get information from Mr. Everclear," I explained, trying not to sound as though I was justifying what I was about to tell him. "His grandfather had hired us and—"

"I can smell the opium." Inspector Evans cut me off. "Is that what you're trying so hard not to say?"

I felt myself flinch. "It was an attempt to win his trust," I insisted, but I heard the defensiveness in my own voice. "I hardly . . ." But I stopped. Nothing I could add was going to make any difference to what had occurred, and the one thing I could not get out of my head was the murderer's accusatory tone as he reviled Quentin Everclear for having smoked. It had cost the young man his life, and I had been complicit.

"It is not my place to vilify or condone whatever it is you think you need to do to solve your cases. You have taken no oath, you hold no office, and you and Mr. Pendragon have proven yourselves a good deal more effective than Scotland Yard on more than a few occasions. So do not think you must explain yourself to me."

"It was foolishness," I said. "It is what set the murderer off."

"And how could you know that? The only thing I wish is that you had been able to extricate yourself faster to get a decent look at the man before he managed to disappear." He turned and stared back down at the rumpled bed. "I'm not even sure how you actually got yourself under there in the first place."

I shook my head and scowled at the memory of it. "Mr. Everclear was quite agitated. I had no choice."

"And what was it the killer said about the women . . . ?"

"He said there were women to be found. That was all. I have no idea what he meant by it, and he did not state anything further. He seemed to care only about the fact that Mr. Everclear had been smoking opium."

"Pity," the inspector muttered with a shake of his head. "You don't suppose the killer might have been making any sort of reference to the murders of the prostitutes on Framingham, do you?"

"That is impossible to say," I answered, though the same thought had already occurred to me. "Certainly that man slit Mr. Everclear's throat without the briefest hesitation. He clearly meant to keep him from speaking to anyone about whatever they were doing."

"Is it at all possible that the killer *knew* you were there?"

I gritted my teeth as this thought had also crossed my mind. "I don't know."

Inspector Evans gave me a nod that did not quite cover his frustration, and for the first time I understood how difficult it was to be a witness to a crime. "*Constable Jenkins!*" he hollered toward the door, and the young man appeared at once. "See that the photographer finishes here, and send for the coroner. Mr. Ross is free to collect Mr. Everclear's remains." He shifted his gaze toward me. "Are you in any hurry to see the autopsy?"

"No. There is no mystery here beyond the identity of the murderer. And if you don't mind, I should like to go to Braxton Everclear's home to tell him what has happened. I feel it is my obligation." Nevertheless, the very thought of it sent my mood spiraling downward again.

The inspector gave a curt nod. "Very well. But perhaps I should come along as an official of Scotland Yard," he added.

"I appreciate that, but Mr. Pendragon and I were hired by Mr. Everclear to find his grandson, and having done so, at least to some degree, I feel I owe him an accounting." Yet another sigh escaped my lips. "And since I was here, mine will not be a tale of conjecture or rumor, but one of my own witnessing. I owe him that. Anything less would be cowardly."

"You know the Yard will send someone out before the night is over anyway."

"Of course. As they should. But he will have heard it from me first, which is the right thing."

"Very well, then. I shall stay here and direct my men to continue knocking on doors. It seems unlikely that this was the first time this man came to visit Quentin Everclear. Perhaps we shall get lucky and one of his neighbors will decide to recollect having seen a nattily dressed man before."

"Let us hope," I agreed, for we had little else to go on. "Perhaps you might also check with a cobbler to try to identify the type of boot I saw. Where it might have been purchased."

"Boots . . ." the inspector groused. "Two murder cases and all we have so far is a bloodied shoe print near Miss Materly's body and the dapper pair you saw at the time of Quentin Everclear's murder. What is it with ruddy shoes all of the sudden?"

I shook my head dourly. "Let us hope that something will come of either one or the other," I muttered, though I felt little cause for hope. "These cases are mystifying and I . . ." But I did not finish my thought. There was no point, as I knew the inspector felt every bit as frustrated as I did.

CHAPTER 15

The rain had let up, but it had yet to stop. It felt almost as though Quentin Everclear's murder had rent the sky with grief, just as it had done to his grandfather when I told him. I was left feeling hollow and spent as the carriage I was riding in clattered back to Saint George's Hospital.

I had gone home to clean up and change before going to speak with Braxton Everclear, aware that I had to bathe his grandson's blood from my face, neck, and hair. My jacket, shirt, and undershirt had been pitched into the trash. I did not want to see any of them again and knew Mrs. Behmoth would never be able to wash the horror off them anyway. She wasn't there when I arrived home, nor did she make an appearance. I had been hoping she might bring news—encouraging news—but I had to be content with the knowledge that if she remained at the hospital, then Colin was still fighting the good battle.

So it was that I went to see Braxton Everclear with that expectation in my head and heart. As I'd told him about his grandson's tragic end, however, I found I could not stay the hopelessness that slithered around my own mind, cracking my voice and causing me to hesitate repeatedly in my telling. For the most part I told Mr. Everclear the truth, though I omitted the fact that

Quentin had been enslaved to opium and that it had ultimately caused his death.

Braxton Everclear had remained stoic throughout my recounting of the event, listening intently but asking nothing. I could not help wondering whether he suspected more to the story. When I'd finished he gave me a solemn nod, his face sallow and his eyes ringed with exhaustion and pain. He'd apologized for not offering me tea, and I took the opportunity to take my leave, but not before telling him that Scotland Yard would be sending an emissary by nightfall to bring him the official report of his grandson's death. I'd assured him that Colin and I would find his grandson's killer and was not the least surprised when he appeared to take little consolation in my statement. I understood.

"Here we are, then," the driver called down to me as he swung the cab around the front of Saint George's.

I was relieved to find no newspapermen milling about. The rain would have forced them into the lobby, where I was certain Miss Kettle had banished them with her assurances that Colin and I were no longer assisting with any Yard matters given his ill health. Colin would be pleased at the chance to work in the shadows again. He would not even care that we had created such a fabrication, for that is what it was to me. It had to be.

Saint George's lobby was small and poorly lit at this time of the evening. That there was little commotion felt comforting to me. I was hungry but had taken no time to eat supper. That seemed like a luxury I dare not afford given how long I had been gone from here.

When I finally let myself into Colin's room, it was to find things exactly as they had been when I had left. Sir Atherton was seated on the far side of the bed, his eyes closed but his head stiffly upright, apprising me that he was not asleep. Mrs. Behmoth was on this side of the bed, knitting something that was spread out across the entirety of her lap. They both looked wearied by the glow of the dull electric lighting. It seemed to cause as many shadows as it chased, though neither was it helped by the darkness of the rain-soaked night. Only the occasional flash of lightning brought the room any further illumination, but even that added little more than a momentary spectral glow.

Colin remained unmoving in the bed like a wax figure from Marie Tussaud's museum. His hair was plastered against the sides of his face, but he did not look to be sweating as profusely as he had been earlier in the day. I wondered if that was a good thing or a bad thing. I did not know anymore.

His breathing had quieted, and for an instant I thought it had stopped. Its shallowness was barely detectable, so I stared at his chest and willed it to keep moving. The ever-present fear that had been my constant companion since I had first brought Colin here accelerated yet again.

"Ethan . . ." The sound of Sir Atherton's voice startled me as I glanced across at him. "I'm glad you're back. I hope the length of your absence portends good things in the Whitechapel case."

There was great kindness evident in his still-handsome face beneath the crown of his silver hair, and there was hope. Mrs. Behmoth, who had turned around to see me, bore a similar expression of assurance, and I was overcome with gratitude to have them there.

"Ya look like shite," Mrs. Behmoth said as she gathered up her knitting and heaved it onto the side of Colin's bed. "Ya 'aven't 'ad anythin' ta eat, 'ave ya?"

"No," I admitted as I dropped into the seat beside her. "There hasn't been time."

She reached down to the floor and lifted up a small basket. "You're lucky 'e ain't woken up yet," she said with a shake of her chin at Colin. "I brought 'im a meat pie and a custard. You can eat 'em. I'll not 'ave 'em go ta waste."

"I suppose I could eat some of it," I allowed, though my appetite was middling at best.

"You'll eat it all," she scolded, shoving the basket into my hands. "I'll not 'ave ya gettin' ill. One is enough."

"What do the doctors say?" I asked as I rooted out the meat pie.

Mrs. Behmoth *tsked* before Sir Atherton answered. "Fairly little. They have changed the leeches twice today and let some blood early this evening. Beyond that they are continuing to in-ject him with fluid and opiates."

I grimaced. "Must they give him opiates? Do they even know whether he is actually in pain?"

Sir Atherton looked startled at my outburst before giving a slight shake of his head. "I don't really know. Do you think I should ask them to stop?"

I looked at Colin and tried to imagine what he would wish. He hated opiates, I knew that much, which reminded me once again of the murder of Quentin Everclear. "Yes," I said. "They're doing enough to him already without the use of those drugs. They can only muddle his mind and his spirit, and I should think he needs both right now."

"Very well. I shall inform them at once."

"Eat," Mrs. Behmoth ordered, giving me the impression that she was glad to have one of us to fuss over.

I did as instructed while telling them of the scene at Delphine Materly's murder. They listened without comment, making me wish more than ever that Colin would stir and have something to add. Harder still was the story I had to share about Quentin Everclear. I told them the truth, all of it, and neither of them fur-rowed a brow at what I had done. It was not necessary for them to do so as I felt badly enough already.

"You should have come to get me before you went to speak with Braxton," Sir Atherton spoke when I had finished. "I could have helped you. You needn't have done that on your own."

"It was mine to do. You belong here."

"That may be," he said with the faintest of smiles, "but if mine is the first face Colin sees when he wakes up, he will most surely be disappointed."

"Tell 'im about the Queen," Mrs. Behmoth interrupted as she began to collect the napkins and plates from the basket, as I'd somehow managed to finish the food.

"The Queen?" I glanced over at Sir Atherton, imagining that she meant to bestow some honor or accolade upon Colin, the very thought of which roiled my insides, as it seemed to suggest he would not get better.

"This latest murder..."—Sir Atherton spoke slowly—"I know it has Victoria at ends. She is aware of Colin's illness and has asked that you and I come to Buckingham tomorrow morning."

"*What?!*" My mind ratcheted up as quickly as my heartbeat. "She wants to see *me*? Whatever for?"

Sir Atherton gave a pained sort of look that made me realize his answer was going to be more complicated than I imagined. "Did Colin never mention to you the reason she had summoned him?"

"She fears that some grand-nephew might be involved in the Whitechapel murders," I blurted without thought.

A thin smile cracked a corner of Sir Atherton's lips. "Yes, I presumed he would not keep it from you, her wishes to the contrary be damned and all that." He cast a sideways glance at Mrs. Behmoth.

"Don't go lookin' at me," she groused. "I ain't listenin' ta either a you. And even if I 'ad, she's got some 'alf a dozen grand-nephews, and that's jest the ones 'er 'alf-sister and randy 'alf brother will admit to. So 'ow the bloody 'ell would I know who you were talkin' about?"

Sir Atherton swung his eyes back to me with a distracted sigh. "Now that there has been a third murder she is going to want to know how the investigation is progressing. Whether you are any closer to determining if this young man could be culpable in any way."

"This is absurd," I protested as my stomach lurched. "This is Colin's case, not mine. I've not been hired to work with the Yard, *he* has. I have no right or reason to discuss any such topic with her. It's out of the question. You shall simply have to explain that to her."

"Well, I'm glad to see you are not letting this rile you," he said with a poorly suppressed smirk.

I glanced back at the bed and begged Colin to open his eyes. "She cannot mean for me to do this. Does she know how ill he is?"

"I sent her word the morning you brought him to Saint

George's. She is a friend, Ethan. I have known her most of my life. She is a monarch, but she is also a woman."

"'At's right." Mrs. Behmoth nodded. "She ain't no different than me."

It was a laughable statement that brought nary a hint of amusement. "But what will I tell her?"

Sir Atherton gave an easy smile. "You will tell her the truth. She will lead the conversation as she sees fit, and you will respond with honesty. Do not trouble yourself over this, Ethan. There is plenty enough of that for all of us already."

"Of course," I replied, not even convincing myself. "Yes." But I felt neither soothed nor placated. I am but the shadow of a man far more capable than me, yet as I shifted my eyes back to Colin, pallid and virtually motionless, I swore that I would do this—for him . . . for me.

CHAPTER 16

The night was fitful with doctors and nurses coming in to poke
and prod Colin—cleaning the wound under his arm and one
time applying new leeches; injecting fluids into his veins; and
recording copious notes about his breathing, temperature, and
heartbeat to the point that had he been awake I know he would
have cursed the lot of them. I remained grateful for their min-
istrations, hoping each time they fussed at him that he would
finally awaken to either grouse or warn them off. But he did not
stir in the least, leaving me to convince myself that as long as
they continued to work on him, there was hope. And that was
enough.

Sleep persisted in eluding me anyway, as I could not stop ob-
sessing over the impending meeting with the Queen. I had no
answers to give her, no consolation to help relieve her mind, and
I could not fathom what Colin might say to placate her concerns.
This was the realm of Sir Atherton, not me, and I could only
hope that he would guide the conversation.

Mrs. Behmoth returned to Saint George's just before seven in
the morning, putting me out of the misery of pretending to sleep
any longer. She carried a small basket of meat pies and scones,
which she insisted were meant for Colin alone, yet she did not

begrudge Sir Atherton and me helping ourselves. I was appreciative for her increased output of baked goods and understood that we each had our own way of keeping busy.

What I did not expect was the nurse bringing in a well-used, slightly dented pot of tea along with three cups and saucers. She had, it became apparent, done so at the behest of Mrs. Behmoth, who popped off her chair and took the battered tray from the nurse. The three of us broke our fast in silence, each keeping company with our own thoughts, and by eight o'clock Sir Atherton and I had climbed aboard his stately black coach and were headed for Buckingham Palace.

We rode without speaking, the clatter of cobblestones beneath the wheels and the tuneless whistling of Sir Atherton's driver, Periwinkle, providing a steady drone of welcome noise. Only after we had circumnavigated Trafalgar Square and Buckingham Palace was starting to become visible between the overhead tunnel of colorful trees did Sir Atherton finally break our silence.

"You understand that this is an informal visit," he said. "Or more accurately it counts as no sort of visit at all."

"I don't understand."

Sir Atherton released a quiet chuckle. "We are not really here," he explained. "There will be no record of our having come, and we will not be presented or greeted in any way. This is a matter Her Majesty wishes treated with the utmost discretion, which means you may tell no one of having come here." He leaned toward me and gave a sly smile. "Mrs. Behmoth notwithstanding."

"Oh . . ." was all I managed to say.

True to his word, as soon as the main gates swung open at the sight of Sir Atherton's coach, Periwinkle took a hard left and we avoided entering the parade grounds. He steered us toward the side entrance instead—the same one Colin and I had used during the Bellingham case—where he pulled to a stop.

"Sir Atherton. Mr. Pruitt." A stiff man of middle years stood just outside the meager service entrance where he appeared to have been waiting.

"Good morning," Sir Atherton answered first, stepping down and taking a moment to glance around, making me realize how foreign it must be for him to enter the palace in this way. "I do apologize if we are late."

"You are right on time, sir," the man responded before turning away and leading us into the building. It was only then that I realized he had not introduced himself. The lack of such protocol left me feeling ever more the interloper than a man who had been summoned.

He escorted us through the unadorned hallways where the guards' offices were, and I could not help peering into the office of Major Hampstead as we walked by, remembering how deceitful he had been during the Bellingham case, but there appeared to be no one there. It made me begin to wonder if the hallway had been cleared to keep our visit entirely covert just as Sir Atherton had warned.

We passed through several other empty corridors before entering an area that I could tell was part of the main structure of Buckingham itself, yet even this passageway remained nearly as understated as those we had just come through. The only real difference was that a few pastoral paintings hung on the walls and the ceiling had lifted another foot above my head.

"If you please . . ." the man beckoned as he arrived at a door and swung it open. "There is tea on the sideboard and currant scones. You are welcome to help yourselves."

"Very good," Sir Atherton answered easily. He seemed to be finding all of this subtlety rather amusing, which left me curious as to whether it had been like this when he had come with Colin.

The room that lay beyond was a sitting room awash in burgundy hues. Its walls were covered in a rich flocked paper of vertical stripes that matched the fabric on the couch and high-backed chairs placed before an ornately carved, dark-oak fireplace that rose all the way to the ceiling. There were tall standing lights arrayed about the room, all of which were ablaze even though the windows on the opposite wall allowed plenty of light into the space. A secretary's desk sat in one corner, made of the same dark wood that surrounded the fireplace, and an ornate sideboard sat against the wall to my left, once again a perfect match to the oak everywhere else.

"Very good indeed," Sir Atherton said again as he moved directly to the sideboard and began to prepare the tea.

I stepped inside and sucked in a deep breath to try to settle my rising nerves, but I felt myself fail when I heard the man ease the door closed behind me. I was about to follow Sir Atherton, thinking some tea might do me some good, when I was startled by the sound of a woman's voice.

"Pour a cup for me as well, won't you, Atherton," she said from out of nowhere.

No doors had opened and no one had entered the room, leaving me to deliberately sweep my gaze back across the space.

"Of course, Mum," Sir Atherton answered without so much as a sideways glance. "And you, Ethan?"

"Please," I managed to blurt as my eyes finally caught sight of the stout but diminutive grandmotherly woman seated before the fireplace in one of the high-backed chairs. The top of her head was some distance from the apex of the chair, which was how I had missed her in the first place. She was dressed entirely in black, which made the starkness of her broad, jowl-laden face look almost luminous. Her gray hair was bound up in a tight bun at the back of her head beneath a small, unbound cap. She was so bereft of height that her feet would have hovered well above the floor had a small matching ottoman not been pushed right up against her chair. On her lap was a billowy pile of navy blue knitting that she was feverishly working on, and upon which she continued to work even as she shifted her eyes to mine.

"Do sit down," she stated.

I did as bidden only to silently curse myself when Sir Atherton came over with the tea tray, angry for not having thought to carry it for him. "You are looking as well as ever," he pronounced as he passed a cup and saucer over to her without having to ask how she liked it.

She gave the ghost of a smile. "I am seventy-six years old. However well could I possibly look at this point?"

Sir Atherton sat down next to me and exhaled. "Need I remind you that I am right on your heels?"

"Eight years is hardly a trivial disparity, as you shall discover in due course," she answered resolutely. "How is Colin faring?"

"There has been little change. The doctors seem to putter over him ceaselessly, but he has yet to stir. It has been five days now."

"His fevers have subsided," I could not stop myself from adding, too struck by the despondency in Sir Atherton's words to allow them to go unchecked.

"Well stated, Mr. Pruitt. Now, you see, Atherton, one must never fail to recognize the smallest of victories." Before he could respond she swept the knitting off her lap to reveal a well-made man's sweater. "I am knitting this for him. Do you suppose he will like it?"

"I can guarantee it," Sir Atherton replied. "You are most kind."

She waved him off with the merest flick of her fingers before pulling the knitting needles free and deftly tying the ends of a few threads of yarn together. "I have always enjoyed knitting and think I must surely have clothed half of the empire by now."

Sir Atherton stifled a chuckle as he reached across and accepted the sweater from her. "I shall very much look forward to seeing Colin wear this."

"He is in our prayers," she said before taking a sip of her tea. "But now you must forgive my indelicacy. With another young woman murdered in Whitechapel yesterday I must know if there have been inroads made regarding the killer's identity." She shifted her eyes to me, and in spite of her age, I found them keen and alert. "Atherton tells me you are leading the investigation at the moment. May I presume that he has confided my concerns to you?"

"Colin did," I answered without thinking. She appeared momentarily vexed, and I remembered that he had been sworn to secrecy, a confidence she now knew he had not kept. "Only because he had sought my assistance," I hurriedly explained, mortified at my foolishness.

Her brow was furrowed and her displeasure evident by the

tight set of her mouth, yet I could not release her piercing gaze as she continued to watch me. "Most irregular," she allowed after a moment, "though I suppose it makes little difference given that you are here now in his stead. Perhaps it was prescient on his part." At last she shifted her eyes back to Atherton. "Most irregular," she repeated.

He returned a wistful smile. "As you know, my son has always had a will of his own."

She gave the slightest nod. "It is a commendable attribute and something I trust he is putting to use right now." She took another sip of her tea before turning back at me. "So what have you learned, Mr. Pruitt? Have you been able to decipher who is at fault for these unforgivable tragedies, and who is not?"

I could scarcely take a breath as I struggled for the right way to answer her with what little I had. "Your Maj—"

"You mustn't." She cut me off with a quick wave of a hand. "I am a woman concerned about her family. Nothing more. What do you know, Mr. Pruitt?"

What did I know?! That the murderer had worn shoes. "I am afraid we are at the earliest stages of the investigation. It is the period when we can do little more than collect facts," I babbled, repeating what I had heard Colin say a thousand times before. "We are also searching for patterns . . . connections . . . between the murders, anything that might tell us something about the perpetrator or his motives. The men at Scotland Yard are also interviewing anyone who might have seen or heard something, or who know anything at all about the habits of the three victims."

"Is there not anyone you have been able to rule out of suspicion? Have you truly accomplished so little at the cost of three lives?"

My mouth sprang open, though what I intended to say I can hardly imagine, as it was Sir Atherton's voice that was heard next. "You expect a great deal to be swiftly gathered about a shadow. A tall order indeed."

She pursed her lips before letting out a rush of air. "It is difficult to be patient under these circumstances. Not only was there a similar scourge over this city just six years ago, but I now fear how closely this could besiege my own family."

"Perhaps if you could share with me why you harbor such suspicions about your grand-nephew . . ." I started to say, which earned me such a ferocious scowl that I halted my tongue.

"It is not an inappropriate question," Sir Atherton spoke in his usual soothing tone. "And it might be helpful to understand."

She set her cup and saucer onto the small table beside her chair and folded her hands in her lap, looking as though she were about to refuse to comply. But after another moment she began to speak in a voice much softer and more fragile than she had used before. "The boy is not well. He never has been. He is ill-tempered and gloomy, and I am well aware that he has been known to frequent the Whitechapel area more often than not. One need not guess at the reasons. I myself have seen him rant more than once. It does not bode well for him. It does not bode well at all."

"Do you know him to have ever been violent?" I asked, hoping she would not find my question impertinent.

"I am aware of some past incidents, but you would need to speak with his father, Prince George, should you wish to learn more."

"Prince George?" Sir Atherton repeated. "But the Duke of Cambridge has never been married. He has no recognized children."

"Do not presume to be so naïve, Atherton. He was as good as married to that actress for forty years, and everyone is quite aware of it. She bore him several children, and there are countless more who have been ascribed to him over the years. These are not the dark ages."

"Nevertheless," Sir Atherton continued to press, "not one of those children is legitimate, so why ever should you care if one of them has lost his mind?"

She gave him a scowl that would have sent a shiver down the spine of a lesser man. "The monarchy has known its share of illegitimacy within those who have reigned, which is why madness has been allowed to proliferate over the years. My own grand-father has been described thusly, but I will not have the family sullied by a murderous lunatic."

"May I speak with him?" I asked once she had settled herself. "May I ask him some questions?"

Once more her brow knit tightly as she returned her stare to me. "You may," she answered warily, "but you shall not inform or involve Scotland Yard, nor will you take any action, should you deem him culpable in any way. You will consult with me and me alone. Do I make myself clear?"

"Unquestionably," I answered at once.

"How much longer do you suppose this will take?"

"Pardon . . . ?"

"To sort these murders out. To arrest the madman."

"I . . ." I glanced to Sir Atherton, hoping he might speak on my behalf, but he was sipping at his tea and looked to have no such inclination. "It would be reckless for me to try to say. I will do everything I can as quickly as possible. You have my word on that." But even as I heard myself speak I feared that my words sounded timid and weak.

She sighed before picking up her cup and saucer again and taking a delicate sip. "Then I can ask for nothing more." Her watery blue eyes held me fast. "Not one word of this to a single soul, Mr. Pruitt. And should Colin regain his health, he will have my displeasure to attend to."

"Of course," I mumbled, but her last words had not slid past me. *Should Colin regain his health,* she had said, stirring the thorny seeds of doubt. Alluding to the possibility that he might not—a possibility I had been consumed with denying, but now our sovereign had dared to voice it.

CHAPTER 17

⟫◦⟪

The moment I pushed the door open I was overcome by the stench of putrefaction and death. It was a smell I knew I would never become accustomed to or achieve any sort of accordance with, which was why I forever distrusted those who did.

"Appalling," Inspector Evans said under his breath as he swept past me.

"This place," I muttered in response, which felt like all that needed to be said about this morgue.

"*Mr. Ross!*" the inspector called once we had reached the counter, the unremitting chill already evident from behind the swinging examination doors to our left.

It was not Denton Ross who barreled into the room with his bloodied white coat flapping about his thighs, however, but his wiry assistant, Miles Kindall, whose slim frame hardly set the doors to any motion whatsoever as he passed through them. "Oh," he said with noticeable wariness when he caught sight of Inspector Evans and me. "Mr. Ross isn't here right now."

"He leave you in charge, did he?" the inspector asked, and I was certain I heard a note of derision in his voice.

"We cannot be everywhere at once," the young man answered, his face colored by a tinge of redness that only further accentuated the pocked scarring littered across his face.

"It does not matter," I spoke up, trying to hide my relief at not having to deal with the reprehensible Denton Ross. "We are here to see the autopsy report for Delphine Materly. Have you finalized it yet?"

"Certainly." His answer was as filled with offense as it was brief.

"Then we would appreciate a look at it," the inspector cut in brusquely.

"It might also be helpful if we could compare it to those of the first two victims, Elsie Barrell and Amelia Linton," I added. "If you would be so kind."

"Yes . . . of course." And this time he sounded far less affronted, perhaps even a bit abashed, as he stepped back toward the swinging doors and bid us follow.

There was a cadaver covered by a white sheet on one of the new metallic tables that had recently been installed along with electric lighting and refrigeration. I noticed Inspector Evans curling his upper lip and realized that he continued to be as effected by the lingering odor as I was. Still, I was pleased not to have to confront the body beneath the sheet for once.

"You can review the files in here," Mr. Kindall said, leading us to Denton Ross's small, cluttered office just beyond the examination area. It was a place I had reviewed many such files on countless other cases, the memory of which provided little consolation. "We have moved the records to a storage room in back," Mr. Kindall explained. "Mr. Ross finds the cold air curls the edges of the papers and isn't at all pleased about it. I'll just be a minute," he added, scurrying off on his long, scrawny legs.

"Odd fellow," the inspector bothered to say.

"I rather doubt this type of job would entice anyone who wasn't slightly amiss in one way or another. Although solving these cases would be a far cry more difficult if we didn't have their scientific assistance."

"That cannot be denied." The inspector nodded. "I've not had a chance to ask how Mr. Pendragon is this morning. Has there been any change yet?"

"There has not," I answered, unable to suppress the sigh that slid past my lips. "He remains unresponsive and, while the doctors continue to clatter about, I cannot see that they are making much of a difference. We are less than five years from the birth of the twentieth century and yet at times it feels like we are no more than a step away from living in caves." I slammed my mouth shut and sucked in a quick breath, embarrassed by my tirade. Good fortune rescued me before Inspector Evans could be made to feel compelled to respond when Mr. Kindall came scurrying back with three files tucked beneath an arm.

"Here you go, then," he said, holding them out with evident pride.

"Very good." The inspector took them and immediately passed one over to me. "We needn't disturb you any further," he continued. "We will let you know when we're done."

"It is no disruption to me," the younger man pointed out. "This case remains our central point of focus. Mr. Ross autopsied the first two victims twice to ensure nothing was missed. We may yet do so with Miss Materly as well."

"Second-guessing himself, is he?" I asked, finding that fact curious and yet undeniably encouraging.

"Oh no," Mr. Kindall answered at once. "Mr. Ross just wants to make sure the Yard . . ." But he did not finish his sentence, as he seemed to reconsider whatever it was he had been about to say.

"I am sure he does," Inspector Evans grumbled anyway. "We shall call you if we need you, Mr. Kindall."

"Of course." The young man gave a stiff nod. I noticed a pinkish hue rise across his face again, making me wonder whether he lived in a perpetual state of flush.

"Comforting to know we have that blasted Mr. Ross looking over our shoulder," the inspector seethed after Mr. Kindall had finally taken his leave.

I flipped open the folder he had handed to me and found myself staring at a photograph of Delphine Materly laid out on the autopsy table, the savagery of her murder wholly visible. "No matter his stated intent, Mr. Ross is also re-reviewing his own work when he takes a second look. Do not let his bombast to his assistant fool you."

If the inspector had anything further to say I did not hear it, as my eyes paused on an underlined statement midway down the first page: *The uterus, fallopian tubes, and ovaries have been excised and are missing.* Exactly as it had been with the first two murders, with the exception that this time there was no length of intestine missing. Even though this third attack had been initiated on the street and appeared to have been interrupted before reaching the grisly conclusion of the first two, the killer had still had the time to remove the victim's womb. Which meant the womb itself had to be a critical impulse behind these murders.

"I am not seeing anything I haven't looked at every other time I have read through these files," the inspector said with a wearied exhalation as he tossed the first file onto Denton Ross's desk and flipped open the second one. "Are you?"

I meant to tell him the truth, to confide what I had realized, but the words that left my mouth were not at all what I had planned. "No . . . nothing." I blamed Colin. Had he been here, I knew he would have answered the same. He was the one who had taught me to hold my tongue when it came to the Yard.

I handed Miss Materly's file over to the inspector and waited to see if he would reach the same conclusion once he'd had the chance to read what I had. "How are we supposed to decipher the mind of a madman?" he muttered as he flipped through her file before tossing it onto the desk and standing up. He removed his hat and rubbed at his scalp as though trying to stimulate some thought.

"Suppose the man is not mad at all," I said. "Suppose his motives are very precise."

"How so? Are you seeing something here?" He leapt at my careless statement at once, but still I failed to confide in him.

"I only mean that we should not concede any possibilities just yet. We are constructing the case, collecting facts, nothing more." Once again I was pleased by how naturally Colin's words rose to my tongue. "Have you and your men learned anything in your questioning of the neighbors yet?"

"Nothing that would appear to have the slightest value. The first victim was a flower vendor and the other two prostitutes. All have been described variously as good women trying to earn a living. They all rented rooms on Framingham Street, but their buildings bear no proximity to one another. Miss Barrell lived near Saint Paul's, Miss Linton was all the way out past Canary Wharf, and Miss Materly was close to Leadenhall Market. So it cannot even be said that this monster is stalking a particular neighborhood. If he means to stalk and kill women who live on Framingham . . ." He shook his head and did not bother to finish his statement. There was no point given the breadth of the city that Framingham Street runs through.

"And so we shall keep pressing. We have Miss Unter's customer to speak with tomorrow night. Perhaps he will have something to say in spite of her insistence otherwise."

The inspector scoffed, and I did not blame him. Had either of us truly believed the man held any viable information, we would never have waited to speak with him.

"Did you want to see Miss Materly's body?" Mr. Kindall asked, startling us both as he reappeared in the doorway. "Her body is in the freezer, but I can bring it out if you would like."

"You needn't do so on my account," Inspector Evans said.

"I don't feel the need, either." I stood up and handed the files back to Mr. Kindall. "Can you say with any certainty what sort of knife was used?"

"Very sharp. Smooth, not serrated. Something a butcher would use, or possibly a barber. Wouldn't be more than four or five inches long, since he would have to hide it while stalking his victims. Could even be a surgeon's scalpel."

I watched the inspector's eyes darken, and his mouth set at the description, well aware that the same had been said of the Ripper. "Are you stating a fact or conjecture?" he spoke up after a moment, his tone heavy with annoyance.

"Fact," Mr. Kindall assured, his voice tinged with its own perceptible effrontery. "I am not paid to speculate."

"I am sure the inspector did not mean to suggest that you are," I said. "Is there anything else you or Mr. Ross has observed about the three victims that we might not be aware of given our far less methodical observations of their bodies?"

Mr. Kindall's eyes appeared to almost burn with keenness, a fact I found simultaneously reassuring and repellent. "The perpetrator is a clever man," he acknowledged. "He has neither revealed himself through his actions nor left any clues behind that might help us decipher anything about him. Not a bit of tissue left beneath the ladies' fingernails, only dirt and detritus. We cannot even tell you the color of his hair, as no such strands were found on any of their clothing or bodies. The only things that can be said with any certainty are that he is a powerful man of greater-than-average height, given the angle at which he inserted the blade into the women's necks as he gripped them from behind, and that he is left-handed."

"Their throats were sliced from right to left, then?" I asked, determined to understand how they had reached that conclusion.

Mr. Kindall looked pleasantly surprised. "Yes, indeed, Mr. Pruitt. Spoken like a true man of science."

He gave me something of a smile, which I supposed was meant to flatter, but like so much about this young man, his boss, and this place, I felt nothing of the sort. "Do let us know if something further should occur to you," I instructed, aware that he might or might not, depending on the whim of Denton Ross.

"Of course," he said, the three files clutched to his chest as though to ward off the inherent cold of the place. "Mr. Ross and I are doing everything we can to help solve this case."

"Just do your job," the inspector snapped back, "and we shall do the rest." He stabbed his hat back onto his head, and I caught the irritation behind his gaze. Without another word the two of us headed out of the morbid place, and I, for one, was happy to do so.

CHAPTER 18

By the time I got back to Saint George's the rain that had been pelting to greater and lesser degrees for the better part of twenty-four hours had finally begun to let up completely. The clouds remained thick and gray, as though the sun had been altogether banished, while the chill that had been dodging about the streets had yet to forfeit its bluster.

As I let myself into Colin's room, the familiar hope and fear wreaking havoc with my heart rate, I found that nothing had changed. Sir Atherton was asleep right where he had been sitting when I'd left, his head thrown against the back of his chair with one arm stretched out by Colin's side, ever vigilant for any sign of movement—anything at all would do. Mrs. Behmoth had clearly suffered enough such idleness as she was polishing the windowsills with a rag and some potent-smelling solution she was carrying in a bucket.

"These women don't know 'ow ta keep a place proper," she growled as I came in.

I could think of no response, so I settled for a nod, though I understood her need to be busy. It was the reason I had allowed Sir Atherton to convince me to throw myself into these investigations. The waiting was excruciating.

"You're back," Sir Atherton muttered, bleary-eyed and worn down.

"I am." I settled myself into a seat and insisted that the two of them go out and get themselves a decent supper. To my surprise they both agreed, and so I was left alone with Colin and my plaguing thoughts—about the cases, about Colin, about what I would do. . . .

My solitude did not last long, as the doctors descended within minutes, injecting Colin with yet another round of saline before fussing with his wound, which, to my eyes, looked just as festered and enraged as it ever had. The sight of it tore at my heart and left me emptied, so that by the time the men scurried off I felt overcome by the weight of my dread and so let my eyelids droop, hoping to find just a moment of solace here by Colin's side.

I hoped that I might dream of him, of better times, of hope and relief, and that would be good. And so I did. I saw him: fit and able, a lopsided smile brightening his face, and he was calling to me, beckoning me to him. It made me laugh, the absurdity of it, Colin repeating my name in an odd and lazy tone, over and over, the sound of it nudging me until my eyes suddenly popped open and I found myself staring into the sea of his azure eyes.

"Did you solve the case?" he rasped, his voice arid and cracked and barely above a whisper.

For an instant I thought I must still be dreaming, but I was not. His eyes were open, staring at me, and though they were filled with confusion there was also wonder and determination nestled within. "Of course not," I answered, almost choking on my laughter as I blinked my eyes repeatedly to prevent them from undermining me. "Would I do such a thing to you?"

"Ever loyal. Where are we?"

"Saint George's. You fell ill Saturday night, and I had to bring you here. It's been . . ." My voice failed me and I said no more as I forced a tight smile onto my lips.

"Saturday?!" he croaked. "What the hell day is it?"

"Thursday. It's Thursday evening."

"What . . . ?!" His eyes bulged with disbelief and he started to shift as though he meant to sit up, only to realize that his left arm was stretched above his head. "What?!" he said again.

I bolted up and grabbed him, settling him down before he could do any damage. "The wound under your arm became infected," I explained in a rapid firing of words. "You went into shock. Your whole body . . . it was septic . . . toxic . . . we thought . . . I thought . . ." I stopped myself again and sucked in a long, slow breath, thankful that he was remaining quiet. "The doctors here . . ." I restarted as I sat down on the side of his bed and seized his hand, relieved to find it warm and firm and exceedingly comforting. "They have done remarkable work. You are the proof of that."

"Then why do I feel as if I'm on a torturer's rack?" he protested.

The door behind me swung open, and I dropped his hand and stood up before looking around to find Sir Atherton and Mrs. Behmoth there.

"Oh!" was all Sir Atherton said, yet the wetness that promptly swelled into his eyes spoke deeper than any words he might have tried using.

"Thank the good Lord," Mrs. Behmoth pronounced in a rush of air before stalking toward us. "Ya 'bout gave us all a feckin' 'eart attack! What in the 'ell were ya thinkin'?!"

I thought I heard Colin starting to choke, only to swing around to find him hoarsely chuckling, the dryness of his throat making it sound more abrasive than merry.

"Enid," Sir Atherton scolded, but there was no conviction to his tone. He finally came forward as well, shaking his head and thumbing at his eyes. "What a sight you are."

"Are ya 'ungry?" Mrs. Behmoth spoke up again. "I got some thin-sliced lamb and roasted potatoes in me basket."

"No," he muttered, looking faintly gray at the thought.

"*Mr. Pendragon!*" I heard someone gasp behind me. Before I could turn, one of the doctors was standing right beside me and Sir Atherton. "You have rejoined us at last," he said, snatching Colin's wrist and checking his heartbeat as though he had expected it all along. "You must take care now. It will not do to tire yourself."

"Tire myself?" Colin repeated in a harsh, grinding way. "From what I have just been told I've done nothing but lie here for the last several days. How could I possibly be tired?" But the discordant sound of his voice betrayed him, making me glad that Sir Atherton was the first of us to speak up again.

"Do not be a fool, boy. We have all of us suffered far too much this past week for you to be heedless."

"You have been fighting a battle for your life," the doctor informed him. "Do not confuse your immobility for inactivity." He turned and looked at the three of us. "I shall ask you not to spend more than ten minutes before you leave him be."

"Sound advice." Sir Atherton was the first to respond again. "And so it shall be, doctor, I can assure you of that."

I snuck a sideways glance at Colin, expecting him to continue his protestations, but I found him already fighting weighty eyelids. The truth of the doctor's words was evident. So the three of us delicately extricated ourselves, promising to be back before he knew we were gone. I, for one, had every intention of continuing to sleep at his bedside. Nothing would drive me away. Even so, the tide had turned and everything quite suddenly had an astounding and lustrous sheen to it.

CHAPTER 19

I recognized the man glowering before me but could never have recalled his name. At the very least I understood the reason Miss Unter had been unwilling, and just as likely unable, to give us his name when we had questioned her days before. That he was a minor representative of the Tower Hamlets borough was known to me only because he had been one of the more vocal critics of Scotland Yard in the newspapers of late, denouncing their inability to secure an arrest in the recent Framingham murders. The more he drew comparisons to the Ripper case of six years past, the more ink the newspapermen accorded him. Which left me with the impression that he was nothing less than a man intent on furthering his political career.

"This is highly irregular," he was insisting, his face reddening while his eyes darted between Miss Unter, Inspector Evans, and me.

"They forced me to do this, love," Miss Unter cooed, sensing a regular customer on the verge of slipping away.

"We are here for one reason alone," Inspector Evans repeated with impatience, and I was certain he recognized the man as well. "For all I know you are here on your biweekly charity visit. The only thing that concerns me and Mr. Pruitt right now is your visit here this past Tuesday night. There was a murder practically beneath these floorboards, of which I understand you may have had some awareness. . . ."

"Awareness . . . ?" The man's eyes continued to flick about as though the inspector had accused him of being the killer. "What are you driving at? What are you trying to say?"

"Mister . . . ah . . ." I hesitated a moment to allow the man to give his name, which, I quickly realized with annoyance, he did not seem inclined to provide. My patience was thin given both the hour—not quite half past ten on Friday night—and the fact that I was worried about Colin. With just over twenty-four hours having passed since he had awoken, he was already sitting up in bed and complaining about wanting to go home.

"Smythe," the man finally answered, snapping my distracted attention back to him. I noticed his eyes flash toward Miss Unter before they shot back to me again. "Mr. Smythe," he repeated absurdly.

"Fine. Mr. Smythe." I forced myself not to roll my eyes, noting that this was not a clever man, apropos for most politicians. "The inspector and I are investigating the murder that took place here last Tuesday night and are seeking any information that might help lead us to the killer. Miss Unter mentioned that she heard some laughter out on the street followed by a brief scuffling while the two of you were together. Do you remember hearing anything like that?"

"The streets are always noisy. Why would I remember that?"

"Because, Mr. Alford . . . Oh, excuse me." The inspector gave a sneer. "I mean, Mr. Smythe." And I was reminded that the man's name was indeed Rex Alford, a name I was not at all surprised Inspector Evans had remembered. "Because the scuffle was a curious-enough sound for Miss Unter here to recollect it. Perhaps it was even odd enough to cause you to stop your charitable work for a minute and listen. After all, there have been two recent murders near here of late."

The man's lips tightened, stretching his dark mustache into a hard line even as his eyes narrowed. He was a fit man who looked to be somewhere in his late thirties, possessing a solid frame for a man of above-average height. I found myself wondering whether these were not precisely the characteristics Mr. Kindall had described of the man who had murdered the three women.

"I may remember having heard something," he allowed after another moment.

"And what exactly would that be?" I asked before the inspector could, finding myself curious about this uncooperative man.

"Laughter, I suppose. Down on the street. Sounded close. But it was just a woman. Could have been anyone. I can't say if it was your victim or not."

"It were Delphine," Miss Unter piped up. "I recognized 'er voice."

Mr. Smythe looked decidedly unhappy at being interrupted. "I didn't hear anyone else. But the woman . . . whomever she was," he added pointedly, "went right on laughing for a good minute or so. It was irritating," he grumbled. "And then it stopped."

"And after that?" I prodded, continuing to find this man's reticence peculiar given that he was with Miss Unter at the time of the murder, which meant that he had an irrefutable alibi.

"I returned to my charitable work," he answered lecherously, sending Miss Unter into a fit of snickering.

"I was referring to outside," I informed him, making certain my irritation was in full view. "What did you hear outside after the woman's laughter ceased?"

He shrugged. "I don't know. The occasional coach clattering past . . . perhaps a person or two strolling by."

"What time did you leave Miss Unter's that night?"

"Who can remember such things? Time gets slippery when you're with the right woman." He leered at her.

"Remove your right shoe, sir," I barked at him.

"What . . . ?!" The man looked from me to Inspector Evans, his face curling up with displeasure, which pleased me. "Whatever for?"

"You will do as Mr. Pruitt asks," the inspector spoke up, "or I shall get a warrant and seize every pair of shoes you own."

"On what grounds?"

"Failure to cooperate with a Scotland Yard investigation. Or maybe I'll just go right for suspicion of murder. One of those will get us what we're after."

"Suspicion of murder?!" Mr. Smythe choked at the same moment Miss Unter gave a startled yelp. And for the first time he finally sounded shaken. "That's ridiculous. You've admitted yourself that I was right here with Miss Unter when that attack took place."

"Your shoe," the inspector repeated.

This time the man did not protest but dropped back onto Miss Unter's bed, the only reliable-looking piece of furniture in the small room, untying his boot and handing it up to me. I tugged my notebook out of my pocket and accepted the proffered shoe before moving over to a large trunk standing in a far corner of the room, a haphazard pile of indeterminate ladies' belongings tossed about the top of it.

"Would you mind . . . ?" I asked Miss Unter as I tore several sheets of paper out of my notebook.

"Oh!" Her cheeks flushed. She scurried forward and swept the items up in a single swoop of an arm.

I laid the loose sheets of paper onto the trunk in a tight, boxed pattern and placed the shoe at the center of it. Pulling my pencil free, I traced the outline of the shoe onto the paper, working slowly and carefully to ensure I got an accurate reproduction. When I was satisfied with the results, I numbered the quadrants of the loose pages so I could reassemble it when needed and then flipped the shoe over to study the pattern of wear on it. The right side of the heel was ground down noticeably more than the left, suggesting that the man turned his feet out slightly when he walked. In general his heel showed greater abuse than the toe, which conveyed further that he carried his weight in a posterior fashion rather than pitched forward on the balls of his feet. I made a quick note of both findings on the bottom of the fourth quadrant and handed the shoe back to the man.

"Thank you," I bothered to say.

"What was that all about?" he asked, slipping the boot back onto his foot and lacing it up with incensed vigor.

"To prove your innocence," I answered as I gathered up my papers and signaled to the inspector that I was done here.

"Whether you like it or not," Inspector Evans told the man, "you are a part of this investigation. As such, I expect you to make yourself available to us again should we wish to speak with you further. And we will not be waiting to call on you here should the need arise."

The man who had bid us call him Mr. Smythe tugged at his mustache and grimaced. Had the situation not been so dire it might have been comical. "As you have already surmised, my name is Rex Alford," he acknowledged through gritted teeth. "I have a wife and children whom I should very much like to protect from . . . this . . . I keep an office on Fleet Street. If you require anything further from me, then I will ask you to see me there. I would be most appreciative," he added, sounding appalled at having to do so.

"Very well," the inspector said. "If you will continue to cooperate we will accommodate your request." He tipped his hat back onto his head and followed me out the door before turning back to face Mr. Alford. "And perhaps you might be amenable to giving Scotland Yard a bit of respect the next time you're speaking with your friends at the press." He gave a grin that was as cold as the night as he pulled the door to Miss Unter's room shut behind us. "That should give him something to mull over."

"No doubt we have ruined his charitable work for this evening," I said as the two of us thundered down the stairs and back out onto the street.

"I should think we have ruined it more permanently than that." He chuckled.

I halted beneath Miss Unter's window, which was hanging just above my head not half an arm's length away, and found myself overcome with a renewed suspicion. "Shall we wait and see just how much damage we have done?" The inspector nodded. "Send your carriage around the corner and ask your man to wait there." He did as I bade, slamming one of the doors for effect, before hurrying back over to me. "Down the cellar stairs," I instructed, and the two of us dashed down the steps that Delphine Materly had been dragged down three nights prior.

The door to the cellar was closed, and I was grateful for it as I pressed my back against it, the police tape stretching across it rustling against my coat. I reached behind and felt the padlock fastened on the door, further relief consoling me. I did not relish seeing that eerie place at this late hour even with Inspector Evans at my side.

Not two minutes later I heard the door swing open and shut at the front of Miss Unter's building, and a set of heavy footfalls tread down onto the street. They paused for a moment, and then several slow, methodical steps could be heard moving in our direction. Mr. Alford appeared an instant later, peering down into the blackness directly at us.

"Looking for something?" Inspector Evans asked in a flat, dry voice.

Mr. Alford jumped and gave a muffled yelp, stumbling back into the street and catching a heel on the curb, nearly sending himself down onto the cobbles.

"It is a great curiosity, is it not?" I said as the inspector and I came up the short flight of steps to face him. "What time did you say you finally left Miss Unter's room on Tuesday night?"

Poor Mr. Alford looked desperate to recompose himself, but I knew that would take some time. That he was so rattled seemed the perfect opportunity to pressure him into answering.

"The time, Mr. Alford?" I said again. "You had your wife and children to go home to. What time did you say that was?"

"A little after one," he blurted, sounding muddled. "I remember hearing my mantel clock chime two shortly after I got home, and I'm not forty minutes from here on the Tube."

"Very well, then," I said with a sniff of indifference. "Have yourself a pleasant evening. I am sure we will be seeing you again."

Mr. Alford nodded his head stiffly and hurried off toward the Tube station at the far end of the block, the opposite direction from the cellar stairs.

"What was that all about?" the inspector asked as we started off to find his carriage.

"I feel like the only honest thing that man told us was what time he got home that morning. And the only reason he did so was because we scared the bollocks off of him."

"That we did," he chuckled.

"The man is hiding something," I stated with a surety I did not necessarily feel and could not have explained. "He knows more than he has admitted so far."

"And why do you suppose such a thing?"

"He headed right for the cellar stairs as soon as he thought we had left. It's not as though he had to pass them to get to the Tube. So why? What was he checking for?"

The inspector gave a low sort of whistle. "Good thought. We shall have to come back tomorrow in the light of day and have ourselves another look around."

"Indeed. Do you recall what time Denton Ross placed Miss Materly's murder?"

He shook his head. "I don't."

"I cannot be certain, either. Aren't we the pair?" All the while I knew Colin would have remembered. He'd never have retained her name, but he would have known the time she had died.

We climbed aboard the inspector's waiting carriage and struck off for Saint George's. I was dropped off at the hospital's front entrance and hastened upstairs to find Colin's room lit only by the lights seeping in from the corridor, him sound asleep. No one else was in the room, and I suspected that either his father or Mrs. Behmoth had left when he drifted off or he'd sent them away first. He had no tolerance for being babysat, as he referred to it, though I had yet to be likewise dismissed.

I lowered myself into the chair closest to his bed and listened for a moment to the sound of his slow, even breathing. His left arm was down by his side for the first time in almost a week, and if I concentrated resolutely, I could almost believe that we were home and I was late in retiring. The thought warmed me, and before I knew it, I too was adrift.

CHAPTER 20

———◦———

I awoke to the sound of a tiger's growl—low, throaty, and filled with menace. If I had been dreaming it disappeared with the swiftness of a candle snuffed in a gale. My eyes rocketed open to find Colin sitting in bed glaring at me, his hospital gown pulled down to his waist with one of the nurses fussing at the still-angry wound beneath his left arm. The nurse looked wholly absorbed as she ministered to the injury, unaware of or unconcerned by the threat inherent in Colin's rumbling.

"How is it looking this morning?" I asked her, hoping to settle him with some good news.

"Irritated," she answered at once. "About the same as him."

I laughed, pleased that she would make such a joke, though Colin did not share my amusement. "You have *got* to get me out of here," he snarled.

"You went home too quickly the last time," I reminded. "I'll not go through this again. Once is plenty for the whole of my lifetime."

"Fine. Then we will get a nurse to come to the flat every day. I will do better there. I will be the model patient."

"You would do best to stay right here," the nurse spoke up as she released his arm and started reassembling her tray of bandages, cotton wads, and medicinal tinctures.

"Thank you for your opinion," he muttered disagreeably, pulling the gown back up over his powerful chest. "I will be sure to take it under full consideration."

"Mr. Pendragon . . ." One of the several doctors who had been attending him came into the room, giving the first smile I had ever seen him muster. "It is a distinct pleasure to see you sitting up and starting to look fit again."

Colin tendered a fleeting smile. "You and your staff have done exemplary work on my behalf and I owe you great thanks, but this idleness cannot continue, as I have two cases that demand my attention and Mr. Pruitt simply will not tolerate such lethargy on my part."

"I must take issue with Mr. Pruitt then," the doctor said, his face collapsing into a frown as he swung his gaze toward me. "Mr. Pendragon has been very ill and requires a spate of bed rest before I can allow him to return to work. He must not be rushed, lest another infection set in. The outcome could be far worse were it to happen again."

"You have convinced me," I said to the doctor, though it was not me who had required convincing. "How much longer do you expect he will need to stay, then?"

"*Ethan!*"

"At least a week. And you should both be aware that it will take some time after that for him to regain his stamina."

"There is nothing wrong with my stamina," Colin snapped, but even so, he sagged back against the pillows as he said it.

A light rap on the door interrupted us, and I was pleased to see Inspector Evans poke his head in. "May I come in?" he asked.

"Yes, of course," Colin answered eagerly as he leveled a pointed gaze on the doctor. "This will be about one of my cases. You can see I have the Yard popping by here at all hours."

"Am I too early?" The inspector hesitated, confusion evident on his face as he fiddled with his hat in his hands.

"Don't be daft," Colin shot back. "It's after nine. The morning is already half over."

"Ah . . ." He allowed an amused smile as he came into the

room, letting the door swing shut behind him. "I can see you are well on your way to a full recuperation, Mr. Pendragon."

"He needs his rest," the doctor persisted.

"I've not come for him," the inspector explained, raising his hands slightly as though attempting to turn himself in. "I am here to collect Mr. Pruitt."

"Where are the two of you off to?" Colin demanded.

I glanced at the doctor and nurse, who were both fussing over Colin from the other side of the bed. "Might the inspector and I have a private minute with Mr. Pendragon?" I asked. "You have my word that we will not cause him any distress."

For a moment I thought the doctor might actually decline my request, before he appeared to reconsider. Heaving a weighty breath that did not belie his irritation in the least, he finally responded. "You may have fifteen minutes, but after that Mr. Pendragon must get his rest."

"Will you *please* stop saying that," Colin snapped as he and his nurse dutifully vacated the room. "I mean it, Ethan." He spun on me the instant the door had swung shut. "Twenty-four hours is all the longer I shall stay. You will get me out of here, or I will throw that blasted doctor out the window and then they will have no recourse but to release me so they can put me in prison."

"All right." I waved him off with a furtive glance to the ceiling, beckoning patience. "We will discuss it in twenty-four hours. But for now the inspector and I must tell you about a third murder that has taken place in Whitechapel. . . ."

"A third?!" he repeated, bolting upright, not a wince to be seen on his face. "How many days ago? Was it under the same circumstances? Why did you not tell me about this yesterday?!"

"Settle yourself, or you'll have the inspector and me evicted."

He did as instructed, leaning back against the pillows though his posture remained stiff and alert. And so the inspector and I caught him up on both the murder of Delphine Materly and the killing of Quentin Everclear. The more he listened, the more riled I could see he became until, just as I was starting to question the soundness of my decision to confess everything to him, he released an aggrieved sigh and shut his eyes.

"I have missed so much."

"You have missed the worst parts of it," I hastened to add. "Much has happened and yet we still know so very little." I glanced at the inspector and saw the same frustration that I was feeling.

"We are mired in two hellish cases," he said, still fiddling with his hat, making his discomfort apparent. "Mr. Pruitt has been working very hard, my boys at Scotland Yard are working very hard, but it continues to feel as if we are running in place."

Colin's eyes snapped open. "Which is why I cannot simply lie here in this damnable bed."

"You will get well first," I insisted, "or you will be no good to any of us."

"I have to concur with Mr. Pruitt," the inspector put in.

"If the inspector will allow, I'll bring Miss Materly's autopsy report and the Yard's files back with me this afternoon, and you can catch up on both the Whitechapel case and Quentin Everclear's murder."

"Of course," the inspector agreed at once. "I shall fetch them myself and bring them round by the end of the day. While I cannot leave them, you can have all the time you need to pore over them. It would be helpful to have your thoughts." He flicked his eyes toward me and gave a quick, self-conscious nod. "Not that Mr. Pruitt hasn't been making a first-rate effort. . . ."

I was on the verge of dismissing his tepid praise when the door opened again, this time revealing Sir Atherton. "Now this looks more as it should," he said with a smile.

"Don't let the doctor hear you say that," I cautioned with a chuckle, "or he'll throw the lot of us out. The inspector and I were just leaving anyway, so you can keep our prisoner here company."

"You're not in the least bit amusing," Colin groused.

Sir Atherton summoned up a slim smile as he set his eyes on me. "Give me a moment before you go."

"I'll wait out in the hall," the inspector said, popping his hat on his head and nodding to Colin before disappearing back out into the corridor.

"Have you kept any confidences from the inspector?" Colin asked almost before the door had finished closing.

"In fact, I have," I answered with some chagrin. "He has been a good and fair partner, and I wonder at my having done so. I rather blame you."

"I'm flattered," Colin said with the flash of a grin. "It is always important that you and I lead the advance."

"If you wouldn't mind," his father spoke up, "I would just as soon not hear your battle plans for outwitting Scotland Yard. I happen to be fond of those boys and think they do a fine job most of the time. Besides . . ." He swung his eyes toward me and quickly continued before Colin could seize on his limited endorsement. "You and I have an appointment to attend to tomorrow afternoon. Victoria has had arrangements made for us to lunch with her grand-nephew. After church services, of course."

"Oh . . ." I caught the distinct tone of distaste in my voice and struggled to right it. "How on earth are we to handle him? We cannot treat him like a suspect and yet she expects us to determine his innocence or guilt."

"I shall be happy to miss that," Colin muttered.

"Need I remind you that I spent the entirety of my career as a diplomat," Sir Atherton said. "I am certain that between the two of us we will handle the situation with aplomb."

"Do you suspect him?" Colin asked.

"At this moment I suspect everyone and no one!" I shot back with more frustration than I had meant.

Colin allowed a tight smile to curl the ends of his lips. "Good that you are keeping your wits about you, Ethan. I can see that perhaps the doctor is right and I *should* stay here another week." He did not try to keep from chuckling.

I bit the inside of my cheek and turned to Sir Atherton. "He is your son. You do something about him." Which simply earned me the slightest of shrugs. With little other recourse I struck off to find Inspector Evans.

CHAPTER 21

Despite the dense, gray clouds looming ferociously over the city, the small staircase that led down to the cellar where Delphine Materly had been murdered looked harmless and banal. Gone was the sense of foreboding from the night before, the feeling that something awful had passed this way. Today it felt like nothing more than ordinary, never mind the bright strips of police tape strung across the door.

"There!" The inspector tugged the lock down and yanked it free. "The bloody thing is open."

"Very good." I turned back to view the black space beyond as the door lazily swung open. "At least we know that no one else has been able to get in and mess about."

"That is a certainty. Which begs the question of what the hell Mr. Alford thought he was doing last night by coming round this way." He stepped inside the earthen-smelling place and set about lighting the few gas lamps that clung to the walls.

"We don't know that he intended to be up to anything at all," I reminded. "We're just here to make sure we've not missed anything and see if, perhaps . . ."

"Yes of course. I wonder if I shouldn't have rallied the lads to bring the electric lights out again. I hate to get the neighborhood stirred up, but I fear this isn't going to be easy."

I stooped at the entrance and ran my fingers along the threshold looking for something . . . anything. "Let us start with what we are already aware of. We know the killer dragged Miss Materly across this area and that her throat had already been cut. Nevertheless, she put up a fight even as she was bleeding out." I sat down on the brick floor, my feet pointing out toward the derelict steps—the last thing Delphine Materly would have seen—and peered over my shoulder. "Come here. Grab my collar and pull me back to the corner where Miss Materly died."

He came up behind me, and I felt his rough fingers curl around the fabric at the back of my neck. "All right."

I closed my eyes for a minute and tried to imagine the scene—her terror as the killer pulled her, quite possibly by the hair, her life and breath bubbling out of the gaping wound in her neck, desperate to do *anything* to save her life. "Go," I muttered.

The inspector's grip went taut and I snapped my eyes open, lifting my rear just enough to allow him to begin pulling me backward. The tie at the front of my collar snapped against my neck, digging in and seizing my breath so that, as I started to slide away from the doorway, I felt a surging panic spring up within my chest, sending my arms flying up and back to try to grab the inspector's hands. He continued to yank me backward, oblivious to my predicament, but I could neither make a sound nor reach his cuffs or wrists, my fingers sliding off the coarse wool of his suit as though it were slick with oil. The most I could manage to latch on to were the decorative buttons running along the sides of his sleeves, though there was little to be gained in such a purchase if I could not reach the flesh of his hands. And then, just as quickly as it had started, the inspector released me, my collar falling back into place with an explosion of air that made me cough several times as I stared back toward the entrance, keenly aware that no such moment had come for Delphine Materly.

"You okay?" he asked, popping his face into view to check on me.

"My collar. . . ." I answered with a laugh, running my finger between the fabric and my neck, and feeling the fool. "I'm fine. It made the experiment more realistic . . . better . . ." I pushed myself to my feet. "I don't think it would have been possible for her to have reached her attacker. Not from that angle. The most she might've been able to do is dislodge a button or tear a bit of fabric, but we're wasting our time if we think we're going to find a man with scratches across his hands. I don't see how she could have done that."

"Mr. Kindall told us that they'd found no skin or such under her nails. The only thing he appears to have scraped free is dust from these bricks."

"I remember." From inside the cellar it was easier to see the fragmented scratches Delphine Materly had left behind as she fought for her life. "When she couldn't reach up and grab him, she had clearly attempted to stop him from pulling her out of sight by trying to gain traction along the floor. It was the only thing available to her." I glanced around the shadowy space and released a frustrated exhalation. "Let us look across the whole of the floor, then," I said, trying not to sound disillusioned. "Perhaps we will find something your troupe of men missed."

The inspector gave a dry chuckle as he looked back at me. "You don't have any more faith in us than Mr. Pendragon, do you?"

I grabbed one of the small, handheld oil lamps the inspector had thought to bring and swung open the small glass hatch to light it. "It is not about faith," I said as the wick caught. I relatched the tiny door, holding the soft light out in front of me. "It is about certainty." I crouched down and started swinging the lamp in a slow arc to the right of the area where Miss Materly had been found. "Have you checked back with Denton Ross about the approximate time Miss Materly was killed?"

"I spoke with him this morning," he answered as he lit the other lamp and began examining the other side of the room. "He places her time of death between one and half past, which makes it precisely the time that Mr. Alford says he heard something."

"Then that is at least one truth Mr. Alford has told us," I muttered, crouching and flicking at something that turned out to be a bit of straw. There were plenty of scraps of matter about, as one would expect to find in a cellar, but there seemed to be nothing that held the slightest significance to Miss Materly's murder. "Have you found anything?"

"Nothing I couldn't find in my own cellar. My wife would attest to that."

"Your wife must be an extraordinary woman to put up with this job of yours. She must worry about you every day."

He chuckled. "I suppose some days she does. Other days not so much. But I've got a boy of ten who wants to be a Scotland Yard inspector just like me. Now, him she worries about."

"How many children do you have?"

"Five," he answered with a groan. "What about you? Ever marry?"

His question, though asked in innocence, struck me hard and made me cringe in the relative darkness. Had we been conversing across a table I felt certain he would have seen me flinch. I had hoped he'd surmised something of my relationship with Colin, that it remained unspoken but understood, but that appeared to be a figment of my own wishful thinking. "No," I answered with a casualness I did not feel. I dropped my gaze back to the floor and was cheered when something abruptly glittered in the feeble glow of my light, catching my eye. "Here's something. . . ."

"What is it?"

I reached out and closed my hand around the very thing I had been hoping to find—a button. I rolled it into the flat of my palm only to feel my disappointment quickly reassert itself as I saw that it was not at all what I was looking for. "It's a button. Most likely from a woman's dress," I grumbled, standing up. It was white and quite small, and it looked to be one of the decorative types placed along the outside of a woman's wrist. "Do you remember the color of Miss Materly's dress? Did you ever see it in any decent light?"

"Pink and white," he answered as he walked around to me.

"Then this will have come from her dress," I said, dropping it into his hand with a sigh. I turned back toward the door, and my eye was caught by another brief flash, although this time I knew at once that it was nothing of any use. "Here then." I stooped and snatched up the dull farthing that had settled against a side wall. "Here's a farthing for your troubles today." I flipped it over to the inspector, and it bounced off his sleeve and clattered to the floor.

"I have to keep that, you know," he scolded, bending down and retrieving it. "Anything collected at the scene of a crime has to be noted and filed until the case is resolved. Maybe you could stop picking up rubbish."

"Sorry." I extinguished one of the hanging gas lamps and the inspector followed suit until we had returned the dismal room to its absolute darkness. "This killer is a clever man."

"Indeed he is."

I waited while the inspector refastened the padlock and straightened the warning tape on the door. "Someone is playing a very dangerous game," I said as we headed back to his carriage. "He cannot sustain it for long."

"Tell that to Jack the Ripper," he pointed out. "Five murders ascribed to him over a two-and-a-half-month period. He may have committed more, for all we know. Eleven women were butchered in Whitechapel between April 1888 and February 1891. We cannot be sure that madman didn't claim more than just the five we have attributed to him." He turned to look at me, his eyes narrowing. "You wouldn't happen to have any further information about any of that, would you?"

"Colin would be flattered to hear you ask such a thing." I gave him a thin smile, avoiding his question as Colin had sworn me to do.

"I always said that Mr. Pendragon should have been consulted, but you know how Inspector Varcoe was. . . ." Inspector Evans grimaced as we climbed aboard his coach and started on our way. "He wasn't always very accepting of Mr. Pendragon's skills."

"It is unfortunate that he and Colin could not find some common ground until well into the Connicle case, and by then . . ." I shrugged and shook my head at the memory of Colin and

Emmett Varcoe trying to appease too many years of animosity. It had been the worst of endings. "And now that I've brought up the Connicle case, have you had any word from the Swiss on Charlotte Hutton?"

"Nothing. It is a delicate process, you know. The Swiss do not like to be pestered, and they value privacy above all else. I am sure it's the reason Mrs. Hutton fled there in the first place. I cannot imagine how Sir Atherton ever convinced them to freeze her assets the first time, but I do wonder if he'll ever get them to do it again."

"He is a master at diplomacy," I agreed. "And we must not discount the possibility that he could be of use again in the search for Mrs. Hutton. After all, she shot his son and nearly killed him. I can hardly think of a better motivation for Sir Atherton to do whatever he can to ensure she is brought to justice."

"True." He released a labored sigh as the coach began to slow. "Be assured that we are doing everything within our means to locate Mrs. Hutton or her daughter. I will not go back on my word to you and Mr. Pendragon. We will see that woman hang."

I suppose I should have been shocked at such a callous sentiment, but I was not. Charlotte Hutton would meet her fate at the end of a noose once we found her again. There would be no further errors.

"Here we are, then," the inspector announced, shoving the door wide and reaching over to pick up a satchel resting on the floor as the coach came to a stop. "This gentleman has worked with Scotland Yard a time or two in the past," he explained while we climbed out into the busy street. "Been a cobbler the whole of his life. I suspect you will find him a bit off, but he should prove of some use."

"Elijah Bagley," I murmured as I read the proprietor's name on the glass door of the small shop.

"Such a keen eye for the obvious, Mr. Pruitt," the inspector chided with a snort as he pushed his way inside. "*Mr. Bagley!*" he called out.

The establishment was not much broader than the width of the door itself, and it was thick with the aroma of leather and wax polish. There was a single chair and a low table to my right, and a counter ran across the wall opposite me, behind which hung a vast number of cubbies, each stuffed with a pair of shoes: men's, women's, and children's all represented in a variety of colors and sizes. They were so neatly plugged into their places that they resembled dollops of honey in a comb.

A slender curtain hanging in the middle of the shoe hive abruptly quivered before parting to reveal a small man with dark curly hair and glasses so thick that they made his eyes look disproportionate to his face. "Who is shouting for me?" he demanded with annoyance as he scurried up to his counter, casting his eyes from me to Inspector Evans. "Oh!" He blinked several times before giving the inspector a fair-enough grin. "Nice to see you, Inspector. Dropping off another pair of boots? Your last pair was woeful, simply woeful."

"No, no," he answered. "I am here on Scotland Yard business today."

"Oh," he said again, and I decided he seemed pleased by the news. "What can I do for Scotland Yard?"

"I would like for you to look at a shoe print and a pencil drawing. Anything at all you can tell us about the shoe that made the print would be most helpful."

"How intriguing . . ." the diminutive man said, rubbing his hands together with exuberance. "Let us see what you have brought, then." He patted the counter that separated him from the inspector and me before sweeping his glasses from his face to give them a quick scrub against the lining of his jacket. His eyes, I could not help but notice, retained their bulging roundness as he did so, revealing a slight penchant for being cross-eyed.

"I must warn you," the inspector said as he dipped a hand into the satchel he'd brought in from the coach, "this first picture is rather disturbing. The print was found in a puddle of blood."

"My, my . . ." Mr. Bagley *tsked* as he slid his glasses back onto his face, focusing on the papers Inspector Evans was holding. "I suppose I should expect nothing less." He held his hands out, revealing short, thick fingers blistered with calluses.

"Right," the inspector acknowledged as he shoved the photograph across the counter first, then unfolded a large sheet of paper upon which someone had copied the print, making a few brief notes along the margins of the silhouette.

"It is the right shoe, of course," Mr. Bagley said at once, though that much we had known. "It is a commonly made sole. Probably out of Leicester or Northampton. Nothing special. Nothing special at all. I see hundreds of these every month." He squinted as he held the print closer to his face for a moment before glancing back at us. "The heel has been replaced. That's not original. See how it has a picture of a tiny cobbler's awl here. . . ." He turned the photograph around and pointed to a miniscule design that had been incused into the center of the heel. "That's not original," he said again. "That's from the Maisling and Hollister Company. They make all sorts of parts for shoes, but they don't make the shoes themselves."

"So he replaced the heel? What significance might that have?" the inspector asked.

Mr. Bagley looked at him a moment, appearing to be almost studying him as though trying to determine whether he was jesting before deciding to answer. "It means that he leans back when he walks. Carries his weight to the back. Look here." Once again he turned the photograph toward us and pointed at the print. "See how the heel leaves a darker imprint in the"—he looked up at Inspector Evans—"blood, you say?"

"Yes."

"That shows you precisely how the man walks. And it's slightly more worn on the right side than the left. I'd hazard a guess that he's probably a bit bow-legged, forcing his toes outward and causing the wear to be the greatest on the outsides of his heels. Very telling. It's all very telling."

The inspector pushed the pencil drawing forward. "Does this tell you anything further?"

Mr. Bagley gave it a quick glance before looking back at the inspector as though it was all quite rudimentary. "It's a drawing. I can't tell anything from it beyond the fact that it's the same size as the shoe in the photograph. It's the wear that tells the story. And the manufacturing."

"Please do not think me obtuse," I spoke up, digging into my pocket and then pulling out the four square sheets of paper from my notebook. I unfolded them with great care. "I understand what you've just explained, and yet I wonder if you might look at this tracing I made and tell me whether it bears any similarities to the print in that photograph."

"As I explained . . ." he started to say as I aligned them at an angle for him to view. I watched his eyes flip between the descriptive notes I had made and the outline of Mr. Alford's shoe. "Well . . ." he said. "I cannot be sure. There is no way I can be sure without the actual shoe, you understand, but if these notes are correct . . ." He looked at me, his amplified eyeballs boring into my own, making it clear that he expected an answer.

"I made those notes myself," I explained, as if that might make any difference to this man.

"If they are correct," he repeated, "then there is a possibility that the same person made both of these prints. But I cannot be certain."

"Unless you can inspect the actual shoe," I finished for him.

"Correct." He shoved his glasses up onto the bridge of his nose and glared at me. "Did you notice whether there was a cobbler's awl insignia on the heel? I don't see one drawn here."

"I cannot say that I did," I answered.

"Then I daren't say more, as it would be nothing but speculation. All I can tell you is that the wear pattern is similar. Very similar." He blinked several times as he studied me before pushing the papers my direction. "Will that be all, then?"

"Actually," I said as I folded up the tracing of Mr. Alford's shoe and pushed the photograph and drawing back to the inspector, "I saw a very fine pair of gentlemen's boots the other evening and would like to know what brand they are and where I might buy them."

"I mentioned that in the note I sent round this morning," the inspector clarified. "I told you that Mr. Pruitt was witness to a crime and saw that the perpetrator was wearing a memorable pair of boots."

"Ah, yes." Mr. Bagley nodded, snatching his glasses and

quickly buffing them again, which I thought odd since we had nothing further to show him. "Did you not think to look up and see the man's face?" he asked me.

"Mr. Bagley," the inspector snapped. "Do you not know whom you are speaking with? This is Colin Pendragon's associate, Ethan Pruitt. I thought I made that clear in my note."

"Please," I interrupted, as embarrassed at his bravado as I was certain that Mr. Bagley had never heard of me.

"Yes . . . yes . . ." He blinked several times and swung his gaze back to me. "I have heard of Mr. Pendergone, but I'm not familiar with you, sir. You will forgive me."

"I take no offense, Mr. Bagley, and neither does Mr. *Pendragon*," I pronounced with a smile. "The shoes I saw were black and highly polished, most certainly leather, and they had gray spats that looked like felt or some other such fabric. But what caught my eye were the tiny pearl-like buttons that ran along the outside of the spats. I cannot say I've ever seen their like before."

"Ah . . ." He nodded resolutely and took a step backward. "A moment, if you please." And then he was gone, disappearing back through the curtain in the wall filled with shoes.

"You were right," I said under my breath in the wake of the man's departure. "But he does seem to know his footwear."

Inspector Evans chuckled. "The wife swears by him. For shoe repair," he quickly added, "not for solving my cases."

"It is a curious thing about Mr. Alford. I traced his shoe only with the intent to disarm him, but now it would seem that we have a most unexpected possibility."

"Do you think he could be our murderer?"

"Anything is possible. But the timing . . ." I shook my head. "What of the scuffling noises Miss Unter also claims to have heard? If we think Mr. Alford guilty, then are we assuming she is lying on his behalf? Why would she do such a thing?"

Before the inspector could hazard a guess, Mr. Bagley came bustling out of his curtained back room, a pair of men's boots held in his hands with all the deference of a man handling the crown jewels. "Here you are, then," he said with an enthusiastic grin. "As you can see, I happen to have a fine pair of Ricci Marinos in my shop at present. An exquisite shoe. The best." He placed them on the counter and snatched up a cloth to buff the spots where his fingers had touched them. "They are made of the finest Italian leather, and their felt is nothing less than combed cashmere wool. Extraordinary work . . . extraordinary . . ."

He took a step back as though presenting them for accolades or a tasteful round of applause. I, on the other hand, could not share his level of enthusiasm, as the boots were a burnished saddle-brown color and the spats the pale tone of a camel's fur. That they resembled the pair I had seen Quentin Everclear's killer wearing appeared only passing at best, and I suppose it was my look of disappointment that made Mr. Bagley speak up again.

"Here," he said, using the cloth to give the boots a quarter-turn push to the side. "Now do you see?"

And indeed I did: tiny, round, white pearlescent buttons glittered and winked at me from their positions along the outside of the spats. "I do," I heard myself murmur, sounding as if I too had glimpsed something inspirational.

"They're real pearls," Mr. Bagley explained. "Ricci Marino is the only shoemaker to place pearls on the sides of their spats like buttons. They cultivate them themselves. In Venice. They choose precise specimens that match most closely to one another. Can you see how extraordinarily similar they are?"

I could not deny what he said. Each tiny sparkling gem looked very much like the one before and after it, and I doubted I would have been able to discern a vast difference in any of them between either shoe. "Extraordinary," I said, parroting his own word.

"Every man strives to have a pair of Ricci Marinos," Mr. Bagley enthused, ignoring the fact that moments ago neither the inspector nor I had ever heard of them.

"They must cost a bloody fortune," the inspector said, eyeing the shoes with wariness.

Mr. Bagley gave a high-pitched laugh that sounded almost

strangled in the back of his throat. "Far too much for a man on a civil service salary, I'm afraid," he answered. "These are diplomat's shoes. Gentlemen's wear. Perhaps your Mr. Pendergone owns them?"

"*Pendragon,*" I corrected again. "I suspect they are not carried in very many shops, then? Would you know where such a pair could be bought?"

"Certainly. There are only a handful of places in this city where they are sold. Unless, of course, your wearer went to Italy to buy them."

The very thought of that seized my gut as I glanced over at the inspector. "If you could jot down the names of those shops, I think we have seen everything we need. You have been most helpful, Mr. Bagley."

"Glad to be of service," he said, scribbling a few notes onto the back of a receipt sitting on his counter. "Here you go." He slid the names over to the inspector and swept the pair of Ricci Marino boots off his counter as though afraid we might try to steal them. "You should bring your shoes for repair, Mr. Pruitt. I can see that you too are hard on your heels. The backs of them are suffering. You scuff your feet when you walk, and you must surely be wearing them down."

"You haven't seen me walk," I pointed out.

"I don't need to," he answered with a satisfied smile. "I heard you coming in." And without another word he disappeared back behind his curtain again.

"He tells me I scrape the toes of my shoes," the inspector groaned as the two of us pushed out of the shop. "He's replaced the soles on almost every pair I own. But he has given us a great deal to follow up on. I will assign a few men to go by the shops on this list and check out who is buying these shoes. If they are as expensive as Mr. Bagley claims, we might have some luck."

"Remember, though, the pair I saw were black with gray spats. It's important that they ask about a pair matching those colors."

"Of course, of course." He waved me back to his coach. "Do you want me to drop you back at Saint George's?"

"If you please." And for once, the thought of going to the hospital made me smile. "I wonder if Colin will be commanding the staff by now."

He chuckled. "That would seem a possibility. However, it will be interesting to hear what he makes of what we've learned today."

I felt a touch of disappointment scrape against my brain as I settled into his coach. Of course he would want to know Colin's thoughts. I myself wanted to hear his consideration, so why would I expect Inspector Evans to feel any differently? "We will discuss all of it with him when you return with the Yard's files and the autopsy reports later this afternoon. He will want to see those more than ever now. And I think you must put a tail on Mr. Alford. We need to know where he goes and who he sees. Perhaps you should do the same for Miss Unter?"

"We are of similar minds." He smiled. "I shall have a tail on Mr. Alford within the hour. Miss Unter could be more difficult to accomplish, since she is clearly not a suspect."

"Nevertheless, she could be an accessory."

"Of course," he said with a nod before falling silent.

His hesitation made little difference to me as I turned to look out the window, already knowing what I would do if the Yard decided it had no justifiable reason to watch Miss Unter. Indeed, the very thought of it made me smile.

CHAPTER 22

Colin was staring at the tracing of Mr. Alford's shoe I had made, including the notes I had placed along the margin, comparing it to the photograph Inspector Evans had given me of the print from the Yard's file. Yet what was most extraordinary was that he was out of his hospital bed, sitting in one of the uncomfortable wooden chairs that the rest of us had been relegated to since the onset of his stay. His color was gradually returning, though it was clear he had lost a bit of weight, and I could tell by the way he was moving that his left shoulder and arm were tender despite the fact that he did not complain about it in the least. It was obvious to anyone who entered the room that he was as pleased to rise from that interminable bed as we were to see him do so.

"I must agree with you completely," he pronounced after a full minute had passed. "Your Mr. Allen . . ."

"Alford," I corrected.

He dismissed me with a flick of the photograph. "Whatever the man's name, there can be no doubt that he left this footprint at the murder scene."

"You cannot be certain of that. . . ." I started to say.

"Of course I can," he fired back, shunting the photograph and tracings back to me in a single sweep of his right hand. "There

are far too many coincidences in these signs of wear to be ascribed to anything less than surety. Have the inspector bring
the man in for questioning at once, and you will crack him like
an egg."

I chuckled. "What a turn of phrase."

Colin did not share my amusement but turned to me with a
petulant frown, frustration and desperation simmering within
his gaze. "You cannot let them keep me here, Ethan. I must get
out of this place, or it will be the end of me."

"This place saved your life."

"I know that," he grumbled, making it clear he did not like
to be reminded of that fact. "But it is time for me to leave now.
It is enough. I need to go home. I need to be with you and Mrs.
Behmoth. I will get better there much faster. You know I am
right."

"You are still weak, Colin. Mrs. Behmoth won't be much help
for you when I'm not there."

"Are you kidding me?! That woman is like an ox. And we can
get a nurse to come in as well in between times. Why don't we
use that lovely young lady who was tending to Adelaide Endicott?"

"You mean Philippa Bromley?"

"Well, I certainly don't mean the other one."

"Just as well, since she is otherwise engaged for some time to
come."

"I knew you would agree," he said, looking well pleased with
himself. "Which is why I have already sent young Paul to get
word to her. I have no doubt that she will have me as good as
new forthwith."

"Oh . . ." I mumbled back at him, realizing he had been playing me all along. This was less a discussion than a directive.
"Then you had best hope she does so as I will not abide agonizing over your health again in this wretched place."

"There. You see? Even *you* find this place awful." He gave me
a sly smile, but I could tell I had made my point.

An abrupt knock interrupted us before the door swung open
to reveal Inspector Evans, hat in hand and several folders tucked

beneath an arm. "Now, there is a nice surprise," he said, his face lighting up at the sight of Colin in the chair. "You are looking positively robust, Mr. Pendragon."

Colin turned to me with the speed of a gazelle. "You see?! You have nothing to worry about." He glanced back at the inspector. "Your judgment is impeccable, Inspector." His face lit with a smile. "The doctors are, in fact, releasing me tomorrow. I shall be completing my convalescence at home. A mere formality, really."

"Well, that is the best news yet." The inspector settled himself into the third chair in the room, opposite Colin and me. "I am sure you both must be very pleased."

"Tell me you have the autopsy report for Daphne Masterson and the three case files that Mr. Pruitt mentioned," Colin stated with almost irrepressible eagerness.

"Delphine Materly," I quickly corrected.

"I have them as promised." The inspector chuckled. "And I'm sure Mr. Pruitt has already apprised you of our astonishing occurrence this afternoon."

"You are referring to Mr. Allwood?"

"Alford," I corrected again.

"I am. The case continues to get more and more confounding." He stared at the tracing and photograph still clutched in my hand. "Have you looked at the evidence yet?"

"I have and I agree. I was just telling Ethan that the two of you should be pounding down that man's door with all due haste. Now is the exact moment to squeeze him before Mr. Ross's autopsy report exonerates him based on the timing of the murder."

Inspector Evans's face sagged. "Whatever do you mean? I have his autopsy report right here." He extracted it from under his arm and gave it a wave. "It corroborates the time Mr. Alford and Miss Unter claim to have heard the scuffling sounds beneath her window." He heaved a sudden sigh. "But then what of it? None of these pieces seems willing to coalesce in the least. Is Mr. Alford our killer and Miss Unter his accomplice . . . ?" He let his voice drift off and flicked his eyes to me, and I could see the same confusion that had been upending my own thoughts as well.

"I have wondered the same thing myself, and yet I cannot help but find it inconceivable to imagine that Miss Unter might have some involvement in these horrible murders."

"You are both missing the point," Colin cut me off tersely. "The two of you are conjecturing about nonsense. The only thing that matters is that your Mr. Alford was at the scene of the murder, as evidenced by his shoe print, and that he was there within minutes of its having taken place, also as evidenced by his shoe print. Consider the facts. If he had stumbled onto the scene any appreciable time later, that thin layer of blood that so indelibly captured his shoe print would have coagulated or dried and would never have retained so crisp a reproduction. Instead . . ." He leaned forward and yanked the photograph out of my hand with such purpose and determination that I did not realize what he was doing until he was waving it at me and the inspector. "Instead he left a print as vivid and rich as the killer himself would have produced. So while it is charming that the two of you cannot conceive of any involvement by your Mr. Alford or his lady friend, I must insist that there is every possibility that one, if not both, of them saw the monster who *did* commit the murder."

"Bloody hell," the inspector grumbled.

"Tell me you have a tail on the man!"

"Of course I do."

"Excellent." He passed the photograph back to me before turning his hand to the inspector, and I realized that he was not using his left arm at all. "Now let me see those autopsy reports."

The inspector handed them over like a chastised child. "You might think I must be new to Scotland Yard," he said with an awkward chuckle that Colin did not join in on.

"I was going to suggest that we have Paul keep an eye on Miss Unter," I spoke up, eager to defend the two of us.

"Who?" Colin muttered without looking up.

"The woman Mr. Alford was with at the time of Miss Materly's murder. . . ."

"Yes. Of course," Colin responded again with a decided lack of interest as he continued to pore over the files. Not a minute later he slammed the last folder shut and thrust the three of them back toward the inspector. "Do you have any reason to believe that Miss Unter is unbalanced?"

"Pardon . . . ?" the inspector said before I could.

"Is she potty? Daft? Balmy? Out of her buggered mind?"

"She would appear to be none of those things," I answered. "She is coherent and as articulate as any poorly educated woman who earns her living on the streets."

"And what of her relationship with Mr. Alford? Does she appear to dote on him? Do you sense that he has any sort of hold over her?"

"Oh!" Inspector Evans spoke up. "You're referring to that character in the George du Maurier book so many people are talking about. . . ."

"What?!" Colin asked, his expression curling in on itself.

"Svengali," I answered. "The book is titled *Trilby*."

"What are the two of you prattling on about?" Colin flicked his eyes from the inspector to me. "I am asking a vital question about the nature of the relationship between that woman and the man who left his shoe print at the murder scene!"

"She is a prostitute, Colin, with a steady supply of customers, of whom Mr. Alford is merely one. She seems no more or less attached to him than anyone else I've ever seen who pays a wage for a night, and I would say she is a woman who is cowed by no one. Would you agree with me, Inspector?"

He nodded. "I'd say that sums her up."

"You see? We have not been sitting idly by while you were ill."

Colin settled back in his chair and released a long exhale. "I apologize if my tone seemed to suggest that the two of you have not been working hard on this case. Nevertheless, I must insist that you interrogate your Mr. Alford this evening. You dare not let another night pass. If he believes himself a suspect in the slayings, you will get him to confess whatever truth he may be hiding. But once the timing of the murder becomes public, you will have no such leverage over him. You must not tarry."

I glanced over at Inspector Evans and could tell he was

weighing the sense of Colin's words against what amounted to the trickery of Mr. Alford, a tact that Colin and I had used on so many occasions. Such was not the way of the Yard, however, and I could see the conflict playing out across his face.

"If I could go myself, I would," he continued, and there was no questioning his earnestness, "but I do believe Mr. Pruitt would raise every possible alarm if I tried to leave here tonight. And"—a sheepish sort of smirk ghosted across his face—"I need him to do me a service before the two of you head out."

"Very well. I shall take your advice, Mr. Pendragon. I can admit to no better notions, and if this scoundrel is hiding something, I shall have it from him tonight. I only hope I will not have to face the consequences of our threats to Mr. Alford should nothing come of it. He does seem the sort of man who would seek restitution from Scotland Yard for wrongful treatment." He shook his head. "A very entitled individual."

"And with little reason to feel so," I added.

"Precisely the kind of man most likely to succumb to such methods," Colin assured. "The more inflated they are, the quicker they lose their air when pricked."

Inspector Evans chuckled as he stood up. "I am going to find a telephone somewhere in this hospital and give the order to the lads at Scotland Yard to have Mr. Alford picked up at once." He gave a shrewd smile. "I have both his work address *and* his home."

"His home?!" I repeated.

"Oh yes." The inspector's smile widened. "I've not been idle either while you've been sitting here visiting Mr. Pendragon." He moved to the door with his files stashed under an arm again. "Take your time, Mr. Pruitt, and I will meet you downstairs when you are ready. I should think it will take the better part of an hour to find Mr. Alford and have him delivered to Whitehall Place."

"I shall meet you downstairs in just a few minutes."

The door swung shut behind the inspector, and Colin's eyes swung toward me with veiled anticipation. "I should very much like to accompany you tonight. I would just sit there like a church mouse and listen. It's even possible that my being there could help by further intimidating the self-important little pox."

I crossed my arms over my chest and stared at him. "Are you finished?"

His expression curdled. "You used to be more accommodating."

"That was before you almost died on me," I shot back.

He flinched, and I saw the vinegar drain from his eyes. "I am sorry, Ethan."

His words stole my breath, requiring a minute before I could collect myself and answer him. "Don't be ridiculous," I heard myself say with absurdly false cheer. "Now, what is it you need me to do for you?"

"Yes!" His eyes sparked again as he pushed himself to his feet and made his way back to the bed. "I need you to tell the doctors that I will be leaving tomorrow. Paul is bound to be back any time now with the good news from Miss Bromley. She wouldn't possibly turn us down."

"Me?!" I protested. "You're the one who wants to defy their orders. Why do I have to take the dressing down they're going to insist upon?"

"Because I have been ill, and you said yourself that I need my rest." He climbed into the bed and pulled the covers over himself. "And make sure you come back as soon as you've spoken with Mr. Alford. I'll want to hear how it went, since you won't permit me to go."

He settled himself and closed his eyes, leaving me little else to do but leave the room.

CHAPTER 23

"I must admit," Inspector Evans muttered as Scotland Yard's main building, Whitehall Place, loomed within range of our carriage, "that I would not have brought Mr. Alford in for questioning just yet if Mr. Pendragon had not been so insistent. It makes me uneasy. I cannot help but believe we have tenuous grounds on which to bring him in, and the subterfuge Mr. Pendragon has suggested—to accuse him of the very crime itself when the autopsy appears to all but exonerate him—is well beyond the protocol within which Scotland Yard holds itself."

"Which is precisely why you must let me do the talking," I instructed, though in truth I wasn't at all sure what I would say. "You cannot be accused of any impropriety if you are but a witness to my interrogation. I shall question him while you listen, and if at any point you feel I have ventured too far afield, you must beckon me out into the hallway and tell me so."

"Yes, yes." He nodded, puckering his face as he seemed to be trying to get more comfortable with what I was suggesting.

If he was concerned about being complicit through his silence he did not say so, and within a handful of minutes we were pulling into the forecourt of Scotland Yard. The two of us went in through the main doors, and Inspector Evans was almost im-

mediately set upon by several of his men, all clamoring about
Mr. Alford, who had apparently just been brought up from the
building's ominous rear entrance and deposited in one of the interrogation rooms.

"The man is furious," one of them warned.

"He is threatening to hire a solicitor," another stated.

The inspector slid his eyes toward me as he shooed his men
away with an angry wave of a hand. "Are you sure about this?"

I wanted to laugh at the fact that certainty was the remotest of
things I was feeling at the moment, but I managed to contain myself. "Yes," I answered, and he seemed satisfied by that response.

He ordered one of his men to take us to Mr. Alford, and the
young constable with his poorly grown mustache and goatee—
clearly meant to hide his evident youth—snapped about and escorted us up two flights. We were led about halfway down a long
hallway that displayed multiple photographs of Queen Victoria
and one of Lord Salisbury. The constable handed over a key before inquiring whether he would be needed to take notes of the
conversation.

"No. That will be all," the inspector answered gruffly, making his ongoing unease apparent to me. "I will fetch you when
we're done."

The inspector did not make another move until his constable
had dashed back the way we had come and disappeared down the
stairs. For a moment I thought he was going to once again question my willingness to proceed, but he surprised me by stuffing
the key into the lock and shoving the door open.

"This is an absolute trav—" Mr. Alford began to holler before
falling silent when the inspector and I were revealed at the yawing door. "You two," he growled, his lips curling back as though
the very sight of us was an offense. "I have already told you everything I know and yet you have dared to treat me like a common street thug. I will not stand for this," he hissed. "You will
have my solicitor to answer to in one of Her Majesty's courts!"

"That is all fine and well, Mr. Alford," Inspector Evans said
as we entered the small room, and he pushed the door shut, "but
I thought you would want to know that we have new evidence.

Evidence that I think you will want to respond to in the relative privacy of this room."

"Evidence?" His eyes shot between the inspector and me, and I thought I recognized the stirrings of concern behind them. "What the bloody hell are you talking about?"

"Sit down, Mr. Alford," the inspector directed, the two of us pulling up chairs on one side of the thrashed wooden table that stood, bowed and fiercely marred, in the center of the tight space. "And do settle yourself. Might I point out that you were not put under arrest when you were brought here. We are attempting to give you an opportunity to explain yourself. Should you fail to take that opportunity, it will be viewed most seriously."

"Well . . ." He huffed with great indignation. Nevertheless, he lowered himself into the chair that sat opposite us.

"Mr. Alford," I began, taking my time to allow him a chance to collect himself. "You mentioned hearing some sort of scuffle on the street beneath Miss Unter's window the night Delphine Materly was killed, isn't that correct?"

"Oh hell," he snapped. "I hardly know what I heard. I told you that yesterday. I was indisposed with Miss Unter and was not of a mind to go snooping about at every sound that drifted in from that bloody street."

"Yes," I agreed, giving him the best smile I could muster considering that I did not like this man and his willingness to dismiss a woman's murder as little more than a nuisance. "I believe you also told us that you left Miss Unter's room somewhere between one and one-thirty. Does my memory serve me on that point?"

Mr. Alford scowled at me and seemed to consider his answer a moment before he finally gave it. "Yes. It was about then."

"About then . . . ?" I pressed, knowing the timing was critical if we were going to impugn him for what he may have seen. "What time did you return home that night?"

Once again I was leveled with a scowl. "I don't know. What is this about anyway?"

"Perhaps your wife might know?" I suggested with a dash of innocence, though I knew he recognized the veiled threat.

"Two o'clock," he seethed, his jaw clenched and his demeanor stiff, which suited me fine. He was on edge, and I had watched Colin disassemble many a man in such a state.

"Ah . . . a late night indeed," I commented for no other reason than to see how far Mr. Alford could lower his brow. "Your wife is very understanding."

"I have business that takes me all over the city at all manner of hours," he shot back. "Now, what does any of this have to do with anything? What of this new evidence?" He shifted his eyes to Inspector Evans as though he might be an ally, but he got nothing more in return than an unwavering stare.

"We have the coroner's report on Miss Materly," I answered, taking my time, ensuring that Mr. Alford's tolerance was pressed to its limits. "It places the time of the murder between one and one-thirty. An extraordinary coincidence, wouldn't you say?"

Mr. Alford jerked back in his chair, and his face tore through a series of expressions from surprise to confusion to fury in the matter of an instant. "What?! What are you saying? What does that have to do with me? Are you accusing me?"

"Accusing you?" I repeated, hopeful that my face could still carry a countenance of utter naïveté. "I don't believe I have accused you of anything. I am simply trying to assemble the timing of events on the night Delphine Materly was murdered beneath the window of the room you were in."

Rex Alford's chin sank down toward his sternum and his eyes flicked back and forth between the inspector and me, dark and infuriated. He looked like a cornered animal, ready to pounce. For once, I truly understood the thrill Colin felt in these moments.

I reached into my coat pocket and pulled out the pages with my tracing and the attendant photograph, moving with meticulous slowness until I could even begin to feel the inspector's annoyance rising beside me. "I have a photograph here," I said, holding it in front of me so that Mr. Alford could not yet see it. "It is a photograph of the print your shoe left in a pool of Miss Materly's blood not five feet from where her body lay. So now I *must* ask you, did you murder Delphine Materly?"

"*What?!*" He jumped to his feet and roared. "This is appalling. You're a charlatan. You are trying to frame me. I will not have this. I won't listen to another word. . . ."

"Mr. Alford . . ." Inspector Evans said in a low, steady tone.

"You have no proof of this. You lot have no bloody idea what you're doing, so now you're looking for the first person to blame . . ."

"Mr. Alford!" Inspector Evans said again.

"Well, it won't be me. You will *not* drag me into your ineptitude. And you will *not* destroy my life with your accusations and . . ."

"Mr. Alford . . . !" the inspector bellowed.

"How dare you accuse me of murder! It is an offense. I know powerful people who make their livings destroying squiggly little vermin like the two of you. I will have your jobs for this. And if one word of *any* of this gets to my wife I will see that the two of you . . ."

But he did not finish his threat before Inspector Evans bolted out of his chair and landed an uppercut on Mr. Alford's chin, sending his head snapping backward and dropping him into his seat. "*I warned you, Mr. Alford,*" he snarled, shaking his hand a moment and rubbing his knuckles. "You will *stop* this bluster and you will *answer* Mr. Pruitt, or I will arrest you now and you can threaten the back wall of your cell for all I care."

Mr. Alford remained quiet, his head listing forward and his eyes blinking wildly. I was not sure whether he had the capacity to understand what was being said any longer, but knew I needed to continue, as our game had taken a decided turn. "You allowed me to trace your right shoe yesterday. You remember this tracing?" I opened the folded pages, already beginning to look distinctly worn, and laid them out before placing the photograph on the table beside it. "It allowed us to match the print you left at the murder scene with what I traced from your shoe. The wear patterns, the size, the make—Maisling and Hollister, correct?"

It felt as if it took better than a minute before Mr. Alford finally lifted his eyes and focused on me. His eyes were rimmed in red and filled with shock. "I . . ." His voice cracked, and he cleared his throat. "I didn't kill her. Jacklyn . . . Miss Unter and I . . . we heard something. . . ." His voice drifted off and his eyes dropped to the table along with his hands, although he gently rocked his jaw back and forth in an effort to assure himself that it had not been shattered. "They were laughing . . . two people . . . a man and a woman. . . . Miss Unter recognized Miss Materly's voice and was going to shout out and tell her to quiet down, but then there was this sound . . . sort of muffled . . . like the sound a baby makes when it gurgles . . . followed by a thump. I don't know how else to describe it. But you could tell at once it wasn't right." He fell silent and sat there, staring at his hands, the only movement now the steady rhythm of his body as he breathed in and out.

"What did you and Miss Unter do?" I finally asked, speaking in little more than a whisper.

"She got herself worked up. Made me look out the window and see if I could tell what was going on. It wasn't top of my mind at the time, but under the circumstances, what with those two recent murders . . . I looked outside and saw two people disappear down the cellar steps and out of sight. They were standing real close, like they couldn't wait to get started . . ." He paused and shrugged, knowing we would fill in the rest.

"And then what happened?"

"Miss Unter, she tells me that Miss Materly has a room upstairs just like hers—so why the hell would she be taking a bloke down into the cellar?" He grimaced and shook his head slightly. "Next thing I know the evening is broken and the two of us are sniping at each other like a married couple. She won't settle herself, so I decided to leave. It was late anyway, and I can get treated like that at home for free." He fell silent.

"When you saw the couple out the window, could you make out the figure of the man at all? Height? Color of hair? Facial features? Anything?" I pressed.

"It was the middle of the night. He had some kind of cap on his head and was leaning way over the woman as if he was whispering in her ear or nuzzling her neck. I don't know. I didn't give a shite what some other couple was getting up to."

"And then . . . ?" I prodded. "How is it your footprint came to be at the murder scene?"

"I got dressed while Miss Unter was haranguing me, telling me to hurry up and go see what's happening. Like if something *is* happening I'm going to do anything about it!" He looked up at the inspector and me, and I realized this man understood his own shortcomings more than I had suspected. "So I pulled myself together and went outside, making a hell of a clamor as I went. I mean, I'm not going to be killed by some lunatic murdering prostitutes. I've got a family . . . a reputation . . ."

"Go on, Mr. Alford," the inspector coaxed.

"I stood there a minute, and I'm lighting a cigar by the front door when all of a sudden this bloke comes bursting out of the cellar. He's wearing that cap on his head, low on his forehead, so I can't see his face. He's pulling on this long black coat, like he's still getting dressed from . . . you know . . . whatever they were doing, only I see he's already got some kind of a coat on, like a tan color or something. And he's carrying a satchel, like something a doctor might use or maybe some kind of clerk or librarian. I don't know. And he races off in the opposite direction like his arse is on fire. He doesn't even bother to look toward me. Just like that." He snapped his fingers as if to better make his point.

"You can tell us nothing else of him, then?" I asked. "How tall he was? Did he appear thin or stocky?"

"He was taller than Miss Materly. I could see that when I looked out the window. He had his head jutting forward, like I already told you, so he must have had five or six inches on her. But I couldn't see anything else. He had the tan coat on and was pulling the other one on top of it. It wasn't even that cold out." He shook his head and fell silent again. The memory of it all, I was certain, was not sitting well for him.

"Is that when you decided to go down to the cellar and see for yourself?" I pressed again.

"Miss Unter had pulled her window open a bit and was pestering me about Miss Materly. I told her to shut the hell up. That everything was fine." He glanced down and rubbed his hands together, the weight of his lie evident. "I should've just gone home. Instead I walked down to that blasted cellar, calling out to the woman, asking if she was okay. . . ." He snorted a grim-sounding chuckle. "There wasn't an answer. I lit a match and held it up, but I couldn't see two feet in front of my face. That's when I stepped in something sticky. It tugged at my shoe and made me jump."

He went still yet again, but this time neither the inspector nor I pressed him to continue. After another moment he looked up at us. "I saw the pool of blood first, and then I saw her. It was black as pitch, and I was holding a buggered match in my hand, but I could tell it was bad. And I knew right then that I should never have gone down there. How could I call a constable? I had no reason to be there. My wife . . ." He left his argument hanging and diverted his eyes, the breath rushing out of his body to leave him sagging and wretched looking.

"Your wife sounds like a formidable woman," I said, hoping he might catch the rebuke in my tone.

"My wife is a baronet," he stated with a hint of misery. "Her position has accorded me a great many things. I would sooner die than betray her trust."

"Commendable," I answered, now certain I could not think less of this man. "So what did you do?"

"The match had burned down to my fingers," he said, holding up his right hand as if to present a badge of honor. "I threw it aside. It must be down there even now. And then I yanked off my shoe and got the ruddy hell out of there, bolting up those wretched steps in two blasted strides."

"You took off your shoe?" the inspector repeated.

"Yes." Mr. Alford glanced at him, and I knew what he would say. "I didn't want to leave any prints behind. I knew I'd stepped in something . . ." He shook his head with a sneer. "I dunked it in a puddle of horse piss out in the street until it was clean, and then I went back to Miss Unter's room. I told her I'd looked around and there was nothing. That she should keep her mouth shut if she expected to see me again. I thought that would work. I never considered that she'd tell you to come back on Friday night to speak with me. A pox on her buggered arse."

I turned to look at the inspector. "We're going to need to speak with Miss Unter right away."

He nodded, and I realized he had already come to the same conclusion. "As to you, Mr. Alford, I shall expect you to make yourself available to Scotland Yard as we see fit, and in return we will continue to seek you out at your place of employment. But if you shy from us, or cease to be of aid, I promise you that Mr. Pruitt and I will visit your wife personally and hurl this entire affair at her feet. Do I make myself clear?"

Mr. Alford nodded with nary a peep, and I suspected he was as wary of being slugged again as he was of having his misdeeds confessed to his wife.

"Shall we take a ride then?" Inspector Evans looked at me.

I nodded. "Perhaps your men could stall Mr. Alford to ensure we reach Miss Unter before he does?"

"I am *not* going to see her," he bristled. "I have told you the truth. Every word of it."

"A sound idea," the inspector agreed as though Mr. Alford had not uttered a word. "Do sit tight, Mr. Alford." He ushered me out, the two of us leaving the venal man in that tiny room with his sore chin and shaken spirit.

CHAPTER 24

If I had imagined that Jacklyn Unter might be relieved to finally share what she knew of her friend's murder, I was sorely mistaken. She made it clear with the instantaneous pucker on her face and drooping of her shoulders that she was not pleased in the least to see either Inspector Evans or me. Just the same, she pulled the door to her room open and allowed us entry.

"You'd better not be 'ere ta drag me down ta that blasted Yard again," she said at once. "People will be gettin' the wrong idea about me if ya don't stop pesterin' me."

"If you cooperate," the inspector informed her, just as he had with Rex Alford, "then there will be little reason for us to keep coming around. But if you continue to play games . . ."

She stared at him a moment before turning her gaze on me, and to her credit, I could see she understood that her lies had been laid bare. "You can sit down if ya want," she invited with a distinct lack of enthusiasm.

I waved the inspector to the room's sole chair, which looked woefully unused in a corner behind the door, before seating myself on the tufted ottoman shoved in front of a dilapidated desk that she clearly used as a dressing table. "We shall not stay long," I assured her.

"'At's good. 'Cause I got a meetin' at the Crow's Nest round the corner with some a the other ladies t'night. Since you Yarders ain't doin' shite about this madman, we're goin' ta look after ourselves." Her tone was exasperated as she stood in front of us, hands on hips, looking as if she had accorded us every assistance and still we had let her down.

"I am *not* an employee of Scotland Yard," I shot back with perhaps a touch more ire than was called for. "No offense to you, Inspector. And I would suggest you start being truthful with us before you try playing the woebegone maiden, Miss Unter."

Her hands fell from her hips at last, and she plopped back onto a corner of her bed. "Mr. Alford told ya wot 'appened, did 'e?"

"We gave him a very compelling argument," the inspector answered before I could. "And you would be wise to follow his lead. I wonder how your friends at the Crow's Nest would feel if they knew you had been keeping potentially vital information from Scotland Yard."

"There ain't no reason ta start talkin' like that. I only 'eld me tongue 'cause 'e told me to. 'E's a good customer, ya know. And they only stay good customers when ya do as they say. A girl's gotta make a livin'."

"Let us save that particular conversation for another day," I spoke up. "For the moment, the greater use of our time can be spent by your telling us exactly what happened the night Miss Materly was murdered."

She looked at me a moment before turning her gaze on the inspector, appearing to be searching his face for something. "Wot did 'e tell ya?" she asked after a few protracted seconds.

I wanted to laugh but managed to contain it. "That does not matter. All we care about is you. What *you* saw and what *you* heard."

"The truth," Inspector Evans reminded from his corner.

She rolled her eyes heavenward before she began. "I 'eard 'em laughin' jest like I told ya. Two of 'em. I recognized Delphine's voice, but I didn't know 'oo the man was." She gave a dismissive shrug. "Didn't really mean nothin'. I 'ear all kinda things livin' 'ere. But then Delphine, she stops laughin' all the sudden.

Like one second somethin' is funny and the next second it ain't. That caught me attention, and it ain't like me and Mr. Alford was jest sittin' 'ere playin' Tiddledy Winks." She gave a full-throated laugh that neither the inspector nor I joined in.

"Did another sound draw your attention or was it the suddenness with which Miss Materly stopped laughing?" I asked, determined to get her focused again.

"There weren't no other sound," she insisted, the smile on her face dropping in an instant. "It jest weren't right—laughin' out loud, carryin' on like they was, and then stoppin' as fast as somebody blowin' out a light." She wrapped her arms around herself and held them there a moment, though I do not believe she was aware she had done so.

"And then what happened?" I prodded.

"I went over ta the window and peeked outside. Made Mr. Alford come along with me too. Did 'e tell ya that?!"

"Go on, Miss Unter."

She tossed me a frown before continuing. "We looked outside and that's when I seen the two a them. 'E were leanin' in over 'er like she's a puppet and 'e's pullin' 'er strings. Men think women like that—'avin' 'em 'ang all over us—but we don't. You two should keep that ta mind. It's like bein' trapped in a box made a hands and arms, all squeezin' and movin' in on ya. Wot makes ya think that's nice?!" she asked the two of us, her frown deepening.

"Can you describe the man?" I asked.

"It were the middle a the night and gas lamps round 'ere ain't worth a shite. But I knew it weren't that skinny shite wot comes round 'ere sayin' 'e's 'er 'usband. I'd a known 'im right off. But the one that night . . ." Her voice drifted off as she seemed to be staring at nothing.

"Height?" the inspector spoke up. "Broadness of shoulders? Type of clothing? Color of his hair? You must have noticed something."

"I noticed"—she bit the words harshly, making it clear that she did not appreciate being pressed—"that Delphine were slumped back against 'im like she were passed out. And that weren't like 'er. She could toss 'em back same as any of us, but ya sure as bollocks don't do that when you is workin'. 'At's a good way ta not get paid fer yer efforts."

"And the man?" I asked again. "You're certain it wasn't the thin chap you told us about earlier?"

"A course I'm certain. 'E's a wisp a nothin' that Delphine coulda flattened anytime she wanted. I told ya I took a turn with 'im meself. That sot couldn't 'urt nothin' and I'd sure as 'ell know if it'd been 'im that night. Now, stop interruptin' me," she protested. "The bugger I saw standin' behind Delphine was wearin' a cap on 'is 'ead, like the ones them lads wear who're always hawkin' newspapers. And 'e 'ad on a black coat that looked more like a cloak it were so large—all billowy and baggy, especially where 'is arms was wrapped around 'er. It didn't sit right with me and I tol' Mr. Alford so."

"What did you say?"

"I tol' 'im ta get his arse out there and see wot the ruddy 'ell was goin' on." She glared at me as though my question was absurd. "When I saw 'im 'aulin' 'er backward toward them cellar steps I 'ad a terrible feelin'. I turned right around and started throwin' Mr. Alford's clothes at 'im. Tol' 'im ta get down there or he weren't never gonna 'ave any reason ta come ta my room again!"

"So he went down?" the inspector prodded.

"Not right away," she admitted, her displeasure apparent. "'E tol' me ta go down there meself if I were so damned interested in wot they was doin', the nob. So I said I would! And that's when 'e finally got 'imself dressed and went out there. But 'e weren't in no damn 'urry, mind you—takin' 'is time lacin' this and tyin' that. I were about ready ta throw 'is arse out the feckin' window!"

"How long do you think it took before he finally left your room?" I asked.

She gave a shrug. "Five or six minutes. Maybe more. And then when 'e did leave, 'e was makin' enough of a racket ta scare off everyone for a block around—bangin' the door and coughin' like 'e 'ad consumption. Then 'e jest stood on the porch like a bleedin' lord and lit a cigar." She shook her head and scowled. "I finally 'ad ta open me window and yell out at 'im. That's when I saw the bloke again."

"The one who you'd seen with Miss Materly?"

"Course. 'E were comin' up the cellar steps pullin' on that big black coat again, even though I could see 'e was already wearin' another one, though that one was shorter and some kinda light gray."

"Are you sure it wasn't just his suit jacket?"

"No." My question earned me yet another frown from her. "It went down to 'is knees, I think. Besides, I know a man's jacket when I see one," she barked. "I've 'elped yank enough of 'em off," she added churlishly.

"Forgive me." I jotted down her description, making note of the ways in which it differed from what Mr. Alford had recollected.

"That was all I saw 'cause Mr. Alford turned around and gave me bloody 'ell, tellin' me ta feck off and shut me window." She shifted her gaze toward the windows, and I could see a shadow of regret ghost across her face. "So that's wot I did 'cause Mr. Alford is a reg'lar payin' customer and I'd already said too much."

"But Mr. Alford came back, didn't he?" I asked. "A few minutes later?"

"Yeah." Her tone had gone cold as if she was trying to seal off the memory of that night. "'E came back and said that nothin' was wrong. Delphine was fine and I needed ta mind me own business." She shook her head and looked down at her hands. "But I could see 'e were lyin'. One a 'is shoes was all wet and 'e were sweatin' like 'e'd jest run a race." It took another moment before she finished her thought. "I knew right then she was dead. I knew I'd seen the man wot killed 'er and those other women. But Mr. Alford jest kept tellin' me ta keep me mouth shut and not say nothin' ta nobody."

"You were impeding an investigation," Inspector Evans pointed out gruffly.

"I let ya come see Mr. Alford, didn't I?! 'E were furious that I'd said that much, but I did it anyway. So don't go tellin' me I weren't 'elpful. It ain't up ta me ta get all yer answers for ya."

"Did you notice anything else about the man you saw?" I asked again, anxious not to allow the conversation to devolve. "Anything at all?"

"'E 'ad on that big coat and cap. I couldn't tell ya shite about 'im except 'e were white and 'e walked fast."

"How can you be sure of the color of his skin if you didn't see his face?"

She looked at me and laughed. "I saw 'is 'ands when 'e was puttin' on that black overcoat."

I nodded, certain we had learned everything this woman had to tell us. Inspector Evans implored her to contact either of us if she remembered anything further, but I rather doubted she would do so. The investigation was impugning her livelihood and, friend or not, Miss Unter would sooner take care of herself.

"Do you still have men watching Mr. Alford?" I asked as we headed back to the inspector's coach.

"I do. Though I suppose now we could better use those resources elsewhere."

"I would suggest you leave them on that duty," I said. "If Mr. Alford is continuing to withhold any information from us, now may be the time we will discover it. These two interrogations with their slightly differing versions just might propel him into some careless action to reveal the whole of what he and Miss Unter saw, or perhaps they themselves could have had a more direct involvement, although these two hardly seem that clever."

The inspector chuckled. "Nevertheless, you are getting more cunning in your thinking, Mr. Pruitt. I do believe Mr. Pendragon will be pleased."

I could not help the thin smile that cracked one corner of my mouth. "He will." We climbed into the coach and settled ourselves, the inspector calling out to return me to Saint George's. "Are your men continuing to speak to the other tenants of Miss Unter's building?" I asked.

"They are. But so far no one is admitting to have seen or heard anything."

"Then perhaps it is time to impress upon Superintendent Tottenshire the need for some sort of reward for information."

Inspector Evans turned to me with a look of surprise as the coach lurched forward. "Are you being coy?"

"What?"

"Mr. Pendragon called the superintendent early this morning to make the very same request. I would assume it has already been done."

"Oh . . ." Of course Colin would have thought of it already, but at least I wasn't all that far behind him. It was enough to widen my smile just a hint.

CHAPTER 25

After a great commotion of angry voices and grave-looking, white-coated professionals spouting dire warnings and assertions of reckless folly, by eleven o'clock that Sunday morning Colin walked out of the hospital on his own. Sir Atherton had been doing his best to stave off the doctors' concerns, and Philippa Bromley, one of the nurses we had worked with on the Endicott case, arrived just before Colin's release to prove that we were not being entirely foolhardy by giving in to Colin's insistence to leave. Her presence alone was enough to finally mollify the primary physician after he had gone through the litany of medicines, treatments, and therapies with her, each of which he swore her to uphold.

Colin had remained uncharacteristically quiet during the morning, allowing his father and me to advocate on his behalf before confessing, once we were in the carriage, that he was saving his energy for the cases. Neither Sir Atherton nor I acknowledged that statement. There seemed little point. I was content to hope that Miss Bromley might be able to persuade him to be reasonable, though I suspected that might be folly on my part.

Given the commotion of the day and our desire to ensure that Colin got properly settled, Sir Atherton moved our meeting with Queen Victoria's grand-nephew to the following day. Several messengers had been sent back and forth before new arrangements could be accommodated, with the last note being dispatched to the Queen to inform her of the change. To my surprise, Sir Atherton received a response from the sovereign not forty minutes later that stated, simply, *I see.*

The day seemed to be taking a notably calming turn, with Sir Atherton even heading home satisfied that we had not been unduly heedless of the doctors' wishes when Miss Bromley abruptly threw our home into utter turmoil. "Which room belongs to Mr. Pendragon?" she asked. "I need to set up his tinctures and supplies."

I stared at Colin with mortification and he at me, leaving Mrs. Behmoth, who happened to be serving tea at that moment, to speak up. "'E's in the room straight back. Mr. Pruitt's room is on the left."

"Very good." Miss Bromley smiled before heading down the hall, black satchel in her hand.

"This isn't going to work," Colin announced the moment she was gone from view.

"It will be fine," I insisted. "She isn't staying nights. She'll not think anything."

"That room looks exactly like what it is, an unused extra bedroom for somebody's maiden aunt to stay in," he persisted, and I wondered if he wasn't angling to relieve her of her services.

"I'll stir the room up," Mrs. Behmoth said with the wave of a meaty hand. "She ain't gonna think shite. She's a nurse, not a ruddy detective."

Colin tossed her a frown but held his tongue.

"I've been meaning to ask you," I said once she had started down the stairs, eager to turn his mind to better things. "Have you ever heard of the shoemaker Ricci Marino?"

"Italian," he answered at once, leaning forward to fuss with the tea things, though I noticed he was still coddling his left side. "Very fine quality. Extremely expensive. You won't find them on my feet, but I'll bet my father has a few pairs. Why?" He handed a cup across to me.

"The man who killed Quentin Everclear was wearing a pair of Ricci Marino shoes. I described them for a cobbler Inspector Evans uses, and he knew what they were at once."

"Did they have tiny pearl buttons running along the sides of the spats?"

"They did," I said with a chuckle. Of course he would know that. "I have since learned they are a hallmark of the manufacturer."

"They cultivate the pearls themselves and hand-select them for each pair. Aficionados insist it enhances the quality and uniformity." He gave a slight shrug. "I don't see why that would be the case. Nature is not known for creating either perfection or symmetry."

"I shall keep that in mind before I buy a pair." I gave him a smile that he returned over the lip of his cup. "So tell me, what does that allow you to deduce about the killer?"

"A great deal," he answered without the slimmest inflection of jest or facetiousness. "Just as I am sure it does for you."

He paused and looked at me, and I knew that in spite of everything he had been through, my education in the art of deduction and investigation had resumed once more. I rattled my brain and tried to fathom what he might be referring to. "The man is wealthy," I stated, comfortable in the certainty of this assumption.

He chuckled before snatching up a cranberry scone and dipping it into the dish of clotted cream, taking an appreciative bite. "I have missed Mrs. Behmoth's cooking."

"That is your own fault. She brought baskets of it to the hospital every day, determined to get you to eat."

"No doubt it was the smell of it that finally brought me around."

"You must tell her that. She'll like it. But what of the man. You laughed when I said he was wealthy."

"Because it is far more likely that while he is a man who wishes himself to be viewed as wealthy, he is overleveraged and exists somewhere near the borderline of collapse."

"What?! You're inventing that. You cannot have any reason to state such a thing."

"Mr. Pendragon . . ." Miss Bromley called from the hallway. "It's time to change your bandage and then I will be off until tomorrow."

Colin's face soured. "Must we?"

It was evident she was not used to being asked such a thing. "Of course," she said after realizing that he had uttered the question in sincerity. "The doctor has given very precise orders. And I will need to show Mrs. Behmoth how to minister to you in my absence."

"You will show Mr. Pruitt," he informed her. "He has had training in health before. He will do the better job."

"Have you now?"

I gave a nod and hoped she could not see my discomfort. Lying was not my strongest trait.

She walked me through the onerous steps of tending to the wound beneath his left arm while Colin fidgeted like the impatient patient he was. Nevertheless, I was pleased to see that he was healing nicely. All signs of infection and redness had eased to the point that my heart fairly soared at the sight.

Only after I had performed my duties as proscribed and could rattle off the medicines and their timings for ingestion did Miss Bromley finally deign to leave us. Several of the tinctures were intended to aid in the relief of whatever infection remained in his body, and two other distillates were to ease his pain. I paid little heed to these last two, as I knew he would never agree to take them. Anything that altered his mind, his ability to think and reason, would no longer be tolerated.

After Miss Bromley had finally taken her leave and Mrs. Behmoth had brought up a fresh batch of tea, I returned Colin to our previous conversation. "How," I asked him again, "can you possibly state that Quentin Everclear's killer is more likely teetering on collapse than wealth?!"

He gave me that thin, roguish smile of his. "You must think back to Wynn Tessler during the Connicle case. A wealthy man with access to vast sums of money. He is *precisely* the sort of man who would be wearing a pair of Ricci Marino shoes. Perhaps he will wear them to the scaffolding," he added with a sneer.

"But when he resolved to remove the people in his and Char- lotte Hutton's way, he did not do so by his own hand, nor was any of it done without careful planning. Yet this man you wit- nessed, whose attire would seem to suggest a person of consider- able wealth and station in life, not only committed cold-blooded murder by his own hands but appears to have done so with little forethought. Sloppy," he said with a grunt. "And that is before we consider the fact that he is in business with addicts and sots. I would say that a man of true breeding would never deign to consort with such types himself. He would have someone act on his behalf. Someone he could trust. Someone who would keep his name above the fray at all times. Someone he would pay very well indeed."

"So you believe him to be a man who aspires to such a station, then, but has yet to reach it?"

"Given whatever nefarious line of business the man is caught up in, I would say he is likely *never* to reach it. What was it you heard him say?"

"'There are women to be found. . . .' Whatever that means."

"It means something. And we shall need to figure out exactly what that is. Does Inspector Evans have his men checking the shops that carry Ricci Marino shoes? There cannot be that many of them in this city."

"He is. I've not yet heard whether they have had any luck, but the cobbler we saw gave us a list of four such shops. Which does not include the possibility that he may have bought them in Italy or elsewhere."

"Do you fancy the killer a traveler, then? Someone who might go from one city to the next while running his questionable business in Whitechapel?" He chuckled, and I knew that dem- onstrated what he thought of that notion.

"I have been taught never to presume anything while in the initial stages of an investigation," I said, archly throwing his own words back at him.

He winced, and for the first time in too long it was not from the pain of his wound but rather from the blow to his ego. "Nicely done." He smirked. "Still, we may be able deduce a few bits of information based on what we do know to be true. But tell me, is the inspector having the people in Quentin Everclear's building interviewed? Is he looking into the clubs and taverns that young Mr. Everclear frequented? It would certainly be most helpful to find someone who knows what he was up to."

"I cannot speak to the clubs and taverns, but I know the inspector was having everyone in the building questioned."

"That's probably the best he'll be able to do anyway." He leaned forward and set his tea down, heaving a contented sigh. "You and I will undoubtedly need to scrounge through the clubs ourselves."

"What . . . ?!"

"You have already proven yourself untrustworthy on your own," he said with the smoothest of tones, his eyes settling on me and locking there. "What was it like after so many years?"

He asked the question so calmly, with such a dearth of inflection, that for a second I thought I had misunderstood what he was inquiring about. But as he continued to stare at me, his gaze unwavering and solemn, my heart dropped, leaving a feeling of deceit and shame in its wake. "How . . . ?"

"You mentioned that Quentin Everclear's killer smelled the opium as soon as he entered the young man's room. That the use of it was the thing that cost him his life. Not following the rules . . . or some such nonsense. So I can only assume that you encouraged Mr. Everclear to confide in you by pretending you were someone very much like him. It is what I would have done. And how better to accomplish that than to partake in his vice? Indeed, you would almost assuredly have failed with him had you not presented yourself as someone he could trust."

My stomach roiled and my heart felt as if it were going to pound right out of my chest if it didn't deafen my ears first. I did not want to lie, but nor did I care to admit the truth. "You were in the hospital and the doctors kept saying we should prepare ourselves for the worst. When Quentin Everclear handed me that pipe . . ."

"Ethan . . ."

I could not look into the deep of his eyes another moment

as I shifted my gaze away, my shame pressing in upon me like a weight. "I *was* trying to get him to confide in me . . . and I tried not to inhale more than was necessary to get him to trust me."

"I'm so sorry," he said.

My eyes bolted back to his face, and I saw the indelible regret there. "You have nothing to be sorry for, and you mustn't worry that I'll need another spell in Needham Hills." I cracked a smile and was pleased to see that he did as well. "I would do it again to solve the case, but I will never fall back into that kind of life. You mustn't ever worry about that. No matter what the future may bring."

"I know. But I shall be careful not to leave you to tackle these cases on your own, just the same. I think us stronger together than apart." He stood up and moved to the landing. "*Mrs. Behmoth!*" he hollered down. "*When is dinner? I'm hungry!*"

"*Are ya really gonna start that shite already?!*" she hollered back. "*It'll be ready when I say so.*"

"Tomorrow night." He turned to me with a wink. "I will rest during the day, but tomorrow night we shall set our sights on Quentin Everclear's killer."

"Tomorrow night . . . ?" I started to protest.

"Don't," he warned. "I have a nurse, I have Mrs. Behmoth, I have my father, I even have a contingent of physicians at that bloody awful hospital. I do not also need you treating me like a fragile bit of crystal on the shelf."

I laughed as I heard the heavy footfalls of Mrs. Behmoth starting up the stairs.

"Ah . . . !" Colin said. "It appears our dinner is on its way."

He scurried down the steps to help, but almost at once I heard Mrs. Behmoth scold, "*I got it. Get yer arse up there and stop it.*"

Tomorrow night, I told myself, Colin and I would be back at last.

CHAPTER 26

———◆———

While strides were being made by the inspector's men with respect to the Quentin Everclear murder, little had yet come of the investigation into the killings of the women along Framingham Street. Even so, I was eager to get back to our flat to catch Colin up on what I had learned at the Yard that morning. I had also promised Sir Atherton I would be ready at eleven to go out and speak with Victoria's grand-nephew, a duty that already had me on edge. I could not conceive how I was going to question the young man without letting him know that his grand-aunt, the sovereign of the empire, considered him a suspect for murder.

"Yer Miss Bromley needs 'er final pay," Mrs. Behmoth announced the moment I stepped inside our flat, before I'd even hung my coat on the coatrack by the door.

"What are you talking about?" I followed her up the stairs while she delivered a fresh pot of tea to Colin, who was sitting quite contentedly by the fireplace.

"'E let 'er go." She gestured to Colin with her chin as she refilled his cup and then hers before glancing back at me. "Tea?"

"If it wouldn't be too much trouble," I rather barked back. "What is she talking about, Colin?"

He sipped at his tea and tossed me a look filled with the innocence of infancy. "We really don't need her. Mrs. Behmoth is already fretting over me like a maternal coverlet, and you can attend to my bandages and wound. It's all very personal anyway, don't you think? Removing my shirt and having her prod at my bare flesh. It's unseemly. Better that you should do it." He took another sip of tea and turned back to the crackling fire.

"She is tending to a nearly fatal bullet wound, not giving a lover's caress," I protested. "This isn't what we agreed upon."

Mrs. Behmoth grunted as she settled onto the settee and handed a cup of tea across to me. "I told ya 'e weren't gonna like it."

"Stop worrying," Colin persisted, still staring at the fire. "I feel better today and will do so every day moving forward. All I need is you and Mrs. Behmoth to continue looking after me."

"'At's right," she agreed. "And I been doin' it nearly forty years now."

Colin pushed himself up and walked over to the windows, peeking down onto the street. "My father is here."

I glanced up at the clock and found that it was ten minutes before eleven. While Colin was forever running late, his father had the habit of always being early. I presumed it to be a function of his lifetime of diplomacy, where tardiness was considered rude, yet I often found this reverse habit equally bothersome.

"We shall see what your father thinks about this," I said, certain Sir Atherton would agree with me.

"Very well." He heaved a sigh that I recognized was a signal that his mind would not be changed.

I hurried downstairs and let Sir Atherton in, rapidly explaining the turn of events as we climbed back upstairs. To my surprise, by the time the two of us had arrived on the landing Colin was standing there with his coat on and a hat in hand.

"Where are you going?" I asked.

"I've been cooped up in this flat long enough. I'm going with the two of you, and I shan't hear a word about it." And true to his declaration he swept down the steps past us. "I will sit quietly by while the two of you ask all the questions. You just might find my presence valuable by the time you're done. A third opinion and all that rot." He stopped at the bottom of the stairs and looked back at us.

"Colin . . ." I spoke in a tone I hoped he would recognize for its seriousness. "You have barely been home twenty-four hours. I hardly think you can refer to that as cooped up. This is precisely the sort of behavior that landed you in the hospital in the first place."

"It was not my behavior that made me ill, it was an infection," he retorted crisply. "My bandages are now freshly changed and my medicines swallowed. I'll not be treated like a bird in a gilded cage. Let us be off. You know how royalty despises being kept waiting." He turned on his heels and went out the front door, leaving it gaping in his wake.

"You know," Sir Atherton spoke up after a moment, "he gets that stubbornness from his mother, not me."

"Ya want me ta drag 'is arse outta that carriage?" Mrs. Behmoth asked as she came up behind us and stared down into the empty foyer below.

I turned to look at her, hands on her hips and a scowl creasing her broad forehead, and most of the fight drained out of me. "I don't doubt that you could," I said with a shake of my head and a dry chuckle, "but he will be incorrigible ever after. Better that we should watch him carefully and choose our fights."

Sir Atherton chuckled beside me and started down the stairs. "You would have made a fine diplomat, Ethan. I have always said that."

A minute later the three of us were under way with nary another word spoken on the state of Colin's health. I told myself that the two of us would revisit it once we were alone, but as much as I tried, I could not convince myself that it would have any impact.

"What did you learn from the Yard this morning?" Colin asked once we had merged into traffic and begun our journey to the outskirts of the city. "Have they made any progress in gathering information on either of our cases?"

"They have made some, though their efforts are not proving to be fruitful enough as far as I am concerned. Nevertheless, they have narrowed the shops that carry Ricci Marino shoes for men to just three. We are hopeful that will make the effort to identify Quentin Everclear's killer the slightest bit easier. Inspector Evans is having the sales records of all three shops pulled for the last nine months. He has asked specifically for the names and addresses of anyone who bought the style of boot that I saw—Conoscitore."

"Pardon . . . ?"

"It's Italian," Sir Atherton spoke up. "It means connoisseur."

"Don't tell me you have a pair." Colin looked aghast.

His father pursed his face and shook his head. "I would never spend that kind of money to put something on my feet. Now, a good hat . . . that's another thing altogether."

I could not help laughing, knowing Colin would never spend any such amount to clothe himself. "The inspector hopes to have the records back tomorrow and has already promised us an immediate review."

"Very good. And what of the other tenants in the young man's building? Have they all been interviewed? Has anyone admitted to knowing anything?"

"They have not completed that duty yet, as many of Mr. Everclear's fellow residents do not seem keen to converse with men from the Yard. They have managed to corner those people who live closest to his flat, but none of them has admitted to knowing anything."

"I find that highly unlikely. Those people's safety depends on knowing what is going on in their immediate surroundings at all times. Someone else in that lodging could very well be caught up in the same business that Mr. Everclear was. His killer would certainly not want to slog all around the East End to check in with his recruits. And it would also explain the indifference with which young Mr. Everclear's life was taken. One is less apt to be concerned about a single horse when there are a dozen more in the stable."

"What an appalling thing to say," his father protested.

"It's just an expression."

"Just the same, it's callous."

Colin shifted his eyes back to me. "See if you can get the transcripts from the people they've spoken with so far. Perhaps we'll have to make a visit ourselves and see if we can be more persuasive."

"May I remind you that you are still recuperating from a catastrophic illness. You cannot be involved in everything. I'll not allow it, and neither will your father."

"Nor will Mrs. Behmoth," Sir Atherton needled.

Colin scowled. "You two aren't the least bit amusing."

"I do have a bit of information about the Framingham murders that you are going to find interesting. They have found another witness, though he is considered unreliable given that he was returning from the pubs at the same time Miss Materly was attacked and dragged off the street. The Yard has already taken a statement from him, which I just happen to have on my person as this very moment."

Colin's face lit up. "You scoundrel. Let me see it, then."

"Just a moment," Sir Atherton cut in. "We are almost at Mentenberg House where Piper lives. I think you had best allow me to give you some details on the young man before you meet with him."

"Piper?!" I echoed. "Whatever sort of name is that?"

"It is a nickname as a result of the pitch of his voice. His given name is Gerhard, although you would be wise to address him as *sir*. He is not officially titled but is referred to as *The Honorable* in introduction and reference, just as so many of Victoria's more distant relations are. He graduated from Eton, so he is educated in spite of his general lack of enthusiasm for most anything, which I am sure you will notice. I have met the lad only a time or two myself. He made little impact on me beyond a noted apathy. Hardly the sort of impact most people are aspiring to, especially when they are just beginning to seek their place in the world."

"You called him a lad," Colin remarked. "How young is he?"

"Twenty-two or three. I don't really recollect which."

"And just why is it that Victoria imagines him capable of murder?" I asked.

"He suffers from a restlessness that has not served him well.

He was censured three times while at Eton—once for entertaining prostitutes in his rooms and twice for opium use on school property. Had his grand-aunt not been our sovereign I am certain he would have been removed after the first infraction, but he has been well protected, perhaps not for his own betterment."

"There must be more," Colin guessed as we pulled onto a short macadam drive that led to a manor home in the Federalist style, complete with a colonnade across the front of its two-story structure. The façade was constructed of huge rectangular blocks the color of limestone, and yet the place was not so big as to rival the homes of our empress or her immediate family.

Sir Atherton gave a sigh as we drew closer to the portico. "He spent some time in an asylum in Scotland while still in his teens and again just before he completed his studies at Eton. He is purported to suffer the affliction of hysterics. When he was in his middle teens he tried to harm himself, which necessitated his first incarceration. A couple of years ago it was a perceived slight by one of his father's footmen that sent him into a fit. He cost that gentleman the use of his legs and one of his eyes."

"Has he ever been known to antagonize women?" Colin asked with the blitheness of a rudimentary conversation.

"I could not say and would recommend that you not ask. You must step carefully around this young man. His mind is not right, and it would seem he believes the circumstances of his birth allow him to behave as he chooses." The carriage rounded the top of the drive and pulled to a stop beneath the large, outstretched arms of the portico. "I will visit with Gerhard's father while the two of you question his son. Neither of them have any notion why we are here other than the fact that Victoria has requested it, so I will be spinning a yarn to the patriarch and ask that neither of you undo anything by speaking to his father out of turn."

A footman was waiting for us, stepping forward at once to open the carriage door the moment we stopped. "Gentlemen," he said. "Welcome to Mentenberg House. If you would please follow me."

We were ushered inside and dispatched to a formal drawing room, where two men were already seated, sipping tea. I pegged them for Gerhard and his father. The older man was tall and lithe with dark, almost black hair, an aquiline nose and a sharp chin. I thought him somewhere in his middle years but could not have guessed more accurately given the heavy lines crisscrossing his face. He looked like a man bearing a cumbersome burden, which I suspected was his son.

Gerhard was also tall, but his middle was soft and his hair not nearly as dark. His face was unblemished, looking free of the encumbrances his father appeared to be enduring. He displayed little reaction to the sight of us and even after the introductions had been undertaken seemed notably indifferent to our presence, leaving me to wonder why he thought his grand-aunt had requested the meeting.

Gerhard reseated himself before his father and Sir Atherton had made their way out of the study, which I found curious and inappropriate. However, it wasn't until the two of them had exited and the parlor door pulled closed by a footman that the Honorable Gerhard even paid us any real heed.

"I must admit," he said, his voice indeed set notably higher and softer than was expected for a man of his height and proportions, "that I had heard you were dead, Mr. Pendragon."

Colin gave a fleeting smile that still managed to contain a glimmer of amusement. "I should think a man of your station would know better than to believe everything you read. No doubt you have suffered under the mischievous pens of the newspapermen as well."

Gerhard snorted a laugh before leaning forward and pouring himself more tea. Only after his cup had been prepared with careful precision—three measured teaspoons of sugar and six level teaspoons of milk—did he settle himself back again and return his gaze to us. "Help yourselves," he invited with the barest hint of annoyance. "I am not here to serve you."

I moved forward before Colin could, intent on saving him the strain to his left arm. He would never permit this young man to see that he continued to suffer, and I would make sure that was so.

"You found my words amusing?" Colin pressed ahead as I handed him a cup made with far less meticulousness.

"The papers do not pester me, Mr. Pendragon. I am nobility, not their fodder. As I am sure you are aware my grand-auntie would never permit such a thing." He chuckled into his teacup. "No," he said after a moment. "I am afraid the real offenses cast against me are bandied about right there on the streets."

"And whatever might those be?"

The young man's face hardened, losing any suggestion of amusement. "You mustn't seek to be cunning, Mr. Pendragon. I know you have been bidden here. Do not dare to propose that you are merely out to pay a visit to the landed gentry. I will not abide such folly."

"What did your father tell you was the reason for our visit?" I spoke up, meaning to wrestle the burden of the conversation from Colin's shoulders.

Gerhard tossed me a disapproving scowl. "You really mustn't speak out of turn, Mr. Pruitt. It is most improper."

"Mr. Pruitt's words are spoken with the same surety as if they had come from my own mouth," Colin scolded.

"What a vulgar sentiment."

"Perhaps our time together would be better utilized if we attend to more germane topics," I suggested, aware that a hint of aggravation had edged into my voice.

"Germane, is it? And what exactly would be germane to your visit here, then?"

"Your whereabouts," Colin stated with a bluntness that startled me. "Have you had any business in the East End of late?"

"The East End?!" he repeated sourly. "One does not conduct business in the East End. One whores, drinks, and dopes there. Hardly the stuff of business." His eyes narrowed as he glared at Colin. "You surely do not mean to suggest that you are a virgin to such pursuits?"

"Do I seem like one?"

The young man grunted a laugh as he turned to me. "And what of you, Mr. Pruitt? What sort of a man are you?"

"What does it matter what sort of man I am? We are not here to discern any of that."

"It matters to me," he shot back. "It matters very much."

"Very well, then. I lived in the East End for a great part of my teenage years through the early part of my twenties. I understand intimately the businesses that go on there."

"Then I shall speak only with you, Mr. Pruitt," he said in a voice suddenly filled with an unnatural burst of enthusiasm. "You are the only one who can possibly understand the siren's song of that enigmatic place. Luring and repelling in a single breath. Promising to fulfill every man's fancy for the flip of a coin. And now . . ." He leaned forward and, for the first time since we had joined him, set his teacup down. "And now our Ripper has come back to reclaim what is his. I am awed." He sagged back and stared up at the ornate ceiling towering over our heads as though the revelation had left him bereft of all vitality.

"You make it sound as though you admire him," Colin said, but he received no response. He slid his eyes toward me and gave the slightest nod of his head, and it took a moment before I realized what he was asking me to do.

"You make it sound as though you admire him," I repeated.

Gerhard heaved a sigh even as his gaze remained fixed on the ceiling. "He is a master. He is Lord Byron, Plato, and Dante. He is a god and a great horned beast. He creates and he destroys as he wills it, and then he dissipates like the fog until he is ready once more. And all the while he is laughing. Laughing, Mr. Pruitt. At you and your preposterous laws. At your cadre of men who think they can catch him." He finally lifted his head from the back of his chair and fixed his gaze on me. "I do not admire him, I revere him."

"You have my fullest attention now," Colin said. "Because it appears that someone is seeking to emulate him, and I now find myself wondering if you dare harbor such a craving."

This was apparently enough to get Gerhard to snap his head toward Colin again; his gaze studied as his eyes raked across Colin's face. "What a disarmingly common man you are. I must admit I expected much more." He turned back to me, and his face immediately softened. "Tell me, Mr. Pruitt, does the inestimable reputation actually belong to you? Are you hiding your repute behind the façade of this incorrigible?"

"Have a care, my good man," Colin spoke again, his voice tight and low. "I will not be so easily dismissed."

"Gentlemen," I cut in, "I fear we are losing our focus again." I captured Gerhard's attention and held his gaze, but I could not decipher what was rumbling about behind his eyes. "Now, I am certain you can understand our concern when you assert such feelings for a brutal killer."

"Understand your concern?" he repeated, making the statement sound preposterous. "Do you profess such concerns when someone states their admiration for Michelangelo or Mozart? Were they not both masters at their crafts in spite of Michelangelo's unnatural proclivities with his own kind and Mozart's appallingly libertine existence?! Yet they are revered for what they accomplished. Titans in their fields. Their successes beyond the scope of most every other man." He cracked a thin, icy smile. "Can we not say the same of our Ripper? Has he not achieved the very summit of his province? Why then must we disavow his extraordinary feats?" He shook his head. "I am afraid we are a pitifully hypocritical species desperate to deny the darkest part of our souls. And yet it remains forever just beneath the surface of every one of us."

I'm not sure when it happened, but at some point during his diatribe I began to hold my breath, though I was not aware that I was doing so until after he had quieted again. I watched as he leaned forward and carefully refilled his teacup, once again adding the sugar and cream with great care and exactitude. After he had settled back, his face as benign and calm as if we had been discussing the pull of the tides, I finally had the inclination to slide my gaze to Colin. I found him staring at me, his eyes heated and full of fervor, willing me to say something. Yet what that might be I had no idea.

"Do you dabble in sculpting?" I blurted after another silent moment. "Or perhaps you have wished to try your hand at writing music?" It was the best I could think to say without blasting this nobleman between his eyes.

He looked back at me from over the rim of his cup, which he appeared to be studying with some interest, before one side of his mouth ticked upward. "No more so than any other man, I suppose."

His coyness curdled my good will. "Have you ever tried either one?" I pressed.

"I have tried a great many things, Mr. Pruitt. As a man who has lived in Whitechapel, I am sure you can appreciate that."

"And when was the last time you were there? If we were to question your valet, your footman, what would they tell us?"

Gerhard's diminutive smile evaporated. "I am tired of this game." He dropped his teacup onto the table and stood up. "I shall tell my father that your visit has concluded." He strode over to the door, turning back just before pulling it open. "You can tell my grand-aunt that she can rot in hell." He yanked the doors wide and disappeared through the foyer before Colin or I could respond.

"What an alarming man," Colin muttered.

"There is little surprise that Victoria wonders after him. But what are we supposed to do? She has sworn us to silence. We cannot very well get the Yard involved."

Colin blanched. "The Yard?! Why ever would we want to involve the Yard? You haven't gone soft while I was on holiday, have you?"

I laughed. "On holiday, was it?"

He waved me off as he stood up and began pacing across the broad parlor. "We shall be far better served employing our urchin brigade and won't owe them the least explanation. And the boys will also be less conspicuous should the Honorable Gerhard decide to make a foray into the East End."

"Do you suppose that likely given our line of questioning?"

"With that man, I would not discount any possibility."

"I do worry about Paul. He seems oddly detached about the loss of his mother to this murderer."

Colin tossed me a curious look as he headed toward the study door. "She was a mother who gave him up before he could even lift his own head." He peeked out into the foyer, no doubt looking for his father to return. "Doing some work, earning some money, it'll do the lad good. He will thank us for it."

"He will thank us for it because he is mercenary."

"And what better reason is there?" He turned back to me. "There is one thing I will ask you to try to accomplish this afternoon while I rest a bit." He flashed a contrite smile. "Will you see if Gerhard has had any medical training of any kind? If he is the one carving up these women, then he has to have learned that skill somewhere. We are most certainly not dealing with a novice."

"Consider it done." My relief at hearing that he intended to relax before we headed out to the East End tonight in search of information on Quentin Everclear's activities was palpable.

"Let us be off, then. My father's coming, so do try not to look so troubled. He'll not want to hear that we have suspicions about this fine young royal." He arched an eyebrow and snickered before stepping out into the foyer.

CHAPTER 27

Having worked closely with Inspector Evans over the past week made it harder to conceal what Colin and I were up to when I went to see the inspector that afternoon at the Yard. Yet, when the sovereign herself extracts an oath of silence, one's conscience tends to become malleable.

True to his word, Colin had retreated to our bedroom once we arrived home, but not before I was trundled off to the Yard with a specific list of tasks to accomplish. Chief amongst them was to concoct a story to tell the inspector as to why I wished to see any records the Yard might have regarding Victoria's grandnephew, the Honorable Gerhard. I settled on giving the least amount of information possible, all of it based around the truth. And because Maurice Evans is a good and astute man, he did not press me for details when I told him that Colin and I were doing a favor for Sir Atherton by collecting some information on the monarch's young relation. He let the gossamer story lie there unprodded, sending a constable downstairs to fetch it from the Yard's records library.

"How is Mr. Pendragon feeling today?" he asked while we waited for his aide to return. "Still raging at his bonds?"

I had to chuckle. "You have indeed come to know him very well."

"One must appreciate his passion for the game."

"A game, is it?" I nodded at his description of the horrors we dealt with in such cavalier terms. "I doubt the victims would define it as such, although I suspect the hunters would."

"My wife has two cats. I am certain they would call it a game if they could talk." He gave a quick snort. "We have had a chance to question the other witness we found to the Materly murder."

"Outstanding . . ." I started to say as I pushed myself upright.

The inspector waved me back to ease with a single nod of his head. "Before you get too enthusiastic, as I told you earlier, the man is known to frequent the pubs down there, and his words seem to be about as fluid as that which he pours down his throat."

"Meaning . . . ?"

"His story is vague and does not particularly match that of either Miss Unter or Mr. Alford."

"May I have a look at his statement?"

He pulled a folder out from under a small, neat pile on one corner of his desk and tossed it over toward me. "I was going to bring this by on my way home tonight. I knew you and Mr. Pendragon would want to have a look even if the man's words must be considered dubious."

I picked up the folder and flipped it open, and a picture of the man's face slid out onto my lap. He looked elderly though his hair was still dark, and I suspected a life on the streets had contributed to his premature aging. That and a predilection to ale.

When I turned back to the file I found a brief description of Milton Wilkinson that placed his age at forty-one. I looked at his picture again and decided he could pass for twenty years older.

"Why do you have a picture and description of this man? Is this some sort of new Yard procedure for witnesses?"

Inspector Evans laughed. "We would never have a witness if we required such things. No. You are holding the totality of the man's file. If you choose to thumb through there you will find numerous reports detailing the many times we have picked him up for drunkenness, vagrancy, or both. He nearly froze to death a couple of winters ago, earning him a convalescence in a work house for a while, but he wouldn't stay. His type never do. They simply won't be confined. They are courting death, if you ask me. And eventually it comes for them."

"Eventually it comes for us all," I pointed out as I pawed through the papers until I came to a single page with the day's date at the top. It was filled with a neat, graceful handwriting, tight and small, that covered most of the page. The story it told, however, was indeed thin and vague.

At some point in the early morning hours of Tuesday past, Mr. Wilkinson had found himself evicted from a pub just off of Framingham Street. Bleary-eyed and wholly pickled, he had wandered down Framingham itself, heading for a bake shop that he knew could be counted on to have warm, yeasty air seeping through the gaps along the bottom of the door long before dawn so he could get some sleep. It was while seeking this goal that he spied a ghoul cloaked in black hovering behind a pretty young woman standing at the corner of a building across the street.

While he watched, the phantom seized the woman from behind and pulled her back into the shadows, the two of them descending toward Hades on devil's wings. I looked up at Inspector Evans. "The man has a vivid imagination."

"I think it more of a rupture from lucidity."

I nodded grimly before returning back to the paper. Mr. Wilkinson could not state how long the specter remained out of his view, because he believed it had enchanted him, freezing time itself, but at some point he saw it rise up again, accompanied by the distinct smell of sulfur. *Somethin' foul,* he insisted, *it'd done somethin' foul.*

This second time, however, it was different. He claimed that the beast had changed its form when it disappeared below. There was a lad's cap on its demonic head, and it wore a leather butcher's apron spotted with the gore of its foul lair. As he watched, Mr. Wilkinson insisted, the thing turned back into a black-cloaked sprite; its arms, body, and head morphing into the color of night, only its great, barbed wings spreading out from the back of its body to glisten in the lamplight.

Mr. Wilkinson had become distracted by a man exiting the building next door, most assuredly Mr. Alford, and was fearful that he too would be attacked by the fiend, but by the time he turned back the beast was gone.

"Did you notice there's an extra copy in there?" the inspector said, pointing to the folder on my lap. "I thought the two of you might be better able to pluck out the facts, so I had the girl make an extra copy for you."

"Facts?" I shook my head. "You are more generous than I." Nevertheless, I grabbed the second copy, folded it, and stuffed it into my jacket pocket. As far as I could tell, the only information that held the slimmest nod to fact was his assertion of having seen a butcher's apron. That made sense. It had been stated of the Ripper and been borne out in a sense, though it had proven to be a barber's apron rather than a butcher's.

"Sir?" The young constable the inspector had sent downstairs poked his head back into the office. "I have the file you requested."

"Very good." Inspector Evans stood and took the file, handing it directly across to me. "You will excuse me a minute, as I have something to attend to," he said before ducking out into the anteroom.

Whether he did or not, I was glad to have some time with Gerhard's file to myself. I did not wish him to see what I was looking at, nor what notes I wrote. He was not a foolish man and would readily decipher what I was up to.

The Honorable Gerhard's file was brief and to the point. The young man had been arrested exactly once—for stabbing a classmate while at university. There had been some sort of altercation resulting in the other boy being stabbed once in the abdomen by Gerhard, but the wound had not proven fatal, and shortly after being released from hospital the other boy had dropped all charges. No doubt the young victim had been enticed to do so, as no one sued the royal family no matter how distant the relation.

What caught my eye was that at the time, Gerhard had been attending the Royal College of Surgeons. His studies, however, had come to an abrupt conclusion with the incident. Gerhard had been remanded to an asylum while his victim recovered, spending two months recuperating himself, according to the brief note at the end of the file, before being returned to the care of his father. No wonder Victoria was concerned.

"Anything of interest?" Inspector Evans chirped as he came back into the office.

"Not much here," I answered as I slid the folder shut without taking a single note. "It would seem he has only passed through your portals once."

"Which is more than most of the Saxe-Coburgs."

"He would actually be a Leiningen," I corrected. "Perhaps they're not as well behaved?"

He gave me a lopsided grin and, to my relief, let the subject drop. "I do have something else that you and Mr. Pendragon will be interested in." He moved back over to his desk and extracted a piece of paper from one of the drawers. "This is a list of the clientele who have purchased a pair of those Ricci Marino boots in the last six months. What were they called?"

"Conoscitore," I answered at once. "Connoisseur."

"If you say so." He handed the list over. "I think you and Mr. Pendragon will recognize many of the names. I know I did."

"Hmmm . . ." I chuckled as I glanced down it. "It would seem the bulk of our parliamentarians have meticulously dressed feet." Beyond them there were also royals, magistrates, and business scions, but there were indeed more than a few I did not know. "May I?" I asked, extracting a pencil from my jacket pocket.

"Please." He gave a wave of a hand as he sat down next to me.

"Colin was very specific about the type of man we are looking for," I muttered as I began checking off the men I was familiar with. I described the conclusions Colin had drawn as well as his reasoning, so that by the time we had reached the end of the list we were down to just under two dozen names.

"That looks better, though we've still got a fair number there," the inspector noted.

"We do." I pulled out a fresh sheet of paper and wrote down the names—twenty-one in all. "Let me see if Colin recognizes any of these men. And you might get your constables started—"

"Checking into the businesses and backgrounds of these men," the inspector interrupted me, pushing himself out of the chair and returning to the seat behind his desk. "You needn't feel compelled to tell me how best to perform my job in the temporary absence of your Mr. Pendragon."

I felt myself flush slightly. "You must forgive me. I suppose I am nothing if not well trained by him."

Inspector Evans gave a good-natured laugh. "As I suspect we all are," he said. "If we are looking for a man living beyond his means, then I think he will not be at all difficult to find." He glanced down the list of unchecked names as I handed it back to him. "Indeed, I rather fear we will end up with more of these names than will easily be dispatched."

I stood up and tucked my copy of the list into the breast pocket of my coat. "If Colin can vouch for any these men, we will certainly let you know right away. And should any of his deductions change that might require expanding the search . . ." I let the sentiment hang there, since I knew neither of us wished to consider such a thing.

"Mr. Pruitt," the inspector spoke up as I reached the door. "I will have a full contingency of men spread around the East End tonight, just as we have done for the last week and a half. Many will be in uniform, but some will not. While you and Mr. Pendragon are scouring through taverns in search of information about Quentin Everclear's recent business activities, it occurs to me that you will need to be aware of the men I have undercover, just as they will need to be aware of you. Might we use some phrase to help you discern one another?"

"An excellent thought. Why don't we keep it simple. How about, *Have you seen my bicycle?*"

The inspector chuckled. "Seems innocuous enough. And the answer will be, *I don't ride.*"

"Very good, then," I answered, turning to leave.

"And Mr. Pruitt," he called once more. "Should you and Mr.

Pendragon learn anything during your endeavors, I will expect to be fully apprised in the morning."

I gave him a somber nod, unable to blame him for having felt compelled to make the statement. "You may count on it, Inspector. And likewise for you and your men," I added, ducking out into the hallway before he could catch my smile.

CHAPTER 28

The evening was not progressing at all as I had hoped it would. Colin and I had already foraged our way through four pubs and two taverns, dressed in ill-fitting, dirty trousers; coarse dock-worker's shirts that itched my skin endlessly; and threadbare coats that provided little in the way of protection from the elements. Yet neither of us had found anyone who admitted to having known Quentin Everclear. Three times I had been told to bugger off when I'd recited the agreed-upon code, *Have you seen my bicycle?* It didn't seem to say much for the charitability of the men and women who lived in this quarter of the city. And Colin was faring just as poorly.

"Blasted, bloody, buggery night," an elderly man mumbled as he slid onto the stool next to mine. "Almost ain't worth comin' out fer a pint. Almost," he grumbled pointedly.

I glanced over at the man, giving him a look I hoped would appear somewhere between disinterested and slightly besotted. He was wearing a large, oversized black coat with a rumpled collar pulled up at the back that accentuated a great scruff of grayish-white hair sticking out in myriad directions. He had a disheveled beard and mustache covering half his face that revealed little more than light crinkly eyes and cheeks that looked round enough to assure me he did not lack for food. Other than that, the only thing I could be fairly certain of was that he did not work for the Yard. "'At's right," I answered before turning back to the ale I'd been nursing since coming into this place.

I was feeling restless and, more than anything, was hoping Colin would finish at the other end of the bar so we could discuss going home. It was already nearing midnight, and I didn't want him up for half the night on his first evening out. His health was far more important than anything we might learn about Quentin Everclear on any given night. Even though I knew he would argue with me about conceding with nothing to show for it, I was not about to be dissuaded.

"'Ave ya seen me bicycle?" the elderly man spoke up again.

I spun on him far quicker than an inebriated man should ever be able to do. "I don't ride," I answered in a tone more questioning than stated.

"I thought that was you, Mr. Pruitt," the man chuckled as he leaned toward me. "Just wanted to be sure."

"Do I know you?"

"I've seen you at Scotland Yard a few times. Sergeant Rutherford." He gave me a nod but had the prudence not to stick out his hand. "I work for Inspector Evans. I sit in the room just outside his office, when I'm there at all. They like to keep me on the streets. I fit in nicely, don'tcha think?" He gave me a great grin, and I noticed he had a few missing teeth, which only added to his authenticity.

"You had me convinced," I had to admit. "My apologies for not recognizing you."

He shook his head, still grinning. "You're not supposed to recognize me," he explained. "My own wife doesn't recognize me when I come in off the streets." He chuckled, well pleased with himself. "But that's not why I've been looking for you and Mr. Pendragon tonight."

"Looking for us?!"

"We finally managed to extract some information from one of Mr. Everclear's neighbors late this afternoon. He told us Mr. Everclear was known to spend a good deal of time and money at one of the opium clubs just off Scarborough near Saint Mark Street. It's a dark red door, the color of clay, with the silhouette of a woman painted on it in black. Very exotic." He chuckled again. "Like that lot is interested in anything besides what they can drag into their lungs. Anyway, Inspector Evans wanted me to find you and let you know."

"I cannot thank you enough for your persistence."

He shrugged and stood up. "It's what they pay me for." He gave me a wink and disappeared into the crowd with the ease of someone who has spent the better part of his life doing so.

"You seem pleased."

Colin's voice drifted over me from behind. I turned to find him standing there slouching, a large stout in one hand and an eyebrow arched skyward. "Tell me you've learned something of value and allow me to share in your reverie."

"Reverie might be a bit high-handed," I cautioned, "but Inspector Evans sent that man to let us know of a place where Quentin Everclear was known to have spent considerable time. They received the information just this afternoon from one of his neighbors."

Colin's eyes lit up and his posture stiffened as though he had just been jolted by a spark. "Outstanding. Then this night might yet prove worthwhile. Where is it?"

"An opium club at Scarborough and Saint Mark's. We're about ten minutes away." I hesitated when I saw his eyes darken. "Unless you don't feel up to it," I quickly added. "Perhaps we'd best go home for the night and start fresh tomorrow. A single night isn't going to upend this investigation and you've . . ."

Colin's eyes narrowed almost imperceptibly. "Don't you start in on me," he warned. "I was actually thinking I might just head there by myself. Why don't *you* go home and I'll meet you there shortly."

I felt my forehead caving down onto the bridge of my nose before he had even finished speaking. "Why ever would I do that?" I shot back, not bothering to evict the displeasure from my tone, since I already knew what his answer would be.

"An opium den is not a good place for you to be. You have

already admitted to smoking some with Quentin Everclear the other—"

"I did it only to earn his trust," I reminded brusquely. "Besides, if you could see into my lungs right now, you wouldn't find so much as a trace of it. I told you, I blew out far more than I ingested."

Colin's mouth ticked at one corner, though his expression did not change in the least. "Well then, we shall simply have to take your word for it, as I am not about to excise your lungs for a look."

"You needn't worry about me. I'm stronger than you suspect."

Colin allowed something of a smile to fleet across his lips. "I believe I know that better than you do," he said before stepping around me and heading for the door.

I followed him out of the pub and onto the street, turning east toward Scarborough. There was a cold wind snaking along the road, and the night sky was bursting with great billows of swollen clouds that blocked out the starry heavens as though a blanket had been cast atop the city.

The two of us walked in relative silence, me worrying about the fact that his treasured energy had to be waning, and him undoubtedly worried that I would need to be consigned to Needham Hills before the night was through to once again rid myself of a compulsion for opium.

As the streets narrowed and the sorrowful brick buildings continued to crowd up against the road, I could tell he was becoming disoriented. The chilled air had summoned a fog that, as it mixed with the ubiquitous soot, made it difficult for anyone to find their way let alone someone who had just suffered the dire illness he had. So I slid past him at the first opportunity and had us standing on Scarborough, just beyond where Saint Mark Street crossed it, without a word.

"That would be it," I said, pointing to a dingy, brick-red door on the other side of the street. There was a blob of black paint about the size of two hands at its center, but try as I might, I could not decipher a woman's silhouette.

"Are you certain?" he asked.

Rather than answer I stepped around him and crossed the street, stopping at the door as I gave it a solid rap. It did not take but a moment for it to be swung open to reveal a haggard Chinese woman who looked closer to her middle years than the youth one would normally expect to see in such an establishment.

"You been here before?" she asked.

"No," Colin murmured as a squat man with broad shoulders and flattened-looking features stepped up behind her. He was meant to keep order in the club, though I could tell by the listlessness of his eyelids that he was at least partially under the thrall of the narcotic himself.

"You pay two shilling you come in," she recited without a trace of inflection. "I get pretty girl to serve you."

I pulled out the coins and handed them across to her. She snatched them from me and to my surprise put one in her mouth, biting down hard on it with her back teeth before letting it drop into her hand with a now pleasant smile. "Come in . . . come in." Her voice suddenly held an almost singsong tonality as she stepped back and waved us in.

"We won't need a girl to serve us," Colin informed her as she closed the door behind us.

"You no want pretty girl?" She shifted her eyes to the lug of a man hanging in the background, and I knew they were gauging us—how much money we had to spend and whether we would try to pilfer any drug once we sat down. Given the worn and rumpled state of our clothing, I realized I could hardly blame her.

"No girl," Colin repeated. "But we are looking for a friend. We understand he comes here often."

The woman's brow furrowed as she stared back at him. "Friend? What friend?"

"Quentin Everclear."

"Who?"

I cut in and described Quentin for her, knowing Colin didn't have a notion what the young man had looked like. "He asked us to meet him here," I concluded my recitation. "With some other blokes." I dug into my pocket and pulled out two more shillings, handing them across to her. "He told me to give you these."

This time the woman snapped them up without bothering to grind on any of them. She half turned to the man still hovering behind her and waved him off with an angry growl; to my astonishment, he moved away. "I know man," she said, looking back at us with what was now a rather stellar grin in spite of an array of crooked teeth. "He not here yet. He good friend. He come often. Always give extra money. Always ask for same girl—Mei Lan. She friend too." She shook her head, and her expression began to change into something that seemed to feign either sorrow or regret. "Mei Lan busy. You too late," she added after a moment, giving her shoulders an oversized shrug.

I tugged a crown out of my pocket, but before I could hold it out to her, Colin grabbed it and began flipping it between the fingers of his right hand, rolling the shining disk with his usual grace and dexterity. "Perhaps we might have a chance to visit with her anyway?" Colin remarked glibly. "And anybody else he likes to visit with while he's here." He twisted his hand around as if preparing to toss the crown, but instead he opened his fingers, the coin held upright in the folds of his palm. "If it wouldn't be too much trouble," he added.

The woman gave a delighted laugh, though I could not be certain whether it was the trick he'd done or the fact that she was able to pluck the crown out of his palm that most pleased her. "Come . . . come . . ." She beckoned us for the second time, leading us out of the entry and into a large central room.

The place was dimly lit by a dearth of gaslights, but even so I could see that the couches and settees placed about were bedraggled and the walls stained by the ever-present smoke. It assaulted my nostrils at once, both familiar and repellent, but it no longer held any sway over me.

"Are you all right?" Colin hissed into my ear as we followed the woman deep into the room.

"You have nothing to worry about. You have to trust me." I

knew he would not like that answer, that such a challenge would not sit well with him, but there was nothing further he could say.

This club was far different from the one we had visited during the Arnifour case. It did not aspire to serve gentry, which was evidenced by the fact that most of the people were sprawled across large grimy pillows tossed on the floor that looked barely stuffed enough to offer any protection from the wood planking beneath. What furniture there was either stood back to back or was scattered about without a hint of sense.

"You sit here." Our hostess pointed at a couch, the original color of which I could not have guessed. "I get Mei Lan."

We did as she ordered, Colin flopping down on one end while I settled myself on the other. The woman did not go far, stopping at an arrangement of pillows just to our left, where she knelt down before drawing an attractive young woman to her feet. She pointed toward us and whispered something into the younger woman's ear, but I did not see her pass over any of the multiple coins I had fed her.

"I am Mei Lan," the young woman said a moment later as she stood in front of us. She had long, straight black hair and a round face with delicate, exotic features, dark eyes, and skin that looked as smooth and soft as satin. "You want smoke?" she asked, holding up a small pipe and a little packet of opium.

"Of course," Colin answered grimly, waving at me to hand over the appropriate sum. "We are waiting on a friend."

"Yes," she answered absently, stacking several pillows next to me before seating herself on them. "You wait long time. Mr. Quentin dead." She said it with the offhandedness of someone discussing the season's rainfall.

"Dead?!" Colin repeated while Mei Lan carefully packed the pipe with a pinch of opium, her movements as rudimentary as someone who has done it innumerable times before, which I was quite certain she had.

She held the pipe up to me and pulled out a box of matches. "All gone," she answered perfunctorily, striking the match and bringing it up to the pipe.

Because of the darkness of the club and the fact that this woman had likely been working here for most of the evening, I was able to make a blustery inhalation sound without actually drawing any smoke into my lungs, and she seemed unaware that the contents of the bowl had not flamed in the least. "We had business with him," I said as I exhaled over one shoulder, forcing a great burst of air out that, had she been paying the least bit of attention, would have further verified my misuse.

Her brow curled slightly, not even enough to puncture a line into her flawless skin. "Business," she repeated, gesturing with her chin that I was expected to pass the pipe to Colin. "My business here. When Mr. Quentin have money, *he* my business."

"Did he have much money?" Colin asked before taking his turn with the pipe, making a far less authentic showing of it than I had.

"Sometime," she shrugged, taking the pipe and dumping the contents onto the floor with a resounding bang. "Sometime no."

"Mister . . ." A soft voice drifted from somewhere over my shoulder. "I got friend of man you waiting for." It was the hostess who had brought us in, bending toward me with a ready grin. "You want I should bring him over?"

"What . . . ?" Colin asked, leaning forward from the other end of the couch.

"Yes," I said to her, sliding a florin out of my pocket and slipping it into her outstretched hand. "She says she's found someone who knew Quentin," I murmured to Colin.

He nodded and looked at Mei Lan sitting idly on the dilapidated pillows. "Again," he ordered her.

Despite whatever level of intoxication she was suffering under, she did not move to refill the pipe until I had dispensed the requisite funds to her. Before she could accomplish her task the hostess returned with a man, slouched and disheveled, and presented him to us with great pride.

"This man you friend," she said, and I knew what she meant.

He stood barely taller than the hostess and had a heavily lined face and peppery hair. That he was much older than Quentin Everclear was unmistakable, and I wondered if he really knew the younger man or if he and the hostess were simply looking to extort more money.

"Ya lookin' ta share that?" the man asked, gesturing to the refilled pipe that Mei Lan was now holding.

"Only if you're a friend to Quentin Everclear," Colin answered.

The man grunted and seized the pipe from Mei Lan, waving the hostess away. "I knew 'im," he said, grabbing the arm of a nearby settee and heaving it toward us with a powerful thrust. Mei Lan rearranged her stack of wilted pillows to allow him space as he hoisted himself onto the unsteady seat and leaned forward to allow her to put a match to the bowl.

"Are you a friend of Quentin's or Chinese Tobacco?" Colin asked while the man drew in a hearty lungful of smoke.

"Mr. Raleigh sit with Mr. Quentin many time," Mei Lan assured us, blowing out the match before tossing it to the floor with the dozens of other spent sticks littered about. "They fight like roosters," she added with a laugh.

"Mr. Raleigh . . . ?" I repeated.

"'At's me. But I'll take another hit before I say a bloody word," he informed us churlishly. "I been on a dry streak and it ain't done me head a bit a good." He shoved the pipe back at Mei Lan, who quickly knocked it against the floor to rid it of its ashes before refilling it.

"Fighting were you," Colin spoke again. "Always the mark of a solid friendship."

"Eh . . ." Mr. Raleigh waved Colin off as he took the pipe from Mei Lan and greedily sucked the smoky product into his lungs while she held the match. "She don't know shite," he finally continued, lazily releasing the smoke and leaning back on the settee with a look of relief easing across his face. "Bugger off, girl."

"You no pay," she snapped back at him before turning on me and thrusting out her hand. "He no pay."

I dug into my pocket yet again and pulled out the requisite coins, handing them over. She banged the pipe on the floor again and then stood up and bowed her head. "You want more, you ask for Mei Lan." With a dazzling smile she backed off and disappeared into the haziness that filled the room.

"Mr. Raleigh . . ." Colin muttered in her wake. "Is that your name?"

"That's wot she calls me," he snickered, flopping his head back and staring up at the smoke-blackened ceiling above our heads. "You can call me whatever the hell ya want so long as ya buy me wot I want. I don't give two shites."

"We'll not buy you another thing if you don't start talking about Quentin Everclear."

"Wot for?" he said to the ceiling. "Wot da ya care about him for?"

Colin surged forward on the couch and pounded the empty seat next to Mr. Raleigh, startling the older man and gaining his full attention in the process. "We just paid for you to talk, so I would suggest you start talking or we shall extract our money's worth another way."

I didn't have any idea what Colin meant by his threat, but then neither did Mr. Raleigh, who forced himself upright before leveling his confounded gaze on us. "Awright . . . awright . . ." His voice had become softer and slightly indistinct. "Ya needn't get yerself inta a state. I'm jest askin' a ruddy question."

"I've paid," Colin shot back. "I get to ask the questions."

Mr. Raleigh furrowed his brow, the expression on his face becoming watchful. "You didn't pay," he said after another moment. "That man did." He gestured at me with his chin.

"Then I shall ask the questions," I snapped. "Were you and Quentin Everclear in business together?"

"Business?!" The man laughed. "Do I look like I'm in business?"

I leaned forward and stabbed a finger at him. "I will leave you with enough coins to feed your habit for the remainder of this day and the next if you start talking. The truth. But I will not sit here another moment and have you continue to play these bloody games. So what will it be?"

The man soured, as I knew he would, but there would be no choice for him. The opium had seen to that long ago. "I weren't in business with Quentin," he admitted as he slumped back in his chair. "He had some kinda shite goin' on, I don't know what, but he were right jumpy about it and I knew it weren't no good."

"A model citizen, are you?" Colin cut in.

"I ain't done nothin' wrong."

"You must have some idea what he was involved with," Colin prodded. "He must've mentioned something."

The man shook his head. "I swear on me mother's grave. But whatever it was, he started havin' money ta flash around. That were nice."

"Did you ever see him meet anyone here? Anyone you knew wasn't a regular visitor?"

Mr. Raleigh shook his head. "Nah. I seen him once with a guy at a pub . . . but never here. Them type don't come ta places like this. They got nicer clubs near Limehouse."

"Types like what?"

"Fancy like. Them that 'as money. Like this guy. He were wearin' fancy clothes and actin' all stuffy when I saw 'im with Quentin." He chuckled. "And I could see Quentin were all stiff when 'e was talkin' to him. Lookin' like a right nob."

"What did the man he was with look like?"

"I don't know. Nothin' special. Brown hair, sorta wavy, and a mustache and maybe a small beard. I think maybe he had some gray too 'cause I remember thinkin' he weren't as young as Quentin. He had a top hat sittin' on the table. That much I do remember. Like a real gentleman. Good for remindin' Quentin that he weren't like him." He gave a snort. "But he was still sittin' in that pub jest like the rest of us. Damn bugger."

"Did you ask Quentin who the man was?"

"I didn't wanna know. Wot's it ta me? I didn't want nothin' ta do with any a that nonsense." He gave a sudden snicker at some remembrance before continuing. "When the man walked by me on 'is way out, all big as ya please with 'is top hat back on 'is head, I noticed 'is jacket were a bit worn at the elbows and there were these little threads hangin' here and there from the ribbon round the rim a 'is fancy hat. 'At's when I knew 'e were full a shite. Weren't no better 'an anybody else there."

"But you never asked his name . . . ?" Colin pressed again, both of us certain this was the same man I had watched slice Quentin Everclear's throat.

"No," Mr. Raleigh repeated with extra force. "I told ya. Ya wanna know about that, you can ask his granddad."

"What . . . ?" Colin bolted forward. "Braxton Everclear? What does he have to do with any of this?"

Mr. Raleigh screwed up his face. "Hell if I know! I told ya that a thousand feckin' times. I weren't involved in none a it, but I knew Quentin hated the old man. Said he were finally gettin' his due. That Quentin owned him." He huffed and settled his head back again, staring up at the ceiling. "Like anybody owns them rich buggers."

The memory of Quentin's words came back to me in an instant: *And do you suppose his generosity is simply a gift? That it comes without any expectation?* I had dismissed them as the resentment of an ungrateful grandson looking for unfettered handouts, but in that same moment I realized that I could just as easily have missed something vital. I turned to Colin and spoke in a low voice. "Quentin said something like that to me. I presumed he was just spouting off."

Colin's eyebrows bristled minutely as he looked back at Mr. Raleigh, who appeared to be on the verge of falling asleep. "Pay him. I've had quite enough of this place."

I shoved a few coins at the man, cursing myself for having dismissed a piece of information without having had any reason to do so. Presumption was a curse, and I had been taught better.

"If Braxton Everclear is involved . . ." Colin muttered as we pushed our way back out onto the street, the chilled, damp air providing welcome relief from the noxious fumes inside. "It is unthinkable. My father . . ." He did not finish his thought. He did not need to.

CHAPTER 29

My eyes sprang open, my heart already thundering in my ears. I bolted upright as my brain tore through what bits of information it could immediately discern: utter darkness, pounding footsteps, Colin missing. As the haze in my head struggled to ebb, I heard someone rushing down the hallway at a fast clip, too fast for Mrs. Behmoth. A sliver of light revealed itself through the gap at the bottom of the door, quickly becoming more luminescent with each approaching step. It had to be Colin.

I pushed myself out of bed and slid a nightshirt over my head just as the door swung wide. "Good," Colin said, "you're up."

"What's going on? What time is it?"

"Just before five. There's been another murder on Framingham. They just found the girl. Inspector Evans is downstairs waiting for us. I'm sure Mrs. Behmoth is plying him with tea and theories, so let us not dally getting ready." As he spoke he removed his robe and tossed it onto a nearby chair before tearing clothes out of the armoire and either pulling them on or pitching them toward me. He was using both arms in his endeavors and, I was ecstatic to see, there was nary a flinch that crossed his face. "He insists he has a legion of men down there," he continued, "all concentrating on the areas around Framingham, and yet the killer has managed to strike again."

"This monster is truly as spectral as the newspapers would have their readers believe. He is just like the Ripper," I added, trying to move my fingers dexterously enough to get my tie knotted.

"Ridiculous," Colin scoffed as he shrugged into his jacket. "Come on, you can do that in the carriage."

I followed him down the stairs and into the kitchen at a pace I would not have thought possible so early in the morning. Just as Colin had predicted, Inspector Evans was standing by the table drinking tea while Mrs. Behmoth removed scones from the oven and freely shared her opinion.

"Men love ta blame women," she was saying. "They think everything started with us. Original sin and all that rot. Like 'ell. Yer lot coulda said no." She looked over at us. "I 'eated these up from last night." She waved her spatula at the scones. "I ain't got time ta make fresh."

"Nothing for me . . ." Colin started to say.

"You are most kind," the inspector cut in as he scooped one up and headed for the foyer.

"You'll take one," Mrs. Behmoth warned Colin, "or ya won't get as far as that ruddy door."

I didn't doubt her word and, apparently, neither did Colin, since he grabbed one before hurrying after the inspector. I followed suit, grateful to have something for my stomach before having to face a scene I was becoming all too familiar with.

"The first report came into Scotland Yard about half an hour ago," the inspector began to explain once we were under way. "They dispatched a constable for me, and I came right here. However . . ." He gave Colin a keen look. "I sent word back that no one was to enter the room before we get there."

"Excellent." Colin gave a clipped nod. "A room you say . . . ?"

"She rents a room on Framingham just off Stepney Way. That's where she was discovered. I believe it was by a roommate, though I'm not certain. By the time word reaches me it has usually been through multiple sources, so there is no telling what we may find."

The three of us fell silent as the carriage sped through the streets, the hour of the day offering us rapid passage. We crossed Philpot Street and began to slow as we neared Stepney Way, turning onto Framingham just before we'd reached the cross street. A throng of bobbies could be seen at once along with a few determined souls, all of them milling about looking anxious and confused. I could not tell whether any of the assembled were newspapermen, but all of them were craning their necks, trying to see anything they could.

"*Inspector!*" a man called to us as we climbed out of the carriage, and as he drew closer I recognized him as the overzealous Sergeant Lanchester whom we had run up against during the Connicle case. "I have sealed the scene as ordered," he announced, reminding me that I had found him arrogant back then. "There are two men stationed outside the door to her room, and no one has been permitted to enter or leave the building since I arrived."

I glanced at the faces of the few gathered people and realized that most of them were likely just trying to get back to their flats. "Very good. Get the names and room numbers of anybody who wishes to enter or leave the building," the inspector directed, "and have a couple of the men escort them in and out. I want to make sure they actually belong here."

"Which room belongs to the victim?" Colin asked.

Sergeant Lanchester slid his gaze to Colin, his disapproval evident, before looking back at the inspector. "It's on the second floor in the back, sir," he answered, speaking solely to Inspector Evans.

"Please make sure no one goes anywhere near it," Colin spoke again.

The sergeant took a moment, apparently considering what Colin had said, before directing a question to the inspector. "Is that your order, sir?"

"Do you have a problem with Mr. Pendragon and Mr. Pruitt,

Sergeant?" the inspector snapped. "Because if you do, I shall be happy to speak with Superintendent Tottenshire about having you reassigned."

"No problem, sir. But this *is* official Scotland Yard business. Their presence here seems unnecessary. Inspector Varcoe—"

"Is dead," Inspector Evans roared. "But before he died you will remember that he sought the help of these gentlemen in solving his last case."

"Of course, sir. Although it still remains for Mrs. Hutton to be captured. . . ."

"That is correct," the inspector answered at once, his eyes narrowing even as his voice smoothed out. "And that is in spite of the fact that you traveled to Zurich with Mr. Pendragon to assist in securing the cooperation of Credit Suisse regarding Mrs. Hutton's funds." He gave a sour leer. "You'd best watch *yourself*, Sergeant. Now, why don't you tell us what the situation is here."

The young man cleared his throat angrily. If he felt censured or admonished, I could not see it in the least. "The victim is a woman in her early forties by the name of Pearl Twickham. We know her name because she was found by her sister, Opal, who's been staying with her." He gestured to a coach pulled up along the curb one building down from the one we were standing in front of. "We've been holding her in there."

"What time did she find the body?" Colin asked.

A look of impatience flashed across the young sergeant's eyes before he answered. "About three-thirty. She was just coming home from work."

"Three-thirty . . ." the inspector repeated. "What in hell does she claim to do for a living?"

"She says she's a seamstress."

"And her sister?" Colin asked.

"A seamstress as well."

"Noble," Colin mumbled as he took a step back and started for the door. "Shall we?"

The sergeant fell in line behind me, so I was relieved when Inspector Evans whirled around on him before we went into the building. "Stay out here," he said, "and make sure my orders are being followed to the letter. It won't be long before the newspapermen show up, and I'll not have them inside this building. And make sure the coroner has been sent for."

"He has."

"Then wait for him."

Sergeant Lanchester nodded his understanding, but there was no missing the discontent on his face as he turned and headed off.

"He's a curious one," I noted as we pounded up the steps toward the second floor.

"Emmett Varcoe was his mother's cousin," Inspector Evans explained from behind us. "You could be the prince consort and he'll still have no use for you."

"Pity," Colin muttered as he reached the landing first and headed straight back to where two constables were standing outside an old door marred with shoe prints along the bottom and myriad scratches, the likes of which seemed to bear out the length of time it had been standing there.

"You will see to it that no one enters this room without my express permission," the inspector reiterated.

"Yes, sir," they both responded, staring openly as Colin grabbed the knob and shoved the door wide.

"Oh . . ." was all he said, his voice low and rumbling, before he stepped inside.

The entry was tiny, and there was a small bedroom off to the right and a slightly larger living area to the left. But one did not need to take a second step to know that something was horribly wrong. There was a smell, not of death but of blood, metallic and sharp. At least part of the cause of this could be seen on the wall directly in front of us, where a framed photo of the Queen had been cast to the floor, the nail from which it had hung still poking impotently from the wall. In its stead had been scrawled a phrase I did not recognize, in a swath of blood about two fingers wide that stretched nearly the width of the entire space.

"What does it say?" the inspector asked, letting the door swing shut on the gaping faces of his two men.

"I'm quite sure it's Latin," I said.

"It is," Colin agreed. *"Ut vadat, ita abscedit.* Was it at the scene of Miss Materly's death?"

"No," I answered first. "But then, that murder was rushed. He didn't even have time to . . ." I let my voice drop, unwilling to finish the thought as I knew we were bound to see the full extent of his madness this time. "Do you know what it means?"

"As it goes, so it goes," he answered. He turned and looked at the inspector and me. "He's taunting us now. Daring us to try to stop him."

"But what the hell does it mean?" the inspector asked before I could.

"Revenge? Retribution?" Colin turned and took a step toward the bedroom but pulled up short as he reached the threshold, his breath catching in an abrupt intake of air. "There can be no doubt that it is him again. Do move with caution, gentlemen. We will want the photographer to capture this carefully, as our madman seems to be speaking ever louder now." Only then did he move fully into the room.

I found that I could hardly breathe as I too sidled into the tiny space, holding my eyes on the small wooden dressing table against the wall opposite the door. It was well used and just the tiniest bit off-kilter, leaving me to believe that one of its feet had been either chipped or split. Atop it rested a hairbrush and a hand mirror, a mismatched pair that nevertheless looked situated just so. There were a few jars of creams and powders, and a couple of tiny pots of what I presumed was rouge or other sort of paint. All of it was neatly arranged as though their owner might come back at any moment to sit down and partake of them again.

I turned my head to the left, toward a small window that was just beginning to hint at the earliest vestiges of dawn, and saw the disheveled bed upon which the body sat propped up. The woman's head was leaning back against the wall, her throat slashed ear to ear as though to form a grisly smile. She was unclothed with her legs akimbo and her sternum split wide from below the neck to well beneath the navel, the skin there sagging flaccidly. Her arms were spread wide with the palms up as if beckoning the viewer to come closer, but to do so meant walking through the minefield of her innards, which had been carefully laid out upon the floor: lungs, heart, liver, kidneys, stomach, entrails. All of it placed just as he meant it to be seen.

"Tell me her sister did not see this," I gasped, unable to force my feet to carry me another step.

"I hope not," the inspector replied in a voice barely above a whisper.

"Check the dressing table and the floor," Colin directed, crouching low by the entrails that had been placed farthest from the body. "You're looking for anything that did not belong to this woman. Something that might have been his."

Inspector Evans moved for the dressing table before I could, so I took my lantern and began to scan the floor looking for a shoe print, scrap of hair, torn bit of fabric, smudge of mud, anything beyond the dust motes collected in the corners. They, at least, attested to a life of normalcy. But I could find nothing. If he had been rushed in the cellar of the Materly murder, such had not been the case here. It made me wonder whether he had known that his victim had a sister who was not expected home until much later.

"Will you check her nails, Ethan?" Colin muttered as he approached the body at an angle to avoid the organs scattered along the floor.

I wanted to protest, to tell him he could do so himself, but he was already there, bent so low over her gaping neck that I thought it a miracle he was not sick. I told myself that if he could view such a wound from that proximity, then I could certainly look at her hands. So I forced myself forward, holding my light aloft so that the viscera on the floor looked more like black masses than what they truly were.

"Don't touch the bed," Colin warned as I drew near. "The sheets are saturated with blood, and we may find something on them."

"There's a dress behind the door and a shawl," the inspector said. "They've got blood on them," he added. I heard a brief rustling of fabric. "And they've been slashed."

"Inspect them carefully," Colin said as he leaned over the rent in her chest.

The sight of his doing so made my stomach flop heavily, and for a moment I had to close my eyes and breathe.

"Are you all right?" Colin muttered softly.

"Of course." I popped my eyes open and concentrated on the pale hand stretched out on the sheet before me. Working with methodical precision I placed my lamp onto the floor and kneeled down, taking great care to disturb neither the bed nor the unseen evisceration that I knew lay behind me. Once I was firmly set, I took up my lamp again and closely inspected her hand. It was cold to the touch and powder white, with just a tinge of blueness beneath her nails. There was no mottling of her skin given that most of her blood had hemorrhaged onto the sheets, leaving her arm looking like that of a life-sized porcelain doll.

Her nails were embedded with grime. None were long, and several were split and ragged, suggesting that she had indeed worked with her hands. I knew what Colin wanted me to look for—the telltale signs of skin or blood—but I could not delineate any such thing. "Denton Ross and Mr. Kindall are going to have to tell us if there is anything of value to be found here," I said as I pushed myself back to my feet. "All I can say for certain is that none of her nails look freshly broken as would have happened in a struggle with her killer. But I cannot speak to what might be found beneath them."

"Very well." Colin stood up with a tight expression on his face and began looking across the bed, swinging his lamp back and forth. "The sheets . . ." he mumbled. "Check the sheets."

I did as he said, moving my lamp slowly, fingering the folds of muslin fabric that had been shoved toward the back of the bed. There was nothing hidden among them that I could see, and after a moment I quit looking when I became aware that Colin had stepped back. "I would suggest you get your photographer in here," he said to the inspector as he picked his way back across the room. "We shall need to study this scene carefully." He moved to the door and turned back. "And be sure your men collect everything with great care. There may yet be evidence to be found. Your Sergeant Lanchester seems up to the task. And—"

"You'll want to see Mr. Ross's autopsy report this afternoon," Inspector Evans cut in sharply.

Colin ticked the briefest smile. "Well done, Inspector. We'll stop by your office late this afternoon. Come on, Ethan, let us have a word with the sister." And then he was gone.

"Does he think I don't remember how to do my job?" the inspector groused, his tone brushed with exasperation.

"It is his habit," I assured as I tread back to the door as carefully yet quickly as I could. "There is nothing personal in it. You know Colin too well now to take offense. You are not Inspector Varcoe, after all." I stopped in the doorway, eager to be out of this flat, and looked back at Inspector Evans. "Do you want to speak to Opal Twickham with us?"

"You go ahead." He waved me off. "Send the sergeant up. I'll see that things get sorted properly here first. But if there is anything she says—"

"You have my word," I answered before he could finish his statement.

Nothing felt better than the crisp, raw air that greeted my lungs when I got back outside. The first tendrils of dawn were stretching across the sky, and a few people were beginning to file past, turning their heads and wondering what had happened during the night while they had slept.

I found Sergeant Lanchester and sent him upstairs, his keenness at being thusly summoned evident, though I knew it would not stay long on his face. Colin was standing over by the coach Opal Twickham had been relegated to, so I made my way over to him.

"The work was very precise," he said as I reached him.

"Are you talking about the wounds?"

"Yes. The hand of a surgeon."

"What about a barber like the Ripper? You'll remember that the one witness, however unreliable he may seem, did say that he saw a butcher's apron under the cloak of the man leaving the scene."

He shook his head. "This is different. A butcher's work is about speed and volume. Cutting down one carcass after another so that women like our Mrs. Behmoth can take their desired parcels of meat home and fashion them into the roasts, pies, and stews their families crave. While I do not detract from the skill of a butcher, it does not equal the care and precision that went into the carving of this woman." His expression looked grave as he reached up for the carriage's door handle. "I fear the worst for our sovereign and her grand-nephew. It is precisely the expertise that he would have learned at the Royal College of Surgeons. I would stake my reputation on it." And before I could say anything, he had pulled the door wide and entered, seating himself across from Opal Twickham.

I climbed up beside Colin and gave a solemn nod to Miss Twickham as I did so. She was a tiny woman who looked some ten years younger than her sister but otherwise resembled her in both her pale coloring and dark hair, as well as the heart shape of her face. It was apparent from the streaks of makeup along her cheeks that she had been crying, and even now she was holding a soiled handkerchief against her face.

"Was it 'im?" she asked in a quivery voice before I had settled myself.

"Him . . . ?" Colin repeated, and for an instant I believe we both thought she might know who the killer was.

"The Ripper." Her dark eyes were bright and terrified as she flicked them back and forth between us.

"No," Colin assured her. "You must trust me when I tell you that Jack the Ripper is no longer a threat. Nevertheless, we seem to have a copycat at work, and it is *he* who was responsible for your sister's death. You have our deepest sympathies."

The poor young woman began to whimper, dabbing at her eyes with the handkerchief even as she seemed to be trying to maintain her composure. "I don't know what I'm gonna do without Pearl. She's been lookin' after me since I were little."

"How long have you been living with her?"

"'Bout a year and a half. Ever since our mum died. She got me a good job, a respectable job, workin' a night shift sewin' ladies garments for a comp'ny wot sells clothes ta stores off Oxford and Regent Streets."

"Very nice. And did your sister work there with you?"

She squirmed in her seat, and her gaze dropped to her lap. "Sometimes," was all she said.

"Did she have other employment as well?"

The woman's hands fidgeted as she seemed to be struggling with her answer. "She weren't much of a sewer," she finally said.

Colin exhaled and leaned forward slightly. "I am not prying without reason, Miss Twickham, nor am I in any position to judge another person's behavior or deeds. I seek these answers so that I can understand where she might have met up with the thief who stole her life."

Opal Twickham's eyes shot back to Colin. "A course," she said. "I just . . ."

"You will serve her best with honesty. That is the only way we will be able to bring this man to justice."

She dropped her gaze again and spoke into her lap. "Pearl just couldn't sit still behind a sewin' machine. She weren't made like that. And she were so much prettier than all the rest a us anyway. So she did wot was easy, but she wasn't gonna let that 'appen ta me. She wanted me ta 'ave a proper skill. We was gonna move outta 'ere. . . ." She dissolved into tears again, pressing the handkerchief against her mouth in misery.

"We are so sorry," I said, hoping Colin would finish this excruciating interview, as I did not think I could take much more.

"Do you know where your sister usually met her . . ." Colin's voice grew hesitant and clumsy as he tried to dance around the very thing Opal Twickham clearly did not want to admit. "Her clients? Was it in taverns or pubs, or was she content to meet them on the street . . . ?"

Miss Twickham looked almost about to swoon before she was able to collect herself again and fashion an answer. "We was both scared about the Ripper"—she glanced over at Colin—"or whoever he is, so I know she weren't bein' foolish. She 'ad 'er couple places she liked, and that's where she met most a the men she en'ertained."

218 / Gregory Harris

"Do you know which ones? Could you give us the names of the establishments she went to regularly?"

"I . . ." She glanced between us. "She didn't want me goin' there, but I went with 'er a couple times. Ya know, jest for a pint."

"Of course, of course," Colin answered too readily, gesturing to my jacket pocket. "If you would . . ."

I jotted down the names and locations of three clubs that Opal Twickham knew her sister frequented. It wasn't much, but it was something. "You've been most helpful," Colin said as he exchanged her well-used handkerchief for the fresh one from his pocket. "If you wouldn't mind continuing to wait here, I know the inspector would appreciate it." He yanked the latch on the door and then stopped to look back at her. "And Miss Twickham, rest assured that we will catch this man."

He popped out, and I did the same after squeezing the young woman's shoulder and giving her an additional word of encouragement. As I clicked the door shut behind me Inspector Evans approached, the grayness of his skin noticeable in the burgeoning light of the new day. I could not fathom how he had been able to stay in that horrid room for so long.

"Did you learn anything from her?" he asked.

"We got the names of a few places she says her sister patronized on a fairly regular basis." He nodded to me, and I tore the list from my book and handed it over to the inspector. "You'll want to have some of your men go round and speak with the proprietors. See if Pearl Twickham was there last night, and if so, who she was with. This could well be the break we have been looking for."

"Indeed!" The inspector's eyes lit up. "And is there anything else I will be wanting to do?" he added with a touch of aggravation.

Colin looked at him with surprise, one eyebrow curving ever so slightly upward. "Nothing I can think of." He gave a curt nod and flashed a thin smile. "Why don't you pick us up when Mr. Ross's report is done. We shall want to go to the morgue to view her remains again. Until this afternoon, then."

"Yes." The inspector exhaled, and I could feel the weight of his frustration as he did so.

"As for you and me," Colin said once we had reached the periphery of the growing crowd, "we have to get word to Paul and have him come to our flat at once. If he and his lads were watching Victoria's grand-nephew last night, as we are paying them to do, then we may well be reaching the conclusion of this journey."

The same thought had occurred to me, though I was too doubtful to dare believe it. So many things could have gone wrong, not the least of which was that we were counting on a small band of scruffy boys to do the work of seasoned constables. It did not sit right with me and, as I followed Colin in search of a cab, I hoped we had not made a grave error.

CHAPTER 30

"I can scarcely think of news that could be worse." Sir Atherton exhaled deeply as he ran a hand through his thinning gray hair. "Are you certain? Is there not *some* chance there could be another possibility?"

I could not remember ever seeing Sir Atherton look as despondent as he did at that moment, sitting in our study staring into his teacup as though it might offer some refuge from the unpleasantness his son had just laid before him. Even the fresh shortbread biscuits Mrs. Behmoth had brought up, a distinct favorite of Sir Atherton's, lay untouched on the plate where she had set them.

"Another possibility?" Colin repeated, and I could tell that his father's distress was not sitting well with him, either. "I would be foolish to state that I was certain of anything just yet. Just the same, Gerhard did not deny frequenting the East End, and I fear that his education at the surgical college leaves him uniquely qualified to have inflicted precisely the sort of damage that these women have suffered."

"But there must be scores of young men who have attended the College of Surgeons," Sir Atherton protested. "Could you not suspect every one of them?"

"I should and I do," Colin answered without hesitation. "But how many of them already have records with the police for acts of violence? One . . . two . . . I should very much like to know, and yet Victoria makes it nearly impossible for me to find out."

Sir Atherton shook his head vehemently. "She was clear on that point. With both of you. We are not to bring Scotland Yard into this business unless expressly requested to do so by her."

"Very well," Colin said, a detectable note of frustration leaking into his voice. "But she is making it damnably hard to prove anything about her grand-nephew, a man she herself suspects, when we are not permitted to use the resources available to us through the Yard."

"Oh hush," his father scolded as a pounding on our front door rang out from below. "It sounds to me like you are going soft. I seem to remember that it was not even a year ago when Inspector Varcoe had the two of you tossed in a cell for your disagreeability."

"It was *not* for disagreeability. . . ."

"I had to call in a favor from a magistrate chum to get you both released. You were perfectly capable of working cases back then without the least bit of help from Scotland Yard. So what has changed?"

Colin pushed himself off the settee and stalked over to the fireplace, snatching up the poker and stabbing at the glowing logs. "You can be so insufferable."

"'*Ey*," Mrs. Behmoth hollered up the stairs as she could be heard pounding her way to the door, "*Don't ya dare say that about yer father.*"

"How the bloody hell does that woman hear through the floorboards?" Colin growled.

"Say what you will"—Sir Atherton set his teacup down and pushed himself to his feet—"but Victoria was clear that her concerns are not to be discussed with anyone. The burden of this case as far as her grand-nephew is concerned rests on the two of you alone. Now, do I head out to Windsor to speak with her or not?"

"Windsor?" I spoke up. "I thought she was at Buckingham."

Sir Atherton turned to me with a wistful smile. "She has been unable to abide Buckingham since Albert's death. It is a testament to her concern about this case that she came in to meet with you,"

"*It's yer urchin,*" Mrs. Behmoth shouted.

Colin slammed the poker back into the rack and bolted for the stairs, his eyes bright with anticipation. "*Send him up,*" he called back.

"Urchin?" Sir Atherton continued to stare at me.

"It is a young man we have hired from time to time to assist us," I explained.

"We have pressed him into service on this very case," Colin added, his voice brimming with anticipation. "He does not ask questions and is more reliable than most anyone we have worked with before. We left word for him earlier today, and I can only hope he has some information for us now."

"Information?" Sir Atherton muttered, concern evident in his voice just as Paul bounded into the room with his scruffy cap in his hands.

"Mr. P!" His face lit up. "Mr. Sir."

"Have you met my father?" Colin asked as he grabbed Paul by the shoulder and led him into the room.

"We are old friends by now," Sir Atherton grinned. "This bright young man seems quite the find to me."

"I ain't that young," Paul protested as he reached over and snatched up two pieces of shortbread. "I'm gonna be thirteen next summer."

"Time is a cruel mistress," Sir Atherton *tsked*. "It is impressive how you've been able to help my son and Mr. Pruitt."

"His youth affords him an almost invisibility on the streets," Colin explained. "Now, why don't you go down and see if Mrs. Behmoth has any other fresh bakes she can shower upon you so you needn't hear our further business."

Sir Atherton nodded as he moved toward the landing. "A sound idea. I do not relish knowing the details of your arrangement."

"Rightly so," Colin agreed with perhaps a touch too much vigor as he joined his father on the landing.

"You haven't told him, have you?" Sir Atherton asked, his voice dropping to the point that I noticed Paul's ears perk up.

"Of course not. Now go downstairs, and Ethan will come get you as soon as we've finished here."

"I shall look forward to seeing you again," Sir Atherton called to Paul as his footfalls receded steadily.

Colin came back into the room, once again moving with impatience. He dropped himself into his usual chair, the one his father had just vacated, and seized his teacup as though ready for a smashing story to be told.

"Wot 'aven't ya told me?" Paul asked before Colin could seize the conversation.

"Frippery," he responded, waving a dismissive hand through the air.

"Huh?"

"Precisely. Now tell me, were you and your band of lads out at the estate we asked you to watch last night?"

"A course." Paul picked up two more pieces of shortbread as I refilled his tea and handed it over. "I was watchin' the front gate and 'ad two a me best blokes hangin' in the alleyway behind."

"And . . . ?"

Paul stuffed another biscuit into his mouth, and a rain of crumbs showered down the front of his jacket as he struggled to answer. "And nothin'. Is that why ya sent yer messenger ta find me? Ya know I woulda come by if we'd seen anything."

"Nothing?" Colin pressed. "No one came or went the entire night?"

"A couple a the staff went out the back in the evenin', but not the man you was lookin' for. And the only one wot came out the front was an old guy 'oo left in a carriage for a couple 'ours. I was by meself so I couldn't 'ave no one follow 'im, but then you said ya weren't interested in any old man."

"That's right," Colin muttered, sitting back and staring into the fireplace.

"Did you get a good look at the man who left in the carriage?" I asked. "Was he elderly? Gray hair and all?" I asked, fearing Paul might consider Colin and me men of age.

"Oh yeah. 'E were real old. He was leanin' on a cane and looked 'bout as dotty as . . ." Paul clamped his mouth shut and I suspected he'd been just about to say Sir Atherton.

"That would have been Gerhard's father," Colin stated. "And what about the people who left out the back. Staff, you say?"

"That's wot they were. Me boys said there was six of 'em altogether. First two women and a man. Then a short time later another man left, and sometime after that two more. Six," he repeated, in case we could not do the math ourselves.

"Are you certain they were all household staff?" Colin pressed.

"That's wot me boys said."

"If I can get a photograph of the man we are looking for you to keep an eye on, will you have your boys take a look to make sure he might not have been one of the men who departed out the servant's entrance?"

"Wot?!" Paul let out a hearty laugh. "Ain't no proper gentleman is nippin' out 'is own back door."

"He might if he was trying to be discreet."

"Huh?"

"If he didn't want to be seen," I clarified.

"Oh . . . Why? Wot's 'e done? Do ya think 'e's the one wot killed me mum?"

"We don't know anything yet," Colin answered. "Which is why we have hired you and your lads to keep an eye on him. See what he's doing and where he's going. Will you continue to do that for us?"

"Well . . ." He hesitated, and I knew what was coming next. "The nights is gettin' colder, which is makin' it 'arder ta get me boys ta do their best work."

"How much more?" I cut him off.

"Maybe 'alf a crown." He gave a sly grin. "Each."

"Fine," Colin said before I could. "And you can be assured that we will find the man responsible for your mother's death."

"I know ya will. She may not 'ave been much of a mum, but no one should die like that. It jest ain't right." He screwed up his face and seemed to consider something a moment. "Imagine if I'd a been followin' 'er around that night like I did sometimes."

"Better that you were not. You don't know what might have happened. This is a dangerous man. A master with a knife. You could have become a victim yourself." Colin leaned back in his chair and took a sip of tea. "Now, I want you to bring your chums back later this afternoon. The ones who were watching the back of the house last night."

"Why? I'll see that they get their share a the money."

"I have no doubt of that," Colin said, biting back a smile. "I will have a picture of the man in question for them to take a look at. I need to be absolutely certain that he wasn't one of the staff they saw last night."

"Wot time do ya want us, then?"

"How about six? The lot of you will stay for dinner. Mrs. Behmoth will be happy to make extras."

"Ehhh . . ." He gave a snort. "I don't think she likes me much."

"You have grown on her," Colin assured him with a chuckle.

"Okay . . . but if I bring them two round, then I'm gonna 'ave ta get a couple more ta watch that 'ouse fer a while. It's gonna cost . . ."

"You needn't worry about the cost." It was my turn to reassure him. "We will pay your mates just as we have always paid you."

"It's yer money."

"Then it is settled." Colin stood up and returned to the fireplace, rubbing his hands absently. "We shall see you all at six."

"Can I 'ave another biscuit?" Paul asked as he stood up.

"Help yourself." I handed him the plate.

He upended it into his cap and gave me a generous smile. "Thanks, Mr. Pruitt. I'll see meself out." He gave a laugh and went bounding down the stairs at a thunderous pace, and not a moment later the front door opened and slammed shut.

"*Could 'e make any more bloody noise?!*" Mrs. Behmoth hollered as I heard her come barreling out of the kitchen.

"We shall find out later," Colin called back, heading for the landing. "I have invited him and two of his mates back for dinner tonight."

"Wot?!"

"Now, don't make a fuss. They're just boys. They can't possibly eat that much."

"A course they can. And will! Now I'll 'ave ta go back ta the market and get another bird ta roast."

"What did he have to say about Gerhard?" Sir Atherton interrupted, the methodical sound of him climbing the stairs punctuating his sentence.

Colin scoffed and moved back to the fireplace as his father reached the landing. "We still have no certainty," he said, frustration marring the edges of his voice. "I need to get a photograph of Gerhard to show the lads. It is entirely possible that he went out through the servant's entrance last night. We mustn't be arrogant enough to think that he is not a clever man."

"I'm certain I have a photograph," Sir Atherton said. "I shall have a messenger bring it by for you. If he is the one . . ." He pinched his face and shook his head. "It will be a tragedy. You must come by this evening and let me know, otherwise I will hardly have a moment's sleep for wondering."

"Of course. I feel at ends myself wishing the case to be solved and yet fearing the worst for Victoria."

Sir Atherton nodded grimly. "I will see you both later, then." His eyes settled on Colin a moment. "I hope you are taking care of yourself in the midst of all this."

Colin grinned. "I am fine. You really mustn't worry. However, we could use a lift to Braxton Everclear's flat."

Sir Atherton's eyes brightened at once. "Have you learned something? Do you know who murdered his grandson?"

"Not yet, which is why we need to speak with him. We have heard a few stories about his grandson and would like to get some corroboration from Braxton. I am hoping they might jog his memory a bit."

Sir Atherton crinkled his brow. "Stories? What kind of stories?"

"The idle blather that one picks up in pubs and taverns," Colin said, grabbing his coat and tossing mine to me. "There is no use discussing any of it until we've had a chance to pass it by Braxton. You know I will tell you as soon as we have learned anything of any real value." He gave an easy smile as the two of them started down the stairs, though I knew our conversation with Braxton Everclear would hardly be so blithe. While neither of us had any tangible reason to suspect Mr. Everclear's involvement in the murder of his grandson, my stomach had soured after our conversation with Mr. Raleigh and had yet to correct itself. And given Colin's evasive answer to his father, I very much suspected that he felt the same way.

CHAPTER 31

By the time we were delivered to the Everclear driveway, the afternoon had turned cloudy and another chill had settled in. The scent of rain was heavy once again, guaranteeing that it would only be a matter of time before the sky released its bounty.

"You can leave us off here," Colin called out to his father's driver. "No need to rattle us up that drive."

"Are you certain, sir?"

"Positive," Colin answered, shoving the door open to prove his point. "A bit of fresh air will do us good." And he hopped out.

"You will let me know as soon as something comes of your investigation into Quentin's murder," Sir Atherton requested as I slid across the seat to follow Colin. I gave him a ready nod. "And Ethan, you have only to ask should you need help with Colin. I know I made something of a muddle in raising him but . . ." He gave a slight shrug.

"You did nothing of the kind." I chuckled. "We shall see you soon." I climbed out of the carriage and caught the crooked smile on Sir Atherton's face as I did.

"What took you so long?" Colin asked when I caught up with him, having already charged halfway down the driveway.

"He would like to be kept abreast of our investigation into Quentin's death."

"You didn't tell him the real nature of our visit, did you?"

"Never. I shall leave that task to you, should it become necessary."

He grimaced, but his pace did not flag in the least. "I must admit to feeling uneasy about this."

"As do I."

"Since I have known him almost the entirety of my life, I wonder if you wouldn't mind taking the lead in this conversation."

In fact I minded a great deal. "If you would like me to," I said.

"Good. Just get him talking. See if you can edge him up to finding out whether he knows more than he has admitted thus far."

"Of course," I answered, though I scarcely knew how I would begin.

He tossed me an approving smile as he leapt up onto the porch and cracked the door knocker hard. "You are beginning to make me feel superfluous." He snickered just at the moment the door was pulled wide.

"Mr. Pendragon . . . Mr. Pruitt . . ." An elegant man in a valet's uniform stepped aside and ushered us in. "Mr. Everclear mentioned you would be stopping by. I have had tea prepared in the study, if you will follow me."

We did as bidden, crossing the elegant foyer with its recessed wood paneling and copper ormolu ceiling in a handful of strides. The man took us toward the back of the house, the damp chill from outside continuing to brush against my face as we proceeded. There seemed little delineation between the outside and the inside as far as I could tell, so I was pleased to find a fire raging when we stepped into the study. The orange and yellow glow from the flames reflected off the deep blue velvet and walnut furnishings set around the fireplace. Just as had been promised, a silver tea set was waiting on a table in the midst of the furnishings with a small plate containing half a dozen butter biscuits beside it.

"Would you like milk and sugar?" the man asked after beckoning us to sit.

"Just a bit of milk for both of us," Colin answered first, which struck me as an inauspicious beginning given the intended reversal of our roles.

The man delivered our tea along with two biscuits each, and before he could withdraw, Braxton Everclear entered. Once again it wasn't his roundness or the full face with drooping jowls that most struck me, but rather his wiry gray and white hair that, just as with the first time we'd met, seemed insistent on sticking out in disparate directions. It lent him a look of dishevelment that was exacerbated by the fact that the bottom two buttons of his vest had sprung open and the collar of his shirt looked ever so faintly threadbare. I could not help thinking that he appeared more the eccentric inventor than a one-time officer of the diplomatic corps.

"Mr. Pruitt . . . Mr. Pendragon . . ." he said with a tip of his chin to his valet, who immediately left, pulling the doors shut behind him. "I am pleased to see you doing so well, Colin. I was delighted when your father told me of your recovery."

"Not nearly as delighted as me." He cracked a hesitant smile. "We do appreciate your agreeing to meet with us during this most difficult time."

"I assume you have information about Quentin's murderer." He gave a burdened sigh as he sat down across from us. "At least this time we will have some tea. I was not up to the task on your last visit, Mr. Pruitt, and can only apologize again."

"You have nothing to apologize for," I insisted. "I brought the worst sort of news that evening, and you cannot be faulted."

"You are very kind." He poured himself some tea and held out the remaining two biscuits toward us. "Would you gentlemen care to have these? I really haven't much of an appetite just now."

"We're fine," I answered. "I know you have a great deal on your mind, and we intend to take up only a few minutes of your time."

He nodded as he sat back in his chair, cradling his tea as

though it was a precious thing. "You may have all the time you need. Now tell me, have you learned anything further about the man who killed my grandson?"

I sucked in a quick breath, fully aware of Colin's eyes boring into the side of my face. "We are only just beginning to get an idea of him, and I'm afraid we are some distance from determining who he is. I wish I had better news for you in that regard. Nevertheless, we are starting to learn more about the sorts of businesses your grandson was involved in, which may also explain why he may have stopped communicating with you in the first place."

Braxton Everclear's bushy eyebrows twitched, his head tilting in a quizzical way as though trying to imagine what I might be about to say. "How ever did you manage to accomplish that?"

It was not the question I had expected him to ask, and yet I appreciated his interest in our methods. "The Yard has spoken with quite a few of your grandson's neighbors, which has allowed us to learn a bit about where he had been going and what he'd been doing."

Mr. Everclear reached forward, picked up one of the biscuits on his plate, and began nibbling it. "What he had been doing?" he repeated, giving me the needling sense that I was being quizzed rather than him.

I paused for a moment, knowing this was the direction we needed to go. "Were you aware that your grandson had been frequenting opium clubs?"

He sagged a bit and nodded his head once. "I suspected. When he stopped responding to my messages I doubted that it was a product of his own sudden good fortunes."

"You were still paying for his room, were you not?" Colin asked.

"I was. But it was not like him to fall silent. Do you believe his opium use had become uncontrolled? Had I lost him like I had lost his father?"

"Mr. Everclear," I said with a flatness of tone I could not control, "there is no such thing as controlled opium use. It is a dangerous drug. I am sorry to say that you almost assuredly lost him long before he ceased his communications with you. Opium is unforgiving. I can attest to that fact myself."

"Oh!" His eyes went round as he stiffened, staring back at me with a look I could not place. "I . . ." He fell silent.

"Forgive my impropriety," I pressed ahead. "I mean only to inform you that there was little you could have done in that regard. But what Colin and I have actually come to discuss with you is more complex than mere opium use. We now believe that Quentin was involved in something very much darker."

He cringed as he continued to stare back at me, his expression tightening as though he was girding himself for something not altogether unexpected. "Darker, you say?" he muttered, taking another sip of his tea before reaching forward to pick up his last biscuit. "What do you mean?"

I watched him a moment before I could bring myself to answer—the way he nibbled at the biscuit, tense and hesitant, his brow knit and his eyes appearing almost skittish. "We were hoping you might have some idea." I finally forced the words from my throat. "That you might have some suspicion or perhaps a bit of information that you did not wish to share when Quentin was thought to be only missing."

"What?!" He dropped what remained of the biscuit onto his saucer and set the whole of it back on the table. "Do you mean to insinuate something, Mr. Pruitt?" His eyes flashed to Colin. "Does he speak for you as well?"

"Mr. Everclear . . ." I spoke up before Colin could. "It is not my intention to make you feel indicted in the least. We are only seeking whatever additional information you might have that, perhaps, you felt inconsequential at the outset of our investigation. Given your grandson's murder we would be careless if we did not re-review every potential resource that could offer even the smallest fragment to lead us to his killer."

He seemed to consider my statement a minute, his brow continually furrowed though his gaze was getting clearer. It took a few moments more before he deigned to give a quick nod as he reached out and picked up his tea service again. "Yes," he murmured. "You are right, Mr. Pruitt. You must forgive my ill temper. It is regret you hear in my voice. Regret for my son's life and now ever more of the same for my grandson."

"You did send money to him every month," I delicately interrupted his prattle, aware that both his protestations and offense felt oddly out of proportion. "We were wondering if perhaps a messenger was ever paid to return news of your grandson to you . . . out of concern for his well-being, of course," I added.

"Oh . . . well . . . yes."

He seemed almost stymied by the obviousness of my question, as I had hoped he might be. I stared back at him, waiting for him to continue, and was reminded of Quentin's assertion that his grandfather had not been paying his rent for nothing.

"Braxton . . ." Colin said in a startling display of familiarity that instantly notified me of the end of any need for a softer approach. "You have been dancing about since our arrival but have yet to say anything of value at all. You hired us to find your grandson, and my esteemed associate here found him. That he was murdered the same night was a grievous injustice and one that we *will* solve, with or without your assistance. You have only to ask my father if you wish affirmation of that fact. So I will appeal to you to cease your evasiveness and confide in us while you can. Because we will not give you a second chance."

The man's eyes went rigid as he glared at Colin, his indignation burning on his face. "The impertinence," he growled. "You have no cause to speak to me with such disrespect."

"It is not disrespect that drives my tongue, sir, it is your lack of honesty." He set his cup down and stood up. "That you know something of your grandson's deeds is unquestionable. And I shall go even further and state that you are yourself caught up in them to some degree."

"This is unconscionable," he roared, and yet he did not get up to leave. "I demand that you explain yourself, or I shall take your defamation to a magistrate and we shall see what *he* makes of it."

"Very well." Colin moved toward the fireplace, watching the flames that had just begun to lie down. "Everything about you and your home speaks of a decided lack of funds. It is as cold inside as outside, suggesting you do not heat it in the least, and this fire was clearly built right before our arrival, as the embers beneath have barely had a chance to collect. Beyond that I can see only two more quarters of wood ready to be thrown upon it, leaving your rack woefully bare.

"The tea tray was already here when we arrived, and I suspect the reason for that is because you have no kitchen help to serve it properly. Is your valet your only staff?" He did not wait for an answer. "The biscuits were precisely doled out, and though you offered us yours, professing to a lack of hunger, you ate them just the same. Which brings me to you, a vision of dishevelment with your frayed collar and discordant hair. But most damning of all is the simple fact that your grandson confided to Mr. Pruitt that your charity toward him did not come without strings. A statement we heard repeated by an acquaintance of your grandson. So why, I must ask myself, would you be doling out copious sums to Quentin when you can hardly afford your own household?"

Braxton Everclear looked stricken, his face gone sallow and his eyes filled with an ache so pronounced that it caught my breath. He dropped his teacup back onto the table, moving with such tentative motions that it looked to be happening of its own volition. After a moment he looked back at Colin. "Is every man so easily deciphered by you?" he mumbled.

"We are not here to criticize or judge," I spoke up. "Our sole objective is to find Quentin's killer. To make him pay for robbing Quentin of the life that should have been due him."

Braxton Everclear shook his head and stared down at his hands as though trying to find some truth there, or perhaps the strength to state what he had been working so hard to avoid. "The birth of my son Henry should have been the grandest day of my life, but I was not there. I was already in Bombay. My wife had gone back to England, refusing to have our child in India"—he gave a burdened sigh—"so I did not receive word of his birth until more than a week later. She never did return with the boy. I did not even meet him until he'd passed his second birthday, and after that I saw him only occasionally. His mother . . . she hated India." He glanced over at Colin with the barest hint of a smile. "Your mother never seemed to mind it, but she had a sense of adventure and was a spirited woman. I was sorry when she passed."

"That was a long time ago," Colin said.

"Yes. But my wife stifled our son terribly, and by the time I returned to England after her death, he was already lost to me. He was attending university but was constantly at risk of failing out. Eventually he just stopped going. I tried to help him find his way, start a career, but he would disappear for days at a time, so there seemed little point to it." He gazed out the windows a moment, and I wondered if he was trying to re-cage his regret. "When I tried to say something . . . do something . . . What right did I have?" He shook his head. "So I gave him money whenever he asked, for every idea that crossed his mind so long as it was legal."

"And what of Quentin?" Colin asked, coming back around and settling back on the settee.

"Henry brought that baby home shortly before he died. The boy was already nearing his first birthday, and all Henry would tell me was that the mother had died. Six months later Henry was gone. I was going to do for Quentin what I had never been able to do for my own son. He was going to attend the best schools and want for nothing. . . ." His gaze shifted far away as a sardonic smile curdled his lips. "My vow cost me everything as such oaths usually do."

"You cannot be faulted for wanting the best for him," I said, trying to comfort him before realizing that his was a trap that had devoured many.

The expression that drifted across his face, pained and regretful, confirmed my own realization. "It took me a long time," he went on, "too long before I understood that it is a fool's goal. A man cannot simply will a thing to be no matter the level of his efforts. My grandson, like my son, had a mind of his own." He tugged absently at his collar. "I wonder if there are those born with the proclivity to fail, whose very nature compels them to undo everything that is right with their lives until they have brought it down like a façade onto the cobbles. Do you suppose such a thing could be the case?"

"We cannot know," I answered.

"Perhaps someday . . ." he mumbled, then fell silent.

"So Quentin spurned your attentions as well . . . ?" Colin prodded when the silence had stretched uncomfortably.

Braxton Everclear hefted another sigh before speaking again. "I mortgaged my home to pay for his university . . . *this* home." His eyes danced about the room with what looked like equal parts pride and remorse. "It has been a part of the Everclear family since the time of James VII. Nevertheless, I was not going to allow anything to keep Quentin from becoming the man I knew he could be. I would earn the home back . . . or better yet, perhaps he would. . . ." His voice broke, and he hastily cleared his throat. "But he proved to be no better a student than his father was, though he was vastly more clever. Heading off every morning, always keeping the routine, coming home with piles of books and retreating to his rooms in the evening. But I did not know that he had left school. He had canceled his enrollment and took the money, the money from *this* house, and pledged it to some scheme he'd come across." He sagged back, dropping his chin, and I feared that he was having trouble breathing. "It took less than a month for him to lose it all," he muttered in a thin, hollow tone as his eyes stayed on the floor. "And more on top of that. That was when he finally came and confessed it all to me." He closed his eyes.

"What did he tell you?" Colin asked. "What had he gotten involved with?"

"He wept when he told me. He was ashamed and repentant, and the sight of it broke my heart. His father had never shown such remorse. Not once." He gave a scornful grunt. "I was a fool."

"What did he tell you?" Colin asked again.

"He said it was a venture out of the East End involving the opium trade. They had found a supply in Persia that they could import for less than half the cost of what was being brought in from China. He believed it could not fail." Again he gave that same disdainful grunt. "Of course it failed. And it took my money with it, money Quentin said he'd planned to return to me twofold. All I wanted was for the boy to get a proper education. I never asked him to earn my money back for me."

"And your involvement?" Colin pressed, though this time with more patience.

"He told me he had reinvested his earnings before there were any to do so with, and those payments had come due. His life, he said, had ceased to have value." Braxton Everclear rubbed the bridge of his nose and stared across at Colin. "With one exception, of course. . . ."

"You," Colin finished for him.

The poor man looked pained as he sat there. "You have shown me to be nothing more than the fool that I am. How quickly you have already seen through what I could not."

"You mustn't be so harsh with yourself," Colin said. "I have spent the better part of my adult life studying and exposing the ploys of these deceivers. If I could not recognize their tricks, I would hardly prove useful in my occupation."

Mr. Everclear nodded solemnly, fidgeting with his teacup. It was easy to see that he was wholly undone. "He brought a man to see me," he went on, his voice hushed and his hands dropping back to his sides as though their very movements had suddenly become too much for him to bear. "I was told that I would be given a sum of money each month that I was to place into my personal accounts, and at the end of every month I was to transfer the money following the precise instructions I would be given. If I deviated in any way or alerted the authorities, my grandson would be killed and I would be ruined. From the small stipend that was left behind each month I was expected to pay my grandson's rent and see that he had enough money to live on. I kept nothing for myself. And so it has been for the past year and a half."

"Has it always been in cash?" Colin asked.

"Without fail. Differing amounts. The least I received was twenty pounds, the most nearly three hundred and fifty."

"And you divided it into separate accounts?"

"Never more than twenty pounds into a single account on any given day. They were very specific about that."

"They . . . ?" Colin asked the question that was foremost in my mind.

He flinched and sagged. "I don't know who they were. I met the one man only once, in the beginning, when he came to explain what would be expected of me."

"Can you describe him?"

Mr. Everclear's face tensed as he stared back at us. "There are some people, some faces, that are difficult to forget. He was one such man. Tall . . . he towered over me . . . with an air of menace about him that set me off my ease at once. His features were sharp, like a rodent's, and nearly everything about him was black—his shoes, his clothing, the great, thick cloak that hung from his shoulders. Even his hair was the color of ink and his eyes set deep, cast in shadows, as if there was only skin stretched over the bones of his face."

"You paint a compelling picture," Colin said, which I scribbled down as quickly as I could. "Did he appear to be a man of wealth?"

"His clothing was very fine—I know, as I have owned such things in my lifetime—but his manner was rough and common. I do not believe him a man born to the gentry, and yet he controlled Quentin . . . he controlled *me* . . . like a skillful puppeteer."

"Did you ever get a name?"

"No. And after he left I never once asked Quentin a single thing about him. I did not want to know."

"So when your grandson disappeared and you spoke to my father, what were you thinking we would find? Why did you hire us?"

"I never wanted to hire you," he said. "But I was worried about Quentin. Since the advent of this . . . arrangement . . . he had been staying in close contact with me. Not more than several days would go by before I would hear from him again. And then, quite suddenly, there was no more money delivered to me. There were no instructions . . . no contact . . . nothing. It worried me, you understand. For Quentin's sake." He rubbed a hand across his forehead and groaned softly. "For my own."

"You suspected the game had changed?"

He nodded. "We had followed every directive without fail, and I feared that something had gone wrong anyway. Quentin was going to look into it. That's when your father..." He held his hands up, and his face went blank.

"My father misunderstood."

"Your father is a good man. I would rather die than have him hear of these terrible things that I have done. Of the foolish old man I have become."

"You have nothing to fear from us," I spoke up. "We have kept the confidences of royalty."

One of Colin's eyebrows snaked up as he cast a sideways glance at me. "How did you disperse the money at the end of each month?"

"Very specific amounts were moved into various accounts. Large sums at a time, usually. But by then I'd already been holding it for an acceptable period of time, so there were no questions."

"The accounts you moved the money into, did they have names attached to them?"

"No. Numbers only. And they changed all the time."

"Swiss accounts," Colin groused. "It is a clever lot you have been dealing with. Did Quentin bring you the money each month?"

"No. I do not suppose that man was foolish enough to trust Quentin with any volume of cash. It was messengers. Lads mostly. I'm sure they never knew what they had."

"Lads..." Colin repeated, an uptick in his voice. "Are we talking newspaper boys? Street urchins? School blokes?"

"A raggedy lot. The kind you'd give a farthing to for any manner of chore and they'd come back to do it again."

Colin flashed a tight smile. "I know the type very well. Did you keep any of the instructions? Do you have anything in writing from that man?"

He shook his head. "I do not. It felt dangerous to save..." He glanced toward his fireplace, and I was certain that's where everything had ended up. "I see now that my errors were boundless."

"You couldn't have known what would come of all this," Colin said. "You mustn't fault yourself for trying to keep your grandson safe."

"You are as generous as your father," he muttered wistfully, his tone as flat as his eyes were hollow. "I will do whatever is necessary to help you catch Quentin's killer. My silence has done a disservice."

"We shall help you make it right," Colin said. "Will you come down to the Yard and sit with one of their artists? If you can describe the man you told us about, it could help hasten the end of this case."

Mr. Everclear nodded his head. "Yes. I will come down this very afternoon."

"Excellent." Colin offered a fleeting smile. "We are headed there now, so we will arrange everything for you with the inspector on the case, Maurice Evans. He is a good man, but you must confess nothing. I will tell them only that you are aware of a man who was doing business with your grandson, a man you knew him to be fearful of."

He swung his eyes back to Colin, and I could see a faint glimmer of something there—warmth, gratitude, I could not be sure, as it was infused with an undeniable sorrow. "Maurice Evans," he repeated.

Colin stood up and waved a hand through the air. "It won't matter whether he is there or not. All you need do is announce yourself and I'll have that Yard lot tripping over themselves to take care of you. You have my word on it."

"Thank you," he spoke almost voicelessly.

We expressed our gratitude and let ourselves out, neither of us surprised when no one appeared to see us to the door. Braxton Everclear's life had become exactly as Colin had described it—shadowy and barren.

"Did you hear what he said?" Colin asked the moment we had descended the steps back onto the driveway. "The money was delivered by a band of lads." A tight smile began to tug at his lips. "If there was a job like that occurring on a regular basis employing a bunch of boys off the street, I will bet that our Paul will know something of it. And if he does not, he will most certainly be able to find out."

It made perfect sense. "Then we are fortunate that you invited him and two of his mates over for dinner tonight. It seems we will have much to discuss with them."

"Let us collect Inspector Evans and get over to the morgue and see what Denton Ross can tell us about Pearl Tinkerton's death."

"Twickham," I corrected.

"Whichever. We may at last be drawing closer to the perpetrator of Quentin Everclear's murder."

I nodded but did not feel the level of confidence he seemed to be enjoying. I only hoped he had good reason for his change of heart.

CHAPTER 32

———◦✦◦———

Electricity was a relatively new and oftentimes dangerous technology, but when it came to the morgue, it was also most welcome. The cloying stench of death and decay was less an offense to the nose upon arrival. One could, in fact, stand directly in the center of the room and detect the astringents and solvents used, as well as a hint of formaldehyde, alongside that of the decay. If one felt truly generous he might even state that it almost allowed for a pleasing experience: It was, after all, still a morgue.

Colin, Inspector Evans, and I were waiting in Denton Ross's cluttered office just beyond the main examination room to get a look at the autopsy report on Pearl Twickham. Mr. Ross was supposed to be finishing it yet at the same time was spending a goodly amount of energy barking orders at his assistant, Miles Kindall, who was preparing Miss Twickham's body for our inspection. I had been hoping to forgo that particular opportunity but was not surprised when Colin had insisted.

"I feel like Mr. Ross is twiddling about," the inspector gripped. "Though I doubt his Mr. Kindall would do us any favors, either. This job seems to attract the damnedest types."

"It most certainly does," Colin grumbled.

"*How are you coming with that report, Mr. Ross?!*" the inspector hollered.

"*I cannot do two things at once,*" came his churlish response. "*You can either wait or come back. I really don't care which.*"

"*We will wait,*" Colin bellowed. "*You'll not be rid of us that easily.*"

"Pity," his response drifted back to us.

"That man is a pip," Colin grumbled. "Surely there must be something else to discuss while we wait. Have your men had any luck with the sales records for those Ricci Marino boots?"

The inspector gave a nod as he dug into his jacket pocket and extracted a folded sheet of paper. "We are lucky these shoes are sold in only three shops. We are luckier still that they are so unique." While he spoke he unfolded the paper and stared down at it, though his expression was one I could not decipher. "Given the specific color and style of boot we were seeking, there were a total of eighty-four pairs sold in the three shops over the last nine months. Of that total, I personally went through and crossed off the men of reputation whom I know of—parliamentarians, nobles, industrialists, and such, who did not fit your definition of living above their means. That winnowed the list to twenty-one."

"Are you certain of those you excised?" Colin asked. "Oftentimes men of perceived means can appear to enjoy great wealth when, in fact, they are mired in debt and obligation." I knew that he was referring to Braxton Everclear.

The inspector gave an amused snort. "I suspected you would wish to see the entirety of the list for yourself. It's all here," he said, wagging the paper but not yet releasing it. "But you shall have to be patient a minute longer." He snapped the sheet back. "Along with the compiling of this list, I had my men verify with the shopkeepers which of the men here keep large accounts that are impeccably paid and which have no accounts or whose accounts are in arrears."

Colin could not keep from smiling. "How very clever of you. And what has that brought the total number down to?"

244 / Gregory Harris

"Eighteen," the inspector answered with great satisfaction before finally handing the list over.

Colin's eyes skimmed the paper once and then went back up to the top and slid down it more languidly a second time. "The names with the checkmarks beside them are the eighteen?"

"Indeed. The ones with the line through them are the men I recognized and could vouch for, and the ones with the *X* beside them are those verified by the shops."

"Excellent work, Inspector. It is an intriguing list. I see that both Archibald Primrose *and* Robert Gascoyne-Cecil are here. And to think that everyone complains of a lack of common ground between our Liberal and Conservative parties. Clearly the heads of these organizations both have an affinity for outrageously priced footwear."

"A fine distinction for our leaders." The inspector chuckled.

"You may also decrease your list by one more. As you know, Edmond Connicle is deceased."

"Oh, for heaven's sake!" The inspector leaned toward Colin and squinted at the list. "I've gone through those bloody names a dozen times. How in the hell did I miss that?!" He snatched the list, grabbing a pen from atop Denton Ross's desk, and placed a careful line through the man's name. "You might think the shop-keeper would have pointed out that fact anyway." He held the paper up and gave it a quick scan before thrusting it back toward Colin.

"Seventeen then," Colin said, glancing over it one more time before handing it off to me. "And with Braxton Everclear giving a physical description to your artist of the man he believes his grandson was working for, we may yet get this list down quite a bit further."

I looked at it quickly, noting the two prime ministers Colin had jested about as well as many other notably powerful figures, but none of the seventeen were at all familiar to me. And in truth, if the boots had been purchased longer ago than the last nine months, we could be accomplishing little more than wasting time. It all felt dreadfully precarious.

"The cadaver is ready," Denton Ross announced with a decided lack of interest from the doorway to his deplorable office. "View it now and I'll get the report finished." He did not wait for a response but turned and walked back out to the main examination area.

"I don't suppose we shall be called twice," Colin said in a dryly mocking tone before standing up and heading out after him.

The inspector clearly felt like me, exhibiting far less enthusiasm as we followed Colin into the main area. Even before Mr. Ross's assistant, Mr. Kindall, could remove the sheet from the inert form, it was plain to see that something was terribly amiss with the body beneath. Where the sheet covered the woman's face, her nose protruded upward, forming a small tented area, just as with the places where her knees and feet jutted up. But any similarity to a typical shrouded body ended there.

Her chest and abdomen, usually filled with gases and easily discernable beneath the confines of the covering, were instead sunken and hung listlessly beyond the outline of her rib cage, making the bones of her pelvis look quite harsh as they bulged so abruptly from the unimaginable gap. It looked as though most of her torso must be missing completely, save for the fact that her arms could be seen running along her sides. Only their mass and form created any visible outline from below her ribs to those sharp pelvic bones.

"As you know she was eviscerated," Denton Ross spoke blandly, almost without inflection, as he waved at Mr. Kindall to remove the sheet. "We have all of her internal organs with the exception of her uterus and ovaries." He pointed toward a line of jars along the far wall. The pieces that the killer had removed from her were floating in a solution of what I presumed was formaldehyde. "We did not keep her intestines. I saw little point, as there is far too much of them and she was not killed by a wound to the gut anyway."

"And what is the cause of death?" Colin asked, the first one of us to approach the body properly and gaze down at the destruction.

Denton Ross pointed to the severed neck, deeply punctured from side to side, leaving her head looking precariously attached.

"When the killer slit her throat he severed both of her carotid arteries quite handily. He did a laudable job—one clean swipe of a razor or scalpel or other such implement. She would have bled out and died in two minutes or less."

"You sound almost impressed," the inspector muttered with the hint of a sneer.

"I'll not deny it. Your killer is not a butcher. He is skilled. See for yourself." He gestured toward the body, offering up a dark bit of a smile as though daring us to do so in spite of Colin's already close proximity.

"Do you have some sort of tool we might use?" Colin asked as he leaned over the gaping chest wound.

Mr. Kindall rolled a small cart over with dozens of slim, silvery tools resting upon it. Other than some scalpels of varying size; a tiny pair of scissors; and a longer, flat saw blade the length of my hand, the remaining items looked indecipherable—picks; clamps; and long, sharply pointed pliers, the use of which I could not presume to imagine.

"Thank you," Colin said, snatching up one of the tools that looked like a pick and coaxing the long medial wound open. "Were any other organs missing?"

"Did I say that any others were?"

Colin looked up and stared hard at Denton Ross, the man's soft, fleshy face set defiantly, his lips pursed with evident disapproval. "Was there anything inside the cavity that should not have been there?"

"Space, Mr. Pendragon. Far too much space."

I feared for an instant that Colin might hurl at Mr. Ross the implement he had been poking into Miss Twickham's deflated torso, but he did not. "What do *you* make of this, Mr. Kindall?" he asked the younger man standing off to the side, well behind Denton Ross.

"It is exactly as Mr. Ross says," he spoke up after a moment's hesitation. "The man who did this is skilled and precise."

"And did you or your knotty colleague find anything within this torso that does not belong there? Anything at all?"

"No, sir."

"Not even a mote of dust, a scrap of dirt, or a strand of hair?"

"Are you suggesting that Mr. Kindall and I are not thorough, Mr. Pendragon? Not capable of doing our job?!" Mr. Ross barked with offense.

"That's enough of that, Mr. Ross," Inspector Evans warned. "Mr. Pendragon is talking about evidence. Evidence that could help us solve these crimes. There is no need for your cheek."

"You are being preposterous," he shot back. "Suppose we did find a single strand of brown hair. Are you going to investigate every man in London with brown hair? There are three men in this room right now who fit that description. So are you going to start with Mr. Pruitt?!" He laughed. "Or perhaps you have no farther to look than yourself. Now, there would be a rub." He scoffed as he headed over to another examination table where a cascade of papers were spread out. "The lot of you are welcome to climb inside and take up residence for all I care," he muttered as he gathered up the papers and stuffed them into a folder. "Here is my full report. It is complete, accurate, and finished. I have nothing more to add, and neither does Mr. Kindall. You may read it and then you may bugger off." He tossed it onto Miss Twickham's collarbone with a flick of his wrist, several of the pages seeping out and threatening to sink into the void just below. "Good day, gentlemen," he added with derision before stalking back to his office and letting the door swing shut with a resounding crack.

One of Colin's eyebrows drifted skyward as he stared after him. "I keep thinking that perhaps I have been a bit harsh with him in the past, but then every time I see him I am reminded of what a pox he truly is."

"He doesn't mean anything by it," Mr. Kindall spoke up, but even his words felt forced. "Is there anything else I can answer for you?"

"Do you support Mr. Ross's summation regarding the cause of death and the swiftness with which it would have taken place?" Colin asked while flipping through the pages and handing them off to me one after the other. I, in turn, gave them only a rudimentary scan before passing them off to Inspector Evans.

"It is exactly as he says," Mr. Kindall reassured, though I would have been stunned if he had said anything else. "The man would have approached her from behind and slid the knife across her throat from right to left since he is a left-handed gentleman. We believe him to be a powerful man, tall and strong, perhaps a laborer or dock worker."

"Fascinating," Colin muttered, his eyebrows furrowing. "And do the two of you have any supposition as to his name as well, given the striking amount of details you have managed to divine?"

"Oh . . ." Poor Mr. Kindall looked noticeably startled. "I didn't mean to presume . . ."

"You're fine." Colin waved him off as he handed the last page of the report to me and turned back to the body. "If there is . . ."

"*Mr. Kindall!*" Denton Ross's voice bellowed from his office. "*I need you at once.*"

"Go." Colin dismissed him. "I would rather not know anything about Mr. Ross's needs."

"Very well." The young man nodded and took a few steps backward. "But if there is anything else you wish to know—"

"Yes, yes," Colin cut him off. Not a moment later the door to Denton Ross's office opened and closed, and the three of us were left alone with what remained of Pearl Twickham. "I don't know whether I feel sorrier for that young man because of the scarring on his face or the fact that he is tethered to that pompous fool. Half of what Mr. Ross teaches him is in error."

"What are you talking about?" Inspector Evans spoke up.

"He said the killer is left-handed and yet you only have to look closely at the wound to see that supposition is wrong." He pointed to the victim's neck as though the inspector and I might find that proof on our own.

"I still don't understand."

"The entry point," Colin said, pointing to the left side of her neck. "It's the deepest wound. It's where the knife was initially plunged in. And then"—he drew his finger across her gaping neck from left to right—"the killer pulled the knife toward himself . . . across her throat to the right . . . making the exit wound, as you can see, slightly less acute compared with the point where the knife first went in. It is precisely the type of incision a right-handed man would make, not left-handed. See for yourself."

While I did not relish so close an inspection, both the inspector and I leaned in, seeing the truth of Colin's observation at once. I glanced back at the report. "That's what it says here as well—right-handed. Mr. Kindall has remembered it incorrectly. Perhaps that is a product of his discomfort at your squabbling with his superior. Don't forget that he is bound to this place and scuttling along behind Mr. Ross."

"Imagine," the inspector said, "the best he can hope for is Mr. Ross's retirement or death. Then all of this will be his."

"The horror," I could not stop myself from adding.

"Nevertheless," Colin said as he started for the door, "let that be a reminder that we are fools if we do not recheck everything. If Mr. Kindall can mix up left from right, then can they both not be mistaken about the mortal wound? The time of death? The order of events in which this woman was attacked and eviscerated? It all matters. Every bit of it. And I will not have those two buffoons be the reason this case drags along." He stopped at the door and turned back to the two of us. "I should like to request that we have a second coroner examine this woman and provide a secondary report."

Inspector Evans rubbed his forehead and rolled his eyes. "This isn't going to sit well with Mr. Ross. He is the senior member of—"

"I know what he is, but this case is getting away from us. The public is not going to sit by much longer without an arrest being made. Need I remind you that your Ripper is still presumed to be at large."

"You needn't," the inspector griped.

"You also are not aware," Colin continued, "that our sovereign has reached out to both Mr. Pruitt and me with her own concerns about this case. You may be assured that she will not sit idly by while your Yard works to assuage the esteem of *that* ridiculous man!" He thrust an accusatory finger across the room with such vehemence that it caused the inspector and me both to turn so that we caught sight of Denton Ross as he emerged from his office, clearly having heard the bulk of Colin's tirade.

"How dare you . . . !" he started to howl, but he was talking to an empty doorway, as Colin was already gone.

CHAPTER 33

The mantel clock had barely ceased its ringing when a sudden and purposeful banging arose from our front door downstairs. I cannot say whether it was the spiritedness of the knock or the persistence with which it was delivered, but I knew without question that it was Paul and his lads arriving for dinner. That they were on time was sure to please Mrs. Behmoth.

"Enough with the bloody racket," I heard her holler as she trudged toward the door.

"I will remind you that they are our guests this evening, Mrs. Behmoth," Colin called down, well refreshed after having fallen asleep for over an hour before the fire.

That she muttered some retort is certain, but I could not make out what it was, which suited me just fine. Colin remained as unaware as he had been of most things since our return from Scotland Yard and the morgue. He was entirely wound up to the point that I was beginning to worry about his newly flourishing health for fear that his continued agitation might set him back.

"Won't you sit down and catch your breath a moment before these boys come pounding up," I beckoned, but it was too late. They could already be heard scampering up the steps, all snickers and thumps.

"I'm fine," he answered anyway, his tone dismissive. "There will be time enough to sit when these cases are solved."

I did not even try to keep from rolling my eyes, though I knew Colin did not catch my reaction as Paul and his band came tumbling across the landing and into the room.

"Evenin', Mr. P's," Paul said with a snort, setting his two companions to further snickering. "This 'ere is me mates wot was watchin' the back a that 'ouse last night. The tall bugger is Chester." He pointed to the tallest of the three of them, a rail-thin lad with coal black hair, sharp features, and a pimply face, "and the short shite is Rufus," he added with a chuckle, waving a hand at the other boy who was well shorter than Paul with a round, owlish face and ever so slightly cross-eyed.

"A pleasure to meet you both," Colin said, shaking their hands and ushering them into the room properly. "Can I offer you a drink? Brandy . . . ale . . . milk . . . ?"

All three laughed as they settled onto the settee, and I was surprised to notice that not only did they all fit, but there was room enough for one or two more their size. "When we eatin'?" little Rufus asked, earning him a nudge in the arm from Paul's elbow.

"Very soon," Colin answered. And to my relief, he finally sat himself down as well. "I hope you lads are hungry, because Mrs. Behmoth has had a couple of hens roasting most of the afternoon."

"I love me a good 'en," the moon-faced tyke replied, his eyes becoming even larger and rounder, accentuating the skewed angle at which they were set.

"Then you are in for a treat. But before we file downstairs, I should like to ask the two of you to look very carefully at a photograph that I have." As he spoke, Colin dug into the breast pocket of his jacket and extricated the photograph of Queen Victoria's grand-nephew, Gerhard, that his father had sent over a short while before. "Paul tells me you saw several gentlemen coming out of the house last night, and I should very much like to know if this was one of them."

He handed the photograph to Chester, the boy sitting closest to him, and I watched the lad take it with his long, spidery fingers. "'E weren't one of 'em," he said at once, passing the photograph to Paul, who took only the slimmest glance before handing it off to Rufus.

"What if he was wearing a beard? Or supposing he had a mustache, or his sideburns had grown out. Can you be certain you do not recognize his face?"

"None of 'em looked like this bloke," Rufus agreed as he handed the photograph back to Paul, who immediately passed it back to Chester. "They was all older."

"Older?" Colin pressed. "How much older? Are you talking about gray-haired men? Were any of them stooped, making it hard to see his face?"

"Nah." Rufus shook his head. "They was all about yer age, I guess."

Colin's spine stiffened as his brow collapsed. "I forget that anyone over twenty is flirting with death to a boy of your age."

Paul snickered.

"This chap weren't none a the blokes we saw," Chester reiterated as he took one last look before handing the photograph back to Colin. "We seen four of 'em leavin' but not 'im, no matter what kinda fuzz ya put on 'is face."

"Do we still get ta stay fer the 'ens?" Rufus asked.

"Of course you do," I answered before Colin could.

"You are our dinner guests no matter what you did or did not see," Colin explained. "It is your diligence that has earned you that right."

"Our wot?" Rufus asked, his little round facing screwing up.

"Hard work," I clarified, trying not to laugh.

As if on cue Mrs. Behmoth hollered up the stairs. *"Yer supper's ready. You can come down and eat."*

Colin hopped up and moved over to the landing before calling back to her. "Will you get Chester and Rufus started please, Mrs. Behmoth? Ethan and I have something else to discuss with Paul."

There was a second of silence before her answer came drifting up. "I ain't the entertainin' committee, ya know."

"I think I have been aware of that the entirety of my life," he responded before returning to the four of us. "You two boys go on down. We've one more quick bit of business with Paul before we join you."

Chester and Rufus did not need to be invited twice, the two of them jumping up and dashing over to the landing as though it was a contest.

"Save some fer me, ya shites," Paul shouted, but I doubted either of them heard as they thundered down the stairs.

"There will be plenty for all of us," Colin assured with a chuckle, resuming his seat across from Paul. "Mrs. Behmoth will not allow any of you to leave hungry."

"It's all right." He gave a nonchalant shrug, acting like the big brother, though I was certain that Chester was older than him. "I can get me own dinner if I need ta. Now, wot's it ya wanna talk ta me about?"

"An unrelated case," Colin explained. "As you recollect, we have been investigating the recent murder of a retired diplomat's grandson. You did some early inquiring for us as to his where-abouts."

"'E was the bloke wot was runnin' through money like 'e made it 'imself."

"That's right. Well, the young man's grandfather, Braxton Everclear, lives out near Gunnersbury Park."

"Gunnersbury." Paul whistled through his teeth. "I ain't ex-actly ever been invited out that way."

"Well, you are really not missing much. However, it has come to our attention that a series of packages were delivered on a monthly basis to Mr. Everclear out in Gunnersbury over the course of the last eight months or so, and those deliveries were made by various lads. Lads like you and your mates."

"It weren't me," he said at once. "But I'd've been 'appy ta do it. Do ya know what kinda coin I'd a gotten ta go all the way out there?!" He shook his head and rolled his eyes. "I'll bet 'alf a quid. Maybe more! Do ya want me ta go out there? 'Cause ya know I'm good fer it."

"No, no. I'm afraid that business is quite done now."

"Bollocks. Why didn't ya tell me 'bout it when 'e needed stuff brought out to 'im?"

"Because we only just found out about it ourselves. And it was very bad business. Not the sort of thing we would ever want you involved with. What I am hoping now is that you might be able to poke around and see if you can find any of the boys who *did* make a run out to Gunnersbury. It could be vitally important for Mr. Pruitt and me."

Paul nodded thoughtfully, acting as though he was considering the possibility, yet I was certain I knew what was going to come out of his mouth next. "I'll 'ave ta ask a lot a me mates, and they're gonna 'ave ta check with their mates . . ."

"We will pay you for your time," I said before he could finish his supposed rumination. "I am certain we can come to an agreement as to a fair sum."

"A course then." His face blossomed into a smile. "I'll 'ave a scrapper in 'ere before a day or two goes by."

"Make sure the boy is telling the truth," Colin reminded. "We'll not pay to have some imp come in here with a tale of nonsense."

Paul scowled, looking as close to offended as I had ever seen him. "I ain't ever done nothin' like that to ya."

"I'm not saying you *did*," Colin quickly backtracked, which I found amusing. "I just want you to be careful that you don't find some boy willing to say whatever it is he thinks you *want* him to say."

"Wot?!" Paul waved Colin off as he stood up. "Ain't nobody pullin' shite over on me. Don't be daft. 'At's wot I do. I know all the tricks. I got eyes like an owl fer spottin' lies. Now, is that all? Can I go eat?"

"We're done." Colin chuckled, and we stood up and watched Paul race over to the staircase and go barreling down. "Well, Victoria shall be relieved now that we have proven her grand-nephew cannot be our killer."

"Which leaves us nowhere again," I lamented. "This case—"

"Ah!" Colin held up a single finger, and a sly smile cracked a corner of his mouth. "Perhaps not. Paul has just given me an idea. We need to get word to Inspector Evans at once. We have to meet him later tonight."

"Tonight? Whatever for?"

"It's what he said. That he has eyes like an owl." Colin chuckled and headed for the stairs. "It has suddenly put me in mind of an experiment we can try that just might help clarify something critical about the killer in the Framingham murders."

"What kind of experiment?"

He turned to me at the top of the landing and gripped my shoulders. "I shall tell you when Inspector Evans gets here." His smile broadened as he squeezed my arms. "We just need to get one of these boys to fetch him. Which do you think? Whoever finishes his dinner first?"

"Colin . . ." I started to scold, but it was too late. He was already heading down the stairs laughing. And in truth, I knew the lads would be fighting for the chance to go as soon as I dove a hand into a pocket and pulled out a few shillings. What I didn't know was what Colin had in mind.

CHAPTER 34

I was standing in the disheveled room belonging to Jacklyn
Unter staring out onto the street below through the single window in her room. She had been furious at the sight of us—Colin,
Inspector Evans, and me—railing that she had nothing else to
add beyond what she had already told us and grumbling that
we would be to blame if she didn't get anything to eat tonight.
Colin suggested I give her a shilling, which did settle her down
a bit, but even so he promised her we would be gone before her
evening could get started in earnest.

"'At's all good and well," she complained, "but unless yer
plannin' on givin' me a crown or two more I'll still need ya outta
'ere before long. Ya pay me that much and you can spend the
whole bloody night if ya want." She gave a great snorting laugh
but was alone in her revelry.

". . . Have the men come out one at a time," Colin was saying
to a constable from the open door to Miss Unter's room, the inspector beside him. "Tell them not to put the overcoats on until
they are coming up the steps from the cellar. And they should
wait for a signal from us before the next man comes out. Do you
have all of that?"

"Yes, sir," the young constable answered, blinking several times as he glanced between Colin and his superior officer.

"Go on then, Wyndall," Inspector Evans barked, and I wondered if he was irritated by Colin's ordering his constable around. "Let's get on with it. We're not on holiday here."

"Yes, sir." He gave a wince before turning about and marching down the hallway obediently.

"Wot is it yer wantin' me ta do?" Miss Unter asked as Colin and the inspector came back to the window.

"You should be right next to us," Colin said, as if there was anywhere else she could be in the tight confines of this space. The only other option would have been for her to be seated on her bed, and given the dingy, rumpled state of it, I was certain it took a particular type of man to join her there.

"All right," she huffed with annoyance, "but wot is it I'm s'posed ta be doin' when I'm right next ta you?" Oddly, I did not hear the least hint of coquetry in her question.

"You will look out the window with the rest of us," Colin answered, tossing her a curious expression. "I shall have some sense brought to this case once and for all. We have not been able to find two people who agree on any aspect of this case, and you shall help us find the exception."

"If ya say so." She shrugged with little interest.

"I insist upon it. Now, we are here to observe these constables as they go about the tasks I . . ." He hesitated for an instant before allowing, ". . . the inspector and I have assigned to them. I am hoping we can jog a clearer remembrance on your part regarding the man you saw leaving the cellar just after Miss Materly's murder."

"I don't know about them other two," she shot back, curling her lips to make sure we knew she wasn't at all pleased with either this exercise or the distrust of her recollection, "I just know what I saw. And I don't need ta stare out me winda 'alf the night ta prove nothin' ta you or nobody."

"Precisely," Colin agreed, flashing a smooth smile. "Which is why we are here with *you* tonight rather than the other two.

Now"—he gestured toward the window where Inspector Evans and I were already hovering—"shall we?"

Her displeasure was well evident; nevertheless she finally came over to us, shoulders flung back and chin raised, clearly unimpressed by Colin's offhanded compliment.

"Wot"—she said in a tone as flat as the street directly below—"the 'ell is it I'm s'posed ta be lookin' at?"

"If you will please, Inspector." Colin turned to him with the ghost of a smile, and Inspector Evans immediately stepped forward, shoved the window halfway open, and stuck his head out.

"You may proceed, Constable Wyndall," he called.

The young constable, dutifully stationed at the corner of the building, gave a quick wave of a hand as he turned toward the cellar where Miss Materly had been slain and called something I did not catch. Before he could turn back to us, Inspector Evans pushed the window closed again and took a step back to allow Miss Unter to move into the vacated space. I was now farthest from the glass, hovering just over Colin's right shoulder, but given my superior height I was still able to see clearly to the street below as well as the steps leading down toward the cellar.

Almost at once the first constable popped out of the darkness therein and onto the bottom step. He was wearing a light-colored vest as he paused just long enough to tug a long, black coat over his clothing, nearly disappearing into the shadows save the pale skin of his face. He was too far away to have been able to describe distinctly, making me realize just how difficult a task these witnesses had faced.

The constable moved up the stairs and started down the block, continuing to head away from us until I heard Constable Wyndall shout for him to return along the far side of the street. As soon as he delivered the order, Constable Wyndall came around and stared up at the window we were all crowded around. This time it was Colin who leaned forward and ratcheted it up partway before calling down.

"Send the next man."

"Yes, sir," Constable Wyndall responded crisply, not waiting for any further word from the inspector.

Colin slid the window shut just as a second man stepped out of the darkness of the cellar, this one wearing a vest that looked a medium gray. He followed the same protocol as the last man, stopping on the first step before pulling on a long, black coat and then bounding up to the rest of the stairs and stalking off in the opposite direction from where we were. As before, Constable Wyndall shouted to the man when he had gotten little farther than two or three buildings, sending him across the street to return.

Once again Colin tugged the window up, this time fewer than two or three inches, choosing instead to bend down and give the order for Constable Wyndall to proceed. A third man stepped out of the shadows, and I could see that he was wearing a lighter vest than the two before, although whether it was cream or tan I could not be certain. The swiftness with which he tugged on the long, black overcoat did not help, and I understood without the slightest hesitation why the witnesses' stories had been so divergent.

Only the fourth and final man proved to be notably different. When he stepped out of the inky blackness I could see at once that he was wearing a leather butcher's apron. It wasn't that I recognized its color or the fact that it was an animal's hide—it was the cut of it, dropping down nearly to his knees, with thick straps rising up from the square bib and disappearing over his shoulders, a bulky belt tied around his waist. He stabbed his arms into the requisite black overcoat and the apron disappeared in an instant, the man coming up the steps and heading down the block just as the three before him had done.

Colin leaned yet again and asked Constable Wyndall to reset the four men back in the cellar and wait for us where he stood, then he turned to Miss Unter. "What did you see?" he asked, a flicker of eagerness apparent in eyes. "Did one of these gentlemen most remind you of the man you saw coming from the cellar that night?"

"I didn't see 'is face, ya know."

"Yes. But what about his height? Or the color and type of vest he wore? Which of these four comes closest to the man you saw?"

She furrowed her brow and stared down onto the street. I watched her expression closely but did not see any flickers of recognition pass across her face. I began to wonder if she had misunderstood and thought that Colin was suggesting one of these men might actually *be* the killer, but after another moment she shook her head and looked back at him. "Well, 'e weren't wearin' no butcher's apron, I can tell ya that."

"And the other three?" he prodded. "What did you make of what they were wearing? Did any of them look similar to the killer?"

She tilted her head sideways and gave a dismissive shrug. "'Is jacket were light. I already told ya that. Could a been any of 'em. They all looked the same ta me anyway."

And in that I too thought she was right. Under the wavering glow from the gas lamps each of the jackets and vests had looked like nothing more than variant shades of gray.

"None of them struck you more than any other?" he asked again, though his voice remained steady and calm without a hint of the frustration I had expected to hear.

She shrugged once more. "The lightest I guess. That's wot I remember. Wot'd them others say?"

"It doesn't matter." He took a step backward and then turned and headed for the door. "All I care about is what you recollect. Now, come along and let us try this again from the street, without the impediment of the glass to distort your view."

"But I weren't down on the street," she protested. "Why do ya want me ta go down there?"

"Humor me," Colin tossed over his shoulder, not bothering to slow his pace as he swept out into the hall.

Miss Unter frowned as she turned to face the inspector and me. "That one is a ruddy ape," she informed us, but started after him just the same.

By the time we all reached the sidewalk in front of her building, it was to find Colin already ordering Constable Wyndall about. The young man, in turn, was herding the other four constables back down the steps toward the cellar. We were, it seemed, about to do it all over again.

"Now watch carefully, Miss Unter," Colin instructed as he drew her up to the corner of the building right next to where Constable Wyndall was once again standing. "We shall have them come out precisely as before, though their order will be changed, and I want you to tell me which of them reminds you the most of the man you saw the night of the murder."

"How many more times are we gonna do this?"

"As many as we need."

"Well, I ain't goin' down inta that bleedin' cellar. . . ."

"That won't be necessary. Now concentrate, Miss Unter."

"I'm doin' the best I can," she snapped. "If it were a week ago, ya know, and these blasted, ruddy street lamps didn't give such a shite's worth a light. It all starts ta look the same color."

"If you would, Constable," Colin said, ignoring Miss Unter's complaint.

Constable Wyndall turned and shouted out for the first man to start. The man in the leather butcher's apron was the first to come out, pausing just a second before sweeping into the long, black coat that covered his body entirely.

"I already told ya it weren't 'im," Miss Unter reminded with detectable annoyance. "'E weren't wearin' no ruddy butcher's apron."

"Move it along," Colin called out to the constable, who in turn beckoned the other three men. One after the other they came—white jacket, gray vest, tan vest—each of them pausing just long enough to slip into their long coats before quickly disappearing up the steps and partway down the street. "Miss Unter . . . ?" Colin turned to her as the last of them completed his routine.

"It ain't the gray one," she said after a moment's thought. "It were lighter than that. It was like one a them other two. And that's all I know. You can parade 'em past the end a me nose and I won't be able ta tell ya nothin' more than that."

"You have told us enough." Colin flashed her a tight smile before turning and thanking Constable Wyndall and his four men. "Inspector . . . Mr. Pruitt . . ." He gestured to the two of us before moving farther down the sidewalk away from everyone else.

Inspector Evans was the first of us to speak up once we had reached a relative distance from the others. "Are you thinking we should drag her client, Rex Alford, down here and see what he remembers?"

"I don't think it would serve much purpose," Colin said with a wearied exhalation. "It is a fact that women's eyesight . . . their ability to discern colors . . . is greater than that of a man. I think Mr. Alford would do little more than further muddle this case. We have so little consensus as it is. Even . . ." He stopped himself and stared out across the street with abrupt intensity, yet when I flicked my eyes that direction I found nothing of note in his line of vision.

"What is it?" I asked.

"Do you have access to the morgue?" he said, ripping his gaze from whatever sightless point he had been contemplating and boring into Inspector Evans.

"Of course. We'll have to stop by Scotland Yard, but I can get us in."

"Then let us not dally," he insisted, already walking with renewed vigor toward the inspector's waiting carriage. "And while we are there we can return the files from the other murders. It just may be that the soul of this case has been lying in plain sight this entire time."

"What?!" The inspector started to protest, glancing at me even as he started after Colin. "What are you talking about?"

"Don't waste your time," I told him. "Colin won't divulge whatever he is thinking until he's certain. The best we can do now is get him what he wants and move out of his way."

"I don't like it," Inspector Evans grumbled.

"Why would you? Nevertheless, we will both be well pleased if his hunch plays out." And in that, I knew I was correct.

CHAPTER 35

⟫━◆━⟪

The place was eerily quiet. I suppose I had thought there would be a night shift on duty, and yet that was the thing about the dead: They had no expectation of service. It was why Scotland Yard had keys to this place. A body retrieved during the night could be wheeled in and placed in refrigeration until Denton Ross and Miles Kindall arrived in the morning. Though in the case of any serious crimes, the two of them were dispatched to the scene no matter the time of day or night.

"I'm putting these down," I announced before dumping the armful of folders I'd been carrying from the inspector's carriage onto one of the pristine examination tables. "I'll put them in order, but Mr. Kindall is going to have to put them away," I bothered to add.

"Do you know how the bodies are stored?" Colin asked.

"The drawers are labeled," the inspector answered even as he ran a finger along the large, metal drawer fronts stacked four high and five across. "Here's Amelia Linton, the second victim. Delphine Materly is over here." He continued to move to the right. "And here's the latest victim, Pearl Twickham." He stopped and looked back at us. "The first victim, Elsie Barrell, is no longer here. Her body was released to her family over the weekend."

Colin's mouth tightened but he did not comment as he swept the drawer open containing the remains of Amelia Linton. "Then we shall start here." He drew the sheet back to just below her collarbone. "Bring her autopsy report over, Ethan. We're going to check everything as though it was the first time."

I did as bidden, joining Colin and the inspector as they huddled around her atrophied face and gaping neck, thankful that I could not see the wreckage of her torso.

"The wound to the neck, we will presume it to be the mortal wound, was delivered in a direction from left to right, just like Miss Materly." He flicked his eyes up to me. "Does the autopsy confirm that finding?"

I flipped past the photograph and began scanning the handwritten notes assembled on the next page. "It does," I confirmed.

Colin gave a nod as he leaned forward and appeared to be inspecting the area around her décolletage, neck, and jawline before once again looking up, only this time letting his eyes fall on Inspector Evans. "Will you help me roll her onto one side just a bit."

"Roll her?" the inspector repeated. "Whatever for?"

"I am looking for bruising," he explained.

"Bruising?" the inspector repeated, but this time he leaned in and helped Colin move her body so that her right shoulder came up off the slab she was resting on. "I can see it from here," he added, and he was right. There were small marks visible on her shoulders, and as they lowered her again I could also see tiny bruises along the soft flesh of her upper chest and under her chin. "How very curious. . . ."

Colin gave a grunt as he pulled the sheet back up over her face. "Is that also consistent with Mr. Ross's report?"

I took a half step back so they could push the drawer closed again before returning to the folder cradled in my hands. "Small subcutaneous bruising evident along the mandibular and mentis regions with minor additional evidence existent inconsistently along the clavicles and scapula." I looked up. "Do you want me to go on?"

"No." He stepped down the row to the drawer marked with Delphine Materly's name. "That covers what we saw. A curious anomaly given what we have been told about the strength of the killer." He yanked open the drawer and rolled it halfway out, once again removing the sheet only from her face and the uppermost portion of her torso. "We know our killer ran out of time with this victim," he muttered. "And it would seem she was able to put up a greater struggle given the scratches the two of you found on the cellar floor and the button that may have been torn from the killer's garment."

"Don't you think that button came from a woman's garment?" the inspector asked as he joined Colin on the far side of Miss Materly's body.

"Perhaps. But I am hoping we will not need to figure that out," he said before, once again, leaning over the body far closer than I would have been comfortable doing. "The wound to the neck has been made in the same manner as the one we just viewed on Miss Linton," he stated in an obligatory fashion. "But this time . . ." He looked up and seemed to be considering something for a moment. "This time there is a great deal of bruising along her collarbone and jaw. The evidence of a struggle. Miss Materly clearly trying to defend herself. But then it is easy to see that she is a younger woman than Miss Linton. I would guess by at least ten years."

"Twelve," I corrected as I checked her age on her report and comparing it to what I had seen on Miss Linton's.

"And the notes on her bruising . . . ?"

"It is as you state. Sustained and consistent subcutaneous bruising along the clavicles, mandibular, and mentis areas, with intramuscular contusions evident along the lateral left deltoid, right anterior metacarpal, and right antebrachium."

"What in the hell does all of that mean?" Inspector Evans cut in, his annoyance evident.

"That Miss Materly was right-handed," Colin answered as

he reached over and pulled her right arm out from beneath the sheet.

"Mr. Ross is referring to having found deep bruises on her left shoulder," I explained, "as well as along the outside of her right wrist and forearm. To Colin's point, she was clearly trying to fight her killer even while she was hemorrhaging from her neck."

"And just how is it that you two know this jargon?"

"Necessity," Colin said. "The late Inspector Varcoe was never good about sharing information with us. If we were fortunate enough to get our hands on an autopsy report or medical chart, we had to know what we were reading."

"Even so, you always had a way of showing him up."

"Fool's luck," Colin mumbled, which wasn't at all true, but I was proud of him for saying it. "The evidence on these women's bodies can tell us a great deal about our killer." He stepped back and pushed the drawer closed. "And where is Miss Twickham?"

"Here." The inspector knelt down and pulled on another drawer, following Colin's lead by only opening it halfway. "This was a bird of a woman." He stated the obvious.

"Nevertheless . . ." Colin crouched down as well, pulling the sheet down to expose her face and upper torso. "You can see there is spotty bruising left behind. Our killer was neither gentle nor, given that bruising, particularly strong. These bodies tell us that he is right-handed and most likely a thinner, wiry sort of man. Given his skill with a knife he is almost assuredly a medical doctor of some sort, which would also be consistent with the witnesses' contention that they saw him wearing a light-colored jacket beneath his coat. Doctors and surgeons wear white coats. And if he *is* a surgeon, then the coat would already be stained with blood should he be stopped along the street. No constable would think twice about a surgeon wearing a coat spotted with blood running from one emergency or other."

"Couldn't he be a butcher or a barber?" I interrupted. "Both of those careers allow a man to become quite capable with a knife or razor."

"And a barber will wear a light-colored jacket," the inspector put in.

"*Ut vadat, ita abscedit.*" Colin repeated the Latin phrase we had found at the scene of Miss Twickham's murder. "Neither of those occupations require a man to learn Latin. But for a doctor or a surgeon, it is a requirement."

"Perhaps he is a failed physician who was forced to settle on one of those other professions," the inspector insisted, and I thought his point deserved some consideration.

"Perhaps," Colin allowed, but without any real significance. "Yet it would seem to me that his skill excising organs suggests that he is practiced and capable." He covered Miss Twickham's face and booted the drawer shut. "Does the autopsy report state anything different? Anything unusual?" he asked as he stood up again.

"It is as you saw." I shut the folder, having found nothing contrary.

"Excellent," Colin said, a dark, thin smile curling his lips. "Then let us go to Denton Ross and wake him up at once."

"Denton Ross?!" I repeated with distaste and surprise. "Whatever for?!" I glanced at Inspector Evans and found him looking as startled me.

"Why, Ethan . . ." And now it was Colin's turn to look surprised. "You are the reason I think we should do it."

"Me?" I looked at the inspector again, making sure I had not missed something obvious, but found him all the more confounded than I already was. "What are you talking about?"

"All the work you did while I was on holiday," he answered, his tone becoming grim at the memory. "Your exhaustive notes. You have them with you, do you not?"

"Of course." And without meaning to, my right hand went to my jacket pocket to feel the soft-covered notebook that I forever carried on my person.

"Then may I suggest that you and Inspector Evans study it while we are on our way to Mr. Ross's flat. He will not take kindly to being awoken at this hour." He gave a husky chuckle. "But it will be the ideal time to catch him unawares." He started

THE FRAMINGHAM FIEND / 269

for the door. "And do bring his autopsy reports, won't you? He may wish to review them again himself."

I felt my jaw unhinge, but when I turned to the inspector once again I saw that he was equally as agape as I knew I must look. "All right," I muttered, Colin having already disappeared out into the hallway. "Let us hope we can sort this out in the carriage."

CHAPTER 36

———◆———

Denton Ross was indeed furious, both red of face and foul of nature at the sight of us at his door. Only after Inspector Evans had stepped forward with his own matching scowl did Mr. Ross even deign to allow us to enter his flat. Had it just been Colin and me, I have no doubt that he would have sent us away without a second's thought. As it was, the spectacle of Denton Ross in bare feet and a fraying nightshirt, which was unceremoniously stretched across his ample belly, allowing his ghostly white, knobby-kneed legs to poke out from beneath, was something I hoped never to view again. However, given the files we had re-reviewed on our ride over, along with the notes I had taken and summarily ignored, it was clear that our present course of action was the right one.

Mr. Ross proved himself to be wholly uncooperative until Colin called into question the quality of work that had been carried out at his morgue. Only then did he finally agree to get properly dressed and accompany us. I had thought Inspector Evans was going to have to take him by force, but it was the defense of his good name—such as it was—that ultimately motivated him to action.

The four of us climbed into Inspector Evans's carriage, something of a tight fit given its greater suitability for three rather than four, and Denton Ross grudgingly grunted directions. The streets were easy to traverse given that the hour had slid past the middle night and was cresting toward one. And though we were nowhere near the East End, I wondered if the recent murders had not impacted the number of people willing to move about in these hours.

"This is a fool's errand," Denton Ross stated, his voice thick with malice as the carriage began to slow. "My only pleasure shall be in watching the *mighty* Colin Pendragon fall."

None of us responded, though I did catch Colin as he booted Inspector Evans's satchel closer to his calves. If Mr. Ross noticed the subtle gesture, he did not comment on it.

"Which building is it?" the inspector asked.

"The black one."

It was the sort of reply to be expected from Denton Ross given that all of the buildings crowding against the street were covered with soot and well blackened. That any difference could be noted between them was minimal at best—the color of the front doors, some with crenellations along the top, others plainly squared off. It was a working-class neighborhood. Very few lights could be seen from the windows on either side of the street, but there was no surprise in that. It was early Wednesday morning and another working day was just hours away.

"Here," Denton Ross grumbled, undoubtedly realizing that if he didn't point out the proper building he would just have to walk back to it anyway.

The carriage drew to a smooth stop, the clomping of the horse's hooves and rattling of the wood wheels falling silent at last, making me aware of just how invasive their echo had been.

Denton Ross grumbled incoherently as he thrust the door open and hefted himself out.

The inspector and I started after him before I turned back to see whether Colin wished me to bring the satchel along. I found him leaning back inside the carriage, one arm buried deep inside the satchel, his hand rummaging around. After a moment he extracted something that was clutched tightly in his fist and, as his

272 / Gregory Harris

eyes fell on me, he gave me a contented smile. He was, I realized in that moment, very much looking forward to this.

We hurried into the building and followed Mr. Ross and the inspector upstairs. "You will allow me to handle this my way," Denton Ross said firmly as he stopped in front of one of the many dark wooden doors lining the hallway, this one branded with the number 614 in dingy brass.

"Up to a point, Mr. Ross," Colin answered. "This is still a Scotland Yard investigation, and I think you will find that Inspector Evans will take exception if you do not accomplish what he wishes."

"Most assuredly," the inspector agreed at once, which I found impressive given that he and I both knew we were following Colin's lead. I had a hunch the inspector's greatest desire was to know what Colin was planning to do, but then I also suspected Colin barely knew himself.

Denton Ross curled his lips down but managed not to say anything further as he raised a meaty fist and pounded it against the door. The sound was deafening in the stillness of the hallway, and I was not the least bit surprised when I heard a door creak open behind us before quickly snapping shut again. It seemed likely that we had disturbed half the floor.

"Mr. Kindall," Denton Ross called out. "It is your worst nightmare arrived at your door."

"Mr. Ross? Is that you?" A hushed voice filled with sleep drifted back to us.

"It is. But what makes it worse is that I am accompanied by three jackals who intend to torture us with malice and fabrications."

"Jackals?" the young man repeated as he pulled the door partway open and peered out at us.

"We need to speak with you and Mr. Ross together, Mr. Kindall," Colin explained. "It is a matter of some urgency or, of course, we would not be disturbing you at this hour."

Mr. Kindall's eyes flicked over to his superior. "Mr. Ross . . . ?"

"Let us in," he answered with annoyance. "We will not get this settled standing out in the hallway, but you can be certain that I will be filing a complaint with Superintendent Totten-shire in the morning." He said the last part directly to Inspector Evans, who did little more than roll his eyes toward the ceiling.

Mr. Kindall stepped back dutifully, pulling the door open and allowing us entry to his flat. The main room was small and cluttered, with a settee pushed against the far wall and two chairs across from it, all three of them covered with small piles of newspapers and magazines. There was a doorway off to the right and another to the left, and I presumed one led to a kitchen and the other a bedroom and water closet.

"Sit down," Mr. Kindall sputtered as he swept the piles of reading materials into his arms before tossing them into a pile beneath one of the two windows on the side wall. "Would you like some tea? I was just about to brew some for myself." And as he said it, I noticed for the first time that he was, in fact, fully dressed.

"It seems like an odd hour to be brewing tea," the inspector noted as he dropped onto one of the chairs.

"Yes . . ." He gave a self-conscious sort of a chuckle. "So I suppose it is, but then I'm not much for sleep. A few hours a night is all I can ever seem to get. It's been that way as long as I can remember."

"Unfortunate," Colin mumbled while casually wandering around the room, poking about as though his opinion of the space had been requested. "It is one of my favorite pastimes. But you mustn't trouble yourself with tea. We've a few questions to ask and will let you be to do"—he waved his hands about arbitrarily—"whatever it is you were doing."

"Study . . . mostly. It is my intention to become a fully accredited coroner. I want to be ready whenever Mr. Ross feels the time is right. Let me get you a chair, Mr. Pendragon."

He darted through the doorway on the right, and as I sat down in the chair beside Inspector Evans, I leaned back and watched Mr. Kindall scuttle into the tiny kitchen, a clutter of dirty dishes and glassware covering what counter space there was. A small table covered with books was shoved beneath a single window, and there were two chairs beside it, both piled with papers. As

Mr. Kindall grabbed one of the chairs, heaving the papers onto the floor, Colin followed right behind him, pausing and looking at the muddle of books arrayed across the table.

"This is certainly some gruesome material you're studying," Colin remarked as he flipped through several pages of one of the books.

"It is not for everyone." Mr. Kindall gave a pained sort of smile as he waited for Colin to finish before following him back out to the main room.

He set the kitchen chair on the other side of me and then went and sat down on the settee beside Mr. Ross. Colin sauntered right past the seat, however, choosing to continue his wandering about the small room before pausing in the doorway and staring back out into the kitchen.

"Have your say already," Denton Ross snapped quite unexpectedly. "I've had about enough of this, and you can be certain my report to the superintendent tomorrow shall state as much."

"Suit yourself," the inspector answered blithely.

"Well said, Mr. Ross." Colin turned back to us with keen agreement in his eyes, startling Denton Ross. "You are indeed a man of detail. Exasperatingly so at times. Which is why I find the discrepancies in your autopsy reports so startling."

"Discrepancies?!" he shot back, his eyes narrowing. "What in the bloody hell are you talking about?"

"Is the killer we are looking for right-handed or left-handed?" Colin asked, slowly making his way back across the small room, trudging along as though trying to dislodge dirt from his boots.

"Right-handed," Mr. Ross blasted at once. "Each of the reports states it. The evidence on the bodies is conclusive. There are no discrepancies."

"And the size of the perpetrator . . . ?" Colin continued, stopping at the doorway on our left and gazing into what I presumed was a bedroom and water closet. "Do you believe him to be large and powerful, or perhaps somewhat smaller and less forceful?"

"Do you need to use the WC, Mr. Pendragon?" Mr. Kindall spoke up.

"Is it through here?" Colin asked, pointing into the darkness beyond.

"To your right. Help yourself."

Colin disappeared at once, leaving Mr. Ross to scowl impotently at the inspector and me. Neither of us felt the least desire to comment, however, until a long moment had passed and I realized I had not heard the door to the WC shut. Colin was almost certainly poking around, and as such I knew I needed to engage everyone before one of them grasped it as well.

"The size of the man, Mr. Ross," I pressed. "What were your conclusions on that?"

His gaze shifted to me, and I could see the loathing behind his eyes. "He is a slight man," he stated, his voice full of condescension. "Several of the women put up quite a fight, and they would not have been able to do so against a tall, powerful man. That is *also* in all of my reports. There are no discrepancies. None. Only facts. You will explain your slander at once, or you will do so before a magistrate before this night is over."

I glanced at the doorway where Colin has disappeared and noticed that a dim light was now visible, whether from a gas lamp or a match, I could not be sure. Whichever the case, I did the only thing I could think to do to continue covering for Colin: I reached into my jacket pocket and slid out my small notebook. I knew where Colin meant to head with this line of questioning, but I had not imagined that he meant for me to be the one to take us there.

"On Thursday last, Inspector Evans and I came by your morgue to review your files and discuss the three women who had been murdered at that time. You were out, but fortunately your associate, Mr. Kindall, was kind enough to share some of the facts the two of you had been able to discern from the bodies. I quickly flipped to the appropriate page—diligently dated— and read, "The man would have approached her from behind and slid the knife across her throat from right to left since he is a left-handed gentleman. We believe him to be a powerful man, tall and strong, perhaps a laborer or dock worker." I looked over at Mr. Kindall. "Have I misstated anything?"

The young man hesitated, a look passing behind his eyes so filled with a confluence of discordant emotions that I could not begin to decipher what might be going through his mind. I turned to the inspector before Mr. Kindall could take the few seconds needed to collect his thoughts and asked, "Is that how you remember the conversation, Inspector?"

"Precisely so," he answered, and whether he truly remembered it or not, he made me believe that he did.

"That is preposterous," Denton Ross thundered, edging forward on the settee to make certain I caught the scornful offense coloring his face. "You are woefully inaccurate in your recollections, Mr. Pruitt. The evidence has *always* been clear. We have *never once* thought the perpetrator to be either left-handed or of any sizeable stature. Just what game are you playing at?" He turned his vitriol to the inspector. "I told you it would be folly for you to cast your lot with these two."

"Am I hearing you correctly, Mr. Ross?" Inspector Evans sallied back, the tone of his voice dropping precipitously. "Do you actually mean to impugn *my* integrity and intelligence?"

Denton Ross heaved an agitated sigh. "I am certain you do not mean to suggest that you are without flaw."

"No more so than you, Mr. Ross. For as confident as you are that your Mr. Kindall would never have made such statements, I will tell you without the shadow of a doubt that he said exactly those words Mr. Pruitt just read to you." And this time I knew that he remembered.

"Oh, bloody hell," Mr. Ross growled, turning on Mr. Kindall with a look of fury. "Tell them yourself, Mr. Kindall."

The younger man blinked twice in rapid succession, his face as blank as a newborn's. "Mr. Ross?"

"Tell them they are wrong and you will swear to it in the Queen's courts, if necessary," he roared. "Because I have had enough of this and will not abide another moment of such slander."

"Gentlemen . . ." Colin glided back into the room without a light or a match in hand but a rigid smile distorting his face. "What has happened to your civility? I can hear you in the WC with the door closed. Especially you, Mr. Ross. You shall have the neighbors banging on the walls if you continue to carry on that way." As he moved toward me he kicked something tiny that abruptly arced up and pinged off the table, landing very near Mr. Kindall's feet. "Oh!" he said. "My apologies, Mr. Kindall."

"It's just a button," he muttered. "It must have come off of one of my examination coats." He scooped it up and shoved it into the pocket of his shirt before turning to face Mr. Ross. "It is possible," he started to say with noticeable embarrassment, "that I misspoke the afternoon Mr. Pruitt and Inspector Evans came by. Right-handed . . . left-handed . . ." And to illustrate the potential for error, he held up the opposite hand from that which he called out, giving a sorrowful sort of half smile as he did so. "But I would not"—he stiffened his spine—"not *ever* have confused our determinations around the man's stature or height. Which would leave your recollections, Mr. Pruitt, and mine equal. I may very well have erred on the one aspect"—he flushed slightly—"but you most certainly misconstrued the other."

"And me?!" the inspector spoke up. "Do you mean to state that the two of us are *both* in error over your words?"

"*Mr. Kindall!*" Denton Ross howled. "Are you telling me that you cannot decipher a man's right hand from his left?!"

"Before you throttle your assistant over a technicality," Colin interrupted, taking a small step back toward the darkened doorway leading to Mr. Kindall's bedroom and WC. "Please allow me one simple question, Mr. Ross."

As to be expected, Denton Ross's eyebrows caved in on each other as he spun his glare onto Colin. "One simple question from you, Mr. Pendragon? I should only live so long."

"Nevertheless," Colin said with an easy smile, though I could not see so much as a flicker of mirth behind his eyes. "Is it the policy of your office to allow specimens to be removed from your morgue?"

"Removed?! Only a man of your proclivities would ask such a thing."

"Mr. Ross—" Inspector Evans began to say.

"Do not trouble yourself, Inspector," Colin interrupted. "For we have a much larger problem, as I fear I smell formaldehyde in Mr. Kindall's bedroom."

Mr. Kindall paled in an instant, his right hand gripping the arm of the settee as though to keep from crumpling to the floor. "Sometimes it gets on my clothing," he started to explain as the rest of us came out of our chairs.

"What the devil?!" Denton Ross stared down at his assistant with the confusion that assured me he had yet to figure out the truth.

"I noticed it when I went to the WC," Colin carried on, but I knew he was lying. "Far too strong for a stain on a pair of pants or lab coat, I'm afraid." As he spoke he sidled to the bedroom doorway, and I saw that Inspector Evans had turned his full attentions onto Mr. Kindall. "Do you mind?" he bothered to ask, but did not hesitate a second for an answer.

"*I mind!*" Mr. Kindall fairly shrieked, the last of us to finally jump to his feet. "You have no right . . . you have no warrant . . ."

"Warrant?!" Denton Ross repeated with absolute mystification. "What the *bloody hell* are you talking about?!" And now he too moved toward the bedroom where Colin had disappeared, a gas lamp having been lit and casting an illuminating glow that filtered out into the main room.

"Stop them!" Mr. Kindall shouted at Inspector Evans. "They're breaking the law!"

"Mr. Pendragon . . ." the inspector called in a decidedly muted tone. "You mustn't be searching the premises without a warrant."

But it was too late. The next sound I heard was the clanging of glass bottles knocking together, followed by the anguished cry of Denton Ross, a lament that about stole my breath.

Mr. Kindall fell to his knees and toppled forward, his forehead hitting the floor and his shoulders shaking with the force of his sobs.

Without knowing that I was moving I found myself headed for the bedroom doorway, and as I drew closer I could see Denton Ross backed against the left wall just inside, his mouth gaping but not a sound issuing forth any longer. He was staring, as was I, at Colin, who was kneeling beside the bed with a large cardboard box opened in front of him. I could see the tops of eight capped jars inside, each appearing to be about a gallon in size, but the last jar, the ninth one, Colin held aloft in front of his face, and within I could see a woman's womb swimming in formaldehyde.

"It wasn't me. . . ."

The aggrieved voice was so close beside me that I recoiled even as I spun around. Mr. Kindall and Inspector Evans had managed to approach me without my being aware, with Mr. Kindall no more than half an arm's length behind me. Both men stared as Colin reached into the box again and pulled out another jar. I glanced back and watched it reveal its matching contents.

"It was them," Mr. Kindall hissed, his eyes darting between the four of us. "They killed me first. One of them did. I don't know which, but they're all the same. She lived on Framingham. I always went to the ladies on Framingham."

"You look very much alive to me," Inspector Evans remarked from his position behind Mr. Kindall.

"It's the pox. They gave me the pox!" he howled as though that fact might explain everything. "They stole my life from me as if it had no value and then they made me pay them for their efforts. So I have done what any respectable man would do—I made them pay with *their* lives. I am cutting out the heart of their womanhood and revealing them for the succubus they are."

"*Ut vadat, ita abscedit,*" Colin recited as he pulled out another jar and set it on the floor beside him.

"*That's right!*" Mr. Kindall effused, his face cracking into a dreadful sort of smile. "You understand, Mr. Pendragon."

"As it goes, so it goes," he translated before pulling out a fourth jar and then a fifth, though that one was empty. "You are making them reap what they have sewn," he added as he stood up, the five jars collected around his feet.

"Yes . . . yes . . . !" Mr. Kindall fairly shouted.

"You have murdered four innocent women, Mr. Kindall, and you sought to confound this investigation by your proximity to it." He absently brushed himself off, though I could see nothing on him. "You will hang for your crimes unless you are found to be mad, in which case, God save your pitiful soul."

He walked over to where I was standing and stopped at my side. "Mr. Pruitt and I will be pleased to help you deliver Mr. Kindall to the Yard," he said to Inspector Evans. "Mr. Ross, I am assuming you can take these specimens back to your morgue. I would hope you will be able to determine which victim each of them belongs to. . . ."

Denton Ross did not answer. He was standing right where he had been when I had entered, pressed against the wall, all color drained from his face, though his mouth was now clamped shut. It took a moment before he finally gave a slight nod of his head.

"I shall send someone back to assist you, Mr. Ross, and get some photographic evidence before these are removed," the inspector instructed. "Please do not touch anything until my men come back." He reached forward and seized Mr. Kindall by the arms, fastening cuffs around his wrists. "I can assure you it will not take long."

Once again there came no answer from the man, but then we did not wait long for one. After only a moment Inspector Evans shoved Mr. Kindall to get him walking while Colin and I fell in at his sides. I had never delivered a man to prison before and did not know what might happen, but there was nothing to it. Mr. Kindall, I realized much later, had already been broken.

CHAPTER 37

———◦◦◦———

"I have never seen such clever maneuvering before," Inspector Evans said as he took a sip of the tea Mrs. Behmoth had just delivered to us. "The smell of formaldehyde, you said." He shook his head, his eyes sparkling. "I didn't smell a thing and yet Mr. Kindall believed that you could. Believes it still, I would suppose, which provides all the difference between your having conducted an illegal search and him having given himself away. It was quite something to see, Mr. Pendragon. It was a thing of grace."

Colin leaned forward and swept up a piece of the Irish soda bread Mrs. Behmoth had made, giving a dismissive sort of wave with his hand. "My nose is very sensitive," he insisted.

Inspector Evans snorted a laugh. "If you say so."

"I cannot help but wonder if we might have brought this fiend to justice sooner if I had paid more attention to the autopsy reports," I cut in. "I looked at them several times and yet did not once notice the discrepancy between Mr. Kindall's words and what was written therein."

"You are too hard on yourself," Colin said. "Why would you ever have suspected Mr. Kindall? It would be like suspecting the inspector himself."

"I am guilty of the same," Inspector Evans admitted.

"Which is where a fresh set of eyes came in useful," Colin persisted. "It was new to me, which made it far easier for me to see. Even so, I did not truly believe it could be him until we arrived at his flat. It simply did not seem possible."

"Well, you certainly proved it," the inspector allowed, "though some of your methods are questionable."

Colin's eyebrows raised, and I could see that his surprise was genuine. "Whatever are you referring to?"

"You mean beyond your astonishing olfactory abilities?" He shook his head with a sardonic bit of a smile. "You took a tiny piece of evidence from the Materly case, the single white button, and brought it into Mr. Kindall's flat. And then you kicked it across the room at him."

"That was not done without purpose."

"Potential evidence from the scene of a crime is not normally removed from Scotland Yard, let alone booted around."

"I sent it directly to Mr. Kindall," Colin corrected with a touch of pique, "and he did just what I suspected he would—he picked it up and presumed it was his. That was nothing less than further proof of his guilt."

"And what if you had kicked it to Mr. Ross by mistake? Or out into the kitchen . . . ?"

Colin's forehead furrowed. "Why are you assuming I have so little athletic ability? It was just a button that had to move no more than the length of a very short room."

"I can see you will not concede the point."

"There is nothing to concede." He flicked the slimmest of smiles at Inspector Evans. "Where is Mr. Kindall being held?"

"He's in a holding cell at Scotland Yard. Processing takes a considerable amount of time these days. This afternoon there will be a bevy of doctors who will come to meet with him and determine the state of his mind. I am sure it will be several days before we know whether he will be charged with the murders or consigned to Needham Hills for the remainder of his life. I rather think it will be the asylum for him."

"I'm not so sure," Colin said. "There are aspects of these murders that show a sound thoughtfulness. He knew enough to wear one of his stained lab coats when he did the killings, knowing it would provide an instant alibi should he be stopped. And then there is the fact that he was feeding the two of you misinformation whenever Denton Ross wasn't around. Shrewd calculation in my mind. There was no madness in those decisions."

The inspector nodded, setting his tea on the table and snatching up a slice of soda bread. "Perhaps it is all a result of his disease. Once the doctors confirm his claim of syphilis, his medical records will be pulled. It may be that his mind has already been compromised."

"Perhaps," Colin agreed, though I did not detect any great conviction in his voice. "But there again, I wonder at his single-minded determination to attack only women who lived on Framingham Street."

A loud pounding on our front door drifted up from downstairs, followed by the heavy tread of Mrs. Behmoth.

"Whether Mr. Kindall earned his illness there or not," he continued, "I should think his focus on the women of that street shows a considerable resolve, hardly the mind of a madman looking to seek whatever revenge he can muster."

Inspector Evans nodded again as we caught the sound of spirited footfalls bolting up the stairs.

"*It's yer urchin. . . .*" Mrs. Behmoth called.

Not a moment later Paul presented himself on our landing, his face bright and smiling even as his eyes fell onto the tea and soda bread on the table. "'At looks good," he said. "Mornin', Inspector . . . Mr. P's. Did yer misses make that?"

We all laughed. "Have a seat and join us," Colin said as he got up and pulled a cup and saucer from the cabinet near the fireplace. "It isn't every day that Mrs. Behmoth makes Irish soda bread." He sat down again and prepared a cup of tea for Paul before handing it over with a plate containing three fat slices of the bread, all of which I knew Paul would finish off. "We have news for you," Colin said.

"Fer me?" Paul glanced up with a mouth full of food, confusion evident in his young face.

"We have captured the man responsible for the murder of your mother. He was taken into custody last night."

Paul's face lit up, crumbs raining down onto his lap. "I knew ya'd do it. The second I saw you was on the case I knew we weren't gonna 'ave nothin' ta worry about."

Colin smiled. "Your faith in us is heartening."

"Well, I got news fer you too," he declared proudly, swallowing the bite he'd been working on in one great lump. "I found the boy wot delivered yer money ta the bloke out in Gunnersbury Park."

"You what?!" Colin sputtered, bolting forward in his chair. "In one night?!"

"Well, ya don't pay me ta sit on me arse now, do ya?" He snickered.

"Are you certain it's the right lad?"

"A course!" he answered with what I took to be an offended frown on his boyish face. "Ain't many a me mates get 'ired ta go all that way ta deliver a package, let alone one a bloody month. And it were one a me own boys too. Never said a word about it ta me. You can bet I gave 'im the shite fer it."

"Was it always the same man who hired him?"

Paul licked his fingers after polishing off his last slice of bread and took a hearty slug of tea. "'At's wot 'e said. A right dandy bloke too. All—" He was interrupted by yet another knock on our door, followed at once by the sound of it swinging open.

"*Hello . . . ?!*" we heard Sir Atherton call out.

"*'Ello!*" Mrs. Behmoth responded, the unmistakable echo of her heavy footsteps heading for the front door drifting up to us.

Colin hopped off his chair and went over to the landing. "Mrs. Behmoth, have you got an extra loaf of soda bread?"

"*Did ya eat that 'ole loaf already?!*" she hollered, accusation in her tone.

"Never mind that," he called back. "Just wrap up the extra loaf for Paul, would you please, and see that he gets it on his way out. He's done the best sort of job for us. And what took you so long to get here?" I heard him add to his father as he began to climb the stairs. I did not hear the response before Colin turned and came back into the room, sweeping up his teacup and planting himself in front of the fireplace. "When can we meet this lad?" he asked Paul.

"I can bring 'im over taday, if ya want."

Colin looked at the inspector. "Are you available to come back at some point this afternoon?"

"I shall make myself available."

"Perhaps by then your constables will have had some luck with the names on the list you ordered them to check on. The ones who purchased those Ricci Marino boots over the last nine months. I should hate to think that Scotland Yard's finest could be so resoundingly shown up by a lad from the East End." He gave a wink to Paul.

"My . . ." Sir Atherton reached the landing and crossed into the room, dropping himself into Colin's vacated seat. "It seems you have quite the gathering here this morning."

Inspector Evans stood up. "Always a pleasure to see you, Sir Atherton. I was just leaving myself. It would seem I have some pressure to apply on my men." He turned and looked back at Colin. "Shall we say four o'clock this afternoon? That should give me plenty of time to assemble whatever information they have been able to collect so far."

"Will that work for you and your mate?" Colin glanced at Paul.

"A course. Owen'll do wot I tell 'im."

"I wish I could speak with such assurance of my compatriots. Nice to see you again, lad."

"And ta you, too, Mr. Sir," Paul replied with a slight flush before hopping off the settee. "I'll be back at four, then."

"Paul . . ." I dug a hand into my pocket and pulled out a near fistful of coins. "For a job exceedingly well done," I said, pouring the lot of it into his open hand.

"And be sure to get your soda bread from Mrs. Behmoth on your way out. She must have it packed and ready by now."

A wide grin covered his face before he turned and barreled down the steps.

"Fetch me a teacup, will you, please?" Sir Atherton said to

Colin after the front door opened and closed behind the inspector and Paul.

Colin pulled down yet another teacup and handed it off to his father with chagrin. "How impolite of me . . ." he muttered.

"Indeed. I should think Mrs. Behmoth raised you better than that." He poured a splash of milk into his cup and then filled it with tea, stirring just a few times before setting the spoon onto the tray and sitting back with his cup cradled in both hands. "Earl Grey is always such a delight."

"And you will be even more delighted when you hear the good news that Ethan and I have for you." Colin leaned back against the mantel looking quite pleased with himself, which he had most certainly earned. "We have captured the Framingham butcher, and it is *not* Victoria's sorrowful grand-nephew."

"Oh, dear God." Sir Atherton seemed almost to swoon. "That is the best news you could have for me. She will be so very relieved." His brow curled slightly. "You are certain . . . ?"

Colin's face fell. "Am I certain?"

"It is just that I would not relish telling Victoria one thing only to have another proven true later on."

"You may rest assured. A man has confessed and been arrested." Colin gave his father the details of our predawn endeavors, telling the story with remarkably few embellishments. "The woman who speaks to the newspapermen on behalf of the Yard . . ." Colin glanced at me.

"Alice Kettle," Sir Atherton and I filled in as one voice.

"Yes." Colin flashed us a tight smile. "She is likely meeting with those men at this very moment. No doubt a special edition will be released within a matter of hours."

Sir Atherton nodded sternly and set his tea down. "Then we had best head out to Windsor at once. She will expect to hear it from us. I know she will be roundly pleased."

"Do you think you could handle her for us? Ethan and I still have our hands full with the case for your friend, Braxton Everclear."

"Have you made progress, then?"

"We have." Another tight smile drifted across Colin's face as he set his teacup onto the mantel. "I am afraid your friend may have gotten himself into a spot of trouble. Overextended himself and been preyed upon for it."

"Oh . . ." Sir Atherton shook his head and exhaled sharply. "Why wouldn't he have come to me?"

"A man has his pride." Colin stepped around and grabbed the teapot to refill his father's cup. "But you mustn't concern yourself with any of it until Ethan and I can learn precisely what has happened."

Sir Atherton waved Colin off and stood up. "No more for me," he said. "I should have stopped with the news for Victoria. I am off to Windsor." He headed for the landing, looking back at us when he had reached it. "Please have a care with Braxton, will you? He is a good man. A decent man. I have known him longer than the length of your life. If there is anything I can do . . ." He let his voice trail off and nodded once, then turned and started down the stairs.

As the sound of his footsteps receded, I found myself hoping that there would indeed be something he could do for his friend.

CHAPTER 38

—➤◆◄—

The sight of Inspector Evans's carriage parked in front of our flat made me quicken my pace as I was coming down our street so that I ended in a near sprint by the time I leapt up the four steps and twisted the doorknob. I went barreling inside and nearly collided with Mrs. Behmoth, who was carrying a tray laden with a large teapot, cups and saucers, and a plate of biscuits too numerous in variety to have been made solely by her. I flinched, as did she, the expression she leveled on me making clear her displeasure at the misfortune I had almost caused. "Ya make me drop this and you'll be explainin' why they ain't got nothin' ta eat and drink upstairs," she growled.

"Let me . . ." I said, lifting the tray from her hands as I let the parcel I'd been carrying drop onto the shelf of the hall tree.

"Well then," she said with a hitch of surprise in her tone, "I s'pose I can bring yer bag up for ya."

"You needn't bother." I started aloft. "It's just a fresh notebook and a couple of new pens. I can bring them up later."

"Eh . . ." She gave a shrug as she assaulted the steps behind me. "I ain't doin' nothin' else."

I could think of nothing to say to that sentiment and so kept quiet until we reached the landing at the top of the stairs. Once there I found the inspector sitting on the settee, his back to me, and Colin pacing in front of the fireplace studying several loose sheets of paper. His concentration was such that he did not even realize that it was me carrying the tray when he barked to have the repast handed out.

"Wot are ya bellyachin' at 'im for?" Mrs. Behmoth scolded as she tossed my bundle onto the desk with the sort of nonchalance that peeved me.

Colin glanced up and gave me a smile. "Because I did not know that you had found yourself a lackey."

"There's enough steps 'ere that I should 'ave one," she shot right back before setting herself to the task at hand.

Colin ignored her as he came over to me in my usual chair and handed over the pages he'd been reviewing. "I am happy to report that our list of seventeen possible shoe aficionados has been winnowed to three by Inspector Evans's fine constables."

"Three?!" I looked at the full list of seventeen names, none of whom I recognized, and the notes scribbled beside each of them. Many of the men were regular clients of the shops they had bought their boots from, enjoying accounts with immaculate payment histories. Several were known to run successful businesses, and a few were the sons of wealthy men whose purchases were linked to their father's accounts and therefore also impeccably managed. But just as Colin had said, three names were men who did not frequent the shops from which they had purchased their Ricci Marino boots. And of those, two had since defaulted on their payments.

"I was thinking of sending a couple of my men around to visit the two chaps in arrears to tell them we had been enlisted by the shops, but I didn't want to proceed lest you had a better notion."

A knock on the door interrupted us before Colin could answer. "That's probably Paul and Orville," he said, heading for the landing.

"Owen," I corrected.

He gave an indifferent wave of the hand as he hurried down the stairs, and I could not help but smile at how astonishing his recovery had been these past several days. Not a moment later I heard Paul's voice, followed by the three of them dashing back up.

"Here we are, then," Colin announced eagerly, and I was surprised to find that he had beaten both boys up the stairs.

"Hullo, Mr. Pruitt," Paul said as he burst into the room, a younger towheaded boy immediately on his heels. "Nice ta see ya again, Inspector," he added as they all came around the settee. "This 'ere is me mate, Owen. He's the shite wot was gettin' paid ta deliver them packages to yer friend out in Gunnersbury."

"I ain't a shite," the boy complained morosely, and I realized he was likely unhappy at being dragged here to meet with all of us. The younger boy was almost a head shorter than Paul and looked as though he might weigh sixty-five pounds wet. Nevertheless, his eyes were bright and held a noticeable keenness. "I'm jest earnin' a little money when I get the chance. Wot's it ta you? You'd a done the same thing."

"'At's 'cause I'm older 'n you," Paul fired back as the two of them perched on the settee next to Inspector Evans, fitting into that single space with room to spare. "It ain't the way things work—ya can't jest run off an' do wotever the 'ell ya want."

"Well, there you have it," Colin interrupted, sitting back down and fussing over their tea. "Even these fine lads on our bustling streets are slaves to a hierarchical establishment."

"Wot?!" both boys squawked.

"It was just a poor joke," Colin muttered as he passed cups to the boys before offering them a chance at the biscuit plate. They each snatched up what their small hands would allow, Owen by far coming away with the shorter end of that reckoning. "We very much appreciate that you agreed to speak with us, Owen. And Mr. Pruitt here will see that you are aptly compensated for your time."

"Wot?" little Owen said again.

"Paid," Paul snapped before turning his gaze on me. "And don't forget that *I'm* the one wot found 'im and brought 'im 'ere. 'E didn't even wanna come, ya know."

"I never said I weren't gonna come. . . ."

"Are you talkin' or am I?" Paul spun on him with a scowl.

"Nothing you boys have done for us is going to be forgotten," Colin reassured. "Now what I would like you to do for us, Owen, is to look at a drawing of a man and tell me if he looks like the gentleman who gave you the packages to take to Gunnersbury."

"A'right." A shower of biscuit crumbs tumbled out of his mouth as he spoke.

Inspector Evans pulled a rolled sheet of paper from the satchel at his feet and unrolled it carefully to reveal the drawing of the man Braxton Everclear had described to the Yard's artist. The man's features were indeed hard and angular, just as Braxton had described them to us, with deep-set eyes that were shadowed by the sharp protrusion of his brow. Just as Braxton Everclear had said, I could not help but think he looked like a man of considerable menace.

Owen flicked his eyes toward the drawing, and I caught the minute cringe that stiffened his spine for an instant. "'At's 'im," he mumbled, stuffing another biscuit into his mouth and trying to look nonchalant.

"Did he give you his name?" Colin asked.

"Mr. Black," he answered, his gaze locked onto the biscuits still clutched in his hands. "But 'e 'ad a mustache the last time I saw 'im."

"When was that?"

"'Bout a month ago, I s'pose."

"What kind of mustache? What did it look like?"

"Fat. Curled over 'is lip a bit, and I thought 'e must chew on it whenever 'e eats." He shrugged. "Nothin' special."

"How did he get hold of you when he wanted to find you?"

"'E told me ta come to the Regency Crest every Saturday night between eight and nine. I was ta look for 'im, and if 'e weren't there I could go on about me business 'til the next Saturday. So that's what I did." He shrugged again as he ate the last of his biscuits. "'E only came by about once a month. Woulda been a waste a me time 'cept . . . ya know. . . ." He tossed a quick sideways glance at Paul before continuing. "When 'e did show up I always got a 'andful a coins."

"Yer a shite, Owen," Paul protested.

"Never mind that," Colin interrupted the two of them again. "Did you ever look inside the packages he gave you?"

Owen shifted on the settee and looked toward the fireplace before he gave his answer. "They was always sealed."

A thin smile fiddled at a corner of Colin's lips as he picked up the plate of biscuits and held them out to the boys again. "I'd bet a tiny finger could pry a corner open and no one would ever know it," he said.

"You can't lie fer shite," Paul ribbed Owen as he scooped up another helping of biscuits. "So ya'd better tell me friends the truth or I'll see ya don't earn another farthin' on the street until yer twenty."

Poor Owen could not even begin to hide the umbrage that stiffened his face. "It were money," he answered with the frustration of someone who has been coerced into doing something they had no intention of doing. "But it were paper, not coins, and the queen weren't on it."

Colin glanced at me, his brow creasing. "Are you sure? What did it look like?"

He gave an indifferent shrug as he too finally grabbed more biscuits. "I dunno. It 'ad a bunch a squiggly lines on it and a lot a writin'."

"Bank notes," I volunteered.

"Could you read any of it? Could you tell what language it was written in?"

Owen froze for an instant before pulling the biscuits closer to his body and sliding his eyes toward Paul. "I ain't sure. I only made a tiny 'ole."

"'E can't read worth a fig," Paul added with a snicker.

"Can too!"

"It doesn't matter." Colin got to his feet and moved over to the fireplace, digging a crown out of his pocket and flipping it between his fingers with his usual dexterity. "The man you delivered it to will know what sort of currency it was." He looked back at Owen and Paul with a gleam in his eyes. "You have both done a tremendous service for us. You should be proud of your-selves." But even as Colin spoke it was clear that Owen was con-centrated solely on the crown flying between his fingers. I knew Colin had noticed it as well. "Here you go, then," he said with a smile, tossing it to Owen. "You've earned that and more."

Paul made a grab as the crown sailed toward him, but Owen was too quick, ripping it from the air before it could slide past Inspector Evans. "I know all sorts a things, if ya wanna ask me more questions."

"I think we are good for today." He gave me a look, and I knew at once what he wanted of me. I dug a hand into my pocket and pulled out more coins, carefully parsing them between the boys, then I placed the remaining biscuits into a cloth napkin that I handed to Paul. "You share them," I warned. "I'll not have Owen telling me you refused to do so."

Paul's face soured as he glared back at me. "A course I will. But we ain't sharin' with anyone else."

"That is up to you," I agreed.

"When do ya want me ta come back? Ya got another case I can 'elp ya with?"

"Come back the day after tomorrow," Colin answered. "Lately it seems we always have something for you to do."

Paul grinned, clearly delighted by that news, and the two boys dashed down the stairs. In less than a moment the front door opened and slammed shut again.

"Crikey!" Mrs. Behmoth cursed from somewhere below our feet.

"Ethan and I will go and see Braxton Everclear at once," Co-lin announced, pulling on his vest and jacket before tossing mine to me. "Do you think you can determine which of the two men on your list is the one in the drawing, Inspector?"

"I can and I will."

"And perhaps an address to go with it?"

Inspector Evans shook his head and chuckled. "Anything else you would like to remind me to do?"

"No," Colin answered plainly as he started down the stairs.

"We shall see you back at the Yard after our meeting with Mr. Everclear. Shall we say an hour and a half?"

"He doesn't even realize what he's doing, does he?" the inspector muttered to me as we followed in Colin's wake.

"He does not." I smiled. The two of us shared a quiet laugh as we hurried out the door after him.

CHAPTER 39

If Braxton Everclear had been notably disheveled before, he looked doubly so when we arrived this time. Where his hair had been in a mild state of disarray before, it now appeared as though he had done little more than run a hand through the gray, wiry mess before agreeing to receive Colin and me. I could only guess that it had been several days since he had last shaved, and though he was properly dressed, his shirttails bulged at his waist and his vest needed a good tug to snap it into shape. It left me with the impression that the whole of making himself presentable had simply been too much for him.

He continued to display the remorse we had seen on our last visit, although it now seemed to have become well seeded, causing a deeper, more inherent sort of shame to be apparent. He did not meet our gazes, his eyes instead wandering from the unlit fireplace to the bookshelves lining the walls to the tall windows, through which could be seen the day as gray and morose as his mood. Even so, he had still proven helpful.

When Colin peppered him about the money that had been delivered to him, he confirmed at once that it was Swiss Francs rather than our own currency. Why he had not thought that fact relevant before was unclear, but I do not believe he'd meant to hide anything anymore. In fact, as he revealed further details to us I could feel his mood brightening, making me hope that the relief of his burden was beginning to provide some sense of liberation for him.

In the end, the only question he had been unable to answer was the total amount of funds that had been siphoned through him. He kept no records, he told us, the sound of his leaden regret surging up in his voice again, because he had not wanted to be reminded of what he was doing. But we had learned enough from him anyway.

Colin remained quiet on our way to the Yard, no doubt ruminating on the things Braxton Everclear had divulged. While the fact that it was Swiss money being funneled into the city complicated matters, there was really no surprise in it. The anonymity afforded by the Swiss enticed a great many illicit activities, and this was just another instance of that. It left me fearing that we would struggle to unravel this case, if we could unravel it at all.

By the time Colin and I arrived at Inspector Evans's office it was to find that he had not yet been able to determine which of the two names on his list belonged to the drawing of the man Owen had recognized. The three of us had been forced to wait another half hour before the information was finally delivered that one of the shopkeepers had recognized the drawing as his customer, Colton Hadley. At last, we finally had a name and an address.

As we were on our way to collect the inspector's carriage, however, a constable flagged us down to inform us that the owner of the second shop had just confirmed the drawing of the man to be *his* customer, Charles Henderson. Suddenly we had two names and two addresses, though they were only blocks apart. We began to wonder if the two names might not lead to the same man, and indeed, when we did arrive at the first address it was to discover that it did not even contain a flat number that matched the one given by Charles Henderson.

"I fear we are chasing a phantom," the inspector said, and

while I shared his concern, I was struck by the fact that Colin kept silent.

The second address was also faded in its appearance. Nevertheless, the only thing that mattered was that this building actually contained a corresponding flat number to the one given by Colton Hadley. That fact alone lifted our spirits as the three of us struck up the staircase.

A rap on the door brought a brief flutter of noise from the other side before it was pulled open to reveal a woman fast approaching her middle years who was dressed in an ill-fitting housekeeper's uniform at least a size too small, which suggested to me that she served as more than just the maid here.

"Yeah . . . ?" she asked, disinterest thick in her voice as she reached up and tugged a loose chunk of black hair back behind an ear.

"We are here to speak with Colton Hadley." The inspector was the first of us to speak up. "Is Mr. Hadley at home?"

"Who's we?" she shot back without a thought, confirming in that instant that we were in the right place.

"Maurice Evans," he answered, sticking his hand out. "These are my associates, Mr. Pruitt and Mr. Pendragon. We are here on Scotland Yard business. Will you please notify Mr. Hadley that we are here."

The woman's brow furrowed with suspicion as she glanced between the three of us. "I'll have ta see if he's here," she finally answered, reaching back to swing the door shut.

"Thank you," Colin spoke up, catching the door mid-arc. "We shall wait inside while you check with him."

If the woman realized his choice of words she did not show it as she staggered backward, allowing him to blithely push our way inside. I let the door snap closed behind me, and the moment it did a man's voice rang out, "Who was it?"

"Colin Pendragon, Ethan Pruitt, and Inspector Maurice Evans of Scotland Yard, Mr. Hadley," Colin called back with amiable simplicity.

The woman looked about to swoon before she took another

step backward, clearly trying to put as much physical distance between us as she could. As her eyes darted to the hallway on our right, a tall, black-haired man in his late thirties or early forties strode into the room, his face alight with too many years of heavy drinking. A paunch was beginning to reveal itself around his midsection in spite of the fact that his face was an accumulation of hard angles and rigid lines, just as Braxton Everclear had described.

"How terribly charming," he said, giving us a smile that lacked even the suggestion of warmth.

"We appreciate your time," Colin replied with his own dearth of congeniality. "We would not bother you were it not a matter of some importance."

"No doubt." Mr. Hadley sniffed as he moved forward, leading us into the parlor at the front of his flat. At the same time he ordered the woman to fetch us some tea.

The parlor very much looked like its owner—charmless, beyond its prime, and possessing secrets it would not easily divulge. There was not one photograph or painting of a personal nature, nor were there any placards, hangings, or trophies denoting any achievements or organizations to which he belonged. If the man read books they were not housed here; however, I did notice a copy of the day's *Times* thrown upon the hearth, ostensibly in preparation for the next fire to be laid. "Please make yourselves comfortable," he offered by rote as he lit a fire and set it to blazing almost at once. "You must forgive my informality, but I was not expecting guests." He turned back to us with the same sort of prickly smile he had offered a moment ago.

"There is nothing to be forgiven," Colin said as Mr. Hadley pulled up a hard-backed chair from behind a desk that had not one item upon it. As with everything else in the room it looked as if it had perhaps once held some intrinsic value before lack of care or misuse had taken their toll. "We have a matter to discuss with you that simply cannot wait for another day."

"Oh my . . ." Mr. Hadley enthused with false bravado. "Then let us not wait for the tea but launch ourselves directly into the mire."

"A mire, is it?" Colin's eyebrows rose toward the ceiling. "Then may I assume you know why we have come?"

"What? No!" Mr. Hadley's glibness failed him for a second before he seemed to just as quickly settle back into his ease. "I am not a seer—Mr. Pendragon, isn't it? I do believe I recognize you."

"How charming." Colin's tone threatened to wither the air in the room. "This is my associate, Mr. Pruitt, and that would be Inspector Evans of Scotland Yard."

"Yes . . . the Yard," Mr. Hadley repeated in a preposterously outsized way. "And whatever is it that brings three such distinguished figures to my humble rooms?"

"Murder, Mr. Hadley," Colin shot back. "And extortion, and the laundering of illicit funds into the British financial markets. Do tell me if I have struck a nerve yet."

Mr. Hadley allowed something of a chuckle to rumble up from the back of his throat. "Why, Mr. Pendragon, whatever are you on about?"

Before Colin could respond, the woman returned carrying a well-polished tea tray with all the necessary accoutrements piled atop. The lot of us fell silent as she parsed out the cups, a beautiful set of matching bone china that nevertheless bore a mar or chip on nearly every piece, attesting to both its age and the fact that Mr. Hadley was apparently unable to replace it.

"That will do, Miss Reeve," he grumbled, and she seemed only too happy to hasten out of the room. "Now, tell me," he started up again, sitting back in his chair with the ease of someone entertaining old friends, "why have you come to see *me* about such disagreeable topics?"

Colin stared back at the man as he too sat back, looking equally tranquil as he seemed to be considering his answer. Only after a full minute had elapsed did he finally reach into his pocket and pull out a sheet of paper that I well recognized. He gazed at it a second, his expression inscrutable, before holding it out toward Mr. Hadley. "Do you recognize this man?" he asked.

Mr. Hadley's response was instantaneous and so fleeting that at first I wasn't at all certain whether I had actually seen the shock rip across his eyes. But in the next instant he looked back at us, that same sardonic smile slowly curling his lips. "Is this supposed to be me?"

"It is a striking similarity, wouldn't you say?" Colin said, flashing his own transitory smile. "It is how Braxton Everclear remembers you. Do you remember him? Out in Gunnersbury Park . . . has laundered a considerable amount of Swiss Francs on your behalf . . . ?"

"Laundered?" Mr. Hadley laughed. "Such an imagination, Mr. Pendragon. I paid him for services rendered. It was a business transaction. There is no crime in transferring funds from one currency to another. Surely you would back me up on that claim, Inspector?!"

"There are limits. . . ." Inspector Evans started to answer.

"And I have *never* exceeded the law. Does Mr. Everclear state otherwise?" His eyes flashed with the first real anger he had shown as he stared back at us. "Does that befuddled old man have records to back any of this up? Proof of any kind? Or are the three of you here on some fool's errand trying to intimidate one of this city's respectable citizens?!" None of us moved, the sound of my heartbeat racing in my ears the only thing I could hear for what felt the longest time. "So I thought," he sneered, and I could feel the case beginning to slide away.

Mr. Hadley made a move to stand up, the expression on his face harder than ever—filled with self-satisfaction—and I knew I was the only one who could stop him. "I saw you murder Quentin Everclear," I said in a single breath, relieved to hear that my voice sounded steady and firm.

For the second time in a matter of minutes I watched the mask loosen from Mr. Hadley's face before he hastily secured it again, a look of astounded disbelief settling in its place. "What?!"

Had I not been sequestered beneath Quentin's bed, Mr. Hadley's response might have given me pause for reconsideration, but as it was, only the glimpse of Colin's startled expression caught in my peripheral vision gave me any pause at all. Still, there was only one way I could move now. "I was there, in Quentin's room. I had arrived not ten minutes before you descended on his threshold. In fact, when he opened the door to find me standing there, it was you he had been expecting."

"*You are out of your mind*," he blasted, yet I could see the one thing I had most hoped to provoke wriggling just behind his eyes—doubt.

"I had gone to see him to get some information," I pressed ahead, aware that both Colin and Inspector Evans were staring at me, though I did not dare glance at either one of them. "You pounded on the door like it was yours to do so and set poor Quentin into quite the dither, sending him into a panic lest you should find me there. So he insisted I hide beneath his bed, that small, sagging lump of sheets shoved against the side wall. I'm certain you remember seeing it." I flashed him my own tight smile, patterning it after the one I had watched Colin throw at innumerable people over the years.

"So I did as he asked and slithered under it while he let you inside. You were so full of bluster that night, threatening to disembowel the poor young man if he ever made you wait out in that hallway again. Surely you remember that?!" I added with a whisper of sarcasm. "You cannot possibly use such threats on a regular basis."

"*I don't know what the bloody hell you're talking about*," he bellowed, but I could tell his façade was cracking.

"You recognized at once that Quentin had been smoking opium. You knew it almost before you stepped inside." I shook my head but did not remove my eyes from him, hoping I could convince him before he realized it would have been impossible to see him from my vantage point. "It infuriated you. You told him you had work for him that night, that there were women to be found, but now he'd broken a rule. Remember that? You asked him if you had been unclear on that point." I halted for a moment to let my words sink in. It did not matter that he remember them precisely, all I needed was for them to ring true.

"Do you remember how he answered you?" I started up again. "He told you he forgot." I shoved out a laugh so devoid of humor that it tore at my throat. "You didn't find that answer acceptable in the least, did you, Mr. Hadley? You told him he was a slave to his habit." I nodded. "You were right about that."

"What is this about?" he interrupted, tossing his teacup onto the table and leering at the three of us. "Are you here to arrest me? I think not. Where are the constables? The handcuffs? What is it you want?"

"The truth, Mr. Hadley," Colin spoke up. "Do not deceive yourself into thinking you will not pay for the murder you committed, but I will give you my word that you will do yourself a service if you tell us the truth. Now, what was the nature of your business with Quentin Everclear, and why did you need his grandfather to launder that money?"

Mr. Hadley leveled his gaze on Colin, the agitation of a moment before slowly draining from his face. "*I am nothing but a pawn,*" he insisted. "These were not my plans . . . my doing. Mr. Everclear did not die on my orders. I was sent there to silence him with the full knowledge that my own life would be ended if his was not. Quentin Everclear was an opium fiend, a gadabout. I, on the other hand, am responsible for an elderly mother and a daughter who is incapable of taking care of herself. I did what I had to do for them, and would do so again, but I am not the fiend you are looking for."

"Tell me the nature of the business you were involved in," Colin said again.

"Slavery. Uneducated women from fifteen to twenty. The kind without a chance for a decent life or any family to speak of. We send them to the Continent, where they are placed in the service of wealthy families. The prettiest ones are married off to the highest bidder. They face hard work, but it's better than living off the streets of this godforsaken city. And those ghastly Framingham murders . . . we were saving them from such a fate as that!"

"Your pride is misplaced," Inspector Evans rebuked. "The killer of those women has been caught and will be hanged for his crimes. The young women you've sent abroad will pay for your hubris for the rest of their lives."

"Who did you work for?" Colin asked. "Who sent the francs to you every month?"

The man's face soured, his expression darkening as he glared back at the three of us, considering his words, measuring his answer. "I'll have your guarantee that I'll not swing for the murder of that addict first," he demanded, his gaze falling on Inspector Evans. "If you expect me to cooperate, I'll have something for it."

"I am neither a magistrate nor a solicitor," the inspector replied, his voice even and considered. "I can guarantee you nothing. However, your cooperation will earn you a favorable light in view of your crimes, and I will give you my word that I will vouch for you in the courts should the information you share prove to be reliable and useful."

"That isn't much of a guarantee. . . ."

"Suppose . . ." Colin broke in, his tone velvety, making me wonder what he was up to. "Suppose there was no witness to the murder of Quentin Everclear?" I wanted to laugh, since his bait was nothing less than the truth.

"What?" Mr. Hadley jumped on the notion, his interest palpable.

"Suppose Mr. Pruitt saw nothing. The case for murder against you would become conjecture. There would be no proof."

The man's eyes flicked to me at once. "I cannot testify about what I did not see," I said as I looked back at him.

"If this is a trick—"

"I am a man of honor." I cut him off. "If I do not have that, then I have nothing at all. And you have two witnesses here." I gave a taut smile. "One of whom is a well-respected member of the Yard."

"Who sent you the francs?" Colin asked again. "You have what you want, so I will have my answer."

"A dead man," Mr. Hadley said with a grin and dry chuckle, clearly well pleased with himself. "He contacted me about eighteen months ago. I had done some work for him before." Again he gave that harsh chuckle. "He and his partner set up this scheme regarding the girls. Very lucrative. Far more than they had anticipated. But they needed someone to administer the process, get the girls off the streets and onto the ships without incident, collect the funds, that sort of thing." He stood up and dipped his head in the slightest of bows. "Which is where I came in. I recruited the help that was needed, mostly low-brow sods who could be easily handled. People like your Quentin Everclear."

He turned and started to wander across the room to the desk. "That type is an easy lot to control. Most of them, like your Mr. Everclear, are already under the thumb of opium, so it takes only the merest nudge from me to enlist their aid. After all, I represented the steady flow of funds, and to these men, nothing matters more."

He leaned back against the top of the desk and looked back at us, a mixture of amusement and disregard evident on his face. I wondered why he had retreated from us, aware that it would take only the simplest of movements to extract a weapon from a drawer in the desk, but he had to know that Inspector Evans was carrying a revolver, and I knew that Colin was as well. Nevertheless, it suddenly put me in mind that perhaps this was not as foolish a fellow as I had thought.

"Everything was working extraordinarily well until about eight months ago." His rakish confidence wavered slightly. "I was earning a bloody rash of pounds and had a select group of street rubbish acting on my every whim. And then your lot arrested the man who was giving the orders," he said to the inspector. "And in a single night, everything came to a halt." He pursed his face and shook his head. "Buggered Yard."

"The francs, Mr. Hadley . . ." Colin warned.

"For a month everything went quiet. I still had the capital delivered to the docks without fail. Sometimes they would be met and taken away, and sometimes we had to let them go. Ruddy waste. But then I got the first telegram." His smile widened indecently. "We were back in business again." He leaned down and yanked one of the desk drawers open.

I felt Colin stiffen beside me, his right hand bolting toward the gun at his side, his other arm poised as though to reach for me, but there was no need. Mr. Hadley shoved a hand inside and extracted a handful of telegrams, holding them up with a flourish.

"Twice a month at first," he continued. "They were instructions on how I was to proceed. And that was when the money changed to francs. I had to get it converted into pounds and dispersed into a series of precise accounts that changed all the time. Your Braxton Everclear proved very adept at taking care of that process for me. And it cost me a pittance." He laughed, the sound prideful and callous. "I was eventually pawned off on a new partner here in the city, but I still receive the telegrams once a month, without fail. And the money . . ." His voice trailed off, and there was no missing the wistfulness in his tone.

Colin was on his feet and moving toward Mr. Hadley before I was aware that he had stood up. "I will see those," he demanded.

Mr. Hadley handed them over without hesitation as he crossed his arms against his chest, that disturbing confidence, or perhaps it was indifference, once again settling on his face. The inspector and I watched Colin paw through the countless pages with increasing speed, his forehead constricting even as his eyes went cold. Not a minute later he strode over to me and thrust them out, a tightly coiled fury rolling off of him like a stink.

"What is the name of the man who instructed you in the beginning?" he asked, his voice constricted and harsh. "The man arrested by the Yard that you referred to as dead?"

Mr. Hadley took a moment to conjure a tight, humorless smile. "Wynn Tessler," he answered. "The Yard hanged the poor bastard not a month ago. Pity really. Brilliant man."

If it were possible I would say that my heart ceased to beat in that instant. Even as Wynn Tessler's name fired across my brain, I glanced down at one of the telegrams in my hand and saw the initials of the sender, a seemingly arbitrary assemblage that might, at first, bring to mind the cries of a kitten: M-E-W. They were from Zurich. All of them. "It cannot be," I said aloud. "It's preposterous."

"It's her," Colin replied, his voice as bleak as death itself.

And I knew he was right. The initials stood for Mary Ellen Witten, the name Charlotte Hutton had assumed when she'd fled from England. "Murder, extortion, slavery..." I glanced between Colin and the inspector. "Is there no foul thing this woman will not do for her own gain?" Neither of them answered me. There was no need. This woman had nearly stolen Colin's life by her own hand right in front of me. I could see no end to her malevolence, which is why I knew I would never stop hunting her until she paid for her crimes.

CHAPTER 40

Morning arrived long before I was ready for it. I much prefer hiding in the nonsense of my dreams or, better yet, sleeping without cognizance at all. Especially given everything we had endured the night before.

Still, I was pleased to wake up and find my head resting on Colin's steadily rising and falling chest, his right arm tucked beneath my neck. We paid for having spent a night in such close proximity, my neck tweaked and aching, and Colin's arm so deadened that I'd had to rub it for several minutes to get the blood flowing back into it, which had caused him no end of prickling discomfort. Yet neither of us complained. It would have seemed ungrateful after the specter of Charlotte Hutton had so abruptly fleeted across our path again. A reminder of what had almost been.

The whole of the day drifted away from us, most of it spent before a crackling fire to ward away the cold of another gray, drizzly day. We did not speak about the cases we had just completed, content to simply be there, Mrs. Behmoth joining us between chores and meal preparations. Of the latter, Colin had insisted on helping to prepare supper, a proposal I knew she did not relish but allowed just the same, and in spite of a wrath of *tsks* and sighs released by her during the process, I could tell she was pleased.

Friday morning brought change along with its blustery winds and blue sky. I awoke to a cup of tea delivered by Colin, who was already up, dressed, and happy to inform me that I had slept beyond normal decency. I reached for him to tempt him further by my indecency but was interrupted by a pounding on our door below. If it was a new case, I informed him as I grudgingly extracted myself from the bed, I would insist we decline. He nodded, but I recognized the antipathy in his response.

My declaration proved unnecessary, however, as it turned out to be Inspector Evans. "They have moved Mr. Kindall to Needham Hills," he told us as we settled in the parlor, a fresh pot of Earl Grey tea and currant scones before us. "The first doctor who examined him said the syphilis had probably begun to curdle his brain already. They've sent him there to determine whether he is incorrigible or not. He'll never breathe the air of freedom again."

"One would hope," Colin agreed. "Though the science of the mind is such an inexact one. Deviation of any type is often judged a perversion of nature and yet nature itself is *filled* with such inconsistencies."

"What are you prattling on about?" the inspector said with a laugh, Colin's allusion to our life lost on him. "And what of Colton Hadley?"

"Mr. Hadley is acting like a man desperate to clear his name of wrongdoing and yet seems to know almost nothing. He insists the initials MEW are simply a code by which he could recognize the sender, and has not wavered in that contention. And he claims to know nothing of the man who took Mr. Tessler's place other than the fact that he is German, or Russian, or Swiss." He shook his head and gave a disgusted grunt.

"He is almost assuredly lying," Colin said. "Some time in prison should incite his willingness to cooperate. Have you gotten a warrant to search his flat?"

"We have, including the room of the woman who worked for

him, that Miss Reeve we met when we were there. She has also failed to provide any but the sparest information. If it is Charlotte Hutton . . ."

"It *is*," Colin insisted.

The inspector nodded his head. "She has, once again, covered her trail exceedingly well."

Another knock drifted up from downstairs. "Are you expecting anyone?" Colin asked me.

"Paul is coming by but not until later. I'd bet he arrives just in time for lunch," I added with a smile.

Colin turned back to the inspector. "Has your office learned anything from the Zurich authorities?"

The inspector shook his head with a grimace. "They seem disinclined to cooperate with us. It has only been because of your father's maneuverings that we've gotten any help at all."

"Well then . . ." Colin's face soured a bit, and I knew he was loath to state his next thought. "I suppose I must ask my father for his aid again."

"Aid in what?" Sir Atherton's voice drifted up the stairs in accompaniment to the methodical sound of his footsteps as he climbed up to us.

Colin popped off his chair and went to the landing. "What are you doing here? Did you know we were going to have need of you? Are you prescient now on top of everything else?"

Sir Atherton laughed as he entered the room, a small package tucked under one arm, and shook the inspector's hand before settling himself into the seat Colin had just vacated. "I bring a gift for you, my boy," he said to Colin with a smile.

"A gift . . ." Colin's eyes popped open as he pushed himself off the fireplace mantel and hastened over to his father. "What have you gotten for me?"

"It isn't from me." Sir Atherton held out to Colin the small parcel that looked about the size of a book but was soft-sided as evidenced by the way it flopped as Sir Atherton handed it over. "It is from Her Majesty."

Even as he said the words Colin had already torn open the

paper to reveal the fine navy sweater that I had seen her knitting. He shrugged out of his jacket and swept the sweater around his shoulders, shoving his arms inside as he moved to the mirror in the hall tree to get a good look. "She has done a remarkable job. It fits wonderfully."

Sir Atherton chuckled. "As she herself says, by now she has knitted something for nearly every man and woman in her empire." He watched Colin unfold and read a card that was attached to it.

"Lovely," he said with a great smile.

"You will send her your thanks," his father prodded.

"Ethan will." He tugged at the sweater as he started back across the room, dropping the card into my lap as he went. "He's much better at that sort of thing than I am."

"She hasn't made me anything," the inspector spoke up, a grin on his face.

"Give her time," Sir Atherton said. "I do believe she is going to live forever." We all laughed, although I noticed that Sir Atherton's face sobered quickly. "I'm afraid my visit also has a far more regrettable reason," he continued as I handed him a cup of tea. "Braxton Everclear was found dead last evening. The poor man hanged himself. It has been sorrow upon sorrow for that family."

It felt like a punch to the gut as I stared back at Sir Atherton, his face filled with its own share of regret. "I'm sorry," Colin said. "How I wish we could have assuaged his mind."

"It's that bloody Charlotte Hutton," I said, my shock having already turned to smoldering anger. "She has cost yet *another* life. *She* is the reason we need your help," I said to Sir Atherton.

"Where that woman is concerned you may be assured I will do everything I can to assist you." He turned to Colin, and his face softened. "I only ask that you do not let her shoot you again."

"You needn't worry on that score," Inspector Evans spoke up. "Scotland Yard will see to the safety of him *and* Mr. Pruitt."

"Well, I suppose that is some consolation," Sir Atherton answered, causing me to wince at the unintended slight to the Yard.

"Then our next task shall be to head to Zurich," Colin announced, a new enthusiasm brimming in his tone. "It is time we have an end to Charlotte Hutton . . . one way or another."

"I could not agree more," I added.

Sir Atherton furrowed his brow. "The two of you will need to give me a spot of time before you go gallivanting off," he warned. "Diplomacy does not work on a schedule."

"Then get to it." Colin gestured to the clock on our mantel. "Time is ever of the essence."

"I shall finish my tea and have a scone first, thank you."

"If you must." Colin chuckled. "And will you do one more favor for Ethan and me?"

Sir Atherton slapped a dab of clotted cream on the end of his scone, eyeing it lovingly. "And what would that be?"

"You remember the lad Paul who has done such good work for us?"

"Of course. I've not lost my mind, you know."

"Do you suppose you could get him into school while we're away? He would do best in one of the academies where he'd be required to live there. Easling and Temple might be nice."

"And who is going to pay for the boy's education?"

"Ethan and I," Colin answered at once.

"I'll take up a collection at Scotland Yard," the inspector said. "He's a bright lad and deserves a chance if anyone does."

"Very well." Sir Atherton gave a single nod. "That will be easy. But I'll still finish my tea and scone first."

We laughed once more, and as I glanced over at Colin, his face alight with joy and satisfaction, I felt like the luckiest man alive.

ACKNOWLEDGMENTS

This marks the sixth adventure for Colin and Ethan, and to everyone who has traversed their journeys along with me, I am most grateful. I have met some warm and wonderful people at book signings and have heard from others via Facebook. To each and every one of you, thank you for picking up the books and joining me.

Special thanks to Kathy Green for taking care of me and for some wonderfully insightful notes. To John Scognamiglio at Kensington, who has been incredibly supportive throughout this adventure. Also at Kensington I must acknowledge the hard work and efforts of Kris Mills, Paula Reedy (and her team), and Claire Hill. They each provide enormous energy and creativity to the product you hold in your hands.

Hats off (if I wore one) to Karen Clemens for her creative input on the stories as well as her terrific bookmark designs. Thanks to Melissa Gelineau for her notes and thoughts. Diane Salzberg provided endless support and I'm pretty sure she reads the books more than I do—thanks, Lovey.

I get a good deal of medical reference help from my nieces, both of whom are nurses—Erin Bertino and Megan Brode. If they ever come into your hospital room you will be in the best of hands.

I work hard to stay true to the time period, so must bear any inaccuracies on my shoulders alone. I would like to give a nod to Queen Victoria for allowing me to put words into her mouth, although she did once state that she thought she had knit a scarf or sweater for every subject in her realm.

Thank you once more for your time and interest.

Until our next adventure . . .

Connect with U s